fashionably
LATE

barcode

fashionably LATE

NADINE DAJANI

A Tom Doherty Associates Book
New York

FASHIONABLY LATE

Copyright © 2007 by Nadine Dajani

A Forge Book
Published by Tom Doherty Associates, LLC
175 Fifth Avenue
New York, NY 10010

www.tor-forge.com

Forge® is a registered trademark of
Tom Doherty Associates, LLC.

Library of Congress Cataloging-in-Publication Data

Dajani, Nadine.
    Fashionably late / Nadine Dajani.—1st ed.
      p. cm.
    ISBN-13: 978-0-7653-1742-1
    ISBN-10: 0-7653-1742-7
    1. Muslim women—Fiction. 2. Young women—
Fiction. 3. Women accountants—Fiction. 4. Cuba—
Fiction. 5. Chick lit. I. Title.
PR9199.4.D346F37 2007
823'.92—dc22

                       2007007009

First Edition: June 2007

Printed in the United States of America

0 9 8 7 6 5 4 3 2 1

To my mother and father,
who flouted tradition
and gave their daughters wings

Acknowledgments

A book sitting on a shelf in a store may seem like any other commodity, a thing to be bought and sold. But to those who write, a book is a dream at the end of a long road, one I might have strayed from were it not for the many people who believed in me and my work, and who anchored my wayward confidence every time it needed it.

To Natasha, who, in her relentless pursuit to represent this book, made the wildest fantasy of every wannabe writer come true for me. To Paul, for taking a chance on a misguided young Arab Canadian with dreams of fashion stardom. To Aryn, Wendy, Jenny, and Dona, for pointing out every superfluous comma, every typo, and every gaping plot hole, and for giving the kinds of pep talks only those who share the joy (and the pain) of writing can give. To Shirine, for reading each and every single draft—and there were many—with no (er, little to no) complaints. To Carole, for the kind of friendship books are written about—from the days she insisted Rageb Alaami lived in her building to our first infamous trip to Cuba together, and to Dara, Christine, and Sharon, for listening to me whine over mojitos and martinis all over the Caribbean and the continental United States. To Basil, my baby bro, for being the brightest light in my life, and to Ghada, the coolest big sister a dorky kid with a 'fro could ask for. Also, a shout-out to the Book Nook crew, who are on a mission to make me a local celebrity, and to Risha, for giving me my first star moment.

And finally to Denis, for being there from the very beginning. Thank you.

Part ONE

1

You know you have a shitty job when your clients would rather slit their own throats with a spoon than return your phone calls.

Which is why today, a crisp early-autumn Friday, I decide it's time for something a little more drastic. Like a coup. One that's going to see me bouncing into the office come Monday morning on the wings of victory, having caught the elusive Ms. Mercier off guard. Before anybody else has.

You'll have to forgive me if I have a tendency to make my life sound more interesting than it is. Accountants will do that. Lawyers get *Ally McBeal, L.A. Law,* and four different versions of *Law & Order.* Doctors get *Grey's Anatomy.* What do we get? Exactly. We're one rung above actuaries on the hopelessly-uninteresting-yet-well-paying-professions ladder, and maybe one down from engineers.

Today also happens to be the day of my cousin Ranya's wedding to self-made import/export mogul Dodi El Hoffi.

Today, in other words, is *huge.*

I duck out of the office at four, a garment bag with my black tulle Behnaz Sarafpour tea dress draped over my arm, strappy Louboutin slingbacks tucked in a corner of my boxy audit bag, and head straight for the client's main office on Sherbrooke and Saint-Marc. Unannounced.

"Ms. Mercier, please." I smile politely at the pretty blonde behind the sleek chrome-accented desk.

"Who, may I ask, is here to see her?"

"Aline Hallaby." I push back my shoulders and meet her stare. "From Ernsworth and Youngston Chartered Accountants." I wait for the intimidation effect to take hold.

It doesn't.

She's one of those button-nosed French girls the Boston college boys like to pick up at the Crescent Street bars when they come up here for a weekend of binge drinking. Her voice is dripping with that brand of New York–meets–Paris snooty you only get in Montreal, specifically from the bone-thin patrons of the shops running down Saint-Laurent Street. You know which shops I'm talking about. Too cool for, you know, *a name,* they carry their teeny tops and flimsy dresses in two sizes: small and smaller.

"Is Madame Mercier expecting you?" From her icicle-dripping tone, you'd think Mercier is actually a code name for Céline Dion, passing incognito through town on her way to her mansion in Sainte-Rose.

It isn't.

Ms. Mercier is just the assistant controller at Fortex Inc., a small paper-products manufacturer that also happens to be an infuriatingly demanding client of ours.

"Yes, of course she is."

Blondie doesn't look convinced. She picks up the phone and dials. "I'm sorry, she's not at her desk at the moment," she says after a short pause, the receiver lodged between her shoulder and her ear.

"I'll just sit over here then." I match her cool stare, professionally tweezed eyebrow for professionally tweezed eyebrow.

I lower myself into one of the deep green leather armchairs facing the gargantuan desk and pull the latest copy of *InStyle* from my audit bag. And wait.

Everybody hates auditors. It's common knowledge. We are to the business community what termites are to antique wood furniture. People vaguely appreciate that even the smallest, slimiest, most apparently useless insect is infused with some higher bio-ecological purpose.

Auditors, not so much.

But, like the lone remora that keeps the aquarium clean by sucking in the muck and waste the rest of the fish leave behind, we auditors do in fact perform an essential service to society, even if the recruitment brochures didn't quite put it that way.

So why would an educated young woman with an appetite for success and a closet full of fabulous shoes be sitting here taking attitude from a glorified coffee girl in a suit that probably cost half of said coffee girl's monthly income, instead of doing something that actually matters? To anyone besides the profit-sharing board at Ernsworth and her mother, that is?

Because those Big Four firms really know how to reel you in, that's why. They're the ones with the coolest booths at Career Day and always give away the best free stuff, like gym bags and chrome coffee mugs emblazoned with their logos, while everyone else is handing out cheap pens. They totally destroy the retail banks and the marketing firms with their professional, glossy brochures plastered with happy people—lots of women and minorities, of course—pointing to laptop screens and smiling like they're looking at the latest dirty joke circulating around the office e-mail instead of a graph comparing different depreciation policies like we're meant to think.

The accounting firms also throw the best on-campus recruitment parties ever, never running short of fine wines, creamy cheeses, and hot young business-school grads just like you rattling on about how great life is on the other side. And if you scored an interview with one of them, then you were *really* in for a treat. Expensive dinners and private boxes at the Bell Center for anything from rock concerts to Canadiens games, depending on the season, courtesy of the partners who squeeze time out of their overbooked schedules to come out and tell you why their firm is the one to work for. And the cocoa dusting on the chocolate soufflé is that even after all this splurging, they still manage to pay the highest starting salaries of all the recruiting companies in any industry.

Unfortunately, the luster of my star status, along with that of every other new hire, faded the very first day I started on the job. That was also the day I heard for the first time the other term industry insiders use to refer to my firm: the Sweatshop.

And they weren't kidding.

Internal controls testing, minutes checking, invoice testing, cash testing . . . It's enough to make you go cross-eyed. Ticking and bopping, they call it. None of us juniors can believe we actually need to go to university and then pass one of the hardest exams ever devised by man to work here. The firm just sends us out to companies so we can harass them with a billion annoying questions about their business. All so we can give the investing public a financial bill of health. Yup, they're clean. Next. Not that our services were particularly helpful to the poor schleps who'd invested in Enron, mind you.

No wonder my clients can't stand the sight of me.

But hey, if glowing career prospects have earned me a small wedge of freedom undreamed of by all my tradition-conscious cousins—overeducated, meticulously groomed twentysomethings still waiting for a man to come along and validate their sheltered lives—then who am I to argue?

I sigh and flip the cover page of my magazine just as Ms. Mercier herself materializes from behind the receptionist's desk, clutching a stack of envelopes against her chest.

"Noëlle, these were supposed to be sorted this mor—Oh . . . Miss Hallaby. I didn't realize you were here." She throws the secretary a not-so-subtle sideways glare.

Noëlle shrugs. "She insisted on waiting," she says, and turns to the mound of envelopes in front of her, disgusted that she actually has to, you know, *work*.

I quickly push the magazine back into my briefcase and stand up, smoothing the creases in my tweed pencil skirt. I'd picked it out on purpose this morning, knowing I was coming here. It's the most demure-looking thing in my entire wardrobe.

"I left a message letting you know I'd be coming today," I lie. "For the invoice testing. I was also hoping you'd have those financials Manny has been requesting ready."

I'm betting my last loonie she'll claim she never got the message anyway. That, or she'll try to pull the "new systems implementation" excuse on me.

"As I'm sure you know, Miss Hallaby, we've been very busy here these past few weeks. We're in the middle of a new systems implementation and—"

What did I tell you?

"I appreciate that," I interrupt as nicely but firmly as possible, "I really do. But this can't wait."

Ms. Mercier eyes me contemptuously, as if through a pair of headmistress glasses slowly sliding off the tip of her nose. Except she's not wearing any glasses.

"I suppose you're already here. . . ." Her voice trails off, disappearing behind a heavy metal door beside the reception area.

I jog to catch up.

An hour later, I emerge from the stout glass building, a thick stack of photocopies stuffed into my audit bag, and waddle-jog toward the Ritz-Carlton Hotel, three blocks down the street. It's all I can manage in my herringbone stilettos and three different bags hanging off various appendages. I check my watch. Five thirty. I'm cutting it close, but I don't care. Nothing is going to dampen my high spirits. Monday morning I get to tell Manny how I got the financials for him. Me. The ones he's been after for weeks. Not five-different-degrees-holding Derek, not senior-auditor-in-charge André, not even unbutton-my-shirt-some-more-and-see-where-it-gets-me Véronique. Me. And in the upwardly mobile world of audit, you never know where these kinds of small victories may lead.

2

I stumble into the hotel at 6:25, fifty-five minutes after the reception was scheduled to start. Most people would consider this late. Maybe even rude.

Not my people. When the Lebanese invite you to something, anything, and tell you to show up at six, they're not realistically expecting to see you standing at their doorstep any time before seven thirty. Seven if they know you're one of those annoying "punctual" types. By those standards, my tardiness would hardly register as fashionably late. I'm downright early.

Seventeen minutes after that, I emerge from the white marbled ladies' room just off the main lobby, makeup refreshed, wavy blond-highlighted hair—prone to the five o'clock frizzles—wound back into an elegant chignon and smoothed down with Ouidad conditioning cream—the only stuff that actually works in my kind of coarse curls. I am the picture of calm, put-together serenity, about to set a well-heeled foot into the mad circus that is a Big Fat Lebanese Wedding.

A Lebanese wedding is pompous affair, even for something as innately pompous as a wedding. For one thing, the actual reception is just the last installment of a trilogy of celebratory events, beginning with an engagement party that, if the bride-to-be were dressed in white, might be mistaken for the actual wedding itself. It's usually only after this extravagant affair that the couple can go on proper, unchaperoned dates. The trade-off is that if the interested parties should, at this stage of the process, come to the realization that they're better off on opposite sides of far-flung continents than together in eternal wedded bliss, they can call the whole thing off with relatively little consequence to their honor or that of their families.

Should they navigate this step successfully, they move on the next round: the actual marriage ceremony itself. This is a much more sober affair, involving a turbaned sheik wearing long layered robes and a deep, serious frown. It's the part where the tearful father gets to give his daughter away and accept the symbolic silver coin the groom humbly offers in lieu of a dowry for taking the girl away from her family. It's where contracts are drawn up and licenses are signed.

You'd think that at this point the groom would be free to rip off his bow tie, roll up his sleeves, and fling his virginal bride over his shoulder and into the nearest Motel 6.

You'd be wrong.

There's still the reception to go through. And it's traditionally a full two weeks to a month after the ceremony.

"You're late."

My mother, the only person who could possibly have noticed this, seeing as the half of the six-hundred-plus guests that made it on time are busy perusing the lavish predinner buffet against a backdrop of soft elevator music and glinting crystal chandeliers.

"Honey, you look beautiful." My dad leans over and pulls me into a warm hug. He smells faintly of ink and chemicals under the new suit and the Paco Rabanne cologne my mother's made him wear.

It used to depress me, that smell. It reminded me of the dingy basement textile-printing workshop he toiled in until all hours of the night with the handful of people who worked for him, none of them speaking a word of English or French. My father would have made a great professor, I think. The cliché could have been modeled after him: mild-mannered, brilliant, and hopelessly absentminded. It would've looked a lot better to my friends, whose dads were VPs of big companies, lawyers, engineers. But first-generation immigrants don't work as professors, even if they come with the best credentials and highest accolades from the Old Country. They don't work as VPs or lawyers or engineers either. They leave that to their kids while they themselves become slaves to their tiny convenience stores, newsstands, or fast food franchises. My dad's lucky, though. He really does love his work. It's his tiny kingdom, a place where the tan shade of his skin and his gruff accent earn him respect instead of scorn or, worse, pity. He's even managed to grow it enough that Sara and Sami, my sister and brother, get to see a little more of him now than I did growing up.

"Brian got here a whole hour ago. How could you be so insensitive to the poor boy?" my mother says in Arabic.

She's talking about my boyfriend, not that she'd ever come out and use that dirty word. To everyone in the Lebanese community he's my *friend* with a meaningful nod and a barely perceptible fluttering of the nostrils, a warning to anyone who might think to question my major breach of decency and good Lebanese manners out loud.

"I was at work, Ma. I had to get some really important documents from a client. Crucial, actually. The whole team was counting on me." There's that tendency to spice up my bland job description again. You were warned.

My mother's eyes soften. I said the magic word: *work*. She loves the idea of my job so much, I wonder sometimes if maybe she should be doing it. With that kind of enthusiasm, she'd go places.

"Where is he?" I ask.

She opens her mouth to tell me, but before she can, we hear commotion coming from the side of the grand staircase.

"Look! Here she comes!" someone shouts above the low rumble of tinkling glasses and muted murmurs. A hush settles over the giant mass of dark suits and gold lamé outfits, buckling under the current of tingling excitement running through the foyer. All eyes in the room turn to the four turbaned drummers at the top of the grand staircase, standing at attention in their traditional white pantaloons and cropped vests as though before a military commander.

An eardrum-shattering ululation pierces the heavy silence, courtesy of the mother of the bride, my aunt Maryam. The first band member, the one with the bright red sash and gleaming black mustache, gives the signal. A quick, snappy shake of his tambourine.

The crowd explodes. So does the music.

The wedding reception has officially begun.

Tum ta ta tum tum, ta ta tum.

They cheer, they clap, they wail. Some of the braver women even try to mimic my aunt's expert ululation and end up sounding like land mammals in the last throes of agony. But it doesn't matter. We're all getting swept away in the living, breathing spectacle in front of us. In the ensuing hoopla, I lose sight of my parents, and still have no idea where Brian is. I start inching my way toward the staircase, craning my neck to get a better view. I wedge one foot between two dark trouser pants but stumble back when I feel the crushing weight of a very large person on my back.

"*Insha'allah*, you will be next!"

Auntie Selma—not so much my actual aunt by blood or marriage, but by virtue of being a friend of my mother's—is definitely a wailer. Overcome with emotion, she'd lunged for the nearest unwitting girl of marriageable age, who happened to be me, and is leaning the whole of her corpulent frame on my shoulder, alternating between sobbing hysterically and blowing her nose in a crumpled up old Kleenex.

Next. Me. SIGNS POINT TO BLEAK, bleats my mental Magic 8 Ball. Especially since I come from a somewhat-lapsed-yet-fairly-traditional Muslim family and Brian is still holding out hope that we'll get to live together like most sensible North Americans do before we hop the late train to Marriage Land.

"Soon, Auntie, *insha'allah*," God willing. The standard Arabic reply to anything from "Are we going to the zoo tomorrow?" to "He's a lovely boy, and you're not getting any younger."

I smile and kiss her cheeks, twice on the right side and once on the left, in typical Middle Eastern fashion, and ease out of her grasp to push, prod, and squeeze myself toward a better view of the staircase.

The procession—led by the band of percussionists; a svelte belly dancer weaving through the throng like a nimble cat, her nipples threatening to pop out of her shimmering bra at any second; and a suave-looking male vocalist with a voice like melted chocolate on a cold Canadian winter night—has made it halfway down the winding marble steps.

Next up are the little girls in white dresses and pink rosebuds in their long dark hair, clutching lit candles taller than they are, followed closely by the bridal party.

Finally, amid the clamor and the pomp, engulfed in an entourage of shrieking bridesmaids in skimpy dresses and Jordan's GDP in jewelry, a cloud of ivory tulle, silk, and organza floats daintily down the stairs.

Somewhere under all that fabric is my cousin Ranya.

My breath catches in the back of my chest. I gasp and take one step back, and slam my elbow right under someone's ribs.

"Oow . . . you're stronger than you look, shrimpy."

I half twist my body around and, sure enough, Sophie, the one friend who'd stuck it out with me through playground politics and teenage acne attacks, is standing behind me, tall and lanky in an ill-fitting Tracy Reese frock her mom made her wear. She still manages to look better than every underfed, overplucked, blond-highlighted, and flatironed-within-an-inch-of-her-life single girl on the prowl for a rich Arab husband in the room. And it's a big room.

"You made it!" I lean over and hug her, taking care not to wrinkle her outfit. "I was beginning to wonder."

"Rush-hour traffic. What's up with the Friday-afternoon wedding-reception thing?"

"Groom's family. It was their idea. Ranya couldn't convince Dodi's mom that a curse wouldn't befall the next seven generations of the El Hoffi clan if they scheduled the ceremony on a Saturday or Sunday like normal people. She insisted they have the wedding on Holy Friday. Even if they had to start a full two hours later than scheduled."

Sophie just shakes her head before her features scrunch up with excitement. "Are you psyched for Cancún, or what?" She squeezes the life out of my arms.

"Oh my God, it's all I can think about." It's true. This vacation will be the first weeklong stretch of my entire existence where my parents won't be following up on my exact whereabouts every fifteen minutes (an exaggeration, but only slightly). I realize that at twenty-two I may seem marginally pathetic, but that's just how it is. It also explains why fantasizing about this trip has overtaken surfing Shopbop.com for the latest in funky clubwear as my number-one means-of-procrastination-when-I-should-be-doing-controls-testing activity.

"Have you talked to Ranya yet?" Sophie nods toward the staircase, snapping out of her rum-soaked reverie and back to the Arab-fest at hand. "How's she feeling? Floating on air? Or does she just want to skip all this and go straight to the Bahamas?"

"What, are you kidding me? She's petrified."

"Of what?"

I gape at her incredulously. "What do you think?"

She stops, her features paused midexpression as though she were giving the question some serious thought.

"Not the wedding night?" Sophie looks genuinely perplexed.

"Of course the wedding night!" I smack my hand against my lips as soon as the words escape them. I don't think anyone heard me. They're still too busy clapping and snapping their fingers to the music. The more obnoxious of the male guests are swinging white kerchiefs over their heads and gyrating their hips awkwardly every time the belly dancer shimmies up to them.

"She can't possibly still be a virgin."

"Sophe, have you *met* my cousin?" I study her for a full ten seconds, denoting just how nuts I think she sounds. "Of course she is."

"But she's been engaged for a year . . . and isn't she, like, thirty?"

"Thirty-one, actually, and up until five this afternoon, still living at home."

Sophie may be my best friend of twelve and a half years, but she's also fifth-generation Lebanese-Canadian, and Episcopalian, so she doesn't get it. One of her uncles married an Italian woman, and a cousin got pregnant by her Haitian boyfriend, kept the baby, and moved to New York to become a catwalk makeup artist. That kind of thing just wouldn't go down in Muslim families, even the more liberal ones like mine.

Except if you're me, and you've been stubbornly seeing your *ajnabi* boyfriend for so long that you've effectively forced your parents to face facts and pray that you'll at least get married soon, before you *really* embarrass them.

"I can't take this anymore, Ali." Sophie slips one foot out of a silver sandal and rubs it against the back of her leg.

"I know. I'd kill for the Macarena at this point."

The waiters weave in between us, relaying back and forth between the ballroom and the kitchen, scooping up gutted remains of custard-filled pastry tulips, the final installment of a seven-course meal that lasted well over two hours. And now, unhampered by a feast fit for a gourmet chefs' trade conference, the guests are in full-blown party mode. Like the seven waifish girls in too-short cocktail dresses, swinging their pelvises in a *baladi* swirl on the parquet dance floor in front of me.

"What is it with Lebanese women and too much makeup?" Sophie tucks her foot back into her shoe and leans forward, squinting to get a better look at the most enthusiastic of the butt-shakers, a woman five inches deep in Revlon Skinlights and navy blue eye shadow.

"You don't remember her?" I nod discreetly at the streaked blonde in a crêpe de chine strapless dress, which is gaping dangerously around her flat chest. "That's Maya, Auntie Suzie's daughter. She's the one who almost choked on a piece of baklava at Halla's wedding last summer when you said you wished you could take a year off from college so you could help build houses for the poor in Africa."

"Oh, right. Her." Sophie crosses her arms over her flat abs. "Did she just come back from vacation?"

"That would be a generous dose of Fake Bake."

Maya flings one hip in our direction, flipping her hair dramatically, and glowers at us as though she senses our presence. We both immediately clam up and grin, baring as many teeth as our outstretched lips would allow us. I contemplate telling Maya she looks anorexic in that dress, but decide against it since she'd most likely take it as a compliment.

Maya doesn't smile back. She just swings her other hip in the opposite direction, where a cluster of admiring males are swaying unsteadily on their feet, looking like they can't decide what to do with themselves.

"She's been up there for five songs in a row," Sophie whispers when Maya's swirls and shimmies have sent her across to the other side of the dance floor.

Given that Arabic songs tend to run about twenty minutes each, that's saying something.

"And she's probably going to stay there until Yasser notices her."

"Yasser's here?" Unaccustomed to three-inch stilettos, Sophie snaps back and loses her footing, almost wiping out in front of all 637—I'd know, my mother helped organize the reception—of Ranya and Dodi's guests. If she'd gotten her way, Sophie would've probably shown up in a Gap turtleneck à la Sharon Stone and a tasteful skirt, with maybe a swipe of sheer Body Shop lip gloss across her lips. Better yet, she wouldn't have shown up at all.

"I have to get out of here."

I can feel the cogs in her brain turning. She's eyeing the white linen tablecloth draped over the nearest empty table like it might hold the key to her salvation.

"Your mother will strangle you, Sophe, and me for letting you get away."

"She must have set this up. I know she did."

"Sophie, you're hilarious. Every single woman under thirty-five in this room is trying to land the last good-looking, Mercedes-driving, engineering grad out there that their mothers would approve of, and you're ready to spend the rest of the night huddled under the table to get away from him."

"He thinks that having money precludes him from the need to have a personality."

"It's a shame—he really is cute."

"And a horrible kisser."

"What? You kissed? When? You didn't even tell me!"

Even as far back as high school, Sophie's had the infuriating tendency of attributing the same level of importance to gossiping that most of us would to shopping for dental floss. She only told me Yasser had asked her out three weeks after the fact, and only because he was the reason she couldn't join me for sushi. A month later, when I met her on campus for a quick coffee, I asked her if she was planning to bring Yasser to the wedding as her date. She said she'd already dumped him two weeks before.

"He slobbered all over me."

"Ugh."

"Yeah. You'd think a guy with that much opportunity would have the technique down by now."

"Look at the guy. Why would he need technique? His mother worships him like a half God and probably has to beat the matchmakers off with a stick to keep them away from her precious son. Look . . . Maya's aunt is over at his table right now, talking to his mom."

"She can have him." Sophie wobbles on her heels and bee-lines for the exit before I can stop her.

How two girls, one with such a deep aversion for anything pretentious and the other with a weakness for haute couture and kir royales could be so close, I'll never understand. Thank God for Yasmin, the third pillar in our social triumvirate, and the only other person I know who thinks of Diane von Furstenberg dresses and Pucci print scarves as valid investments.

The music switches from an upbeat Arabic tune to the first chords of "I Will Survive." I decide it's probably a good time to head back to my table, where I presume Brian's been waiting since Sophie and I had left him for the dance floor. He's not exactly what you'd call a dancing enthusiast. I gave up begging him to join me at the clubs a month into our relationship.

Sure enough, he's exactly where I left him, slumped in a velvet-upholstered chair, and left to nurse a glass of orange juice by himself.

Not a screwdriver. Plain orange juice.

Of the dozens of decisions involved in planning a party of this scale, this one had to be the dumbest. In keeping with strict Islamic tradition, the groom, a clean-shaven pretty boy in a fabulous Armani tux and white silk tie, had flatly refused to indulge his not-so-holier-than-thou guests and those of us who may have sought refuge from the shrill music and the need to spend an evening with a roomful of virtual strangers in a tumbler of brandy or a glass of champagne.

I hate him.

But he's marrying Ranya, so for her sake, I've kept my mouth shut for the entire length of their year-long engagement. That's probably why my recent conversations with her have had all the emotional depth of a nutritional label on the back of a bag of Doritos.

Ranya and Dodi, short for Mohammad, weren't engaged a full month when he took to lecturing me about the importance of keeping "our traditions" alive while conspicuously glaring at my Catholic boyfriend out of the corner of his eye.

Whatever. I may never understand what the girl sees in him other than a penthouse in Westmount and an expedient way out of possible spinsterhood, but then again neither will I ever comprehend why she bothered with a university education if the Grand Plan was to get married and raise babies all along.

I pull up the chair next to Brian and lower myself onto it, smoothing the full skirt of my dress under me so as not to crease it. Brian looks bored, but breaks into a smile when he sees me. I smile back. It really was sweet of him to be here with me, knowing he'd be surrounded by so many curious glances and raised eyebrows.

"Your brother told me some guys just came back from the liquor store around the corner. They're standing outside the hall, spiking people's drinks. I brought you some." Brian slides a crystal flute topped up with bright red liquid across the table. Under the tablecloth, his hand grazes my silk-draped knee.

"Hey, watch it!" I pull my leg away furtively. "My whole family's here."

"Sorry." He turns sheepishly away from me and looks around.

Okay, so maybe I overreacted. Still, Brian ought to know better than to touch me in front of a roomful of people who feel as warm and fuzzy toward premarital sex as Dr. Laura does about gay pride parades.

"Nice place." He makes attempt number two at civility.

He's right. It is a nice place. More than nice, actually. With a vaulted ceiling as high as that of the Notre-Dame Basilica where Céline wed René the first time around, verandas and enclaves jutting out from behind thick brocade drapes, and soaring silk panels around the sculpted ballroom, it's almost *regal*.

It's the kind of venue befitting a modern-day aristocrat, which is exactly what my cousin looks like in a Reem Acra made-to-measure gown that she flew to New York City sixteen times to get fitted for. With her fiancé picking up the tab, it didn't matter. She'd even let me tag along a few times.

"So this is the kind of place you'd like to get married in, huh?" He doesn't say this with the dreamy wouldn't-it-be-nice-if-that-were-us-up-there kind of look, but more of an I-hope-you-don't-think-this-is-what-I'm-spending way.

The band picks this precise moment to launch into a popular *dabke* number, the Middle Eastern take on the circle dance.

"I love it when you get all romantic." I push my chair back, about to get up to join the circle.

"Aline, what is it? What did I say?" I hate it when he uses my full name. Only my mother does that anymore.

Speaking of whom, I catch her eagle-eye stare from Auntie Selma and Uncle George's table. That woman doesn't miss a beat.

She gives me The Look. The one that says stop being nasty to the poor boy before he gets really fed up with you and dumps you once and for all and then where will you be?

Not terribly marriageable, that's where. At least not among those who view a three-year-strong attachment to an *ajnabi*, with no sign of a big sparkling rock anywhere, as a serious affront to good manners. Lebanese society can eerily resemble a BBC period piece in situations like these.

Still, watching the hurt expression on Brian's face, I feel guilt start to nibble at the outer corners of my brain and I plop back onto my seat.

I love Brian, I really do. He's sweet, and sensitive, and he never loses patience with me despite my monumental mood swings. And my mood's been swinging a mile a minute ever since the other juniors around the office started getting their UFE results.

Oh my God. I'm going to puke. I clutch my stomach, feeling it contract into a hard, painful knot. I'm suddenly aware of the ventilation buzzing around the room, and I realize that the armholes of my dress are soaked through with sticky sweat.

UFE. It sounds like a cross between a wide-eyed alien obsessed with phoning home and fifties-style flying saucers straight out of an Ed Wood horror flick. The ominous abbreviation stands for Uniform Final Examination, and it's every bit as scary as it sounds. It's to accountants what the bar exam is to lawyers. In other words, its results can send you soaring up the corporate ladder to the world of stock options and golden parachutes, or sink you into the dungeons of anonymous bookkeeping. Like being an accounts clerk for a corner grocery store or the neighborhood dentist.

"Honey, are you okay?" Brian's fair brows are knitted in alarm.

"Um, I just—"

An enthusiastic screech cuts me off.

"Come here, my little duckling. You look wonderful." Auntie Selma has waddled over to the table elbow in elbow with my mother, who looks down at my bright red punch glass with tight lips. How did she know some of these were spiked?

"Brian, welcome. It's very nice to see you here. Should I start shopping for a new evening gown soon?" Though Auntie Selma says this last bit in Arabic, the pronounced wink in Brian's direction has turned him as red as the roses on the ushers' lapels. She leans over to him and offers up her cheek. One kiss . . . two . . . Whoops, he forgot that pesky third one. He flusters, not sure whether to go in for the third after she'd left her face hanging awkwardly in the air a couple of seconds too long. He opts for slumping back into his chair and studying his lap intently.

I want to pat him on the leg as a show of solidarity, but can't risk something so intimate in this setting. Instead we sit side by side, as mute as the stone gargoyles perched on the ledges of the cathedral across the street, fidgeting uncomfortably.

I really shouldn't complain. I brought this on myself. I'd asked Brian to attend the wedding as my date, which, where I come from, is tantamount to an engagement announcement in Rochelle's society column in the *Gazette*. Except we're not engaged.

My mother opens her mouth first. "No one's thinking of these things yet, Selma. Aline hasn't heard about her exam results. And they're still very young, you know." She tut-tuts her friend and tries to lead her to another table where respects are yet to be paid and gossip is yet to be mined.

"Of course she'll pass, Muna. Don't be silly. Better start thinking ahead. You know the waiting list for this hall was eighteen months long. . . ."

Auntie Selma's voice fades under the last chords of the *dabke*, and Ranya's yelps as both her plush velvet Louis XVI armchair and that of her new husband are lifted into the air by four men each and paraded around the dance floor.

Ranya is absolutely petrified.

Only after the poor girl has exhausted all her shrieks and nearly fallen off the chair a half dozen times do her assailants set her down.

"Ali . . ." Brian nuzzles his nose against my ear, tickling me.

I smile tenderly at him. I should push him away before anyone, especially from the groom's side, sees us, but I can't help it. This kind of sweetness would wear down even the sourest mood.

"What is it?" I let my leg graze his under the tablecloth.

"Let's go outside for a bit."

"Why?"

"Because we haven't been alone together for one second all day." He presses closer.

"It's my cousin's wedding—they're going to wheel out the cake any second now." I pull away.

"She hasn't even tossed the bouquet yet. Come on, just for a few minutes."

I open my Stila Berry–tinted lips in protest, but I'm all out of arguments. The idea of fooling around anywhere within a five-mile radius of any member of my family is making me nauseated. But really, an innocent little stroll around the hotel grounds isn't going to hurt anybody. I need to get over myself.

"Fine. Let's go. But you'd better not try anything."

I follow him through the giant French doors of the ballroom and out to the lobby.

It's much quieter here. From the middle of the elegant Versailles–meets–Martha Stewart décor of the foyer, I can still see the whole inside of the hall. No one seems to notice Brian and me standing behind the massive mahogany table in the middle of the room, crowned by the biggest floral arrangement I've ever seen.

"What do you want to see first, upstairs or the Royal Tea Room? If you want to go outside, then I'm going to need my coat. . . ."

The music coming from the cavernous hall screeches to an abrupt halt. The DJ's voice booms across the entire first floor of the hotel, ordering the single women in the room to come out to the dance floor.

"Ali . . ."

"Brian, she's going to toss the bouquet!"

"Ali, there's something I need to ask you."

Ha! There's Auntie Colette dragging a beet-red Sophie to the floor, where a horde of giggling girls, none that needed to be asked twice, is standing at attention. They look like they might really believe that in catching the bouquet they might also catch the eye of a prospective husband.

Hopeless, I tell you.

"What is it, sweetie?"

One . . . two . . . Oh God, look at Sophie. I swear she'd rather be roasting on a spit than be up there right now.

"Three!"

At the DJ's scream, twenty-five squealing girls lurch into the air.

"Ali, will you marry me?"

At the precise moment Maya's feet bounce against the ground, clutching the small bunch of white orchids and calla lilies high over her head like a victorious Olympian bringing home the gold, the zipper at the back of her bodice comes undone. The whole upper half of her dress flops over, leaving her little brown breasts jiggling and exposed before the entire room.

And I burst into tears.

3

I never thought there was anything wrong with marrying the first man you ever had sex with. Even as I got older and the grip my culture had over my senses eased, I still thought the idea had merit. Especially when that guy also turned out to be the one person I got along with the most. So what if the perfect guy came along a little earlier in life than I expected? Did that make him any less perfect?

Brian's one of those soft-spoken guys, the type you may not have noticed right away in a crowded campus bar or a sleek Saint-Laurent Street lounge if it weren't for his understated good looks and kind eyes. He's one of those guys who stays sober when everyone else gets hammered, looks straight into your face instead of at your boobs when they ask you your name, and offers to take you home just to make sure you get there okay.

And then there's the way he listens. He remembers things even I've forgotten I said. Like the time I mentioned—totally in passing—that I was sad I'd let whatever modicum of artistic talent I once had go to waste, and he showed up at my house the next day with a set of professional watercolors, complete with paintbrushes and an instruction manual.

Now that's love.

But then again, how would I know when there's never really been anyone but Brian? I didn't go out on my first date until I was fifteen, and the whole time I was terrified someone would see me and tell my mother.

I did manage to fall head over heels for this one guy during my last year of high school. He was tall with dark wavy hair and tar-black eyes. Completely the opposite of Brian. I would read *Macbeth* Cliff's Notes to him under the big oak behind the school while he dozed in my lap, right before our English Lit class. It lasted three months, or until he couldn't hide me from his Italian mother any longer. Apparently, she wasn't too crazy about Arabs. Maybe he wasn't either, but I was too heartbroken at the time to ask.

A year later, still not quite over my Italian Stallion, I met Brian. He loved my "exoticness," and I loved that he could carry on an intelligent conversation for longer than five minutes. He was older, more mature, and well, I guess at nineteen, I was starting to get curious.

We never ran out of things to talk about—we still haven't—and he doesn't cringe when I bring the latest issue of *Cosmo* to bed and ask him to contort himself so I can achieve "ultimate sexual fulfillment."

Another thing Brian and I agree on is that neither of us believes in soul mates, or fate, or any of that New Agey crap. We're both sensible accountants. We believe only in what we can see, touch, count. And I see two people who really enjoy being together, who laugh at the same jokes and cringe at the same politicians.

So today, the day Brian's *finally*, after three whole years, asked me to marry him, has to be the happiest day of my life so far.

But then why do I feel like I'm starring in one of those cheesy-effect movies where the walls are slowly closing in on the hapless screaming woman in the middle of the room? Shouldn't I be elated?

"Ali, honey . . . You haven't said anything."

Shit, he's right. I wipe the corners of my eyes without once looking at him. Could I pretend I'm crying out of joy instead of sheer terror?

"Brian, I . . . I'm so . . . Jeez, I don't know how . . ."

Now it's his turn to look like he's about to puke.

What would he say if I told him I needed more time? That if I didn't know after three years, then time may not be what I need, that's what he'd say. Then what?

A cold shiver races up my spine and forces the hairs on my arm upright.

I'd lose him.

I draw a deep breath. There's only one way to answer this. It won't be pretty, but I don't see any other way out.

"Brian." He is looking at me with those warm gray eyes, usually so clear, you'd think you could see straight through to his soul in them, now clouded over like a depressing winter day.

I am such a bitch.

"Brian," I start over. "How could you possibly be so selfish?" I pause dramatically.

The man looks absolutely gobsmacked. I silently promise God to feed my spiked punch to the plants and stay off the booze for a whole month if this works. He still hasn't managed to recover from the blow. I move in for the kill, cursing myself with every beat of my wildly racing heart.

"The UFE scores are due out any day now. I've never been under so much stress in my entire *life*, Brian, and this is the time you pick to ask me this?"

There. I did it. Surely, my lowest moment ever. I can't imagine what I'd have to do to top this. At least what I said was the truth. Not the whole truth perhaps, but that's not going to help anybody right now.

Brian goes ashen. His bottom lip quivers a tiny, almost imperceptible bit before he bites it.

I am Evil Incarnate. I had no choice.

"You're right." He straightens himself, running a hand

through his hair, and tugs his suit jacket into place. "Of course you're right. I have no idea what I was thinking. . . . I was just . . . nervous, I guess. Ali . . . I know you're the one. I also know that there's no way you're ever going to move in with me if we don't get married. I guess I didn't want to waste any more time."

My mouth opens and closes, like a fish gasping for life on a fisherman's deck. I want to say yes. I want to hold him so tight that I crush every last one of my lingering doubts. But I can't. Something inside me won't let me say what I always imagined I would at a moment like this. And yet I can't fathom a life without Brian.

He lifts his eyes tentatively at me. "This isn't a no, is it?"

"Oh baby, of course not!" I lunge for his neck and pull him into a tight hug. My heart squeezes painfully in my chest. I just managed to stop bawling a few seconds ago, and now I'm afraid I'm going to start all over again. My beautiful dress deserves better than to be paired with raccoon eyes and blotchy skin. And Brian deserves better than this. Better than me.

"I just want everything to be perfect." I kiss his forehead and slowly, I release him.

"I can live with that." He rubs his thumbs over my hands one more time before letting me go. "But now you've ruined the surprise."

"Not necessarily . . ." I snap my head around and make sure no one's looking. I think everyone's still reeling from the Bare Breast Scare to have noticed my conspicuous absence. I lift myself onto the balls of my feet and without any warning I kiss him long and loud on the lips. When I pull back, his eyes are still open wide with surprise.

"I haven't seen the ring yet," I say from under mascara-coated lashes.

I blow him another kiss and turn back toward the ballroom. I need to get away. I need to be around people.

"Ali . . ." Brian's fingers brush against my bare shoulder. "Don't get yourself sick over this. You're going to pass."

I smile tightly and break away from his grasp.

I wish I could be so confident.

Brian didn't bring up the M-subject again all weekend. And I didn't call up the girls and suggest we meet up at Carlos & Pepe's for nachos and strawberry daiquiris. We could stay up all night, any night, talking about everything and nothing in partic- ular, but when the biggest thing that's ever happened to me comes along, I don't tell a soul. I wonder what they would think of me if they knew.

I floated through the two days as if I were on drugs, not eating much, saying even less, but when I woke up this morning, I'd snapped out of it. The dark gloomy cloud looming over my head dissipated just as suddenly as it had appeared. I could think of only two things.

I'm going to Cancún in one week. With McGill's entire grad- uating class of the Diploma in Public Accountancy program. In other words, everyone who'd written the UFE with me. They're a lot more fun than they sound. Really.

Though in general the exam's failure rate hovers at a chilling 70 percent, at McGill, one of Canada's top universities, it's closer to 5 percent. If you can get through the program, the logic goes, you'll pass the exam. End of story.

Well I got through, so no reason to panic, right? Right.

Cancún is going to be fabulous. Better than fabulous. But since the trip is meant to include only those brave few who'd suf- fered the anguish of the certification process, I'd sort of breached tradition a bit when I asked Sophie and Jaz to tag along. I didn't think my classmates, mostly guys, would object to two extra fe- males on the trip. They didn't, but Brian did. I'd managed to weave in the revelation between bites of steamed mussels in spicy tomato sauce two months ago at L'Académie. It hadn't gone over quite so smoothly as I'd hoped. . . .

"I don't get it, Ali. You make a huge deal when I suggest that I could take the week off, you say it's the first time you get to travel without your family, and then you go and ask your friends to go with you?"

The man was seriously *pissed off.*

"But won't we have the rest of our lives to vacation together?" I countered. "When am I going to get another chance to go on this kind of trip with my best friends without giving my parents a conniption?"

He eventually came around, and now he's almost as excited about my trip as I am.

Almost.

For some reason he keeps telling me to make sure I watch out for myself and always, *always* stay with the girls. Oh, and that he trusts me. He makes sure to tell me that every so often too.

I did mention there were two things I was excited about on this bleak Monday morning, didn't I?

The other one's work-related. Shocking, I know.

This morning I get to show everyone at the office just how indispensable I am.

"Hi, everyone!" I say, and march over to my cubicle.

Cubicle. Cube farm. Box.

For all its derogatory monikers and negative connotations, the word itself implies one solitary silver lining.

Four walls.

Privacy.

At least you would think so.

But not the cubes at Ernsworth. Our cardboard-and-Styrofoam jail cells are made up of three sides of "half partitions" whose only virtue consists of the lack of even the pretense of privacy. The fourth side is, of course, a wide-open space.

"Hey, sexy, aren't we cheerful this morning? Love, love, *love* that cropped jacket, by the way, although it looks like it might fit my five-year-old niece," a Fran Drescher–pitched voice calls to me as soon as I plop down on my swivel chair.

"Thanks, Aphro. I think."

A Greek girl with an unfortunate nickname (which I'm sure her parents didn't anticipate when they named their baby daughter after the Greek goddess of love) who, at twenty-nine, still lives with her profoundly traditional family and shares my weakness for small-label designers, Aphroditi is my absolute favorite person at the office. When we're not out on audit engagements, we spend most of our time musing on how a good day at work is one where we're too swamped to remember how much we hate our jobs, debating the pros and cons of the bias-cut skirt, and openly drooling over Tom Stephanopoulos's ass. Plus, I suspect Aphro is the only one of my colleagues to appreciate my attempts at livening up the requisite accounting professional uniform: the polyester/cotton–blend navy blue suit.

"Wanna hear the latest stupidity to come out of Jessica Simpson's mouth?" Aphro looks up from a copy of *In Touch* with genuine enthusiasm.

"You need to lay off those gossip rags. They'll rot your brain cells worse than crack. You'll have none left for consolidating financial statements."

"Yeesh. You couldn't sound more like my mother if you told me I need to find myself a nice Greek boy and settle down before my tits sag like Grandma Maria's and my ass expands to the size of Crete."

"I'm a nice Greek boy, what's wrong with me?"

We don't need to turn around. We know exactly who it is. Aphro blushes deep fuchsia first, then recovers.

"In your dreams, Macedonia boy. I don't date descendants of goatherders. Bad karma. Besides, I think our villages might have been embroiled in a feud involving sheep and the fucking thereof circa third century B.C. Sorry."

He laughs. A gorgeous, guttural, straight-white-teeth-baring roar of a laugh.

Tom. Short for Athanasios. Ernsworth's resident Greek god, and everything you'd imagine Apollo himself to have looked like if any one of his marble likenesses were to suddenly spring to life.

"And what brings you to our little corner of audit heaven? It's a long way from Corporate Recovery." Aphro glances up at him from under mascara-soaked lashes batting faster than a set of hummingbird wings. I love how she can switch seamlessly between biting wit and shameless flirt. I generally just clam up around guys this hot. Remnants of a chubby childhood, I suppose.

"Just need to pick up some valuation docs from Manny. One of your audit clients is filing for Chapter Eleven. That's my turf."

As Tom speaks, I notice female heads leaning back ever so slightly in their swiveling chairs, eager to catch a fleeting glimpse of our own personal Jude Law.

"Well, I haven't seen Manny this morning, but you're welcome to pull up a seat and wait for him here." Aphro cups her heart-shaped chin, her lips slightly pouted. On anyone else, it would have been Danielle Steel novel–grade cheese, but Aphro comes off as smooth as a Kate Spade calfskin handbag.

"You know I'd love nothing more than to spend the morning in such lovely company." He returns Aphro's mock-flirtatious stare. "But duty calls right now, I'm afraid. I'll have to think up another excuse to come back here."

Shameless, shameless flirt. But virtuous boyfriend, if the gossip-mongering admin assistants are to be believed. Because for all the double entendres and bedroom stares that are exchanged between these drab walls, no one's ever known of Tom cheating on his longtime girlfriend. He's been with her for the past two years and as good as married as far as anyone here is concerned.

"You'll tell Manny I came by?"

"Sure thing," Aphro purrs in a tone worthy of a seventeenth-century Castilian señorita inviting her beloved to climb up her balcony for a midnight romp.

Tom flashes us one last Don Juan grin and backs toward the hall. Just as he's about to leave, he catches my eye, and very, very discreetly, he winks at me, and then walks away.

I feel a flush rising in my cheeks, and I snap my head around quickly and pray he didn't notice.

I've never told anyone, not even Aphro, but I have a recurring fantasy involving Tom. It started right after the Christmas party, about the time I first began working for Ernsworth as an intern.

Spouses and significant others, as well as "life partners," were not welcome at this particular gathering. I'd already caught glimpses of him lugging thick files and his beat-up old laptop around the hallways. I'd also already been warned by the secretarial staff not to bother even glancing in his direction, that even if he were to break up with his girlfriend, I was about seventy-fifth in line. But since said girlfriend was absent that night, and copious amounts of free alcohol were being passed around quickly and efficiently by the penguin-suited waitstaff, Tom was unanimously declared, with meaningful stares and muffled sounds, fair game for one and all. One of my favorite songs blared across the loudspeakers late into the evening. "I Just Died in Your Arms Tonight," by some defunct eighties pop group. I'd used up all ten of my free drink vouchers by then, as I'm sure Tom had, and I did the unthinkable. I asked him to dance. To my utter shock and disbelief, he agreed. And as if that wasn't bad enough, I plowed on. My mouth seemed to run on a different engine from the rest of my body, asking him how his girlfriend was doing.

"Fine," he said. "She's doing fine."

Ever since, I've taken to asking him, every so often, how his girlfriend is doing. I don't know her name, and I have no idea what she looks like. I'm not even sure why I ask, since I'm in a great relationship myself.

Like some sort of complicit code between us, he always says the same thing, but in a tone that suggests he'd rather be saying, "Come, the broom closet's this way, and wouldn't you like me to give you a private tour?"

This is where the fantasy part comes in. One day, he comes to the audit staff room on some errand or another. We flirt, and I ask him the usual question. Except I imagine him saying this instead: "My girlfriend? Oh, we broke up." And then follow it up with: "I was hoping I could take you out sometime."

I wonder how many women in the office have some variation on this scenario. I won't speculate. Just because I'm in a relationship doesn't mean I can't be curious. It's normal, right? Maybe it's a test to see what I'm made of.

At least it's one test I can safely say I've passed with flying colors.

"Oh, shit!" Aphro whacks her open palm hard against her forehead.

"What?"

"I forgot to tell you. Manny was looking for you last Friday. I hope you have a good story—he looked pretty pissed."

Ah. My moment of reckoning is finally here. Because I like Aphrodite so much, I'm even more eager to earn her respect than Manny's. I wince dramatically.

"I don't, but I've got something better." Here it comes. Either she's going to jump up and kiss me for making her life, and the lives of our entire audit team, easier, or she's going to be jealous she didn't beat me to it. I'm not worried. Aphro's not the jealous type.

"The Pirelli contract?"

"Okay, no, not that good. But still really, really good!"

"What?"

Maybe this'll get me promoted from junior- to intermediate-level auditor. In just under a year! At this rate I might just make manager before I hit twenty-five. Maybe that'll shut my relatives up at the next wedding. Who am I kidding? They'll just ask me why I haven't made partner yet.

"I—" I pause for added emphasis. "—was at Fortex Friday afternoon."

"And what, pray tell, were you doing there?"

"Getting those financials we've been after for over a month now."

"You didn't!"

"Not only did I, but I've got them right here for your drooling pleasure."

"Ohmigod! So the old witch just handed them over to you, just like that, after she'd been giving Manny and me the runaround?"

"No, actually, she just let me into the archives room and told me I could photocopy whatever I wanted but that I'd have to look for it myself."

"Let me see, let me see!"

I want to toy with Aphro, savoring my victory a little while longer, but she snatches the navy blue folder from my grasp before I can sweep it out of her reach. Her face is lit up with the same expectant enthrallment I imagine it does when she beholds the expensively dressed windows of Holt Renfrew, Canada's version of Saks, before it twitches in puzzlement, screws up into a strange sort of grimace, and promptly falls.

A tight rope of anxiety begins to wind itself into a knot in my stomach. I wait for her to say something.

"Aphro . . ."

"Oh, Ali . . . These are last year's financial statements. It's the ones from the year before they won't give us."

4

I'm not incompetent.

I'm not. I just don't care. There's a difference. Accounting did this to me.

Aphro throws the papers away, the dozens upon dozens of papers I'd photocopied, right there in the cardboard recycling box under her desk without saying a word.

If I didn't feel like a complete shit a few moments ago, I do now. The only person I actually respect and enjoy working with is now mad at me. Maybe just disappointed. Oh God, that's worse.

"Where is Manny, anyway?" I ask just as the man himself hurries into the audit staff area, spring in step and latte in hand, looking overly excited in my opinion over something so hopelessly banal as an interim audit review.

I brace myself for the avalanche of grievances and accusations that he's sure to hurl at me once he spots me trying to contort my body in such a way that it's completely hidden behind my laptop screen. He marches down the narrow passage at the far side of the room. Nothing. I study his face for signs of the reprimand storm to come. Still nothing. If anything, it's smug and self-satisfied, and if I didn't know better, I'd think he just had a roll in the tax files with his secretary in the archive room.

I hold my breath as he continues to march down the aisle,

seemingly impervious to my attempts at self-concealment. Oh, God, please . . . If he forgets to ask where I was Friday, I promise, no, I swear, I'll be nicer to my mother the next time she curses me out for coming home past 3 A.M. from a night of hardcore clubbing. Better yet, maybe I'll just stay in for some quality family time and skip socializing altogether this weekend.

His torso hovers above the partitions, navigating the maze of cubicles toward his office as though infused with a will of its own. Going . . . going . . . going . . . gone.

That was close. He's obviously forgotten about my mysterious whereabouts Friday afternoon, and what he doesn't know won't hurt him.

"You must have a horseshoe up your ass or something, because he just got back from a meeting with the bigwigs, and from the looks of it, it went well," Aphro says. "Swear to God, some people have all the luck. . . ."

She's talking to me! She's even smiling. I feel a bit better. Still, knowing that I disappointed her stays with me like a rotten aftertaste. I'm not used to disappointing people.

"You won't tell him where I was Friday, will you?"

Aphro mimics zipping her lips together, turning an imaginary key, and tossing it behind her, her massive citrine cocktail ring casting a kaleidoscope of shadows on the wall behind her.

Perfect. I can breathe.

"Drinks on me this Friday," I say.

"Don't sweat it. It happens."

She's right. Friends are so great for that. Giving you perspective, I mean. So I made a mistake. I'd gone out on a limb anyway. No one had even asked me to do it. I was trying. And I'm not going to dwell on it.

I relax and reach for my planner. Time to see what glorious accounting adventures I'm scheduled for on this gray Monday morning. I scan the tiny boxes under today's date from top to bottom. Hmm . . . no client visits today, goody, just "audit planning"— the technical term for play-hooky-and-get-off-early. Maybe I could even take the afternoon off and engage in some well-deserved retail therapy. It does seem a bit odd, though, this audit planning, seeing as it's busy season. I scan the rest of the page and . . . Oh.

Holy. Fucking. Shit. I forgot.

How could I? I'm usually so meticulous about these things . . . but I did.

I drop my head onto my desk as visions of lunch at Café République and an afternoon jaunt along the Saint-Laurent Street shops fizzle out and die like an overbleached patch of hair. My turn has come to face the dreaded semiannual performance review.

My first one, in fact. Another one of corporate life's annoyances, like unpaid overtime, stingy vacation schemes, and company-wide pay freezes. And at four o'clock, right about the time I would've been strolling into Stylexchange to check out the latest in Euro streetwear. It's not so much the interview I'm dreading, but the interviewer: Evil HR Lady.

Her name is actually Diane Cloutier, and she is the most terrifying person I've met in my entire adult life, which I must admit isn't very long, but it's an impressive feat nonetheless. Diane doesn't simply represent the firm—she lives and breathes it, as a walking, talking, individuality-crushing energy force.

Diane *is* the firm.

"Good morning, Ali. Nice weekend?" Manny says, plopping his head over my cubicle wall.

Shit. And I thought I was in the clear. Still, no need to panic just yet.

"Yes, lovely, thanks. I checked out this new place with my—"

"Sorry, Al, I've got to run, senior manager meeting. I just wanted to mention that you left a little early on Friday without alerting the group. We might have used your help, and we certainly don't want to have a situation where some people are working harder than others. I'm sure you understand."

"Err . . . sorry, Manny, I just thought that . . . I mean, well . . ."

Aphro keeps her gaze firmly fixed on her screen. That girl would destroy at poker.

Manny is now glaring at me, left eyebrow arched.

"Right. Sorry. Won't happen again."

That might have smoothed things over slightly, as he nods and takes off for the main boardroom.

For the second time today I feel I should whip the Banana Republic scarf from my neck and throw it over my head, drop to my knees, and pray to God for having pulled me out of a potentially sticky situation. Per usual, the urge is short-lived.

I draw in a deep breath instead and reach for the first folder on top of my in-tray. I open it to the Outstanding Issues page and read the first point: *"Fees previously applied to the unpaid principal protection dividend, accrued as at 2005 and incurring foreign exchange gains or losses should be marked to market at each net asset period date."*

Right. I can almost feel the yet-unexamined copy of *Marie Claire* burning a hole through my audit bag, pleading to be let out and enjoyed with good female company and a steaming cappuccino. I can ignore its nagging pleas for only so long. I glance at the annoying entry one last time before shutting my planner and leaving my cubicle.

Why am I being so negative, anyway? Besides this morning's debacle—which no one but Aphro knows about—I haven't done anything wrong. I haven't taken any sick days (just one, but I think having your period should count for *something*), only occasionally consult the Internet for non-work-related matters (it's not my fault I live in Montreal and have to get my Jimmy Choo fix online), and usually cap social calls to other cubicles at fifteen minutes each—tops. With some luck, I could still squeeze in some window-shopping before the stores closed. After all, how long could it possibly take to say, "Keep up the good work"?

It's never a good sign when the person holding your fate between her French-manicured fingers makes you wait in the hallway for twenty-three minutes on your miserably high-heeled shoes while she mercilessly attacks someone else via the telephone.

"Aline!" She eventually motions me in, but not before hurling one last insult at the poor plebeian on the other end.

"I don't care if she was a good candidate, Jerry. They're entry-level auditors, not rocket scientists. You don't wear a pantsuit to an interview and expect me to call you back! Who does she think we are, Urban Outfitters? This is a world-class consultancy, for Chrissake. Call me back when you have someone decent."

Slam.

Oh my God.

I look down at my outfit. Tasteful beige blazer and trusty tweed pencil skirt with Chanel-esque black-tipped shoes. At least my fashion sense was showing some foresight.

"Well," she says, motioning for me to take a seat. "Thank you for taking the time to see me this afternoon."

Like I had any choice in the matter.

As if to physically signal the end of the niceties, she snatches up a red folder from a pile on the corner of the desk and drops it on the space in front of her with a saturated thud.

It's curiously thicker than I had imagined.

"Tell me," she says without looking up, "how have you enjoyed the past few months here with us?"

"Great! Really great experience. And I've met so many great people." I suddenly wonder if she's going to break into a lengthy tirade against my overuse of the word *great*.

"Really?" She squares her shoulders and studies me, her face contorting somewhat. It might have been a smile. "Well, that's certainly encouraging to hear. But is that your honest opinion?"

What? *Honest opinion?* Is she kidding me? What is this, a police interrogation?

"Um . . . Well, I've been on some very interesting audits lately, and—"

"Which ones?"

"Which what?" I try to fan my shirt collar discreetly. It's getting rather hot in the room.

"Which interesting companies have you audited recently?" Diane taps her pen against the desk without taking her eyes off me. Not even to blink.

"Er . . . well. There was AlCorp Mining a few months ago, that was a real gas . . . ha, ha, no pun intended . . ."

Diane sighs, somewhat aggravated, I think.

"And, um, I've also had a chance to travel, which is really cool." I'm desperate, grabbing at straws, hoping she will move to another line of questioning.

"Travel? A junior? Where to?"

The only company "traveling" I'd done on the firm's dime was to the water-purification plant in Beauharnois, a gray slab of steel and concrete in the middle of rural Quebec.

It qualified as official travel only because of the extra couple of kilometers that made it cheaper to spend the night in a run-down, side-of-the-highway motel rather than expensing the gas involved in commuting back and forth to Montreal. There wasn't even a McDonald's in sight, for which I would gladly have broken my self-decreed commandment of not eating anything containing over two thousand calories per serving. I had to settle for *poutine*, a local specialty of french fries and cheese curds drowned in thick brown gravy, also known as Cardiac Arrest in a Dish, à la Québecoise.

"Well?" Diane snaps.

"Um . . . you know that picturesque little town by the Beauharnois canal, the one with the quaint bed and breakfast overlooking Lake Saint-Louis?"

Diane sighs and shifts her gaze back to the folder in front of her. "If you're not going to be frank, Aline, then I will. We've been quite disappointed with your performance since you joined Ernsworth and Youngston last spring."

My stomach shrinks and curls on itself as though someone has poured acid on it. How dare she say that about me? I'm Aline Hallaby, proud daughter of Muna and Omar Hallaby, winner of the grade five spelling bee, permanent fixture on my high school dean's list, and all-round straight-A student. Except in my accounting courses. My record in that department isn't quite so luminous. I was able to hide that fact from the recruitment reps by having been smart enough not to take the tough classes in my first two years of university, so all they could see were my sparkling A-minuses and B-pluses in things like Consumer Behavior and Business Communication. My D-minus in Advanced Cost Accounting and C in Principles of Consolidation were buried in my GPA calculation for all of time.

"I don't know what you're talking about," I say, looking straight at the tiny piece of Scotch tape stuck to the wall behind Diane.

"You don't? Okay, then, let's see what your manager has to say about your performance, shall we?

"Aline exhibits a lack of professionalism in her conduct through extensive use of e-mail and the Internet for non-business-related matters. Furthermore, her work betrays a lack of understanding of many key accounting principles and their applications. She is distracted and as a result her files are replete with careless errors. I do not feel the results of her efforts are at par with our expectations of a typical Ernsworth employee, and I would hesitate to select her as part of my audit team in any future engagements."

Each one of her words falls on my ears like a heap of dirt on a coffin. I squeeze the sides of the chair to stop my hands from shaking. I must be the color of vomit. Come to think of it, I'd rather *be* a splat of vomit on some underaged and partied-out kid's shoe, puking in a bathroom stall of a campus bar, than sitting in this chair across from that woman.

I had no idea Manny felt that way. How come he never told me? Was I supposed to divine his true feelings by reading the dried-up coffee stains decomposing at the bottom of his crusty Alouettes mug?

"So," Diane continues, completely oblivious to my shock, "I've been consulting with the audit partners, and none of them really want you on their engagements anymore." *Oh, God please kill me now.* "But since your probationary period has already passed, we can't really let you go without a warning, unless you decide to leave by your own volition."

She glares at me.

I blink a few times. A vision of me confronting my mother with the news that I'd been fired clouds my brain, all hazy and flash-forward-like. The vision then implodes in a poof of hysterical shrieking and threats of deportation back to the Old Country.

Ha. If Diane thinks I'm going to make this easy, then she's got another think coming.

"So—" She exhales sharply and eyes me one more time for good measure. "—we're going to offer you another chance to prove yourself. In the Corporate Recovery department. You can start fresh. As of tomorrow. New manager, new clients, new assignments. Let it not be said that Ernsworth isn't a caring company, committed to the advancement of our employees."

Advancement toward the social security office, more like it.

"Thanks, Diane, I really appreciate this. I won't let you down this time." I squirm in the uncomfortable modern-design chair. I need to get out of here before I succumb to a nervous breakdown, right this moment.

She studies me again, her eyes narrowing into hard slits. "I'd like to remind you that your UFE results should be in soon. Some people around the office have begun receiving them already." She clears her throat. "You are aware that

Ernsworth reserves the right to terminate your employment with us if you fail? It's in your contract. I'm very proud to say that as long as I've been working here, we've never had to resort to that clause. We boast a perfect success rate, thanks to a rigorous selection process."

Surely this can't be legal, to make someone feel so utterly small and replaceable. I don't know whether I should just quit and figure out how to explain it to my parents later, or drop to my knees and beg for mercy.

"Yes, Diane, I'm aware. Thank you. I studied very hard and I'm hoping for the best," I mutter, trying not to betray my anxiety while droplets of cold sweat snake down my back. I pull myself to my feet. There can't be any more to this ordeal. I couldn't take it.

"You *will* be providing me with a copy of the results as soon as you get them, won't you?"

"Of course I will." My voice comes out stilted and squeaky instead of indignant. "Why? Are you suggesting—?"

"I'm not suggesting anything at all. I have no doubt you'll do marvelously. That's why we hired you."

I let out a snort, which I try to muffle with a cough. "No, of course not. I have no doubts either. That I'll pass, that is. It's just a bit of an unpredictable little test, what with the seventy percent failure rate and all."

"Are you saying you don't consider yourself to be somewhere in the top thirty percent? That I made a mistake in taking you on?"

"That's not what I'm saying at all. It was a general observation, stupid, really . . . ," I stammer. Something inside my head is pounding, and my vision is beginning to blur. I need to get out of here. "Well if that's all, then I think I'd better—"

"Actually, there is one last thing, Aline. This one's a little more . . . Let's see, how shall I put this? *Sensitive* . . ."

Is she kidding? After all that? I can't wait to hear this.

"Please take a moment to think about what I'm going to say

before you react. Feedback is an important tool that guides your career path. It's up to you to decide which criticism to act upon, and what to disregard."

Please get to the point. I'm still feeling faint from the preceding barrage of insults, and I don't know how much more of this I can take. I need time to pull myself together. Now.

"It's been noticed around the office that your attire is, well, rather inappropriate for our company image. You should consider wearing clothes that aren't quite so . . . *fitted.*"

And that's when I break down.

5

Tears sting my eyes as I try to figure out the quickest, shortest way back to my desk and out of the building. Something in my suit pocket rattles as I push open the heavy door to the fire escape. No sense taking the elevator with my face looking like this.

Coins!

I'd forgotten the change from my breakfast muffin this morning and I couldn't be more grateful for it. No need to go back for my purse then. Or my audit bag. Or my cellie. Okay, so maybe I'll go back for that. I'll be in and out. No one will see me.

"Ali!"

Crap. Jean-Pierre from Tax. He's standing beside the water cooler right next to the twenty-fourth-floor staircase entrance, almost as if he *knew* I was going to waltz out of there this very minute.

"Getting your daily exercise in, eh? You'll never guess what I . . . Hey, are you crying?"

"Crying? Me? Don't be silly," I say, wiping the moist spot at the outer corner of my right eye. "Allergy season. You know how it is."

"What are you allergic to, exactly?"

As it happens, I've never been allergic to anything in my entire life, and I don't have the first clue what to say.

"Ragweed."

"Ragweed? Isn't that more of a spring kind of—?"

"And pollen. Dog hair . . . all pets, really. And dust, too, come to think of it." Dust! Why hadn't I thought of that first? There isn't a dust season, is there?

"Oh, well. Sorry to hear that." He stares down at the cardboard cone in his hand, looking a bit confused. "*En tout cas,* as I was saying." His eyes suddenly fill with a bright glow, as though recalling something particularly pleasant. "The UFE results. Just got 'em this morning."

"And?" I ask, mustering up all the fake excitement I can manage, even though the answer is oozing out of every pore in his overjoyed body.

"Two forty. Just made it."

"Well, you know what they say. It really doesn't matter what you get just as long as you pass."

Two forty. What wouldn't I give to see those three digits on CICA letterhead delivered to my doorstep? Sorry, my parents' doorstep.

"You're telling me. *Aïe-oye!*" He pretends to wipe sweat from his brow, and breaks into a broad grin. "I was beginning to get a little nervous. Especially since I'd signed the mortgage agreement on the house and everything."

"Oh, you had? Congratulations, then!"

"Thanks. Definitely a huge step. Nerve-racking, you know? What about you? Get anything yet?"

"No, nothing."

"I wouldn't worry about it. You should see how fat the envelope was, stuffed with all kinds of applications for credit cards, life insurance, pamphlets about the Order, all kinds of crap. It only takes one thin little piece of paper to say you flunked, though. Fat envelopes take longer in the mail. Don't sweat it."

"Yes, that makes perfect sense." It does, doesn't it? But then how come he got his fat envelope and I didn't get mine? Despite

Jean-Pierre's platitudes, the narrow hallway is beginning to suffocate me, and fresh tears are threatening to flow down my cheeks again any second now.

"Thanks JP, but I've really got to go. Catch you later!" My voice sounds unusually shrill.

"Yeah, good luck anyway." He calls after me as I run into the stairwell, "And take something for those allergies!"

I burst outside into the cool autumn afternoon and stop to catch my breath. Diane's voice is still echoing in my head, blowing my self-esteem to smithereens before dealing the lethal last blow: mocking the way I dress.

I can still hear her imparting words of wisdom to me about reconsidering some of the more "questionable" items from my wardrobe while she fanned my green face with her red folder.

I start walking, eyes fixed on the dry yellow leaves stuck between the cracks in the sidewalk, trying to avoid passersby's inquisitive glances while they watch me wipe the few renegade tears from my lower lashes.

I need to get home. I wonder if I could call in sick tomorrow. Tempting though that may be, it's probably not the best way to kick off my new stint at Corporate Recovery.

Corporate Recovery. It's really just a euphemism for flatbroke-and-about-to-fork-over-their-last-dime-to-us department. *Corporate Recovery* just sounds better. It's all about image, even in the high-flying world of high finance. Our clients prefer "recovery consulting" over bankruptcy services, just like Joe Blow would rather say he's getting "stress management counseling" before breaking down and admitting it was either the shrink or the straitjacket.

Another thought occurs to me: What if I fail the UFE? I battle another wave of nausea and scan the street for the nearest garbage can, just in case.

What then? I'd most likely end up at one of the small mom-and-pop audit firms, filing tax returns and doing inventory counts for things like underwear and toothbrushes. I shudder.

Diane's right. I've got to try harder. At least I can make a fresh start at this department. I'll dazzle them with the new, improved, über-professional Aline Hallaby.

And I'll need a whole new way-too-important-to-be-talking-to-you career-woman wardrobe to go with my new image, of course.

Finally, some positive thinking.

Plus—and I could kick myself for actually thinking this when my entire future is hanging by a proverbial thread—maybe I'll even get to sit next to Tom.

Just then, as I'm about to turn the corner to the metro station, I feel cell phone vibrate in my purse.

"Hello?"

"You are *never* going to guess what that little shit did to me."

The word *never* comes across the airwaves so loud and shrill that I'm sure it's caused some sort of inner ear damage.

Yasmin doesn't wait for me to venture a guess, or even say hello, before continuing her verbal onslaught. "That's it, Al. It's over. I know what you're thinking and I don't want to hear it. I'm really serious this time."

"Calm down, Jaz. Just tell me what happened."

"I caught the fucker talking to his ex at Rouge last weekend."

"Oh, Jaz, I'm so sorr—"

"I don't give a shit about that!" she screeches before I have a chance to properly commiserate. "I knew he was screwing Jessica behind my back even though I told him I didn't care if he was and that all I ever wanted from him was the truth. I saw him at a bar, Ali, on Crescent Street, a gazillion miles from Hampstead on a *Friday night.* All these months he's been giving me that bullshit about keeping the Sabbath and how he couldn't go anywhere on Friday nights unless he walked—and I swallowed it! You should have seen me. I just gave it to him

right there in the middle of the dance floor. In front of everybody."

"You made a scene in the club?"

"I don't care! I hope he's so humiliated, he never steps out of
his fucking house again! Why would he do that to me? Why can't
he just tell me the truth? It's not like I'll stop sleeping with him.
All I want is for him to take me out once in a while. Is that too
much to ask?"

"No, sweetie, of course not. What did you tell him, though?"

"I confessed to sleeping with Andrew at the Christmas party
last year."

"You didn't!"

"I did."

"Jaz! What's Andrew going to do when he finds out you ratted
him out to his own best friend?"

"He denied the whole thing, the prick."

"Wait a minute. . . . When did this happen?"

"He was standing right there beside me when I went off—"

"I can't believe you did this."

"Why should I spare anyone's feelings? Ben didn't even bat
an eyelash, the fucking, fucking asshole. And that's not even the
worst part."

"There's more?"

"Well, now that Andrew isn't speaking to me, I have no way of
knowing what Ben is up to with that slut anymore. What the hell
am I supposed to do now?"

I open my mouth to offer some words of solace, but I'm at a
complete loss. What I really want to say is that she deserves a lot
better than that douche bag who wouldn't know a good thing if it
slapped him in the face with a pair of black satin elbow gloves. I
don't. Because I know I'll live to regret it when Jaz and Ben get
back "together" this time next week, in as far as two people can
get back together when their entire relationship amounts to a series of booty calls.

"Ali? You still there?"

"Oh, yeah, sorry, Jaz. I'm really sorry. It just hasn't been the best day for me."

"Why not? What happened?" The venom in her voice completely dissipates and is replaced with genuine concern.

In semicoherent sentences and between congested sniffles, I tell her everything, in as much detail as someone standing outside a busy subway station at rush hour can. I start sobbing all over again when I get to the part where Diane insinuates I dress like Julia Roberts in *Erin Brockovich.*

"Shit, that's horrible. We need to get you drunk."

"Can't. Work tomorrow."

"Me too, so what?"

"Your boss doesn't notice when you're drunk *on* the job, let alone the night before. My situation's a little different."

Jaz has the coolest job ever. Okay, I'll admit to being somewhat biased here because my career happens to be only marginally more captivating than one of sweeping animal feces at the zoo. Still, being a sales rep for a major pharmaceutical company does come with its perks, like getting to ply big money on potential clients over expensive dinners and fancy cocktails, access to a generous expense account, and hefty bonuses at the end of the year.

Oh, and having a backbone and personal style is actually considered a good thing in her line of work.

"So what are you doing tonight then?"

"I dunno . . . call Brian, rent a movie, maybe order in."

A hot flash travels through me at the mention of Brian's name. I still haven't told Jaz, or anyone, that he proposed. I have no idea what I'm waiting for. It's almost like if I don't talk about it, I won't have to seriously consider it just yet.

I don't hear anything for a full minute. I wonder if the line's gone dead.

"Jaz?"

"What if I told you I could maybe—maybe—don't get your hopes up, score tickets for the Nadya Toto show tonight?"

All the usual buzz and hum of my internal organs' normal functioning grinds to a halt. Suspended.

Did she really just say Nadya Toto? Nadya Toto, star of the Montreal Fashion Week Nadya Toto?

I think a pool of saliva might be forming at the corner of my mouth.

"How . . . ?" I can't finish the sentence. I never had any idea who you had to call, see, or blow to get into one of the Fashion Week shows, but they had always seemed completely closed off to the general public. Usually, by the time I heard that they were going on, the shows were already over.

"Paige is doing PR for the events. And Jim owes me," Jaz says flatly.

Dr. James "Jim" Caldwell III. Neurosurgeon of twelve years and divorcé of one and a half. The vision of Jaz in her low-cut Diesel top and Paxil order sheet was the welcome mirage to the desert of his bitter divorce proceedings. He had the cozy Mount Tremblant ski lodge his ex-wife had conceded, and she was going through another rough patch with Ben. It didn't seem to matter to either one of them that Jaz and his daughter Paige were around the same age.

"Jaz, I don't know what to say. . . ."

"Nothing. Just do me a favor and show that tight-assed HR bitch just how much you care about her fashion advice and buy yourself something fabulous tonight. I hear the featured designers are keeping their stores open late for some after-hours shopping. I'll call Sophie, you just meet me at the Old Port in an hour."

And she hangs up.

6

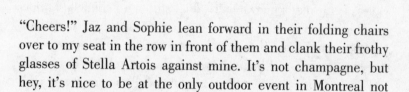

"Cheers!" Jaz and Sophie lean forward in their folding chairs over to my seat in the row in front of them and clank their frothy glasses of Stella Artois against mine. It's not champagne, but hey, it's nice to be at the only outdoor event in Montreal not sponsored by cheap Molson or Labatt beer.

"How do you like your spot? Can you see anything?"

At this short notice, Paige couldn't get us three seats on the same row. But Jaz made sure I got the best of the bunch.

"Jaz? Did I already mention that I love you?"

"Only twenty-five times since we got here. Just sit the fuck down and enjoy the view."

And what a view it is. Front row at the seventh annual Mercedes-Benz Fashion Week, set up along a cobblestoned Old Montreal street against a backdrop of the river glinting under the pink sky on one side, and a two-hundred-year-old cathedral on the other.

This is so cool.

Even more so are the young dressed-to-kill PR reps passing out gift bags full of MAC samples from their upcoming winter collection. I peek into my logoed black chamois pouch. Summer-fête, a tube of rosy-gold SPF 15 tinted lip conditioner, and a sample-size moisturizer. If I didn't still have lingering urges to puke up my lunch after this afternoon's encounter with Ernsworth's resident Medusa, I'd think I was in heaven.

The woman sitting next to me, clad head-to-toe in a hot pink power suit worthy of Samantha Jones herself, is checking her watch and sighing furiously. I giggle like a giddy teenager on her first date. My first fashion show ever, and just like in my fantasies, it's running an hour late.

I twist in my seat to face the girls.

Sophie, who'd been forcibly plucked out of the McGill campus library by Jaz, is clearly unfazed by her glam surroundings and looks as relaxed as if she were hunched over an Advanced Optics textbook on her kitchen table. Her hair is bunched up on top of her head in semblance of a bun and would have been held together with an old pencil, pockmarked with evidence of compulsive chewing, if I hadn't persuaded her it wouldn't clear the fashion security check at the door. She finally relented and took my antique silver barrette instead.

Next to her, Jaz seems uncomfortable and fidgety, something I've gotten used to over the ten years we've been friends. Though half-Lebanese, Jaz is not exactly what you'd call a proud Arab. She insists that she's *Phoenician,* a tribe of merchants that plied its trade along the shores of the Mediterranean back when Jesus was still trying to break into carpentry.

She's right though. That's who the history books say our ancestors are. Still, it's like Britney Spears saying she's half Visigoth, half Burgundian, with a sprinkle of Macedonian from her mother's side.

Jaz even replaced the surname she'd inherited from her father, Khoury, with that of her Canadian mother when she turned eighteen. It can totally throw you off if you come face-to-face with Jaz's barely confinable auburn curls and wide espresso-brown eyes instead of the pale freckled skin and button nose you might have been expecting with a name like Yasmin McGregor.

"Hey, don't look," Jaz says, completely deadpan. "I think that might be Ben and Jen over there."

I swing around wildly. "Ben Af—"

"Shh! I said don't look! He's up here shooting a movie. It figures."

This is so surreal. I don't care how sappy this makes me look, I have to do it. I fling my half-twisted body back and try to pull Jaz into a hug.

"Are you going to be this sappy in Cancún? Because if you are, I just might have to reconsider this trip."

Sophie's eyes light up at the mention of the C-word. And my stomach turns.

"Props, Ali, for the best idea ever!" She smacks her knuckles against mine, ghetto-style.

"If I'm going to spend my first tropical vacation away from my best friends, I might as well just soak in an inflatable kiddie pool in my backyard and save on airfare."

I force a smile and pull it off rather well, considering there isn't going to *be* a Cancún vacation if I don't pass the UFE. As if I'd subject myself to a whole week of "You'll get 'em next year!" and pitying sideways glances. But how am I going to work up the nerve to tell them that? Jaz even booked a manicure/pedicure/all-over-body-wax appointment at Spa Diva in honor of the occasion.

"Have you packed yet?"

"Jaz, the flight's not until Sunday. That's another six days."

She opens her mouth to say something, but suddenly, a blinding spotlight illuminates the makeshift catwalk, and what sounds like two thousand watts of Daft Punk blasts through the narrow street. The show has begun.

"That was fun." Jaz picks imaginary lint balls off her DKNY trench coat.

"Really? You couldn't pay me to wear half that stuff," Sophie says. "And the other half probably costs more than my annual tuition for what amounts to a few yards of see-through fabric."

Jaz purses her lips at Sophie.

"What?"

"Never mind." She sighs. "Ali, honey, what did you think?"

I was absolutely mesmerized. From the moment the first model placed one brightly painted toe on the catwalk, I felt like I had come home. These were my people. Any one of them could give you a complete rundown of the Proenza Schouler spring collection at the drop of a Lulu Guiness hat, and all could appreciate the sublime genius of Karl Lagerfeld in a way that no one else I knew could, not even Jaz.

I glance around the bustling alley. The rows have nearly emptied of beautiful and/or highly connected people, they've all flocked to the catwalk, clinking glasses of Stella and San Pellegrino, greeting one another with air kisses in a cloud of Chanel No. 5. And though I'm only twenty-two, half of them don't look a day over eighteen. If I somehow managed to switch careers without having my mother die of shame (I can hear it now: *We didn't come to this country so you could work in a clothing shop*), I'd still be an old fogey next to these young upstarts. There's simply no place for me among them. I don't belong.

"Thanks for the tickets, Jaz. I'll try and find you a hot single audit senior to make up for this. I have to get going now, though."

"What about the after-hours shopping? The bar's still open."

"I'm sorry, I can't. I'm starting in that new department tomorrow. I can't show up hungover on my first day."

"I'm not letting you go home before you buy something to cheer yourself up."

"She's right, Ali. Live a little." Sophie bounces up next to me and hooks her arm through mine. "You know, I still haven't bought a swimsuit for the trip?"

"Sophie! You're horrible! How did you manage to get into McGill with that brain?" And not just any old McGill major, might I add. Electrical engineering. The crème de la crème of higher education. Unfortunately, the same program her parents were so thrilled she was accepted into—without any thought to how she felt about it herself—has erased any semblance of a social life Sophie might have had. It's also liquefying her gray matter and will soon be serving it up scrambled, just like in those "this is your brain/this is your brain on drugs" ads from the eighties. Except in Sophie's case, it's academia she's overdosing on.

"Why don't we just pick one up tonight? We're borderline drunk, about to go on the trip of a lifetime together and have the best time ever. How could things possibly be more perfect?"

I could think of a few ways. Like a cool 400 score on the UFE. I'd settle for a passing 240. And a nice, convenient way to give myself more time to think about my future with Brian without running the chance of losing him altogether. But if this night was cutting through even Sophie's school-induced stress, maybe I owed it to the girls to lighten up.

"Hey, look, guys." Jaz points to an illuminated shop on a street corner we'd just wandered around. "Let's try that one first. It looks new."

We walk up to the windows and peer inside.

The sign above the heavy glass doors reads AÏSHA SAINT-JACQUES.

Interesting.

"Yeah, why not?" I say. The familiar tingle of anticipation I get from really orgasmic-quality shopping overtakes the looming dread in the pit of my stomach. We swing open the door, releasing the sweet scent of vanilla into the cooling outside air, and walk in.

Like most high-end stores, the space is uncluttered and the ambience hints at modern minimalism. I turn to look at the racks of clothing running along the walls and gasp under my breath, hoping the sales clerk didn't hear me.

It's like someone had taken a CAT scan of my brain while I was sleeping and translated the contents into actual clothes.

Club wear, resort wear, trendy evening wear . . . There's even a wall of really cute swimsuits that Sophie ambles to.

"Whatcha think?" She holds up a saffron halter bikini with wooden ring clasps at the sides.

"Very cool." I flash her two thumbs up, and she scampers off to the dressing room.

I wander to a rack of brightly colored dresses, totally perfect for Mexico, at one side of the store. I nearly swoon at a high-necklined pink paisley dress with a plunging keyhole that would show off half my chest.

"See? Told you this would be a good idea," Jaz says before meandering over to the accessories corner.

I pick up a backless khaki silk-blend dress, slit up to the thigh, and mentally prepare myself for the price. The label says AÏSHA SAINT-JACQUES, just like the store name, so I'm hoping it won't be too exorbitant. Still, the quality is clearly top notch. It's only a matter of time before this up-and-coming designer becomes a household name, so I figure even if the dress is in the four figures, it would still be a steal, really. Why, a similar Armani dress would be priceless. I take a deep breath and turn over the tag.

What? I blink twice and lean in closer. There's got to be a mistake. This can't be right. It's not possible. Maybe the sales clerk didn't realize she'd tagged it wrong. I'll just inconspicuously walk over to the cash register and . . .

"*Bonjour. Vous aimerez l'essayer?* Would you like to try it?"

Damn. So close. The saleslady is looking at me expectantly.

"Um, is this really the price?" Totally gauche, I know. My curiosity just has to be satisfied.

"Yes. I am afraid I cannot go lower."

"Oh, no! I didn't mean—I mean . . . It's just that, well, I kind of expected it to be more expensive."

The young woman smiles. "That's not my philosophy. By doing everything myself—almost everything, that is—I cut down on the costs and pass the savings on to my customer. Plus I'm just starting out, so I need to build my name before I can charge couture prices."

"Someone should tell that to Marie St-Pierre a couple of doors down." I snort, and she starts laughing. She's got the milkiest, most flawless porcelain skin I've ever seen, pink lips and cheeks that scream "I run five kilometers before my breakfast of nuts and berries every morning." And then there's the hair: gorgeous thick black hair that hangs halfway down her back in one sleek, perfectly straight layer.

"So that must be your name on the sign, then?" I say.

She holds out a dainty hand. "Aïsha Saint-Jacques. *Enchantée.*"

I want to ask her a million questions, like how did she get into this business in the first place? Can she support herself, or is she some kind of heiress living off a trust fund? How did she decide to go against her better judgment and do something this risky instead of be a teacher or a nurse or take whatever predictable office job? Or did she know all along that this was her path? I have no idea. I just know I want to talk to this woman again, maybe another time when Sophe and Jaz aren't around.

The three of us continue browsing, and by the time we finally decide to move on, I've gathered an armload of new clothes, shoes, and accessories for Cancún on top of the ones I already had neatly stacked next to my Guess monogrammed carryall, with their tags still attached.

As Aïsha waits for my credit card info to register, she wraps my new pink satin d'Orsay pumps and matching confetti-beaded purse in lovely blue carrier bags that look handmade, and fastens them with a taffeta ribbon.

We leave with a promise to drop by again sometime soon and tell everyone we know about Aïsha Saint-Jacques.

Halfway to the next shop, I realize I've just blown my entire clothing budget for the next three months without having bought a single new conservative piece for the office.

Great.

Jaz drops me off at home well past one that night in her shiny
new Jetta. After all the shops had run out of complementary
Stella and closed for the night, we'd wandered over to Jello Bar,
where we spent a few more hours dreaming out loud about foam
parties and banana boats while we clicked martinis in between
glasses of water.

"Thanks." I hug her. She's done her best to get my mind off
my horrible day. And had succeeded for a while. But the sinking
feeling in the pit of my stomach is back, muddled with the anxiety of having to face my first day at Corporate Recovery tomorrow hungover.

For the second time today, I wonder if I could call in sick.

In the darkness, I feel for the keyhole of my front door. It
takes me a few tries, but I manage to get it open, pushing *v-e-e-e-ry*
slowly so as not to wake anyone up.

I'm too tired to bother with the lights. Or with brushing my
teeth. I just kick off my shoes in the hallway and take a step
across the kitchen, toward my bedroom in the basement.

"Busted."

"Wha—!" I nearly jump out of my skin. Sami is sitting in
front of the TV in the living room playing Xbox or PlayStation or
whatever the latest video game console upgrade he managed to
finagle out of my parents is.

"Sshhh! You'll wake up Mom and Dad!"

"How was work?" he continues, unfazed.

Despite barely repressing an urge to wrap his entire head in
duct tape, I walk over to the couch and lock him in a huge bear
hug.

My baby bro. Maybe it's an ethnic thing, or the fact that we
could bond over the misery of having to adhere to insane rules,
but my siblings and I grew up close.

He lets me hug him for about three seconds.

"Are you finished?" he says without taking his eyes off Grand Theft Auto on the screen.

"What are you still doing up?"

"What are you doing walking in at one in the morning on a Monday?"

"Okay smart-ass, do whatever you want." I say, limping toward my room, "Uh, Sami?"

"Huh?"

"You didn't notice any mail for me today, did you?"

"Dunno, check the mailbox."

"Thanks a lot."

I trudge back upstairs past the kitchen and the foyer, and one more time, with the utmost care, I ease the front door open. By now my buzz has completely dissipated.

At barely five feet three inches, I can't see over the box, even standing on my tiptoes. Luckily, my mother is barely five feet at all.

I swing open the flap and reach in, feeling every inch of the box I can reach. Nothing.

Wait a minute.

There's something that's been flattened against the bottom of the box. Probably just a supermarket flyer.

I stretch myself higher on my toes and reach in again. This time I pull it out.

It's an envelope.

Like a woman on death row, I float back through the door-frame and, still in zombie mode, flick on the lights.

The Canadian Institute of Chartered Accountants crest on the upper left-hand corner is unmistakable.

I hold it in my shaking hands for inspection, and feel that it's really very, very thin.

And I want to vomit.

7

I am the Goddess of Inner Poise and Confidence. I am Self-Possession incarnate. I can do this.

Who am I kidding?

I weave among the black trench-coated, briefcase-clutching mezzanine crowd, as I do every weekday morning, my fist clamped over my mouth, fighting the urge to throw up as memories from the night before bounce off the inner walls of my pounding brain. Maybe it's just the hangover. I position myself in front of the appropriate set of elevators and wait, my heart wallowing somewhere in the vicinity of my lower intestines.

Ms. Hallaby, We regret to inform you that . . .

Maybe not.

Two thirty-five out of four hundred. All I needed was two hundred forty. I was *this* close. How I'm going to divulge this information to my parents, I don't know. They'll both drop dead from cardiac arrest before I can finish my sentence. Right after they remind me how the only reason they left the Old Country in the first place was to give me, Sara, and Sami the best possible future, and how I've now gone and deprived their entire lives of purpose, and what's the point of even going on anymore? And that's being optimistic. Next they'll have to fess up to the entire Canadian-Lebanese community that their eldest daughter and The Keeper of The Family Pride will most probably end up an assistant manager at McDonald's rather than vice president of a

Fortune 500 firm, as the Cosmos originally called for. After which, they will promptly proceed to banish themselves from the immigrant-parents-with-psychotic-expectations-of-offspring club forever.

For some people, this is a fate worse than death.

I am a Goddess . . . Inner Poise . . . binge shopping tomorrow . . . I continue chanting my newly adopted mantra in my head. It's all I can do to keep myself from passing out completely.

This is it. Corporate Recovery. My last chance at redemption. In the midst of her corporate-speak ranting, Diane had made one valid point, a breath of fresh air in a fully stocked organic fertilizer emporium. I could, in theory, impress the pantyhose off my new manager, and (please note that extreme stress may be rendering me delusional) possibly be granted another chance to write the UFE next year. No Ernsworth junior has had to suffer the humiliation before, at least according to Diane, but there's a first time for everything.

Though that still doesn't help me deal with the twenty other people in my class, all of whom most likely passed. How am I going to put up with them for a whole week in Mexico? Maybe they don't know yet. That's right. How would they if I didn't tell them?

I adjust my suit jacket, lift my chin, and take a deep breath as the chrome elevator doors slide open, close, and open again to gradually unveil the black marbled floors of my new second home on the twenty-fifth. Instead of the morbid silence that usually haunts Ernsworth and Youngston's halls, two women are duking it out, right here, in the middle of the lobby.

"What? You can't quit! What about your two weeks' notice?" says the tall blonde, waving several folders of various sizes and colors around.

"I don't care! I can't believe you have the nerve to ask me to cancel my vacation—again! You owe me big-time, Soula, and if you think I'd miss the chance to tour with MetalHead just to stay here and take any more of your crap, you're insane!"

Glued to the wall, I try to decide if I'm better off ducking behind the large chrome ash can by the elevators or the reception room sofas until the monsoon blows over. All of a sudden, the red-faced freckled girl in the black pleather pantsuit and bright orange pigtails whizzes past me in a cloud of fury and four-letter words (and some colorful five-letter words too). Still clutching the ominous-looking files, the blonde, most likely in her early thirties, trails after her, threatening legal action, expulsion from the business community for the foreseeable future, and a plethora of other menaces, if Pippi Longstocking did not come to her senses.

The young woman doesn't look fazed by the Oscar-worthy scene she's partaking in and calmly waits for the elevator as an avalanche of expletives is hurled at her. In fact, she looks downright smug. Some seemingly interminable minutes later, she slips into the elevator and is whisked away from Ernsworth and Youngston's offices for what I gather will be a long time.

It takes Soula a few moments to compose herself.

"Well," she begins, tugging her gray shift dress into place. "I'm sorry you had to see that. Our office assistant has just discovered her calling as a groupie for heavy metal garage bands. She won't be with us anymore. It seems she prefers touring rural Canada aboard a Greyhound in the company of unemployed ex-lumberjacks and hog farmers."

"I say you're lucky she had her epiphany before you promoted her to office manager," I reply.

Soula gives me a harried smile and extends her hand.

I think I've won her over.

"I'm Soula Adrian, assistant manager, Corporate Recovery. Can I help you?"

"Aline Hallaby, pleased to meet you," I say, not without some anxiety. Doesn't she know about me? "I've been transferred to your department. . . . I thought maybe Diane would have told you."

"Oh, yes, actually, we were expecting you." Her expression darkens a shade. I can imagine what that shrew Diane has made me sound like. Someone who needs to be babysat and put to minimal use until she commits one cardinal accounting sin or another and can be safely disposed of.

Thanks, Diane. My first day, and already the boss hates me.

"Follow me," Soula says, a little stiffly.

She leads me down a narrow hallway, done in deep greens and mahogany tones and decorated with expensive-looking aboriginal art. Not bad. Certainly an improvement on the drab cubicles I'm used to in Audit. I'd had no idea gray came in so many different shades.

At our first left, we turn into a large corner office. It's bigger than Manny's. It also has a lot more artwork. Just like Manny's, though, it's strewn with big fat green files. The gold-plated plaque on the door reads SID COHEN, so I'm a tad confused. I take a second to study the large canvases on the burgundy walls, the family pictures depicting an older man, a stylish blonde at his side, scattered around the room. The chocolate brown leather armchairs are looking particularly inviting since I'm wearing my cream-colored, black-tipped slingbacks, specially reserved for interviews and situations of comparable importance.

Except for the pants, I think Diane would approve of this outfit.

I look to Soula for some indication that I may take a seat, but she's busy skimming through her files. She's quite pretty, and skinny for her height too, but in a clumsy sort of way. More Olive Oyl than Kate Moss. Her dress-and-jacket ensemble looks expensive but hangs awkwardly off her frame, and those shoes would have looked better on my grandmother. They suck all the dignity out of the outfit.

"All right . . . these should get you through the day," she says without looking up. I have no clue what she's searching for, but a few more minutes' worth of thumbing pages appears to satisfy her.

"I had planned to get you started on some of our Chapter Eleven clients, but since you've witnessed the . . . *episode* . . . with Stacey for yourself, I don't need to explain why I'd like you to fill in for some of the more urgent administrative work."

What? Is she allowed to do this? Isn't that what receptionists are for? I am a quasi-certified accountant, and there is absolutely *no way* I will do this.

It's preposterous.

"Um . . . what kind of administrative work do you mean . . . exactly?"

"Oh, just odds and ends, really. Listen, Eileen, I don't have time to discuss this. Penny can fill you in."

"Aline."

"I beg your pardon?"

"It's Aline, not Eileen."

"Yes, well. I need to be getting back."

Maybe it's the hangover talking, or else I'm having a strange reaction to Stacey's display of self-assertion, but I feel emboldened enough to say, "But I was hoping I could do more . . . you know, accounting work. Get some real experience."

Soula freezes. She lifts her head and stares straight into my face, her eyes bulging as she speaks. "Aline, how long have you been working here?"

"Well, if you count my internship last summer, nine months." I have a hard time steadying my hands as I say this.

"Do you think that nine months and a disappointing track record give you the right to argue about your assignments?"

Ouch. Point taken. Way to make a good impression. I know she's right, but I had to try. I shift my gaze to the floor and stare at my pretty shoes. They were a fabulous buy and worth every cent I had paid for them. Unfortunately, their therapy-via-retail powers haven't managed to prevent my newfound confidence from leaking out of me and oozing to the floor around Soula's unbecomingly clad feet.

I'm relieved when she shows me to my new cubicle and leaves me with a stack of invoices that need to be filed in their corresponding client folders. Stacey had gotten up to *F* when she had her breakdown.

✺

Maybe it was the enormous amount of filing I did that day, but the next six hours sped mercifully by, with little further interaction with Soula or any of my new officemates. They mostly eyed me with morbid curiosity, stopping briefly to introduce themselves, asking a few inane questions about my prematurely demised stint in Audit before scuttling back to their desks. That suited me just fine.

The only person who'd made any effort at meaningful human contact was Penny, an "accounting trainee." That title means she was either too lazy to bother with an accounting certification, or maybe, like me, she tried and failed. Maybe she could smell the familiar stench of failure on me and figured we could bond over our shared lowliness on the corporate food chain.

As Penny tells it, she followed her bartending boyfriend here all the way from Brighton, England—I'm not exactly sure why. She sounds just like Elizabeth Hurley, although she could moonlight as a body double for the chubby one on *The Facts of Life*.

And then, of course, there's Tom, a few cubicles away. All he did when I walked in this morning was smile kindly at me. No smirks, no nosy questions about how I got here. Nothing. He just pointed out where the kitchen and bathrooms were and told me to let him know if I needed anything.

I quietly grab my purse and metro pass and head for the elevators.

On the front steps of the mirrored building, my cell phone breaks out into an electronic tango number. Cheesy, I know, but more apt to still hold appeal after the 150th ring than the latest Kanye West. The caller ID confirms my suspicions. It's Brian.

"Hey, babe. How was your first day at Corporate Recovery?"

"I don't think I'll be able to handle the excitement."

"They didn't put you on photocopying duty, did they?"

"Worse. The secretary quit this morning. I'm filing indefinitely."

"Oh, honey . . . Listen, why don't we go out for dinner? How does Toqué sound?"

"You'll never get reservations," I say.

"It's Tuesday. Not only will they get us a table, but it'll be the one right at the window so the vision of you could bring in some business for them."

I indulge him with a halfhearted laugh.

"I've been in and out of accounting files all day. I'm sweaty and dusty, and I'm wearing my stuffy interview outfit. I doubt I could drum up business for a cigarette shop at a men's penitentiary, much less a hip five-star restaurant.

"But I love you for saying that," I add.

"Have you heard from the Order yet?" And as simply as succinctly that, the spell is broken, and I'm plummeted back into the nightmare from whence I had briefly arisen.

"I, er . . ." This is it. The point of no return. Once I confide in Brian, the nightmare will slide from a nook in my brain to a firm, tangible place in reality. But I can't outright lie to my man, my best friend, my for-all-intents-and-purposes soul mate. How would I feel if he ever deprived me of the chance to be his Rock, to test the depths and lengths of our love?

"I haven't heard a thing. Fat envelopes take longer to post, they say." *Oh, to have a spine.*

"You should call them tomorrow. This is getting ridiculous. Weren't they supposed to get back to you last week?"

"Yeah, well. What do you expect out of our socialist government?"

"The CICA is not a government organization, honey. You're paying for this, or at least you will be when you get certified."

"*If* I get certified, Brian. If."

Brian exhales audibly. "I hate it when you say things like that. You have absolutely no faith in yourself."

I commend Brian for his unwavering support of me and everything I do, I really do. But I suddenly feel faint and queasy like the first time I ever gave blood and neglected to grab the complimentary doughnut and juice box afterwards. I'm sure Mrs. Gupta didn't anticipate my reaction when I passed out in her history class, right after she'd announced a pop quiz.

"I'm sorry, sweetie," he says. "I know you're nervous. I was a complete mess when I was in your shoes. I'll splurge on the wine tonight."

"Brian, I can't. I . . . I just remembered I'm supposed to catch a movie with Jaz tonight. I promised."

"Can't you call it off? Say you've got to work or something."

"She'd find out, hunt me down, and impale me. You know how she is."

"I know. I don't want you to cancel on your friends on my account, it's just been so long. . . ."

"Rain check for this weekend?"

"You'll be in Mexico this weekend," he sighs. "Without me."

Right. Just five more days till the trip. Plenty of time to break into the Order's headquarters, hack into their computer system, give myself five extra points, and produce an official letter attesting to my blinding success. No problem.

Come Friday, I'm no closer to McGyvering a way out of this mess than when I found that fateful flat envelope sitting in my mailbox. What's worse, I've had to contend with the stream of freshly stamped Chartered Accountants whizzing past my lowly cubicle, tooting their proverbial horns, as though infused with a newfound sense of worth. Just before rushing off to the nearest BMW dealership, of course. And the ladies all bought matching commemorative Fendis. It's enough to make a fashion-minded professional failure such as myself want to puke.

I miss Aphro. I've taken to calling her once a day for the latest on juicy office gossip and to make sure she doesn't forget I exist. Oh, and to remind her that Tom and I share the same corner kitchen now. And water fountain. And air.

"I hate you. You get to put your mouth right where Tom's saliva could still be. You might as well have made out with him," she tells me today.

"You're so gross."

"What's gross about Tom's saliva?"

"I'm not dignifying that with an answer. Tell me, how's everyone over there?"

"Everyone's the same. Bored to the point of self-bludgeoning. I want to hear more about Tom. What does he say to you?"

"Not much. He's pretty quiet around me, actually."

She sighs. "Any chance he'll break up with whatsherface anytime soon?"

"I have no idea, Fro, but if I ever find out, you'll be the first to know. I promise."

"I'm holding you to that. Whoops, I gotta go. Manny is rearing his ugly head. Have fun in Mexico, babe. I want pictures."

My stomach lurches.

"Thanks, Aphro. I'll try and remember to if I'm not too hammered." Or dead.

After surreptitiously watching the arrows on my wristwatch snail-race their way to 5:35, I feel safe enough to call it a day.

"Had enough?" The jingle of my keys as I threw them into my purse must have given my intentions away to Tom.

"Well, the filing's all done, I've sorted Soula's mail, alphabetized it, and then I flipped her Best of Surrey Gardens desk calendar over to the right day. What do you think, should I polish the spare pair of shoes she keeps under her desk, or is that too much?"

He leans back in his chair and laughs. "She's just testing you, don't worry. I know it's shitty, but you've got to hang in there and prove your mettle."

"Or rank fifth nationwide on the UFE like you did two years ago and skyrocket my way to the cool assignments?"

"Is there really such a thing as a cool assignment in accounting?"

"Excellent point. On that note, I think I'll head over to the ninety-nine-cent pizza place before going home."

"I've got a better idea. A bunch of us from the office are meeting up at La Cage aux Sports at six for happy hour drinks. Interested?"

I'd planned on staying in and watching movies with Brian tonight, but the prospect of ducking more of his attempts to get me to call the Order and find out what happened to my scores is too daunting an effort to undertake. I need time. I also need the security of a group so as to prevent suicide from being an option.

"Sure. Sounds good."

"Great. Just gimme a second here to turn this thing off. . . ."

La Cage aux Sports is the kind of establishment that considers a floor carpeted in wood shavings a viable decorating option. That, and autographed hockey jerseys encapsulated in glass frames all over the wall, requisites to any self-respecting sports bar. A blaring Habs game competes with deafening dance music for the patrons' short attention spans made even shorter with the presence of three-for-one Molson Ex beer.

Everyone in the office under thirty-five is here. Even Aphro managed to escape Manny's watch to make an appearance.

"Ali! Didn't know this was your scene. Rock on, man!" Jean-

Pierre holds up two open beer bottles in front of my face, and I'm afraid he's going to play air guitar with them still in his hands.

"Hi, Pierre, celebrating your UFE victory, I see."

"We all are. Just about everyone's gotten their scores by now, I think."

Uh-oh. This is my cue to head for the exit. JP's alcohol-induced loss of short-term memory makes this easy enough. I turn around, hoping to catch a glimpse of the main entrance, but a sea of loose ties, rolled-up dress shirts, and strewn audit bags blocks my way.

"Oops, sorry! Pardon me. . . . Oh, hi, Isabelle. . . . You passed, *mais c'est fantastique!* Gotta go. . . ."

I push and prod my way to what I think may be the exit, until I feel someone catch my arm.

"Don't tell me you're leaving! We're doing kamikaze shots at the bar."

"Aphro, I really have to go. I'm sorry."

"But we just got here, like, not even an hour ago!" She points to her Gucci watch for emphasis.

"Look, I know but—"

"CANCÚN! RAAAA!" Great. Now a choir composed entirely of Auditors-who-can't-hold-their-liquor-Anonymous members has just broken out into rhythmless song. A song about a vacation I won't be going on, to a place I won't be going to.

"Just one shot, Ali, to celebrate you joining our department." Penny materializes behind me holding four glass test tubes in each hand, brimming with toxic yellow liquid.

"I don't know about that. . . ." But it's already too late. Somehow a shot tube is rammed into my palm, and the choir's chorus morphs from "Cancún!" to "Chug! Chug! Chug!"

I have to oblige.

The drink is citrusy, cool in my mouth but warm in my throat, all at the same time. I don't even taste the alcohol.

"I chugged, okay? I'm going."

I execute a less-than-graceful 180 and smack myself firmly against a thick chest in a ribbed wool pullover.

"Wow, watch out there." Tom grabs me by the arm to steady me.

My knees weaken at the closest contact I've ever had and am ever likely to have with the office god.

"Need some help?"

That look. That bedroom tone. This is definite flirtation, and I'm not going to stand for it. I'm going home.

"I'm fine, thanks. I was just on my way out."

"Are you sure? Can I get you anything?"

I guess one more drink won't hurt.

"I'll have another one of these shooters. They're actually pretty good."

Tom smiles and turns toward the bar, with me in tow.

At 2:45 that night (or should I say the next morning?), La Cage aux Sports announces last call. By now only serious, hard-core partygoers are left. And me. I exclude myself from this category because I have never, ever stayed out to drink this late on a weeknight since I started working. Many of my colleagues still manage this feat, despite the fact that our carefree college years are a thing of an almost mythical past.

But not me. My system just can't take that kind of punishment anymore.

Tonight, though, I'm on a completely different level of pain. If I go home, if I happen to find myself alone, if only for a second, I'll have to face it head-on with nothing or no one to cushion the blow. Both Aphro and Tom have repeatedly offered to drive me home, but I wouldn't budge from my barstool, which I fear may bear the permanent mark of my ass in its cushion from now on.

"Guys, the paper's out!" A random drunk guy whom I vaguely recognize from the office pummels through the door.

"Whoopdee-do," I mutter to no one in particular.

Tom hears me. "Don't you want to see?"

"See what?"

"The UFE results. They're going to print them today."

"*What?*"

"Didn't you know? Anyway, everyone should've gotten them by now."

"*Cancún—Here I come! Whoo-hoo!*" The same drunk guy shouts after leafing clumsily through the newspaper.

"What do you mean, they're going to print them? Who's going to?"

"The Order."

"I thought the audit firms did that. And not until later."

"Ernsworth will take out a spread congratulating all the employees who wrote on passing just as soon as Diane gets everyone's results. Anyway, why does it matter? Let's go see your name in print!" Tom takes my hand and pulls.

"Let's not." I'm suddenly overcome by the same urge to puke up all the alcohol and pizza I've been ingesting for the past ten hours. I pull against him, but he's too strong. He's already dragged me halfway across the bar to the echo of "Cancún, baby!" coming from various parts of the room.

"When are you guys leaving again?" Tom asks amid the clamor. "The year I wrote we took off just a couple of days after the results came in."

I manage to break free from his grasp only to find myself trapped in the throng of anxious junior auditors, all vying for a chance to see their name among the chosen few.

"Gagné, Gendron . . ." Being quite a bit taller than me, Tom begins calling names out to me from his vantage point. ". . . Hadley, Hubert . . . Hey, wait a minute. . . ."

His voice fades into the distance as I finally catch a breath of cold, outdoor air. I feel the acid bile rising in my throat. I don't want to see these people again. Not on the plane. Not in Cancún. Not ever again.

୶◌

I step out of the Air Canada jet on Sunday afternoon and squint under the first blazing rays to reach the cabin's interior. Instantaneously I feel my flatironed hair seize, tighten, and then quintuple in size at its first contact with the stifling humidity. From behind my dark, oversize glasses, I see Sophie and Jaz float down the aluminum stairs ahead of me, light and bouncy as twin champagne bubbles. And I fight back the tears. Again.

I have to be the sorriest person ever to set foot off this aircraft.

Sophie stops on the tarmac and waits for me to catch up. She squeezes my arm when I reach her, and drapes her own arm around my shoulder as if to steady me.

Don't worry. You're going to make it, her eyes say.

I'm not so sure.

Together we follow the crowd to the arrivals terminal.

The surly officer buzzes us into the customs booth one by one. I let Sophie and Jaz go ahead of me. They can't speak Spanish, and I want to make sure I can see them in case anything goes wrong.

A few minutes later, it's my turn. I walk up to the booth, and the door buzzes shut behind me. The brown-faced customs officer with a flat nose and olive green beret tries to meet my stare, but I keep looking away. I don't want him to see my red puffy eyes.

"Buenas tardes," he says, his eyes boring through me. "Please remove your glasses."

Maybe the "born in Lebanon" line in my Canadian passport is making him nervous. I should probably cooperate. I slide them off and hope the red blotches have subsided.

"Buenas tardes." I manage a weak smile.

"*¿Hablas español?*" He looks impressed. I guess most of the tourists he sees are here for the booze and not so much for the culture.

"*Sí, un poco.*"

"*Bienvenido.*"

And with that, he stamps my visa with angry, official-looking red ink.

"Welcome to Cuba," he adds in English, and hands me back my papers.

Part TWO

8

Two words. Cancellation insurance.

Cuba hadn't been my first choice for a tropical escape. But sitting across from Jocelyne of Travel Cuts, our on-campus budget travel agency, a mere twelve hours before I was scheduled to board the plane to Cancún, I couldn't care less. The multipierced, hemp-clad Jocelyne could have suggested the far side of the moon and I would simply have asked if my cancellation policy covered it.

"We'd like to change the destination on these tickets."

"Anywhere specific in mind?"

"As far away from Cancún as you can send us."

"That would be Thailand, but you'd have to pay an additional thousand plus hotel," Jocelyne said with a smart-assy look about her that made me want to yank one of her fluorescent pink dreads right off her head. I was *not* in the mood to listen to smart-asses.

At this point I felt someone tugging at the sleeve of my Gap hoodie.

"What is it, Sophe?" I wasn't in the mood for anyone getting between me and the farthest possible location from Cancún either.

"I can't afford another thousand dollars. Not to mention hotel . . . Ali, I have no income."

"Don't worry. We'll just rent a hut on the beach for ten bucks a day or something ridiculous like that when we get there." I patted her hand, but she didn't look convinced.

It was all I could do to keep myself from having a nervous breakdown right there in the middle of the cramped office.

"What about Cuba?" Jocelyne seemed to be following our little exchange quite attentively. "I just received a special offer for an all-inclusive four-star resort in Varadero Beach. And it wouldn't cost you anything extra." She looked hopefully from me to Sophie to Jaz.

"Ugh" was Jaz's input. "I'm not going to a third world country." She tossed her curls away and sank lower in the orange plastic chair.

Jocelyne returned the comment with a dirty look. I had a feeling backpacking through the planet's most destitute third world countries was this particular travel agent's idea of heaven.

She swiveled her seat around to face a filing cabinet, rummaged in the top drawer, and pulled out a handful of colorful brochures.

"Look, all drinks, meals, snacks, and water sports are included." She pointed to a photo of a stretch of beach lined with kayaks, sailboats, and all manner of water toys imaginable. "And trust me, girls"—she huddled in closer to the three of us—"Cuban men are something else."

With that, she shoved the brochures across the desk toward us and crossed her arms in triumph.

Jaz picked one up that showed a picture of Havana. It looked like it might have been snapped sometime in the fifties. "Hmph. It *is* all-inclusive . . . ," she said.

"And it won't cost a penny more. . . ." Sophie turned to me, her eyes wide and pleading.

I looked over from Sophie to Jaz, and then back to Jocelyne, whose mouth had turned upward at the corners. The pitiful commission she'd be getting on this booking couldn't possibly be responsible for the bolts of sheer glee escaping from behind her eyes. . . . I wondered exactly what Cuban memory she was reliving through us.

"There's only one problem." She tapped at her archaic keyboard.

"What's that?" I said.

"The return flight on Sunday is fully booked. I'd have to get you on the Saturday-morning plane. Does that work for you?"

Would it raise suspicion with Brian and my mother? I'll just play the yes-I-did-so-tell-you-and-you're-the-one-who-forgot card and pray. I had no doubt it would work on Brian, at least. As for my mother . . . I just couldn't be bothered. I didn't want to talk details. I wanted out.

"Fine. Sold."

"You won't regret it." Jocelyne beamed.

Varadero Beach, Cuba. So far everything appears normal; that is to say I don't notice any barbed wire anywhere, no machine-gun-wielding police, and the tiny José Martí airport shows no visible signs of socialism-induced decay. Then again, the inside of a hog pen might look better to me right now than the glitziest of hotel bars in Montreal. We haven't been here a full half hour, and yet twinges of jealousy are already tugging at my heart. For Sophie and Jaz, as for all the other passengers on the bus to the resort, this is a vacation. A proper one. For me, this is like the last hurrah between posting bail and waiting for trial.

I watch the scenery scuttle by as the aging charter bus heaves along the highway, flanked on one side by tall, powerful palm trees with thick, upright trunks, reaching far up to the skies, their fruit barely visible under long, dense leaves. They also bear a mysterious swelling somewhere around their midsection, almost as though they were pregnant. The other side of the highway stretches out blue and endless into the horizon, glistening here and there under the haphazard kisses of the sun.

In Montreal, November has already brought with it the first frosty winds of winter and taken away the last of the autumn leaves, but here the sun is shining strong and steady, and I can feel my skin burning under its rays even through the double-paned glass windows. Only a few fluffy clouds, not at all like the sweeping gray smog we get back home, litter the sky.

Slowly, people and structures come into view, beginning with an old man on a rickety cart pulled by a donkey, against a backdrop of run-down buildings with remnants of bright pastel paint covering the decaying walls, then concrete industrial structures, some stores, and a decent-size town square. I guess they'd call it *plaza* here.

It's a lucky thing I chose Spanish over German in high school. So far, a couple of strategically injected *gracias* and *por favor*s have worked wonders with the immigration officers whose personalities, true to form, were about as warm and welcoming as a pack of pit bulls. Which made their transformations that much more surprising. As soon as I mumbled a few words in broken Spanish, their expressions warped. They looked like they had been smacked across the face by Pamela Anderson's boobs.

After passing the Arenas Blancas beach resort, the Sol Meliá, the SuperClub Breezes, and the Beaches Varadero resorts, we reach our own. It looks just as impressive as the others from the outside, with lush landscaping and plenty of mermaids and tropical fish statues spouting water into large stone fountains. All the hotel façades are painted in the same pastel colors I saw on the old buildings in the town of Matanzas, and I'm beginning to wonder if everything in Cuba is either baby blue, petal pink, or daffodil yellow. At least the abundance of vividly hued bougainvillea and hibiscus shrubs escaping from every nook and cranny, like indomitable dandelions, lend the place a semblance of authenticity. I can skip pinching myself; I really am in the Caribbean.

Sophie and Jaz had spent the previous night at my place so

we could help each other get up at the crack of dawn and make sure we didn't miss our six o'clock flight, which, by the way, was delayed. Two hours. So when the bus jerks to a stop and all fifty passengers clamor toward the exit in a mad dash to be the first to make it to the check-in line, we are, I believe, justifiably disheartened. The staff is cheerful and indulgent, but in no more of a hurry to attend to us than if there were only two of us in line. A full forty-five minutes after we first set foot in the hotel, we are shown to our room.

On such short notice, Jocelyne couldn't finagle us a large enough room to accommodate the three of us comfortably. We have to contend, instead, with a "junior" suite, composed of two double beds, a vanity table, a small closet, and a television set, which to Jaz's dismay, appears to be broadcasting Spanish-language programs only. "I bet they get HBO in Cancún," she mutters under her breath.

"This is nice, isn't it?" I claim the bed closest to the balcony by dropping my canvas-tote-cum-beach-bag onto the floral bedspread, and wait for any objections.

"Hey, where's the third bed?" Jaz turns to the bellboy loitering next to the door, waiting eagerly for his tip.

"*¿Cómo, señorita?*"

"Oh, for Chrissake." Jaz dumps her luggage onto the floor and makes for the bathroom, leaving Sophie and me to deal with the hapless bellboy, his face a mask of candid confusion, still shifting his weight uncertainly under the doorframe. By the time the snag is cleared up and a narrow cot is wheeled into the room, the sun is already beginning to set. It's six o'clock in the evening. All we have left to do is to unpack, shower, and change for dinner.

An hour later, we are seated in the main restaurant, the one serving "international" cuisine. After perusing the buffet, I'm beginning to think this is a euphemism for "barely edible" cuisine. I'd previously heard that Cuban food is less than inspiring but didn't think it to be quite so bad. Perhaps due to her lack of pretension, Sophie has managed to find enough foodstuffs to fill her plate (mostly beans, broccoli, and corn—I don't envy any potential dance partners she's going to have tonight), while I've decided to stick to salad and ice cream, the only two items from the extensive buffet that I could both identify and stomach. Oxtail and cow tongue just aren't for me.

"So, what are we doing tonight?" In a short blue gingham dress, Jaz appears to be going for the Dorothy look tonight.

"I don't know. I'm kinda tired," Sophie says, leaning dangerously close to her plateful of veggies. Her eyelids are already beginning to flutter, and I know I'm not far behind. Jaz fidgets in her seat and averts her eyes from us, scanning the dining room.

"Look, Jaz, I know it's a great evening for going out, but I'm tired too. It's been a really, really long day, not to mention week, for me. If you let me sleep tonight, then I promise you, I'll be up for anything tomorrow." I don't mention that the simple thought of doing anything social is making my stomach turn. Just last night I had to deal with lying to everyone I care for in my life—present company excluded—about my current whereabouts.

As if on cue, Sophie lays her fork down, snapping out of her jet lag–induced daze.

"How did Brian react last night? Do you think he bought it?"

"Yeah, Ali, he's going to ask to see pictures. And word's going to get around the office that you weren't on the Cancún flight. It'll get to him eventually." Jaz eyes me, right eyebrow arched, and washes down a mouthful of salad with a gulp of white wine. "What are you going to do?"

I grab my temples and slump forward, pounding my head against the table. "I. Don't. Know." I chant to the rhythmic banging of my forehead against the cold marble.

"It'll be okay, sweetie. Don't worry about anything now. You have nearly a week to figure it out." The contact of Sophie's hand with my shoulder makes me feel a teeny bit better. At least I've still got my friends, my surrogate family. The entire world could crumble around me, and I'd still have them. I'd have had Brian too, had I not thrown the entire last three years of my stable-if-somewhat-lackluster relationship down the crapper. The worst part is that I had every intention of telling him, I really did. But when I called last night and he immediately asked me if I'd gotten my results, I just froze.

"Baby, I just know you passed, don't worry about it. You're so bright, have a little faith."

"I know, Brian, but, you know, what if—?"

"Stop it. I believe in you. Now believe in yourself."

"'Kay . . ."

After that exchange, I just couldn't stomach telling him. Not just out of morbid dread of his impending disappointment in me, but because saying something so utterly horrible to someone other than Sophie or Jaz would make the nightmare real somehow. He's my boyfriend, the love of my life, and potential future fiancé, and I know we're not supposed to have secrets from each other—I know that—and this was just meant to be a temporary fib anyway. I just needed to clear my head first, figure out what I was going to do. Which is what I'm doing now. Then I'll tell him. Really.

When he insisted on driving me to the airport the next day, I said I'd already organized something with the gang at work. I mentioned something about team building and camaraderie, and he relented. He insisted I call him as soon as I arrived in Cancún, and fill him in on every detail.

"So? You're telling me you don't want to do *anything* tonight? We're on vacation, for fuck's sake." Jaz attacks the last bit of her lettuce and glares menacingly from Sophie to me. She looks as though she might add something, but bites her lip instead.

I know exactly what she's thinking. As much as I want to stay in and sulk, I realize that having dragged my innocent best friends all the way over here, I owe them to at least pretend I'm having a good time.

"There's a club here. La Bamba, I think it's called. I thought I saw the entrance somewhere by the lobby. Wanna check it out?"

The power of inducing genuine emotion through the mere act of pretending must extend beyond faking orgasms, because just as I'm trying to squeeze a few droplets of enthusiasm out of the deepest corner of my psyche, I feel the first stirrings of anticipation building inside me. I even find myself hoping Sophie will agree to come along.

"Sounds good," says Sophe with a hint of excitement in her voice as well. "What are we waiting for? Let's go!"

Jaz lets out a high-pitched squeal and squeezes us both in a group hug. "I knew you'd come around!"

"You know what, guys?" I break away from Jaz's grasp, taking one of her hands in mine, and doing the same with Sophie. "You just . . .

"I . . ." I rack my brains in search of the words that would convey to my best friends just how much what they've done means to me. "I can't imagine anyone else coming along with me on this crazy ride, and I can't believe we're actually here. I just wanted to tell you . . . no matter how I've felt this past week, and no matter what happens five and a half days from now, I promise you, we're going to have the best girls-gone-wild vacation there ever was. Deal?"

"*Deal!*" they both screech in unison, and hug me again.

"This isn't working. Oh, man, you guys, this is horrible! I'm going back to the room."

Sophie grabs me by one of my halter top straps and pulls me back inside the club. "Your hair looks *fine*. Stop touching it."

"It so does *not* look fine. Look at it! It's pulled a Jack Nicholson and gone flying over the fucking cuckoo's nest!"

Sophie ignores my ranting in favor of the bar she's just discovered on the far side of the club. My coarse Middle Eastern hair, meanwhile, has morphed into some sort of hydraulic force field, sopping up every drop of moisture in the atmosphere and ballooning into monumental proportions. The result isn't pretty. And this despite the five different anti-frizz products I splattered onto my head just minutes ago. Short of winning the Ouidad curly hair makeover sweepstakes, there's nothing else to be done.

"Just put it up in a ponytail or something," Jaz offers, helping herself to a free piña colada from the bar.

It isn't fair. All three of us share the same ethnic background, yet Jaz's hair manages to wind itself in pretty, tight curls while Sophie's follicles are as smooth and well-behaved as Gwyneth Paltrow's. Mine is at a rather unattractive median between the two, though back home I manage to fake the *Baywatch* Babe mane with the help of the most cutting-edge, overpriced, celebrity-tested creams, serums, and lotions known to the fashion magazine—reading world. Except today none of them are working, leaving me feeling stark naked and at the mercy of every physical insecurity I've ever had.

"So these are the Cuban men that Jocelyne chick was raving about?" Jaz tosses her hair to one side and pops the bright magenta cherry off her drink and into her mouth.

One glance around the sunken dance floor and I can immediately second her sentiments. Not one reasonably attractive male specimen to be seen.

Not that it matters to me, of course, I'm spoken for. But eye candy is always nice.

"Hey, ladies, we thought we heard some English coming from over here. Figured we'd stop by. I'm Paul." The freshly introduced Paul offers an outstretched hand to me since I'm sitting at the end of the booth closest to him. He's wearing a gray fedora à la *Godfather*, with a large gold crucifix hanging over his wife-beater. "This is Mike." He points to a diminutive guy behind him, this one wearing a Hawaiian shirt over his white cami and too much gel in his blond spiky hair.

Mike's hand beelines straight to Sophie's without a hint of hesitation in either my or Jaz's general direction.

"Hey," he says in a way that makes my mind flash back to Nick, the renegade boyfriend from *Family Ties*.

"Hey!" The three of us nod cheerily, but not so much so that our friendly salutation might be construed as something more inviting.

No such luck. The boys take seats at either end of our booth, squishing the three of us in the middle.

"Where are you girls from?" Mike asks Sophie's breasts.

"Canada." She flashes him the same innocent smile that never fails to get her in trouble.

"No way! Us too. Toronto."

"Montreal," I say.

Jaz looks everywhere except in either guy's direction.

"You girls having fun?" Paul nods at a tall, European-looking woman at the bar as he says this, and pulls a thick cigar from his pocket, nipping one end with a pocketknife and taking long, full-throttled puffs to light the other.

"We just got here. We're still a little jet-lagged, actually, so don't mind us if we're a tad on the boring side tonight." I mime falling asleep.

"What? Are you kidding me? How could three good-looking ladies like you ever be boring? Now, maybe if we were a couple of fags—"

"Okay!" I bolt out of the plushy seat and pull Sophie up with me. "I'm really sorry, guys, but we've been dying to dance ever since we got here, and . . . ah, this is my favorite song of all time! Jaz, you coming?"

Paul steps aside, letting the three of us pass.

"God, that is some nerve." Jaz hisses once we're on the dance floor.

"Did you see the look on their faces when you said that?" Sophie wails, looking like she might wet her pants. "You don't even know what song this is, do you?"

"Somebody had to do something, and it's not like either of you were any help. They're still looking. Smile." I turn toward Paul and Mike, who are still eyeing us from the booth, and I break into a fake grin. Sophie follows my lead, and Jaz ignores them completely.

"I need another drink," she says once the song is over. She leaves us and heads toward the bar farthest from the guys.

Sophie and I continue to groove to the best of our abilities, letting the little bit of alcohol we've consumed so far seep into our bloodstreams, and scan the dance floor for prospects. The club is nice enough, nothing special by North American standards, but not dingy either. The vibe is friendly, and that's a welcome change from the cutthroat see-and-be-seen Montreal bar scene.

A few songs later, I notice Sophie's being more quiet than usual, a faraway kind of look painted on her face.

"Is anything wrong?" I yell over the music, now a pulsing techno Kylie Minogue remix. "We usually go nuts when this beat comes on. What's up?"

"Nothing."

"Sophe, come on. Tell me."

She leans over and tries to say something, but it sounds all garbled and unintelligible to me. I've never been one of those people who could carry on a conversation in a club. When I see someone on a crowded dance floor with a cell phone glued to their ear, looking as though they can actually comprehend what's being said to them, I am in complete awe.

"I can't hear you, sweetie. Let's go sit down."

"With those guys? Ugh."

She scrunches up her finger in a reverse come-hither gesture, our secret alternative to the loser *L* to the forehead, to in-
dicate to each other when we're annoyed by a given guy's
advances.

I laugh, loving this vintage Sophie from our younger clubbing
days.

"I'll tell you later," she mouths.

"Sure."

Jaz picks this moment to join us, squeezing herself past a trio
of prepubescent boys in grungy oversize pants and shaved
heads, who've been practically undressing us with their glares
for the past fifteen minutes.

"I'm glad this place is finally picking up. Let's par-tay!" She
hands each of us a shot glass filled with clear liquid, clanking
hers against each of ours before knocking it back. I down the
colorless, odorless drink and wait for the alcohol to warm my
throat. It doesn't take long. My mouth puckers and I wince in
disgust.

"Man, this is gross! What is it?"

"Dunno. Who cares? I just told the bartender we wanted to
have a good time."

She's right. Who cares, indeed. It's not like I have to get up
for work or anything tomorrow. In fact, after this vacation, I may
not be getting up for work for a long time to come. The thought
hits me like a punch to the gut.

"I think I could use another one of these."

"No, Ali! Stay! It's Usher, your favorite. Your *real* favorite,
this time!" Sophie giggles, clearly on the verge of total intoxication. It doesn't take that girl much.

"I need a break. Just for a few minutes." I turn around, pushing and prodding my way to the bar, trying my best to avoid any
sudden eye movement in the direction of the booth where Mike

and Paul are still nursing their free drinks and choking on their cheap cigars.

And that's when I see him.

The most beautiful man I've ever seen in my life. And all I can do is stand there, gaping and salivating like an idiot.

9

Don't panic. Do. Not. Panic.

He hasn't seen me staring, so there's really no reason I can't just spin my heels, head back to the booth, and enjoy a stimulating conversation about the merits of *Rocky I* versus *Rambo III* with the moron twins.

Except that, for some unfathomable reason, I can't seem to move. The music that was so stimulating to me just a moment ago now rings too loud and tinny in my ears. I become acutely aware of being pushed and elbowed by every overdressed, underaged, intoxicated reveler in the joint.

It's dark, and although not terribly crowded, there are enough people milling in and out of my field of vision to block my view. A giraffelike blonde in a zebra-print tube giggles and pulls a decidedly less-than-amused friend off his feet and onto the dance floor, and now I'm wide open.

I keep staring. He is absolutely exquisite. Not the kind of exquisiteness you can have carved, nipped, tucked, and then charged to your MasterCard at your nearest cosmetic surgery clinic. Nor is it of the too-smooth, metrosexualized, coming-soon-to-a-theater-near-you variety. It's better. More real. And it's sitting on a barstool, enjoying an easy laugh with the bartender, not ten feet away from me.

"Ali, I think Jaz wants to leave."

I nearly jump out of my skin at the sound of Sophie's voice. "What? Why?"

"She's bored. And she thinks all the guys here are repulsive."

"She's the one who dragged us here." I act more indignant than I feel. What I'm really hoping to do is buy some time so I can stand here and stare in silent admiration for a few more minutes.

Sophie tilts her face away from me and tries to stifle a yawn.

Great. Now she's got me feeling guilty.

"Why don't you guys go ahead, and I'll pop by in a few minutes."

"Why?"

Good question. I quickly glance back at the bar, and my heart stops short in my chest before slinking slowly toward my gut. Mystery Man is not alone. A tall brunette who reminds me vaguely of Xena the Warrior Princess (in a late-thirtyish, heavily-made-up, surgically enhanced sort of way) is leaning closely toward him, mouthing something into his ear. One hand is pushing a dark shiny curl away from his forehead, and the other one is draped casually over his knee.

"You know what? You're absolutely right. I'm just being stupid. Let's get out of here."

We "please" and "sorry" our way to the middle of the dance floor, where Jaz is sluggishly swaying back and forth to some Sean Paul.

"Where's your drink?" she asks me.

"I didn't end up getting one. I wasn't that thirsty."

"So, are we going or what?" Sophie stifles another yawn.

Jaz's swaying slows down to barely a shoulder shrug, and she huddles against Sophie and me. "Guys? I'm really sorry, but can we stay?"

"But I thought—"

"Oh, please, please, *pleeeeease!*" she pleads. "Listen, don't look, but there's this guy, I swear, he is *so hot,* you'd freak. One fuck, and I swear, I am *beyond* over Ben."

Oh, God. Oh My Fucking Lord, no. Please let her not be referring to Him. I don't ask for much, really, and I've already flunked the UFE and all, so why can't I have this? Not that it matters, anyway—he's with someone else. But what if she's a hooker? What if she's leaving Varadero tomorrow? A girl can hope, can't she? Plus I didn't come here looking for any action, but . . . I don't know. I guess I could still admire him from afar in the same sort of way I did Jordan Knight back when I was twelve. But if Jaz has the hots for him, then it's over. Fully, unequivocally, and irrevocably over. I'd be guilty of thought crime if I so much as fantasized about brushing up against him on the dance floor.

"Hey! I said don't look!" Jaz's uneven, short nails dig deep enough into my forearm to draw blood as I spin to see who she's been ogling. A surge of relief swells my chest and fills my head. It's not Him.

Mystery Man No. 2 has got to be about six feet two, maybe even three. His hair has the kind of dark, disheveled look you know had to have set him back at least two hundred bucks. The kind you can get only at a salon owned by fashion's latest bad-boy hair artiste. But it's the arms that really get me, *très* post-*Troy* Brad Pitt definition. And you can tell he knows how to work it, since he's chosen to highlight them in a buttoned-down, cut-off black shirt. He's ordering a drink from the bar at the opposite end of my own Mystery Man. He reaches for the glass, and just at that moment, he turns around, as though sensing the three pairs of dilated pupils on him, and for just one second, my eyes lock with his.

Sometimes, a second is all it takes. I pray this is not one of those times.

Jaz, thank-the-Lord-above, doesn't seem to have noticed.

"We're staying." She picks up the pace of her hip-hop grooving, this time to some Latin mix, wiggling her butt with a great deal more purpose and determination than before.

Sophie reluctantly follows suit, and pretty soon the three of us are dancing almost as though we really mean it.

We slink, slide, and swoosh to a few more songs, the last chords of each one melting into the opening beats of the next. I glance over at Jaz, wondering exactly what she's got planned. Nothing. She's busy looking up to the ceiling, at her feet, from side to side. Everywhere, except in his direction.

"Jaz?" I fake a salsa step and sashay my two-left-footed self closer to her. "Do you think maybe you should go talk to him?"

"Are you insane?"

"Okay. Fine. Don't kill me. Look, he's still at the bar. Alone. I don't think you'll get to talk to him if you stay on the dance floor. Why don't you get a drink? We'll stay here."

"What, and do this alone? What kind of friend are you?"

"You don't need a babysitter, Jaz. Besides, Sophie's going to pass out any second. We can't stay here all night."

"Come with me, pleeease!" she whines.

"The three of us will just scare him off. Look." I wave my hand and turn toward his side of the room, about to instruct Jaz to march over there and get this over with, and catch him gazing steadily at me. I think. I could be wrong. Maybe the tall blonde in the zebra top is standing right behind me.

I'm afraid this time Jaz may have noticed too, because she sort of steps back, eyes me for a second like she's trying to size me up, and then looks away.

"Guys, I really need a break." Sophie takes one step forward and fumbles, like she's lost her footing. If I hadn't left her side all night, I'd swear she was drugged. The girl cannot hold her alcohol to save her life.

"Sophie, man, how much have you had to drink?" I guide her slowly toward the booth where Mike is still sitting, his head thrown back against the cushions, his mouth open in a ridiculous

O as he attempts to puff smoke rings with his cigar. Paul is nowhere to be seen. Jaz follows right behind us, and we all slump into the comfort of the seat.

Mike barely registers our presence, lost in the beginning phases of intoxication himself. A few minutes go by in complete silence. Jaz doesn't seem to be interested in talking to me, and Sophie's having a hard enough time keeping her eyelids open.

"Where's Paul?" I have no idea what else to say to Mike, and the awkward silence is getting on my nerves.

"He's chattin' up that older broad over there." He nods his chin over to one side. Paul is standing by the same Euro-chick I'd noticed earlier, who although she may not be my age, looks more in shape and put together than I've ever been. Her outfit looks like it was purchased straight off a Milan runway, and she's laughing at something Paul is saying, tossing her long, poker-straight hair behind her, as if he were the wittiest man alive. She must be more desperate than she looks. Or maybe she has deep-seated sexual memories associated with the wife-beater/gold crucifix combo. Hard to say from here.

Having dried up the conversation well with Mike, I turn to Jaz and open my mouth, waiting for something mildly engaging to come out of it. Before I've even uttered a single syllable, her eyes widen, and she looks at me like I might have spontaneously sprouted a goiter.

"What?"

She nods to something behind me, and I turn around.

It's him. Not my Him, the other Him. The blue-tipped-hair dude I was hoping would relieve Jaz of her unfortunate Ben fixation.

"Um . . . excuse me, I'm sorry, I really didn't mean to bother you or anything, but I was wondering if you'd like to dance."

"Aahh . . ." Okay. So this is just a tad awkward. I don't dare look at Jaz, and Sophie is smiling from one antique silver drop earring to the other. It might just be the booze.

"Sure." I have a very hard time shooting guys down, especially when they look like this. I'll just casually explain to him that I have a boyfriend and leave the field wide open for Jaz. I ease myself slowly out of the booth, praying silently that a certain someone doesn't see me, even if that someone was more likely to have his tongue jammed down a certain Lucy Lawless look-alike's esophagus than scanning the dance floor for me right now.

We join an eclectic mix of people on the floor, some that look too young to be in such close proximity to an open bar, and some that look too old to belong here at all. We dance at a safe distance from each other, and when the remixed version of "Sexual Healing" comes on, he doesn't try to jam his pelvis against mine or grind me from behind, which I find pleasantly refreshing.

"You know I've been looking at you for a while now, trying to work up the nerve to talk to you?" He has to practically double over to be in whispering distance of my ear.

"Are you serious?" I don't know if it's the song, or the ultra-laid-back ambience, or maybe even the fact that I'm too smitten with someone else right now to care much for this guy's physical appeal, but I don't feel any of the usual inhibitions I normally would if a good-looking guy had just up and shown his interest in me back home. Maybe it's because those guys are too busy being cool to show they're into a girl who may not look like a contender for Model Search USA.

"Yeah. You're sitting there with your girlfriends, and one of them keeps staring at me in a strange way that's kind of scaring me, actually, and I don't know what the deal is with those guys. . . . I was too shy to come up to you."

I break out in hysterics. Totally gauche, I know, but I can't help it. He's so open and frank and too endearing for words. Plus I can't believe someone who looks like that could fall prey to the same insecurities I do.

"I think you're talking about Jaz, and . . ." I'm not really sure what to say here. And she laid claim to you first and may be plotting my demise as we speak? "And she's really great once you get to know her. She's just a little shy too. And don't even talk to me about those guys. Ugh." I roll my eyes and shake my head.

"See, now that's exactly why I didn't want to be too aggressive. I have a lot of female friends, and they're constantly telling me about how annoying it is when they can't get rid of guys like that."

I want to tell him that with his looks and pleasant attitude, he shouldn't ever worry about coming off as "guys like that." I just smile instead.

"You didn't tell me your name," he says.

"Aline. You can call me Ali, though. You?"

"James."

"Hmm." I glance around the dance floor surreptitiously. Is he watching? I wonder. He isn't. Thank God. Xena the Warrior Princess is leaning in even closer, if that's at all possible. I turn back to James. "Where are you from?"

"W-e-e-ll . . . it's a little touchy, actually."

I can't imagine how in this day and age there could be a "touchier" place to be from than pretty much any country in the Middle East. Take your pick.

"Come on, James, you can tell me. I promise I beat you hands down."

"You don't even know where I'm from."

"I'll bet you anyway."

He lets out an easy, unassuming laugh. "Come, I want to give you my undivided attention. Let's get a drink."

"I, uh . . ." I was having so much fun, I almost forgot that my too-apparent enjoyment might be getting some unwanted attention. I sneak a glance at the booth where I left Sophie and Jaz, and sure enough, Jaz is eyeing both James and me like she may already have picked out a burial site for me.

But my hesitation comes just a half second too late. He's already lunged for my hand and we are halfway to the bar. He orders a glass of Cristal, the local beer, and I'm served the first daiquiri of my life that actually tastes alcoholic.

"You didn't answer my question," I say, trying hard not to sound flirty (difficult under the circumstances).

He takes a deep breath. "New York."

"City?"

He laughs. "Yes, New York City, New York State, United States of America. Precise enough now?"

"But—I don't understand. . . . How did you get here? Aren't you afraid they'll cuff you as soon as you get off the plane in the States?"

"I drove up to Toronto and flew from there. Lots of people do it. Or they go from Jamaica, or hop a European cruise liner. And the Cuban government is totally cool about it. They may hate our government, but they love us and our tourist dollars. I guess they're just anxious to show off their country and culture and make Washington look like the bad guy."

"But isn't the government going to know when you get back?"

"How? Cuban immigration doesn't stamp our passports when we get in the country. They know the drill. As far as the department of Homeland Security is concerned, I'm spending some quality time with our northern neighbors right now." He leans back against the bar and takes a swig of beer. "Your turn." He puts his plastic cup down.

"I'm one of those northern neighbors of which you speak. The French Canadian variety."

"You don't look Canadian. You have this accent I can't place."

"It's ethnic Montreal."

"What kind of ethnic exactly? Italian?"

Do I tell him? A New Yorker, to boot? Even before 9/11, you never really knew how people were going to react. Like many North American Arabs I know, the instant I saw that second tower crumble under a giant mushroom of dust and debris, my mind sprinted to thoughts of World War II Japanese internment camps. I'd wondered if they had those camps on Canada's west coast too. Honestly, I'm not sure I wanted to know.

"Nope. Not Italy. But close, geographically speaking."

"Greek?"

"Getting warmer."

"Israeli?"

"You're going to kick yourself for that one when I tell you, but keep guessing."

"That's it. I'm done."

"I'm Lebanese." I wince.

"Lebanese? Really?"

"Yeah, really. And no, my father doesn't own a falafel stand, and I don't condone any part of what happened on 9/11."

He looks taken aback. "Why would you?"

"I don't know. . . . I think that people always wonder that about Arabs. Which camp we're in. But whatever beef we may have with America, some of us live there too, right? It could've been us, you know, in those buildings." I feel myself getting hotter and hotter under my halter top. I don't know how we got into this conversation, but I'm dying to end it.

"Look, I'm American, I know, but I'm also here in Cuba, at a bar, trying to get a cute girl to dance with me. And I didn't run for the hills when she told me where she's from. In fact, I'd like to get back to the dance floor, if there aren't any more revelations she wants to share."

"W-e-e-ll . . ."

"Oh no, what now? You have a cousin in Hezbollah?"

"Worse. I have a boyfriend. I left him in Montreal to come down here for a girls' vacation. Am I horrible?" I wince again.

He laughs, drops his head, and lifts it back up, smiling. "Naw, I'm glad you told me. At least I didn't keep my hopes up for too long."

"Both of my girlfriends are single, though. . . ."

He smiles even wider and shakes his head. "I've already hit on you, Arabian princess. Too late."

At least I tried.

"It was lovely meeting you, James." I mean it. "We're here until next Saturday. I'm sure we'll bump into each other again." And I'll make sure Jaz is right by my side when we do. A guy like this is exactly what she needs.

⌒

"It's about fucking time," Jaz spits when she sees me.

"Look, I'm sorry about that. I told him I had a boyfriend anyway, and that you guys were single—"

"You *what?*"

Oh, boy.

"What? It's cool, don't worry. I didn't make it sound like you were desperate or anything. It was casual, you know."

"No, I don't know, since I wasn't the one who spent an hour with him on the dance floor when I was specifically informed by my best friend that . . . Oh, just fuck it. Let's just get the fuck out of here. I can't stand the smoke anymore."

I want to argue but decide that this is neither the time nor the place to do so.

"Where's Sophie?"

"Some guy just asked her to dance."

I turn around and, sure enough, a very green-looking (and I don't mean fresh-out-of-Saskatchewan green) Sophie is hip-hopping to the musical stylings of Shakira and Alejandro Sanz. And having a hard time staying upright.

"How could you let her go up there, Jaz? She looks like she's going to puke."

"Oh, so now you're concerned about us?"

I throw my hands up in exasperation and go to fetch Sophie.

"Time to go, sweetie." To the dismay of her scrawny, bespectacled partner, I pull her away from him and head to our table.

"Ali, I don't feel so good—"

"I know, I know. Just hang in there a few more minutes." I'm propping her up by her elbows, as she's having just the teensiest bit of difficulty walking. Suddenly she lurches forward, missing her step, and both of us would've tumbled to the ground together if a hand hadn't grasped my shoulder and steadied me. A very strong, very manly hand.

"Iss you frien' okay?"

My head swivels at the sound of the heavy Cuban accent. My legs go much in the manner as Sophie's, and I nearly pass out from the blood draining out of my brain and into my face.

I couldn't have conjured up such beauty in my imagination had I tried. He's almost as tall as James, with glistening caramel skin and eyes as dark and rich as his thick wavy hair. And whatever his cologne is, it's making me physically swoon. My eyes furtively scan the area behind him for signs of Xena, and sure enough, she's surveying the scene from a nearby barstool, twisting her fingers in her lap and tossing her thick black hair self-consciously from one side to the other. I focus back on the two hundred pounds of pure man-ness in front of me and try to take a mental snapshot of this visual feast in case I never see him again, try to etch the density of his lashes and the plum pinkness of his lips into my memory.

Of course, as go the cruel laws of the universe, I myself could not possibly have looked worse, sweat oozing out of my every pore, bags down to my chin, and hair expanded to the size of the Northwest Territories.

"Ali, is everything all right?"

Oh, no. No, no, no, *noooooo*. James's voice pounds clear and hard over the music, and he puts a protective hand under my arm.

"Is this guy bothering you?" he asks loud enough for everyone within a few yards of us to hear.

"I'm sorry, *amigo*, I didn't know you are with her. Sorry." My vision, my dream-come-to-life holds his hands up in a peaceful gesture and retreats to the bar.

I want to die. Right here, right now. God, please take my miserable soul.

"Let's get your friend up to the room." James gently nudges me.

"Don't worry, I can take it from here." I sigh. "Good to go, Sophe?"

"Mmm?"

I take her dazed answer as a yes, and motion to Jaz that I'm heading for the exit. The three of us trudge out of the club and into the elevator, in complete silence, save for the deafening ringing in our ears.

10

Ohmigod.

Brian.

I haven't called him yet. I promised I would as soon as I checked into the hotel.

What if he thinks I and the rest of the UFE-passing posse went out and got so hammered, we missed our early flight and that I'm still in Montreal, passed out in bed, the results of the previous night's overdrinking clearly visible in dried chunky globs all over my clothes? What if he goes looking for me and finds out I never got on that plane to Mexico? What if he tells my parents?

I push back the covers and jolt upright in bed, ready to lunge for the phone on the nightstand. I fall against the pillows instead, a headache ripping through my head and obliterating any receptors except those responsible for acute pain transmission.

I am hopelessly, shamelessly hungover. I hadn't drank that much, really, but then again, I'd never been exposed to a place that served unlimited rum and Cokes consisting largely of a brownish, pale concoction of about 90 percent rum and 10 percent actual soda. Cuba Libres, the bartender had called them as he handed me my order. That, and the fact I've never felt so stressed and hungry in my life, would probably explain my current state.

"What time is it?" Sophie squeaks from under her covers.

"I don't know. I can't get up."

"Neither can I."

I close my eyes and wait for the rugby match going on in my brain to go into halftime. I suddenly become aware that my throat and chest feel like a twelve-year-old chardonnay. Dry to the point of burning.

"Sophie?"

"Huh?"

"Can you please check what time it is?"

I hear her heave herself up from the bed and fumble with something on the nightstand.

"Ten thirty," I hear, along with the sound of Sophie's skull hitting the headboard. "Oww."

"Hey . . ." This time the drowsy voice is coming from Jaz's cot. "Didn't they tell us when we checked in that breakfast is from eight to eleven?"

"Shit!"

The next ten minutes are a jumbled mess of confusion, tossed underwear, and exposed boobs as the three of us tackle each other to the single bathroom, our inhibitions gone the way of our evaporated hangovers from just a few minutes ago.

We just barely make it in time for breakfast. The omelet chef doesn't seem too pleased with us, seeing as he's already putting away his assorted props and utensils. But it's not like there's anything remotely edible at the buffet, so we're not backing down, no matter how many dirty looks he gives us.

The three of us set our half-empty plates on a table by the window, in silence. I stab my eggs, and a greasy liquid line oozes out onto the white ceramic. They're undercooked. Fabulous. I settle on a piece of stale bread and a lukewarm cup of tea instead. I can see that it's bright and sunny outside, and there's nothing I want more at this moment than to be out there, holding a sweating glass of something sweet and frozen, and drenched in rum. If only to take the edge off my lingering headache.

Jaz hasn't said much since we woke up. Sophie looks decidedly uncomfortable, as though not sure what to say to lift the tension.

She decides on, "Well, I had a blast last night."

"How could you? You were barely conscious," I tease.

"Hey!" She feigns outrage.

"Well, how much do you remember, then?"

"Uhh . . . there were those two annoying guys."

"One of whom was totally into you, but anyways, continue. . . ."

"Really?" Sophie says this as though it happened to someone else.

"Yes, Mike, the short one."

"But weren't they both short?"

"The short blond one."

"Oh. Right. Wasn't there another one, though? A really tall, hunky one in combat pants and—"

"Right! I'm done, and I'm absolutely *dying* to get some sun. What do you think, Jaz?" With my eyes, I plead with Jaz to forgive me and let this go.

"Actually, Ali, I wanted to see you upstairs for a sec. D'you mind?" She tosses her napkin on the table.

Oh, shit. I really don't need this right now.

"Don't you want to go check out the beach?" Poor Sophe. She looks like a kid trying to smooth things over between warring parents.

"We'll only be a minute, sweetie. You get out there." Jaz grins back, nicely if a tad strained.

Whatever. I haven't done anything wrong, so why should I give her the satisfaction of acting as though I had? If Jaz really wants to make an issue out of this, there's nothing I can do about it.

I push back my chair, stand up, and follow her out of the International Buffet restaurant, past the wicker loveseats in the lobby, and in the elevator up to our room.

When Jaz slides the electronic key into the designated slot and pushes the heavy door open, I brush past her and plop down onto the edge of my bed. I blink a few times, stare at the peach-tiled floor, and try to run my fingers casually through my hair—except they keep getting caught in the knots, completely destroying my attempts at nonchalance.

Jaz doesn't sit. She looms by the bamboo dresser, arms crossed, and stares down at me.

"What happened yesterday?" she finally says.

"Nothing happened that you didn't see yourself."

"You told him you had a boyfriend?"

"Yes, of course. What do you think I am?" And what kind of question is this? I want to add. If anything, Jaz is the one who's been trying to get me to break it off with Brian, saying things like "He's not your soul mate" or something equally ridiculous. Does anyone still believe in soul mates in this age of soaring divorce rates? And what does she even know about the subject anyway, having never been in a relationship that lasted beyond a blowjob in the cramped backseat of a sporty car, or a few booty call encounters? The only time I'd seen her genuinely smitten is with Ben, and even that relationship never fully blossomed past the fuck-friend stage.

"That's not what I meant."

"Jaz, I didn't set out to hurt you. It was no big deal. He's really nice, actually, and if you'd given me the chance, I would've introduced you." I glare back, willing her to believe me. "And frankly, I'm the one who should be pissed off. Do you remember why we came here in the first place?" If she didn't, it might be time someone reminded her.

"I do." She turns away from me, facing the dresser instead.

"That's why I got you this. I was hoping it would cheer you up."
She digs in the drawer and pulls out a blue carrier bag, fastened
with silver ribbon, slightly misshapen and bent around the
edges from being squished in a suitcase. "I wanted to give it to
you yesterday, but I didn't get the chance. Here." She hands me
the unmistakable package: Bleu Comme le Ciel, my favorite
jewelry store ever. I had worked there a few summers while I
was finishing up my undergrad. When I was recruited by
Ernsworth in my final year, I persuaded the owners of the boutique to pay me my last few weeks' wages in merchandise, since
I'd be raking in the real dough at the firm soon enough anyway.
The massive mother of pearl cocktail ring and antique pendant-
on-sky-blue-ribbon I'd bartered on that occasion still garnered
their fair bit of compliments.

I raise my chin toward Jaz and see the girl who, when we were
in high school, would bake me a cake every year on my birthday
and bring it to class with her, along with confetti and Happy
Birthday balloons. Someone who, despite working the same
dinky part-time mall job as the rest of us, would somehow manage to buy me the latest jeans I'd been coveting, the likes of
which my mother adamantly refused to finance on the grounds
that two hundred dollars was a preposterous sum of money to
spend on anything denim. The same girl who always thinks to include me, whether it's for a by-invitation-only L'Oréal after-
hours clearance sale, or a limousine-and-red-carpet event at a
hip Saint Laurent Boulevard club, even if she's got hordes of
other Zac Posen–clad office acquaintances to schmooze with.

The thing is, with Jaz, if you can bear to weather the mood
monsoons every once in a while, you are left with a sweet girl
whose need for love and belonging hasn't dulled with age or
achievement. Why else is she only too happy to act as Ben's personal toilet paper? If nothing overly special, the guy is at least
the embodiment of Fitting In—aspiring stockbroker, healthy interest in posh sports like golf and tennis, wealthy exclusive-

neighborhood-dwelling parents, and handsome enough. And reasonably witty too, as I discovered on the few occasions where he deigned to be seen with her in public.

I take the bag from her outstretched hand and tug on the silver ribbon. Inside, in a purple velour pouch, is a triple-strand Swarovski crystal tennis bracelet.

"Jaz!" I gasp. "Why? You must have spent a fortune!" I've seen this bauble before, and I know for a fact that she did.

"You've had a pretty shitty run lately, and I just wanted you to know that things are gonna turn around for you. Look at you, you're so beautiful and talented, and everybody loves you! Fuck those fuckers at Ernsworth. And the fucking UFE too." She slumps beside me and squeezes my shoulders. "And that guy, whatshisface—"

"James."

"Whatever. He's no Ben anyway. So we're okay?"

"Are you kidding? We're *so* okay that I'm going to get on getting you and James together by the end of this vacation, or else. You need to get over Ben. Seriously."

I regret the words the instant they leap off my lips. The tension I thought had dissipated seeps back into the space between us.

"What exactly is your problem with Ben?" she hisses.

That he's as enthused about you as one is toward the prospect of catching crabs. That in the time you've been "together," he's made fewer public appearances with you than Paris Hilton would at a Wal-Mart.

I'm aching to speak my mind, but such a display would only result in (a) the belittling of the state of my own love life, again, and (b) hurting Jaz's feelings in that messed-up kind of way that comes from caring about someone enough to want the best for them and yet not be able to trust their judgment. "Nothing, I'm being an idiot."

She's quiet for one long moment, before composing herself.

"All right, fine." She exhales. "Let's go get our asses a tan. Sophie's already got a lead on us."

I shuffle to my feet without looking her directly in the eye.

"Hang on, I need to call my parents." In the midst of the mini-drama, I'd managed to forget. "My mother's probably got me lying passed out naked in a dirty Mexican back alley by now." I grab the phone and search the Spanish wording on it for dialing instructions. "Great. You have to go to the lobby for international calls." Defeated by my second attempt at avoiding impending doom, I slam the receiver in its cradle and throw myself back onto the duvet.

"Can we please see the beach first? It's already noon, and no one's home anyway. You'll be calling to talk to the answering machine."

"Even better."

"Just a peek, Ali. Aren't you anxious?"

As a matter of fact, I am. Needles of excitement are prickling the back of my neck, the bottom of my spine, and nerve endings all over my body. It's hard to imagine that you can be filled with so much dread and so much anticipation at the same time.

"Okay, but I'll just help you find a good spot on the sand. Then I'm off to the lobby."

I store the bracelet in the safe by the closet, give myself a once-over in the full-length mirror, and we practically skip downstairs to join Sophie on the beach.

They say the Caribbean was named after the native tribe that inhabited this area centuries before Columbus "discovered" the Bahamas. I wonder, looking out at the endless span of sapphire blue before me, speckled with diamond-white flashes where the sun joins the waves, if the natives had the slightest clue they owned the best little piece of real estate on the planet.

Even Jaz is impressed.

"Wow. I've been to Jamaica before, but the beach wasn't like this. This is *huge.*"

Unlike the featured beaches of *Miami Vice*–type TV shows, which showed seemingly hundreds of glistening sunburned bodies baking under the smoldering sun, the shore here is virtually bare, except for patches of thatched-roof parasols dotting the pinkish-brown sand.

I breathe in the heavy, coconut-oil-and-salt-scented air, and close my eyes to focus on the sound of the surf breaking somewhere out in the sea instead of on shore.

So this is why people back home buy CDs of this stuff to help them fall asleep. But I don't need a CD. I'm right here, and already memories of Diane, the UFE, my parents, and even Brian are steadily being picked up and tossed around, like the fine sand particles at my feet, and carried far away from me by the waves.

Now that I'm here, I can't picture that I ever existed anywhere else, or that I'll ever have to leave. It can't be normal to feel this way about a place I'd never laid eyes on, or even really stopped to think about until a mere forty-eight hours ago.

"There's Sophie." Jaz jogs ahead of me, waving at a silhouette under a straw umbrella in the distance.

Jaz scolds her. "What are you doing under there? I thought we were here to tan."

"I've never seen anything so amazing, you guys," Sophie says in total Zen mode. "It's like, how do you describe this?"

"You don't have to, sweetie," I say, patting her stone-white leg. "I hear you."

We both gape at the ocean, trying to soak in as much of this as we can.

"It's just water, guys." Jaz spreads out the green-and-white towel we'd procured from the hut marked TOALLAS at the edge of the beach, and plops down on her stomach, her silver iPod by her side. Moments later, she's dozing off to what sounds like Nirvana from the screeching that I can make out through her headset.

"I checked with reception before I came out here," Sophie says. "They're expecting clouds this afternoon and tomorrow. Maybe we should check out the list of excursions they offer."

With the question of my very existence on Earth after the two phone calls I'm about to make still weighing on my mind, I can't say contingency planning for the next few days figures high on my list of priorities.

"Listen, Sophe, I really need to get to a phone. I'll let you and Jaz figure it out." I take a deep breath of resignation and turn toward the hotel.

"Good luck," Sophie calls after me.

I trudge heavily through the sand, my gaze trailing the footprints I leave in the snowlike texture. Within a few minutes, the tips of my toes make contact with rough crabgrass, the edge of the resort property. In Cuba, all beaches are supposed to be public (or so says the guidebook), even though I have yet to come into contact with one local not employed by one of the hotels lining the strip.

"Where are you off to so early?" A shock of spiky blue-tipped hair and molded arms I manage to remember through last night's drunken haze passes me along the faint overgrown trail.

"James!" I execute a less-than-graceful 180, my feet landing on something thorny. "Ow."

"Careful, there's tons of these prickly weeds out here. I have no clue what they are." He takes my arm to steady me. "So?"

"So?" I'm not entirely sure what he's wondering about.

"Had enough of the sun?"

"No, no. Man, if only you knew . . . I can't believe I'll have to leave all this in six days and get back—" To my personal version of the reeking pit of Hades. "—um, home." No sense coming off as a deranged psychiatric ward escapee to someone I just met last night.

"How's your sense of adventure?"

"Excuse me?"

"What would you say if I told you there's a resort dive course starting in a few minutes?"

"Err . . ." Do I admit I've never even snorkeled and have no idea how a resort dive course differs from a regular dive course, risking certain ridicule?

"How much is it?" Genius. I'll say I didn't bring much cash on me.

"It's free. Didn't you read the brochures?"

Uh, actually, no. I was busy trying to weasel my way out of being sold into serfdom by my parents for daring to achieve something less than total perfection.

Maybe that's not entirely fair. Flunking the UFE isn't exactly a hair away from the shining luminescence of success.

"Why, no, I must have overlooked them in my sheer delight in being here." I bat my eyelashes and try to mimic a Playboy Bunny who's just heard she'd been invited to Hugh Hefner's bedroom suite.

"Well?"

I take a deep, long breath. Well.

"I was actually on my way to make a phone call. Maybe tomorrow."

"I think someone's being a chicken."

"Am not! You don't even know me."

"Why don't you come do this thing with me, and you can be my buddy, and maybe we can talk politics over a couple of daiquiris after."

Okay. I'm definitely beginning to see some weirdo vibes emanating from this guy. I mean, what adult actually asks another to be their "buddy"?

James's eyes narrow a little. He tilts his face slightly to one side and looks at me. "*Buddy* is a diving term. We need to be in pairs to dive. Safety precaution."

Oh. I knew that. Makes perfect sense.

"Yeah, but my friends—"

"Ask them to come along," James offers, matching my weariness with his enthusiasm. He lifts his eyes off me and waves to someone behind us. I swing around and find Jaz waving back. Under the surface of nonchalant sweetness, I sense a Look.

I know that Look.

It's the I-thought-we'd-settled-this look. I need to do something, quick.

Mandatory buddy system. Hmm.

"So you say we need to be paired up?"

"Absolutely. Unless you end up being the loser nobody picks and have to dive with the instructor . . ." His eyes laugh at me.

"No, I think I'm all set for 'buddies.' You say this resort course is starting now?"

"So you're coming? Great!"

My heart is pounding so hard now, I'm not sure anymore how much of it is attributable to the phone calls I have yet to make, the cunning plan I've just concocted, or the mortal fear that's gripped me now that I may potentially be facing death at the hands of an air tank and the deep blue sea.

My voice a tad shaky, I say, "You don't suppose I have a minute to make a phone call?"

"Class started five minutes ago."

"Let me get the girls."

∽◌

"The first thing you need to learn about diving," begins the tan, broad-hipped Aussie divemaster Deanna, "is that you have more chances of having an accident in your bathtub than you do underwater." Her *water* comes out sounding more like *wa'er*.

"And if you do end up crossing paths with a shaa'k, consider yourselves very lucky. These magnificent beasts are a rare sight."

Lucky? Is she kidding me?

When I'd proposed the plan to the girls a mere few minutes

ago, I thought Sophie was about to detonate with joy. A tae kwon do black belt and an all-round avid athlete, she has an unusually low tolerance for lounging about for more than a few minutes at a time, and even then, only to catch her breath from whatever sport she has just immersed herself in.

Jaz, on the other hand, having been blessed with a much higher fear-of-bodily-harm quotient, had been significantly harder to convince. I suspect I wouldn't have met with any success at all had James not been waving in our direction when I did the asking.

So by 1 P.M. on this stifling hot, partly cloudy November afternoon in Varadero Beach, I've learned all about the effects of air density on my lungs, the joys of neutral buoyancy, where the air pockets in my body are located, and what to do when the pressure inside them builds. (Equalize, equalize, equalize!)

"Now for the practical portion of our course," says Deanna a little too enthusiastically after having droned on forever on what sounded like a high school physics lesson to me. "We'll see how well you were paying attention!"

Uh-oh.

Walking into the slanted, rectangular pool is like walking into bathwater.

"Do you think they heat these things?" I whisper in Sophie's general direction.

"Why would they heat the pools? It's like five hundred degrees."

"So you think the sun alone makes them this warm?"

She shrugs.

Well, whatever it is, we need more of it in Montreal.

"Okay! Are we all psyched to dive yet?" I swear, all that Deanna is missing is a pair of hot pink pom-poms and pigtails.

I'm definitely feeling something right now, although it's more along the lines of impending doom than being psyched. There's a reason evolution left us devoid of gills, and even this "shallow" dive of thirty feet is chilling me down to my bone marrow.

"Chino and Miguel will bring out the equipment and supervise while you assemble your sets."

I look up from where I'm waddling gracelessly in ill-fitting fins, my eyes squinting under the blazing sun, and freeze. Dead. In the water.

From the rear view, both of Deanna's assistant divemasters had looked alike. Their bare backs are both baked a light brick brown, lending them an air of having spent the better part of their lives yachting along Mediterranean shores. Both are wearing trunks in the lemon-and-turquoise colors of the resort. And they both have the same muscular builds, their biceps bulging as they relay wetsuits, steel air tanks, and bulky canvas vests from the dive hut to the side of the pool. But when I look up into their perspiring faces, I see that the one Deanna calls Chino has slightly Asian features blended in with his high Cuban cheekbones and strong jawline.

The other one is Him. Him from last night. And this time Xena is nowhere in sight.

I know he recognizes me because he smiles as soon as he catches me gawking and says, way too casually, "How are you?"

"Ah . . ." My mouth seems to have gone completely numb. "I'm good," I croak. Oh, the wit, the exquisitely sparkling repartee.

"Good," he replies.

Good. Good, indeed. Then why am I so flustered? Why is my chest heaving ever so slightly at every vibration of that unnervingly deep masculine voice?

"I see your frien' is okay," he continues.

"Err . . ." I draw a complete blank, until I catch him waving at someone behind me. Sophie. Oh. That. "Yes, she's fine. A little hungover, but otherwise functional."

He smiles wryly and resumes tending to the air tanks. I want to turn away, to stop gawking like a sex-starved spinster, but I can't.

"Okayyeee!"

Please shut up, you squealing Australian baboon on steroids.

"I'll need you all to buddy up now, so we can assemble our equipment and do our safety checks like we just learned."

Out of the corner of my eye, I spot James slicing through the water toward me. Okay. Just like we'd planned . . . Now, where is that girl?

James is inching closer. Any second now, he's going to ask me. His mouth is contorting in the shape of an *A*. Shit. She's too late.

"Ali? Ali!" Sophie dog-paddles up to me. I could kiss the girl. "Wanna be my buddy?" I exhale a sigh of relief and hope that both James and Jaz are catching our devious little exchange.

"Sure, bud. I hope you were listening when Outback Jane here was explaining all that BCD, regulator, buoyancy crap, because I wasn't."

"You should've told me that before you agreed to be my buddy."

"You should've asked." I sense James is right behind me now, and I feel so guilty, I can barely scrape together enough courage to turn around and face him. But I have to. Phase Two of my plan depends on it.

"Hey, James, have you met my friends Jaz and Sophie?" A quick glance around the pool area reveals that everyone seems to be conveniently pairing up. Jaz has turned a bright classic YSL lipstick red, and James isn't looking any more comfortable. I can hardly bring myself to look him in the eye. Though it was never said, it was plenty implied that we were going to pair up. But he'll get over it. I'm not entirely sure Jaz would have.

I do, on the other hand, steal a quick glance in Miguel's direction. Is it just me, or is he smirking at me?

⁓♂◯

The pool exercises were either a total disaster or a marginal success, depending on how you looked at it.

The first time I assembled my BCD, the suffocating vest that serves as a flotation device when puffed up with air, I had my regulator, the octopus-like contraption you have to breathe into, strapped on backwards. The second time, I couldn't muster up enough strength to snap the tank firmly enough against the back of the BCD, and had all but given up on the whole operation, when Chino came by and gently prodded me through the whole process again. By my third attempt, I was in the wa'er, as Deanna would say, practicing breathing through a regulator for the first time. This, in fact, turned out to be kind of thrilling. The next task, a little less so.

In the unlikely event that the regulator slipped out of our mouths sometime middive, we were required to learn how to calmly retrieve it, put it back in, and inhale, all without going into a panic seizure.

My first five attempts yielded immediate shoots up to the surface as soon as I'd lost contact with air for longer than two seconds.

"I can't doooo iiiit!" I wailed, hoping to garner enough sympathy that I'd be set free from this afternoon from hell.

No such luck.

When I finally found the fucker and put it in my mouth without incident, I adamantly refused to breathe in, no matter how many times Deanna patiently repeated that I would not, in fact, swallow any wa'er if I remembered to exhale first.

It took another couple of aborted missions before I was convinced, and at long last, I was ready for my first ocean dive.

We break for fifteen minutes before taking the Plunge. Out of the corner of my eye, I can see that Jaz and James are engaging in some awkward-looking conversation, both shifting their weight around, gazes roaming everywhere but on each other. This isn't good. But hey, at least I tried. I turn my attention back to my dive buddy, who, despite having been excitedly attacking every instruction Deanna Dundee had barked at us, was now slumped by the edge of the pool, shoulders drooping and lost in thought.

"Hey there," I say tentatively. "Do you feel ready? I sure as fuck don't."

"You're such a girl, Ali. Get over it." She sighs. "Speaking of being a hopeless girl, how do you think Jaz is doing?"

We both glance over in Jaz's direction, and see her and James sitting together in complete silence. Ouch.

"Should we go rescue her?" Sophie asks.

"Give her another minute. We haven't really had a chance to talk since we got here, just the two of us. So tell me, how've you been, bud?"

She shrugs. Not a good sign.

"Sophe?"

"There's something I didn't tell you before we came here. You had enough shit to deal with."

Oh, God. She's pregnant. And Yasser is the father. Now she's going to have to bring up the baby on his family's camel ranch in Jordan and trade in her green sweatsuit (and I'm not talking Juicy Couture) for floor-sweeping embroidered Bedouin robes and headscarves. Seriously though, I can't imagine anything going wrong in Sophie's G-rated life beside her getting a B (gasp!) rather than her usual A-pluses in, say, Advanced Microwave Emissions class.

"What is it?"

"I've been offered a scholarship into the master's program."

Silence.

We both swing our feet in the lukewarm water for a few long, quiet moments.

I'm racking my brain, wondering how I could possibly ask

how this is a bad thing without coming off as condescending, when she volunteers: "I just can't take it anymore. What's the point?"

I don't feel any closer to the heart of the problem than I did a second ago. Take what anymore? The dismal state of the North American education system? World hunger? And what's the point of what, exactly? Life?

Being a certified Dreamer, Sophie often questions such philosophical conundrums as the problem of third world poverty, separation of Church and State in America, or whether or not Michael Jackson is merely eccentric or just plain nuts. I gear myself up for the existential debate to come.

"What do you mean, sweetie?"

"I mean I can't go on doing this. Going to class every single day, wishing I were anywhere else. Sometimes I feel like I'm having trouble breathing when I wake up in the morning, like I can't imagine getting dressed and going to *that place* one more time."

By "that place" I can only assume she means campus, but we could just as easily have been talking about me, and "that place" could very well have been Ernsworth.

"But you're doing so well—"

"That's just it!" Sophie cries. "My dad keeps telling me and anyone who'll listen how proud he is of me, and how he can almost taste the day I'm heading up my own Internet company while my mother just wants me to get married and have babies, and . . . and . . ." Her voice breaks off, and I think she's about to cry. This is definitely not like her.

"And what? Oh, honey, it's okay, tell me." I rub her back, not knowing what else to do.

I'm sure she's going to burst into tears now, but she doesn't. She swallows hard, and her face regains all former composure. "And I don't want any of it. The thing is, Ali, there's so many things I want to do, I don't know where to start. Electrical engineering is *not* one of them. I want to feel like what I'm doing matters somehow. If I tell my parents this, they'll throw their arms up in the air and wonder why someone who has come this far in their field goes and throws it all away for stupid pipe dreams."

"It sounds to me like you need to take a year to find yourself, for lack of a better term. You know, make like a young yuppie and backpack through Europe or Tibet, or whatever."

"I've only got a month before the scholarship offer expires. It's just enough time to finish my last undergrad semester, maybe get a week off, if I'm lucky. Yay. Plus we're Lebs. Can you imagine telling your mother that you're quitting your job at Ernsworth to find inner peace in Mongolia?"

I'm just about to protest when Deanna the Deranged Dingo claps loudly, calling us to attention. "Now that we've all got our equipment assembled and are roaring to go, help your buddies into their BCDs, do your final safety check, just like we practiced, and follow Chino, Miguel, and myself to the beach. Let's go!"

"We'll continue this conversation later," I whisper, and begin the ordeal of sliding into the medieval torture device I've just put together. I turn my back to it, wriggle my arms around for a bit until I get them through the armholes, and hoist the vest onto my back. My knees nearly buckle from the sheer bone-crushing weight of the metal tank, and an intense flash of pain sparks at the base of my spine and shoots all the way down to my right foot.

"Oww!"

Deanna is looming next to me, watching me stagger and writhe. She doesn't offer to help, despite my pitiful, beseeching puppy-dog eyes. "Can I maybe have one of the smaller tanks over there? . . ."

"You have to learn to dive with the adult tanks. Go on. Let's do that safety check together. What's the catchphrase we learned today?"

I wince from the pain. All I want is to put this piece of shit down.

"Err . . . Bruce Willis . . . aah . . . Ruins All . . . Movies?"

"Right! And what does that stand for?"

I'm breathing audibly now, and a trickle of sweat is snaking from my temple down to my chin.

"BCD . . ." I clasp the vest. "Check. Weights . . ." This time I go for the fifty pounds of pure metal strapped to my waist. "Check." And so on and so forth until I've gone through all the motions and diving jargon, and Deanna finally releases me.

One wobbly step at a time, I follow Sophie and the group onto a deck leading out into the sea, tucked away from the casual bathers and snorkelers. One by one, each resort course attendee takes one long stride off the edge of the deck and plunges fins first into the water.

My turn comes. I spin around and gape at Sophie behind me. She gives me the thumbs-up sign. Miguel is standing right beside her, ready to give me a hand if I need it. No chickening out now. I close my eyes, take a hard, nostril-flaring breath, and leap.

My webbed rubber fins break the water first, then my wetsuit-clad thighs. I feel so heavy, I'm sure I'm going to sink faster than Enron. But as soon as I hit the water, I become instantly weightless, and everything that's strapped, squeezed, and clasped onto my body finally feels like it actually serves a purpose. Just as I was taught, I spurt some air into my vest and watch it expand and carry me to the surface of the water where everyone is floating idly. This isn't half bad, really.

"Everyone ready?" Deanna performs a quick numbers check, and when she figures we're all accounted for, leads the pack toward a bright-orange-painted buoy, some fifty feet out to sea. We paddle backwards, laughing and chatting the whole way. Within a mere five minutes, we're ready to go under.

I can do this. Everything is going to be *fine*. With trembling fingers, I deflate my BCD a tiny bit, and my heads sinks beneath the gently rocking waves.

We descend, slowly . . . slowly . . . Deanna is giving a thumbs-up under the water. So far, so good. I check my depth gauge. Ten feet. My ears are beginning to hurt from the pressure. I've gone too far too fast. No problem. I pinch my nose and exhale in spurts. The pain subsides, and I give Sophie the okay to keep going deeper. The enormous plastic mask pinching her cheeks and her lips clasped shut over her mouthpiece make her face look like that of a chubby sea turtle. I can't help but laugh silently, even as I can only imagine what I must look like right now. Before I know it, our fins hit the underwater sand in a small poof of dust.

Oh. My. God.

I'm thirty feet below sea level, and I'm breathing. Fish, coral, vivid colors are exploding all around me. The water is so clear, I can see for what seems like a mile ahead of me. I feel like an alien with my mask and the multihued tubes sprouting out of various holes in my BCD, but none of the fish milling around seem to mind my invading their space. I crouch down on the ground to watch as a silvery one digs for food in the sand. It doesn't flinch, even though I'm not half a yard away.

A loud banging noise, metal on metal, calls me to attention. Deanna is rasping on her air tank in an effort to show us an enormous stingray somewhere out in the distance, flapping its wide wings in the teal underwater sand dunes.

I observe the bubbles spilling out of my regulator, and think about how surreal all this is. Two days ago I was sitting at my desk, depressed, wondering what the hell I was going to do with my life after its unexpected turn for the worse. Now I'm in feeding distance of a swarm of black-and-yellow-striped sergeant majors, blue angel fish, and half a dozen different kinds of coral.

The group moves forward, following the upward slanted slope of the dunes, stopping every now and then to gawk at whatever marine curiosity we happen upon. The minutes pass too quickly, and slowly, we begin our ascent. I'm feeling lighter and lighter, and loving it. We float leisurely through a small cave, and I try to take in every little creature, every plant, and every strange object around me. I don't want to forget a single thing, not the hollow, mechanical sound of my breathing, not the huge urnlike life-forms clinging to the rocks, not the myriad of different fish ignoring us as we pass over them.

I check my gauge and see that I don't have much air left. We must be nearing the end of the dive. Looking for Sophie, I turn my head from side to side, my peripheral vision constrained by the mask. But I can't see her. I look up, nothing but blue. I turn my head down, and there she is, somewhere below me. As a matter of fact, so is most of the group. I'm floating too high.

I flip myself over in an effort to fin my way down, but it doesn't help. In fact, the more furiously I bat my legs, the higher I'm being sucked. I exhale to empty my lungs of air, just as I was taught, but I keep floating up. By now I'm on the verge of panic. I don't know what else to do. Why can't I sink like everyone else? What's happening?

I grab at my vest, now dangerously inflated, searching frantically for the lever that lets the air out. I find it and squeeze the release button as hard as I can. Nothing!

I want to scream out to them, but the best I can do underwater is grunt, and they're way too far now to hear me. Where's Sophie? Isn't she supposed to be watching out for me? And Jaz? James? Hasn't anyone noticed I'm missing? I feel like I'm having one of those nightmares where you open your mouth to call for help and nothing comes out. Except this is really happening. . . . I can't run. I don't know what to do to help myself, and I can hardly breathe anymore. The water closes in on me like an airtight coffin even as I'm being pulled by a violent antigravitational force faster and faster toward the surface. I've lost complete and total control. There's nothing I can do except pray I don't smash into a boat when I break the surface.

I kick and scream noiselessly, and kick again, when

something—someone—grabs me from behind in a crushing grip, grinding me to a suspended halt. I can't stop kicking. I don't care who it is, I don't care what's happening, I just want to get out of here. I want to breathe proper air.

I sense that we're still edging toward the surface, except at a much more reasonable speed, up, up, and up until we break the surface and I spit out my regulator, gasping for the most welcome whiff of oxygen of my entire life.

I didn't die. I'm okay. Shaken up, tearstained, and probably snot-smeared, but alive.

"You forget to let your air out when you start to ascend, and you lose control."

I turn my head around, and find myself staring straight into Miguel's beautiful face.

11

"Ali? Ali, are you okay? Oh my God. Al, open your eyes. How many fingers am I holding up?" Sophie slumps into the patch of warm sand where I'm sprawled out, half denuded of my wetsuit and still panting.

"Give her some air! Can't you see she's choking?" Jaz sprints toward us, followed closely by James and Deanna.

"Two fingers, Sophe. I'm just a little freaked out, not retarded. I'm fine." I prop myself up on my elbows and pull myself into a sitting position.

"Crikey, what happened hea'?" Deanna hovers over me like a rabid wildebeest about to pounce. Her eyes are bloodshot, and I'm almost certain she's happy to see I survived just so she could get the privilege of throttling me herself.

My eyes furiously comb the beach, but I can't see him anywhere. After we surfaced together, Miguel dragged me to shore without so much as a grunt of strain, heaved me up on the surf, and undid the suffocating zipper on my wetsuit, pulling it down halfway. I had neither the time, energy, nor presence of mind to perform a quick boob check to make sure nothing was hanging out of anywhere, or to pull my bikini bottom out of my ass crack. I just lay motionlessly on the beach, while he disassembled my equipment and carried it away, mumbling an inaudible, muffled "Thanks for saving my life" in between gasps for air.

Now I want nothing more than to be lying under a warm comforter, with a steaming mug of tea next to me, and reruns of the entire final season of *Sex and the City* playing on TV. Alas, I don't think they have TBS in Cuba.

"I'm sooooo sorry, Ali! I was just looking at this incredible little fishy—it was long and sinewy like a snake, and it looked like it was stuck to this other fish. . . . Oh, crap, I'm doing it again, I'm sorry! I'm such a crappy buddy! I don't blame you if you never speak to me again." Sophie wails, burying her head in a mound of sand.

"I don't know what to say, Ali. . . . Geez, I'm sorry too." James runs a hand through his hair, looking genuinely embarrassed. I can almost see him mentally crossing "demonstrate physical prowess with superior diving skills as means of impressing females" off his repertoire of pickup behavior. Poor guy. At least if he and Jaz have something to talk about now, my near-death experience has served a higher purpose.

By now a not-too-small crowd of curious onlookers has gathered around us, and I'm feeling like I've provided enough entertainment for one day. I pull myself to my feet, waving the specks of clotted sand off my butt, and trudge toward the hotel.

"Sorry I sort of messed up your afternoon, guys. I'll catch you later." I glance back without breaking my stride.

Sophie and Jaz immediately follow me, having shed their respective equipment in record speed and left it lying on the sand.

James stays glued into place. "Yeah, um, catch you later. And I'm the one who's sorry."

Poor, poor James.

"Okay, so I've got us booked for Havana tomorrow!" Sophie screeches from the doorframe as she crosses the threshold into the room and shuts the door behind her. "The bus is picking us up at eight thirty sharp, so no sleeping in tomorrow. We've got to make this."

I move from the lying-down-on-the-bed-propped-up-by-five-pillows position I adopted an hour ago only to plop a Lindor milk chocolate truffle, one of the five we've rationed between the three of us, in my mouth. It's warm and sticky, and just barely makes it the 0.5 seconds between the wrapper and my tongue without disintegrating into brown goo, but at least it's familiar, and it's sustenance. Between the unidentifiable buffet grub of last night, the runny eggs this morning, and the bloody hamburger I didn't touch today at lunch, I'm astounded I've managed to eat anything at all since we've gotten here.

Sophie slides out of her flip-flops, crawls onto her bed, and adopts a Zen pose reminiscent of Madonna in her Buddhist phase. She grabs a pair of tweezers from the dresser and begins to pluck away at the tiny hairs around her knee.

Ten minutes later, she's still at it.

"Sophe, man, if you need to borrow a razor, just say so."

"No, I like this. It's like beauty yoga."

"Beauty yoga?"

"It's relaxing. You should try it."

"Mmm . . . no, thanks. I prefer shopping yoga. Enlightenment through Ungaro, if you will."

"There's always sex yoga." Jaz steps out of the steamy bathroom with a towel wrapped around her head. "Inner peace via the art of bonking." She plucks a Lindor from the stash nestled beside me.

"Hey!" I slap Jaz's lunging hand away. Seeing as I almost died today, I'm feeling more than a little entitled to them.

"I think the dudes who wrote the *Kama Sutra* beat you out on that one, Jazzie," Sophie says without looking up from her painfully slow project.

"Okay . . ." Jaz eyes me tentatively. "So now that you've had a chance to relax and everything, you're going to get dressed and come out with us tonight, right?"

To the casual observer, I may indeed appear to be in a calm

state. But really, I couldn't be further from it. There's no avoiding those two phone calls anymore. It's six o'clock, and I've officially been in a foreign country for over twenty-four hours. I'd never left my parents' sight for that long, let alone the whole continent. What the hell would I say to them? To Brian? So far, I hadn't so much lied as neglected to mention a few, um, developments. As soon as I picked up that phone in the lobby and opened my mouth, anything that would come out of it would invariably be an outright, undeniable lie.

And to add to my heaping pile of steaming shit of a life, I had to go and make a complete ass of myself today. I'm sure everyone from the German skinheads to the restaurant staff knows all about the ditzy Canadian tourist who lost it in the water today and had to be rescued by a big hunky Cuban. Gag me.

"No, I'm not really in the mood to go out."

"But what about all your new outfits?" Jaz pulls a gorgeous Tahari purple strapless number from the closet, complete with a knee-skimming flouncy hemline. I remember thinking how I'd destroy all the other girls at Señor Frog's when I picked that up expressly for Cancún. "Or this?" She holds up an ultra-tight ruby red Theory tank dress with white trim. "Wouldn't this look incredible with your BCBG sandals?" Also a Cancún-related purchase.

I look at my suitcase on the floor at the foot of my bed and think about all those clothes I had bought, many that even my best friends haven't seen yet. I had so many plans, so many elaborate fantasies. What would I be doing when I donned the drop-waisted French Connection creation? Would it be Cavalli or Chloé to Coco Bongo, the biggest, wildest club in all of Latin America? And the shoes . . . I had planned fourteen different pairs of sandals for half as many vacation days.

I hadn't been crazy. Just excited. Hopeful. Ambitious.

So things didn't quite turn out as I'd planned. How much does that really matter? Was it too late to shift gears? Maybe even—

shudder—go back to school and study fashion just like I've always wanted? Was this life's not-so-subtle way of telling me to make a limoncello martini with the lemons it had hurled my way?

I contemplate telling my mother the truth. I picture her having coffee with my aunt Maryam, discussing so-and-so's son's latest promotion, and how he's now planning to build his parents a vacation home in Dubai. I then imagine them being interrupted by a phone call. Long distance.

Right. Maybe not.

"Ali, you can't just sit here and watch Spanish TV all night." Sophie looks up from her plucking just long enough to cast me a pleading pout. "It's not even subtitled."

"Why not? It's great practice."

She makes an exasperated face. "Well, for one thing, you still haven't thanked that dive instructor who caught you mid–nautical flight. You know, for someone who's just been rescued by a guy who could pass for Enrique's bigger, buffer, mole-less sibling, I don't think you're being appreciative enough."

"She's right." Jaz chimes in, "That was one delicious—"

"Okay! Okay, enough. Fine." I huff and puff and pretend that I'm doing this for their benefit, but really, the thought of possibly seeing Miguel again, this time with advance notice and properly dolled up, is shooting every one of my central nervous impulses out of orbit. I'm already here, aren't I? Moping isn't going to give me back the five points it would have taken to pass the UFE. And I've got a suitcase full of fabulous clothes beckoning me. Failing to heed its call would constitute a bigger sin than indulging in bacon washed down with beer on the doorsteps of our neighborhood mosque.

But before I can relax and attempt to enjoy myself, there's still something I need to do.

"What time is dinner?"

"The by-reservation-only restaurants were all full for tonight." Sophie says, "So I guess it's the buffet again. Sorry."

"Perfect," I mutter to no one in particular. "Now if you'll excuse me, I'll be back in a minute, ladies." And with that, I slide my feet into a pair of cork-wedged mules and trudge downstairs to the lobby.

✥

"Three *pesos convertibles* a minute! Are you serious?"

The impassive look on the receptionist's face tells me that she is. I fork over three crisp bills of the just-for-tourists currency, and step inside the privacy of the public-style calling cabin. I'd given the mustached Cuban woman my home number as well as my Visa information and I'm now waiting for her to connect me. A few seconds later, the phone explodes into loud, shrill ringing.

Breathe. Again. This time like you mean it. Okay, I'm ready now. Really.

I pick up the receiver and wipe my damp forehead with the back of my hand, the sweltering heat of the lobby compounded by the rank, suffocating four sheets of glass surrounding me. The phone keeps ringing, except on the other side now. *One, two, three rings* . . . Oh, God, please let the machine pick up. Please, please, ple—

On the fourth ring, someone gets the phone, just before it goes to the machine. "Yo." My seventeen-year-old sister's casual voice comes streaming across the airwaves in one short, carefree note.

"Oh thank God it's you!" I let out in one breath, nearly melting with dehydration and fatigue.

"Ali? Is that you? What's wrong? Are you okay? Have you been mugged? Do you need money?"

"Relax, I'm okay. It's nothing like that."

"What is it, then?"

As much as it pains me to utter the truth at this point, I could never lie to Sara. Even if my job and her hectic social life meant that we didn't get to bond so much anymore, together we had weathered every phase our still-adjusting-to-Western-life parents had gone through over the years. From clandestine trips aboard the subway back in the days my mother was persuaded the Montreal public transportation system was, in fact, the Devil, to the times we'd sneaked a few sips of the cognac my dad kept hidden in a far corner of a high cabinet, away from my mother's anti-alcohol raids and our own inquisitive eyes. Lying to Sara would be like Bonnie lying to Clyde. We were in it together, whatever It happened to be. We were the younger, hipper, better-dressed Lebanese expatriate community's answer to Thelma and Louise. And Thelma and Louise don't lie to each other.

"I don't really have time to get into this now but . . ." I drop my head against the hard plastic of the phone. "I'm not calling from Cancún."

"*What?*"

Fuck. If this is the reaction I'm getting from my cooler-than-thou, ultra-laid-back sister, then I just can't wait to talk to my mom.

"Where the hell are you, then?"

"Relax, I just had a slight change of plans. I'm in Varadero with Sophe and Jaz."

"Varadero, *Cuba?*"

"Know any others?" I chirp. "Anyways, Sara, don't worry, we're at this really cool resort, and I'll be back next Saturday. I need a huge favor from you, though."

"What?"

"Tell Mom I called and that I'm okay, and please, please, please don't let her or Brian pick me up from the airport! You do it, *capisce?*"

"You haven't told Brian *either*? Are you retarded? You don't think he's going to figure it out?"

"Of course I'm going to tell him, duh!" I say with a whole lot more conviction than I feel. "I'll explain later. I really have to go now—there's a lineup for the phone. Remember, give Mom and Dad my love and tell them I'm doing great. That's it. Don't volunteer any extra information."

"Ali, I can't believe you're doing this to me again. Remember when you were fifteen and Spyro broke up with you and Mom demanded to know why you were crying so much and you wouldn't tell her? She locked me up in my room and grilled me for—"

"Yeah, no time, sis. Gotta go. Love you." I hang up.

One down. And the easy one at that.

I motion to the receptionist to dial the other number, and again the phone rings, loud and shrill. I pick up the receiver, this time waiting for Brian's voice to come across the airwaves.

Something inside me wonders if it's normal that I don't miss him yet. We'd never gone a day without at least speaking to each other since we started dating, so you'd think I'd feel at least a tinge of excitement, relief, eagerness to hear the voice of the man who's been my crutch, my confidant, my sounding board for every injury to cross my mind, whether real or imagined, for three whole years. But I don't. Instead I feel dread and humiliation at having to lie not to a parent, but to a peer, a friend, my supposed soul mate.

There's also something else lurking somewhere deep in my gut, something more intangible. A resentment, I think, at being pulled out of the vacation mode I've temporarily nestled into, to face the twin responsibilities of Home and Reality. Couldn't I just go on vacation and let loose like everyone else? Isn't that what they're for? Why do I feel like I have to answer to not one but *two* people, one of whom I'm not even related to, who feel they need to know my exact whereabouts at every single point in time? Isn't my mother enough?

One, two, three rings. I feel a wetness seeping through the armholes of my body-hugging Nevik T-shirt. *Four.* I look at my

142 * NADINE DAJANI

watch. Six twenty-five on a Monday night. He could still be at work. Actually, he most probably is.

On the fifth ring, a hollow, mechanical version of Brian's voice answers.

"Hi, you've reached Brian Hayes. Please leave a message after the tone, or, if this is urgent, please call my mobile phone at . . ."

I slump against the glass panes and fan my damp face with my fingers. The next few words to come out of my mouth are possibly the most crucial of this entire week. I have to be careful to hit just the right tone of upbeat (but not so much so that he thinks something is up) and cheerful (sans overkill, so he wouldn't get the idea I'm having too much fun to miss him) and comforting, so he can relax and forget I exist. At least for another five days.

"Hi, Brian, it's meeee!" Definitely too hyper. "I'm, uh, having a really nice time over . . . um, here." This is so not going well. "The weather is fabulous. I even went diving today, can you believe it? I'll pick you up a book with pictures of all the fish I saw down there. We're going to Hav—" Shit! Shit, shit, shit, *shit!* "Heaven. We're going to club Heaven tonight, and we'll probably be out shopping all day tomorrow. I hope everything's okay back home. I miss you a lot, okay? Bye." And I hang up.

That could not possibly have gone worse. I failed to mention that Sara would be picking me up from the airport on Sunday, that it would be too expensive for me to call him again, and I didn't even tell him I loved him. Unfortunately, it's going to have to do for now.

I glance at my watch again and realize that the girls must be all dressed up and ready to go, and I still haven't even showered or fixed my hair.

12

Tonight's dinner at the International Buffet restaurant was perhaps even less inspiring than it was the night before. I'm beginning to wonder how a place so famous for its spicy dancing could
have such bland cuisine.

Decked out in our finest, the three of us meander to the piano
bar, where we sit down on rather plain-looking wicker chairs to
decide what to do with our evening.

"There's always La Bamba again." Jaz sips a rum punch the
meaty bartender has just handed her. She's looking great in a
black beaded top and pretty floral skirt.

I shudder at the thought of going back to the same spot we
first met. Could he be there tonight? What about the Lucy Lawless double? Is she going to be with him this time too? All questions I should not be asking myself, seeing as none of them bear
any relevance to my non-single status.

"Hey."

I know that *hey*. We don't need to swing around to see who is
"heying" us. We already know it's one of the Rocky Wannabe
Boys.

"Hi, Paul. Hi, Mike . . . oh. Hello . . ." Paul has obviously
scored with the tall European woman from last night. Towering
about a foot over him, she seems to have Krazy Glued herself to
his arm, seeing as she doesn't let go even as they pull up chairs
beside us.

"I am Donatella," she says with a heavy Italian accent. "It ees nice to meet with you."

"Nice to meet you too." I nod politely.

"Donatella here's from Italy."

Thanks, Paul. Very enlightening.

"Milan, to be precise. That right, babe?" He turns to her and smiles. She nods approvingly.

I don't believe this. I cast a furtive glance at my friends and see that their mouths are also slightly agape with disbelief. I'm not sure if it's the air, the water, or whatever else down here, but there's definitely something going around messing with people's heads. Either that, or every single woman in Italy must be a su-permodel, if Donatella feels this is the best she could do.

"Mind if we join you before hittin' the pageant?" Mike says directly to Sophie's breasts.

"Pageant?"

"Yeah, the resort's beauty pageant. It's tonight's entertain-ment."

"And who's in it?" I can't believe I didn't know about this. Things could get ugly.

"Why, sweetcakes, you wan' in on the action?"

I feel like smacking him upside the head like they do in all those mobster movies.

"No, I simply wanted to know which areas of the resort to avoid tonight."

"Why? What's the big deal? You look fantastic." He holds his hands up like he can't believe I'm arguing with him.

"He's right, Ali. It sounds like so much fun!" Jaz hasn't been excited about much since we've arrived here, and who knows, maybe I'll get another crack at getting James and her together. "Come on," she continues. "We all look great tonight."

In my efforts to appear presentable in case we ran into a cer-tain someone tonight, I'd decided on a very pretty, very feminine BCBG slip dress and Charles David barely-there silver sandals.

It had actually been a tad breezy when we'd come down from the room, so I brought a cropped lavender cardigan along. My brand-new Swarovski bracelet from Jaz completed the look.

Even Sophie had made an effort, borrowing my yellow Bebe micromini and pairing it with a simple white tank and mules.

"What do you think, Sophe?"

She fiddles with a strand of her longish bob for a second. "Well . . . it's too early to go to the clubs, and it does actually sound like fun. . . ."

"That's it, gang up on me," I say, even as I push my chair back and stand up. "Let's go."

The stage area is set around the outdoor pool-bar-cum-grill, and consists mainly of white plastic lawn chairs arranged in about a dozen rows facing an elevated set. There are only a handful of tourists present besides Jaz, Sophie, and me, the two Torontonians, and Donatella.

I walk up to the bar, about to order myself another Cuba Libre.

"Where are you going?" Jaz says, tugging at my elbow.

"The bar. What's the problem?"

"Let's sit up front where we can get a better view."

"Whatever. I don't care. You guys coming?" I ask Rocky I and II.

"Naw, we're gonna hang out back here," Paul says before turning to the bartender and ordering a round of rum punches.

"I'll catch up to you ladies in a minute," Mike says, conspicuously ogling Sophie and her tight top.

"Take your time." I head for the farthest seats from the bar possible, the ones closest to the stage.

A bunch of young guys I recognize as hotel staff are patrolling the stands, asking every female between the ages of fifteen and fifty they come across if she'd like to participate in the show. When the polite request for volunteers comes up three contest-

ants too short (the number of intended participants being three),
they begin scanning the aisles and a few minutes later, one of
them discovers the three of us huddled together in the front row.

"*Hola, muñequitas,* why you are so shy?" It's Chino, the
half-Asian half-Cuban dive assistant from this afternoon. "Ah, I
remember . . . ," he drawls when he sees me. "You are okay
now, *sí*?"

"Yes, thanks. Much better now." I can just see my cheeks
turning beet red.

"You are going to be in the show tonight?" he says.

It comes out sounding more like a statement of fact rather
than a question.

"Uh, no. I don't think so." I sink a little lower in my plastic
lawn chair.

"No, you muss'." He tries to pull both Jaz and me to our feet.
Out of the corner of my eye, I make out another staff member in
the background heading in our general direction. We're being
ambushed.

Chino tugs harder, making me lurch forward.

"Noooo!" I'm squealing, fighting back with every ounce of my
physical strength. For a second I really think I'm winning.

Until the unthinkable happens.

Jaz manages to pry herself free from Chino's one-handed
Arnold Schwarzenegger grip, and with Sophie's help, they propel
me into his arms.

I've been bamboozled. Two-timed. I can't believe it. My own
friends. Naturally, they both find this so amusing, they can
hardly stop themselves from convulsing with laughter long
enough to whip out their disposable cameras and snap pictures
of me being hoisted over Chino's shoulder, my butt in the air,
arms and legs flailing, screaming out for lost dignity. He crosses
the row of seats to the main aisle, climbs the five steps leading to
the stage, and drops me in one of the three awaiting chairs, all to

a soundtrack of hooting and whistling from the sparse crowd, the loudest of them being Jaz and Sophie.

At least he was gentle. He politely asks if I'd like a drink, and I even detect a hint of embarrassment behind his smiling eyes.

"No, I'm going to need my wits about me." The *Braveheart* reference is completely lost on Chino. He retreats to the safety of the area behind the stage.

Facing the smattering of drunk, obnoxious tourists, all howling and snickering in their Cristal beer, I decide to get through this with as much of my dignity as I can salvage, and then put it behind me.

Until the time comes to torture my so-called friends, that is.

So I smile and wave like a young Princess Diana in a signature Oscar de la Renta gown might have done, while two other women are being dragged on stage kicking and screeching.

A blast of loud Spanish pop music interrupts my stately stance, and I take that to mean the show has begun. In turn, each member of the entertainment staff steps forward and introduces him- or herself. There's Chino, the Latin-Asian stud responsible for my present misery, followed by Lisette, the five-foot-two girl with long chestnut pigtails in charge of the children's pool, Pedro, the ebony-skinned masseur with a body that would put Michelangelo's *David* to shame. His only flaw is a badly chipped front tooth, ruining what would otherwise have been a perfectly white mega-watt smile. Another girl, this one a blonde, follows with a huge grin and an elaborate curtsy.

And then I see him. Behind one of the other contestants, two chairs and several yards away, he's standing, clapping for his colleagues as they step forward. He affects a slight nod when it's his turn to introduce himself.

Miguel.

I'm afraid the audience might have seen me swoon when he said his name while standing tall in the background, as kneeclatteringly stunning as ever in blue jeans and a thin chest-hugging pullover. His hair is slicked back and glistening under the hot-pink stage lights. My heart is still pounding, and this time I'm not sure if it's because I'm terrified of what I can imagine I'm going to have to do in front of all these people, or if it's because he can see me. I turn back and mouth obscenities at Jaz and Sophie before Pedro announces the first event of the contest.

"*Damas y caballeros,* ladies and gentlemen, welcome to our show." Pedro translates this in both French and German before going on. "We are going to begin with our first test. The beautiful ladies here are going to do a fashion show for you. A *sexy* fashion show!"

As soon as he says *sexy* with that low, suggestive tone he seems to be very good at, the small gathered crowd howls. Jaz is doubled over in laughter, Sophie is winding up the disposable camera while squeezing her legs tight to hold back from peeing. And I'm just about ready to cry. How did I get myself into this?

Oh, yeah.

I was thrust into the arms of Humiliation by my own best friends, who are going to pay very, very dearly.

Guylaine (that's how she's introduced herself) swaggers across the stage first in what looks more like a light jog than a runway strut. Not very model-like. And not very sexy either, for that matter. Mireille's sashay is similar, except she stops midway to bend down and wiggle her flower-print bum at the audience. In the stands, a balding middle-aged man I can only presume is her husband hoots and pumps his arm Arsenio-style.

My stomach had been churning since I'd first been hoisted on stage, so now that my turn for complete and total degradation is upon me, I'm feeling a tad disconnected from reality. Very New Agey, out-of-bodyish type thing.

A little faint and wobbly at the knees, I start strutting my way across the stage when, by some strange enlightened state—

which in retrospect I can only explain as Divine Intervention—
I'm inspired to slip off my sweater as seductively as I can manage under the circumstances and toss it at the audience.

They go wild, and the entertainment crew claps approvingly. I
have salvaged act one.

I don't dare look at Miguel.

For the next task, Pedro kneels next to Mireille and asks her
to name her favorite male singer. She spends the next five minutes affecting confusion, bouts of uncontrolled guffaws, and in-
comprehensible exchanges with her posse in the front row before
she finally decides on Antonio Banderas. No one is in the mood
to tell her that Antonio is actually an actor and wait for her to
come up with a more appropriate name.

I'm up next. I can't think of a single name. Pedro looks at me
expectantly. I'm breaking into a sweat. How could I not know
this? Think, Ali, think!

"Enrique Iglesias!" I have no idea where that came from.
Maybe I saw a picture of him locking lips with Anna Kournikova
in Jaz's copy of *Star* earlier today.

"Enrrrrrrrique Iglesias!" repeats Pedro, waving his arms en-
ergetically at the audience and rolling the *r* like a Telemundo
sportscaster announcing Brazilian soccer players' names.

That was close. This really isn't so bad. I fold my arms in my
lap and hold my chin up, pleased with my performance. I've
been quite the little natural, really, when you think about it.

Just as I'm beaming with smug self-satisfaction, Pedro turns
to the three of us, a mischievous grin on his face. "*Y ahora,
bellas,* you have to choose a man from the audience who looks
the most like you favorite singer. Go, go, go!"

Spurred into action by his spastic hollers and wild arm ges-
ticulations, I jolt out of my seat, but my feet stay nailed to the
floor. Through the petrified lens of terror-induced slow motion, I
watch both the other contestants pull their partners from their

chairs and onto the stage. My arms and legs feel like they're acting on a will all their own, and my mind is drawing a bewildered blank. I can think of only one thing to do, something no other stimulant in the world could have induced me to do—not twelve shots of tequila, not a yearlong prescription to Prozac, not even crack cocaine.

Stage fright.

Thankfully, the too-bright lights make it impossible for me to see much. And my brain has long since stopped functioning.

In long urgent strides, I lunge toward Miguel and take his hand, without once looking up to his face. I can't fathom what he must be thinking. Only when I'm back at my seat do I dare to peek at him. He's smiling. So broadly and so sincerely, you'd think he was one of the uniformed navy officers chosen to accompany the Miss Universe contestants down the fake stairs during the evening gown competition.

"And now, ladies and gentlemen, Miguel and contestant number one will dance a salsa for you!"

I have never danced salsa in my entire life. Or waltzed, or tangoed, or sambaed, for that matter. Or any other dance requiring actual presence of mind.

I could die right this minute.

Miguel leads me into the spotlight as the DJ plays a sultry song on the loudspeakers. His feet encircle mine, moving gracefully to the beat while I struggle to keep up.

I am so mortified, it's a wonder I remember to breathe. This is punishment for all those times I asked the waiters to slip me some vodka in my orange juice at my mother's friends' daughters' weddings. I thought I had a deal with God: no pork, ever, in exchange for unlimited booze and sex. Clearly this was unacceptable, and He'd picked today to send me the memo.

Miguel must have sensed my discomfort because he slows his footwork down to a pelvic-gyrating hip-hop groove. I melt into his arms as he pulls my waist toward his body. Shockingly, I begin to relax despite the glaring lights and a crowd I can't see but I know is out there, watching me, willing me to trip.

Pedro yelps some Spanish instructions I don't understand, and Miguel pulls me closer to him, and down toward the ground. He's so close that I can breathe him in, and he smells incredible.

"Gracias, Miguel. Thank you, *señorita*. Thank you very much."

The music stops; the small crowd assembled around the pool bar and the few people in the stands cheer. Miguel pulls his arms from around my waist, and something in my heart drops. This can't be it.

He leads me back to my seat, thanks me, and smiles warmly before returning to his spot on the stage.

The rest of the pageant goes along seamlessly. After we're asked to perform the de facto Cuban national anthem, "Guantanamera," impersonate our favorite celebrities, and drag as many men on stage as we can, Pedro lines us up for the final judging. The audience's applause is supposed to determine the winner. Try as they might, Sophie, Jaz, Paul, and Mike can't muster up enough whistles, catcalls, and loud hooting to counter Mireille's relatives' cheering. She is declared the winner, and I can finally scurry back to my seat.

I'm elated.

Just as I am about to climb down the stairs, I feel a hand on my shoulder.

"Miss . . . Where are you going now?"

I can barely hear Miguel over the cacophony of jumbled jeers and laughter coming from the bar.

"Ahh . . . I'm not really sure. . . . I was just going to see my friends over there. . . ." Jaz and Sophie wave frantically as they make their way toward me.

"Would you like to meet me at La Bamba after the show?"

I could end it now. This second. Thanks, Miguel, I know I'll never come across such male beauty in my life ever again, but no thanks. I have a boyfriend, but I'm sure any one of the nubile young ladies that parade through this resort every week would be happy to oblige. Just not *moi.*

My knees shake a little and my voice cracks ever so slightly when I turn to face him. "Umm . . . Yeah, sure." I flee toward the girls before he has a chance to reply.

13

"Ali, that was *hilarious*!" Sophie squeals, joining me as I descend the steps.

"We got the whole thing on two cameras. I can't wait to see the pictures!" Jaz flashes me a self-satisfied grin. "And what did that stud want just now? He's fucking gorgeous."

"He wants me to meet him at the club."

"Oh. My. God. You're not serious, are you?" Sophie's eyes are wide and her hands are clasping mine, as though she's the one who's just been asked out by Julio's lesser-known offspring.

"I know, I can't believe it either. . . ."

Under any other circumstance, I'd expect my best two friends in the whole world to jump in at this point and remind me how *he* should be so lucky to be my arm candy, regardless of what either really feels. That's exactly what I'd do for them. But they both remain tellingly silent, and grace me with the eye-and-shrug "Can't argue with you there, sista" combo.

I can't say I blame them.

"Guys, what am I doing here? What about Brian?"

"What about him?" Jaz glares at me the way she usually does when I suggest that she might be putting out for Ben too easily, considering she's trying to get him to actually date her. Not happy. "You haven't done anything wrong."

"Not yet," I mutter under my breath.

"What? What was that? Don't think I didn't hear you." She smirks. "So it's just a matter of time now, is it?"

"Jaz, you're really not helping. That's not what I meant. Of course I didn't . . . I mean, I wouldn't . . . at least I really hope I wouldn't . . . Sophe, what do you think?" My eyes beg her to bring me back to my senses.

She bites the corners of her bottom lip and gives me an apprehensive, wide-eyed stare. "I don't know, sweetie. How do *you* feel about it?"

But the mischievous expression behind her features says it all. This is the adventure of a lifetime, and I'd be a fool not to go along for the ride, even if I have to restrict it to the merry-go-round level rather than the full-blown Space Mountain caliber it has the potential to be.

At least that's how I'm going to rationalize trailing after Miguel tonight to myself.

When the three of us walk past the bored-looking bouncer in a cheap white shirt and crooked polyester bow tie, we find Miguel chatting with a woman at one of the bars. All I can see of her from this angle is a sheet of long black hair and too-tight black pants under a tacky silk shirt, but when she flips her shiny locks, fake-giggling at something I presume Miguel's said, her Lynda Carter blue eyes steal a disdainful sideway glare at me.

It's *her.*

So she hasn't left Varadero, and it's looking less and less like she's a hooker.

No problem. He asked *me.*

With small hesitant steps, I inch toward him and tap him gently on the back.

"Hi. We're here," I say as casually as I can manage with a pulse that seems to be operating directly out of my eardrums.

Wonder Woman snakes a hand over Miguel's arm. He doesn't seem to notice.

For the second time today I'm assaulted by his thousand-watt white smile.

"Would you like son'thing to drink?" His demeanor is open and unassuming. He could say anything and it would come off as sincere.

Realizing that this may very well be his most disarming secret weapon, I try to rein in the furious little butterflies in my tummy. "Yes, thank you. I'll have a piña colada, please."

"Can I suggest you son'thing else?"

"Um . . . oka-a-y . . ." My mind flashes back to the tequila-laced-grape-Jell-O shots of college days and the furious vomiting that would usually ensue, not to mention that I really had my mind set on the syrupy sweet coconut brew, but I don't want to seem unadventurous or prudish. When in Cuba—well, I'll find out soon, I guess.

Miguel leans over the bar and says a few Spanish words to the bartender, his arm brushing lightly against my shoulder. A heat flash so intense rushes through me, I think I might break out in hives. Moments later, he produces two tall glasses filled with clear liquid, ice cubes all the way to the top, and a sprig of something green and leafy.

I'm going to regret this.

"This is a mojito. Iss' very popular in Cuba. One taste, and I promise you will not forget it."

I don't need the drink to know that a lot of things from tonight will be etched in my memory forever. I sigh and take a sip. He's right. The stiff drink is the perfect mix of refreshing, sweet, and strong. Very memorable, indeed.

"You want to sit down?"

"Yes, please."

He excuses himself from Amazon Lady, who purses her lips

in a forced smile and fades into the shadows of the club. For someone who looks so eager to score with this guy, she relinquishes him to me a bit too easily, but to be fair, I'm not sure what I'd do in her Choos. Right now, though, I can't be bothered to care.

Holding both of our drinks, Miguel leads me toward a booth facing the dance floor. We sit in silence for a few minutes, watching Sophie and Jaz boogie to 50 Cent with a couple of tourists. There appear to be a few failed attempts at communication that can either be attributed to the language barrier, or else to the rapper's 150 decibel crooning.

Out of the corner of one kohled eye, I catch him staring. And shockingly not at the cleavage spilling out of my slip dress. This would probably be a good time to bring up Brian's existence.

"Listen, I . . . um." Do I say it? What's the worst thing that could happen if I don't? Oh God, just *thinking* about that sends a sharp, pointed burst of longing right in that spot. I haven't felt electric shots there in years. I'd begun to think I'd left those behind with the last flickers of adolescence. "I have a boyfriend."

There, I said it. All I have to do now is wait for him to make inane small talk, requisite to any successful exit strategy, and then politely excuse himself. I'm down with it. I know how it works. I'd personally witnessed the phenomenon enough times to know.

"If you were my girlfriend, I would no let you go to Cuba alone."

This is a trap. Under no circumstances whatsoever am I to flirt back.

"What's that supposed to mean?" I might have actually met with some measure of success had I not simultaneously cast him a coy, mock-stern look, rather than try to hide how much his comment had melted my insides.

He doesn't reply, just shrugs and shakes his head to one side, telling me with one long glare that neither one of us is stupid and that I ought to know exactly what he meant. "I would no let you go."

I was afraid of this. He's definitely a Category Two grade of cocky. At least. Which means he's going to give it a few more tries before he throws in the *toalla*. A Category One would already be hitting on someone else by now. I'm usually quite adept at fielding the Category Twos and up, mostly because I find their cockiness repelling. Unfortunately, Miguel's brand of self-assuredness seems entirely devoid of pretension, and so has the complete opposite effect.

"He trusts me," I say.

Miguel's eyes are dancing, laughing at me. Like he's heard that line enough times to know how little it means. Part of me is offended. I mean, how dare he make these assumptions after what I'd told him? What does he know that I don't? The other part is crying out for surrender before this battle of wills gets too ugly. It has already broken out. In the surreptitious way our eyes fleetingly meet, the way we're sipping our drinks and purposefully turning our bodies away from each other, we've each declared war on the other.

And me with myself. The caged Arab girl within, raging against outdated mores and irrelevant traditions, seeking vengeance for every time she'd met a good-looking guy at a club and wanted so much to leave her ingrained morals behind for one night—one night only—but couldn't bring herself to. And the other Self, the one with sensible dreams, goals, responsibilities, and people to answer to. The one who'd be left to clean up the mess.

After we finish our drinks, he leads me to the dance floor. We spend the next hour dancing at a safe distance, the ease we'd felt on the stage just minutes before all but evaporated. I feel awkward and two-left-footed, and I keep looking over my shoulder wondering why he isn't dancing with this or that girl, who I'm convinced is taller, thinner, and all-around better than me. I haven't been this self-conscious around a guy since I graduated high school, and I hate it. But in spite of the lingering feeling that my body's been swapped with that of a Snuffleupagus, I sense that Miguel and I have hit a certain comfort level, like we've known each other longer than we actually have. Maybe it's because I've shared more traumatic moments with him in the past twenty-four hours than I have with Brian in the past year, I don't know.

"Ali?" A gentle nudge prompts me to turn around. Sophie's staring back, looking slightly embarrassed at interrupting me. This in turn makes me flush a little, not knowing what she and Jaz must be making of my behavior. "We should probably get going. It's already one, and the wake-up call's for seven."

Havana. Right. Which means I won't be seeing Miguel all day tomorrow. Something inside me sinks, and this in turn makes me angry. I didn't come here to complicate my life further. All I wanted was to get away, think, regroup before I had to go back and explain to everyone I know that I'll have to write the UFE again next year, and grovel to keep my job.

"Miguel, *lo siento,* I'm sorry I have to go." I want to grab him by his shirt and pull him closer to explain about the daylong excursion tomorrow, maybe even get a deep whiff of his cologne I can take with me to bed and dream about all night. But his face remains impassive, and I don't feel confident I can get the message across the loud dance music and over the language barrier. Besides, like a shark sensing a drop of spilled blood somewhere in the sea, the tall brunette emerges from the shadows and is bopping and swaying a few meters away from us.

I don't need this.

She can have him.

I spin on my heels and take three steps away from him. Jaz and Sophie have beaten me to the exit. I stop, my senses oozing down my spine and out of my open-toed sandals. I turn back, grab his collar, and hoist myself up on my toes to leave a kiss on one of his dimpled cheeks. Before I can run away, I catch a tiny glimpse of his startled expression and scurry off the dance floor without looking back.

14

The next morning the three of us sleep right through the wake-up call, and so we are the last people to get on the Havana-bound tour bus. This, and the fact that we are the only set of young, unaccompanied women amid a straw-hatted, Bermuda shorts and sensible walking shoes–clad middle-aged crowd, quickly establishes our troublemaker status. But save for a couple of sideway glares and a snicker or two, the bus is soon sailing along a wide highway, passing familiar foliage and the odd skin-and-bones heifer along the way. Paul and Mike had opted to stay behind, and I'm feeling somewhat jealous because the sun is shining strong and bright, and I'm wondering what I'm doing freezing my ass off on the arctic air-conditioned bus when I could have been working on my tan.

"Good morning." A petite, youngish Cuban woman dressed in mustard culottes and a gauzy white shirt wobbles to her feet and stands next to the driver. "My name is Ana, and I will be your tour guide today." Her English is spoken slowly and carefully, each letter drawn out and pondered upon. "And this is Lenin, our bus driver." She leads the sleep-sedated group into a half-hearted applause.

"*Bueno.* Welcon' to the Havana day tour. You are excited?" From the gleeful expression on her face, I gather we're supposed to clap and raise our fists in the air, hooting and cheering. But it's just way too early. Maybe on the way back. Ana, however, is clearly not one to give up easily.

"Come on, people! Are you excited?"

A splutter of weak *yay*s and muffed claps greets her enthusiasm. She laughs at us, no doubt used to the patheticness of the gringos that file past her every single day, flashing a fistful of *pesos convertibles* in the hopes that this cultural detour sandwiched between hours of baking under the sun will make worldly travelers out of them.

"The trip to *la Habana* will be two hours. We will stop for a break in one hour for you to take son' pictures at the canyon, and buy souvenirs if you wish. Today we will do a walking tour of *la Habana Vieja*, Old Havana, and see places like the Capitolio, the hotel Ambos Mundos, where Hemin'way wrote *For Whom the Bell Tolls . . .*" Ana's voice drones on while I notice a few of the tourists' heads roll to the side. Jaz and Sophie are among them. And while I really am interested in the tidbits of Cuban trivia Ana is imparting, I'm finding it hard to concentrate.

Did Brian get my message yet? What must he have thought about it? Did he suspect something was up? I wonder. Who am I kidding? He would have noticed my name's conspicuous absence from the UFE pass lists, no doubt circulating in all the newspapers by now. Had my parents noticed? Of course everyone at work knows. Even if by some miracle Ernsworth doesn't fire me as soon as I show my face at the office on Monday morning, I'll still have to put up with the pitying stares, the *don't worry*s, *you'll get 'em next year*s, and fleeting guilty looks every time I pass a gathered group reminiscing over drunken Cancún nights and days spent passed out sick on the beach.

Almost as soon as I start thinking of Brian, Miguel's face pops into my head, looking down at me as I lay panting for air on the beach. Has he noticed I didn't come out to the pool this morning? Or is he too busy hanging out with the Amazon Lady? This last thought instantly flushes my cheeks with guilt.

Where do I get off being so possessive over this guy? And why have I latched on to this poor woman, guilty of nothing more than poor makeup-application skills, and who has every right to be going after a studly resort employee whose entire raison d'être is to keep guests happy and entertained? At least she's probably single, and if she isn't, well, that still doesn't give me the right to be praying for her early demise every time my brain conjures up her image.

I have a boyfriend who loves me. I'm just not sure why I've had to keep reminding myself of this fact ever since I got here.

We used to be happy. We still are, most of the time, but in a different kind of way. I mean we used to be *really* happy. The kind of happy you don't have to think about. The kind that just is.

Meeting Brian for the first time wasn't exactly the bodice-ripping, when-Heathcliff-met-Cathy, love-at-first-sight sort of experience I'd envisioned in my prepubescent youth. Or even the heart-thumping, hormone-unleashing infatuation of my teen years. It was more of a sensible attraction, very Bridget–spots–Mark Darcy–pre-Rudolph-jumper kind of thing, and it took us both by surprise. Not in the least because we were—are—very different people. I mean, look at me, a free-spirited aspiring fashion designer trapped in a curfew-abiding, "good family" upbringing, sensible-career-path-following Lebanese girl's body, dating a born and bred Montrealer, with city streets and local convenience stores alike bearing the name of his ancestors. Though my mother and I had always had completely opposing ideas of what the right sort of man for me would be like, Brian came squarely out of both of our left fields, so neither one of us knew what to make of him at first.

It happened at a wine-and-cheese party hosted by the audit firm Brian was working for—and there he was, a wide-eyed audit junior, helping to snag the best and brightest of the even wider-eyed undergrads in his employer's net before a rival firm scooped us up. I was dating someone at the time, a totally random guy I'd met at a club one Saturday night, good-looking enough to warrant a few consecutive dates but too empty-headed for anything more. Out of prudishness, a misplaced sense of loyalty, or perhaps just for the thrill of saying the word *boyfriend,* I confessed to having one in mid–small talk with Brian, between discussing McGill's performance at the UBG games and the ample travel opportunities provided by the Big Four firms.

Unsurprisingly, Brian didn't ask me out that night, but the accounting world being as small as it is, and with him still finishing up his Chartered Accountant training part-time, I knew we'd run into each other again. So, when my so-called relationship with Rocco met with its predictable demise, I set about tracking and hunting Brian down. No girlfriend with a free nanosecond between partying and cramming for exams was spared in the effort. In turn I dragged Sophie, Jaz, a slew of my classmates, and even Sara a few times to any recruitment cocktail, keg party, or football game where I had a chance of spotting him.

It wasn't long before he got the message and asked me out. First to a crowded bar with a bunch of friends, then to a cute Crescent Street café right by campus, and finally to dinner. By the end of the first date I knew that he'd started out studying microbiology, science being his first love, but was daunted by the prospect of spending seven more years at school in the hopes of one day, maybe, earning the privilege to teach for a pittance. So he switched to accounting, which at least appealed to his thoughtful, analytical side.

I loved spending time with him. It seemed like we could talk for hours, especially when he launched into science-speak, getting all worked up over the evolution debate, and telling me about the projects and experiments he used to carry out in Quebec's nature reserves. There was something unnervingly sexy about his Matt Damon dimples, his excited gray eyes, that I had no trouble picturing him as a tweed-jacket-wearing, pipe-smoking young Indiana Jones–professor type, stepping out of a classroom full of admiring debutantes.

And I fell in like with him.

We held off dating seriously until recruitment season had passed and I was snapped up by Ernsworth, a rival firm of his. We couldn't get enough of each other back then. My favorite Saturday activity became telling my mother I was going to spend the day studying at the library and scurrying off to his downtown pad to spend twelve consecutive hours having sex, watching TV, having more sex, going out on a beer run, more sex, and eating takeout pizza followed by semi-successful sexual activity, depending on how Brian felt at that point.

It was bliss.

Until busy season came along. That should have been my first clue to get out of accounting. As the endless Canadian winter wore on, Brian's workload increased to the point where if I saw him once every three weeks, I'd be lucky. And when we did see each other, rather than screw like squirrels in heat like we used to, or even venture out to any one of Montreal's hundreds of gourmet restaurants, we stayed in, me watching TV and Brian playing the latest version of Madden, his addiction to which increased in proportion to his work-related stress.

I longed to see the inside of a club with him, but he tended to avoid them like one avoids contracting malaria. And so began the cycle of resentment for his not taking me dancing, guilt for when I did venture out with Jaz and Sophie and succumbed to the lure of flirting with attractive strangers, and more resentment, wondering if I'd committed the biggest sin of Singletondom: settling. Too soon, too quickly, too young, too inexperienced.

The thing is, I can never picture myself with anyone I ever meet at the clubs, on the metro, at work. Not seriously, anyway. I just get a kick out of flirting and feeling wanted. Nothing had ever shaken my faith that Brian is the One.

Until now.

I'd never felt anything so physically strong. But really, what could I do about it? What do I know about Miguel other than that

he's a hotel employee? The naïve tourist and the suave Latin local. So clichéd, it's going to make me puke.

Let's just pause for a second and imagine that I lived in some
parallel universe where ending my three-year-strong relationship with a great guy and taking the plunge with someone I
know nothing about—except that he makes every nerve ending
in my body tingle every time I think about him—was actually
fathomable.

What would we do? Even if we spent a couple of days of sheer
bliss, I'd be back to my cozy, Miguel-less life in no time, anyway.
What then? If we decided to go for the whole long-distance-
relationship thing—which I'm convinced never works, even under less outlandish circumstances—how would we go about it? I
highly doubt the man has access to potable water, much less
e-mail. He can hardly afford to call me, let alone visit. Not that
he'd be allowed to, anyway, unless of course we were married,
which would explain why a man who looks like that is coming on
to an only slightly-better-looking-than-average (though exceed-
ingly well-heeled) girl like me. And how long would it take to
send letters to Canada from Cuba? I'd have to look into employ-
ing carrier pigeons.

The clincher being, of course, that my poor mother would
never dare show her face in public again. If having an upstand-
ing, well-educated-though-*ajnabi* boyfriend was bad, how will
she ever live down my taking up with a poor, developing-country
hotel employee with absolutely no prospects?

This is so hopeless, it makes Romeo and Juliet's relationship
issues look like a case of simple misunderstanding. All this for a
man I can hardly communicate with. I may be losing my mind,
but I'm not crazy.

15

After almost an hour of rolling lazily in the same direction, the bus veers abruptly off to the side of the road, jostling me out of semiconsciousness. In the seat beside me, Sophie stirs and rubs some of the sleep out of her eyes. I hear Jaz yawn from behind me.

"Are we there yet?" Sophie yawns in turn.

"I don't think so, sweetie, but you should definitely see this."

The bus is perched at the rim of a huge canyon, densely covered in greenery. I stare into its crater-deep, cavernous belly when I spot an eagle swoop down somewhere in the lush emptiness below me.

"*Bueno,* we will stop here for a few minutes," Ana's voice bellows from the front to the rest of bus, "so you can take pictures. Please don' be late."

One by one, we waddle to our feet and file out of the charter bus. A few of the passengers recognize me from last night's pageant and smile. Alexei, another entertainment crew member, even wraps his arms around me and pronounces me Miss Beauty Queen.

"You know, Alexei, I didn't actually win."

He dismisses my objection with an insulted wave of his hand. "It should have been you. The other woman just whine too much."

I laugh and wonder how hard it would be to move down here.

⚬◯

"Okay, move over . . . a little more to the left . . . I meant right . . . I know I said left, just move, will you. Just a little more . . . Perfect!"

Snap.

"Jaz, that's enough," I say while Sophie tries to beeline it back to the bus.

"One more."

"No. I'm sick of this." I swear, the girl can't blow her nose on foreign soil without stopping to capture the moment on film. Barely two days into a resort vacation where there's presumably nothing more than sun, surf, and sea, Jaz's already filled two rolls' worth of, among other things, the departure lounge at Mirabel Airport, our Air Canada carrier, the interior of the plane, the arrival lounge of José Martí Airport, the luggage handlers, and every bus we've been on since we took our first steps on Cuban soil. That's beside the real pictures of the hotel, us in our hanging-out-by-the-beach wear, dinner wear, and clubbing wear, and naturally, the beach.

"You're going to thank me when you have the best vacation album ever."

"No one's ever going to see these pictures, Jaz. Unless you manage to get the Cancún Grand Oasis in the background somehow."

"You're such a drama queen. As if you could keep a secret like this from Brian."

I gag on my bottled water. "Jaz! I'm serious. Don't you dare ever tell anyone!"

"I wasn't going to, but you're seriously delusional if you think you're going to get away with this. I'd start coming up with a story right now if I were you." She snaps a shot of Alexei's derriere and follows the rest of the pack back onto the bus.

I don't follow her right away. A large bird, a vulture maybe, swoops down and perches on top of a skinny stump not two feet away from me. A frightening chill rips through my body. But it has nothing to do with the menacing creature that's staring me down. It's from the realization that Jaz is right.

The second leg of the ride is much livelier than the first. Ana's convivial chatter accompanies our excitement. Before I know it, the hazy green hills flatten out into open pastures, which eventually funnel into modern highways and a network of tunnels snaking into the edge of the city. I can now distinctly see the beginning of a skyline—dusty, sand colored, and low.

"Those buildings look like they're going to fall down," Jaz says when the bus emerges from the tunnel and into the city, across from a wide stone boardwalk separating the petulant waves of the ocean from the road.

"How can you say that? They're beautiful. Look at the architecture . . . it kind of reminds me of somewhere . . ." I can't quite put my finger on it, but I have the distinct impression I've been here before. Like in another life type of thing. Which, of course, makes absolutely no sense.

First of all, the semi-crumbling buildings around me have nothing of the pastel-colored quaintness about them I've seen in other people's seaside vacation photos or on television. Plus I'd never been to anywhere in the Caribbean area, much less Havana, Cuba. In fact, the only other place I'd ever been to, beside the handful of family road trips to Cape Cod as a teenager, is Beirut. And only when I was very young, when I still had family there, before they all moved to their respective far-flung corners of the earth.

And that's when I know. Something about the distinctly Arabic curve of the asymmetrical arches of the doorways, the latticed windows, and the broken stone of the sidewalks sends the floodgates of my mind crashing down under a torrent of memories.

Jaz veils her wrinkled nose behind her palm. "What's that stench?"

"Diesel fumes." Just like many cars in Beirut, so old that every conceivable part seemed to be recycled from even older, more decrepit vehicles, every Chevy, Ford, and Lada we come across here leaves a thick trail of black smoke in its wake. I close my eyes and inhale. How many years had it been since I smelled that?

"You're actually enjoying this?"

I shrug. This has always been a toughie. How do you tell someone for whom war and suffering are just things they see flashes of on TV, in between sitcoms, about the pockets of pure happiness and peace among the ashes of pain and loss? Jaz and Sophie have never known war or even immigration. They were born Canadian. They think, just like any other native North American, that people like me must be scarred, our view of the world permanently warped. They think that we wake up every day thanking God that we'd left behind whatever hell we'd come from. But things are seldom so black-and-white. In leaving Lebanon, I'd also left behind the freedom of finding joy in the simplest of everyday things, in having breakfast surrounded by my extended family, in watching people stroll the old dusty streets, in a car ride through the mountains. It's precisely this kind of freedom that's eluded me since I started worrying about grades, the UFE, my career, or whether or not Brian is the One.

It's this vibe that's making Havana seem so familiar to me—like people here know to steal their happiness wherever they can find it.

By every conceivable indicator of the industrialized world, the Lebanese didn't have much during the civil war. But somehow my cousins, their neighbors, everyone I saw when my mother would take us for our annual visits to the Old Country, all managed to smile through it, as though their awareness of life's simple pleasures was heightened by the misery that surrounded them.

On those trips, Sara, Sami, and I would revel in the power outages that were a frequent occurrence during the war, electricity being rationed, and use this time for people-watching from our balcony, or wandering the ever-bustling streets, scouting the area for the best, cheapest falafel sandwiches. And when the power did come on, things like popping a movie into the VCR, listening to music, or even showering with hot water took on new meaning, and we relished every moment of every small thing we did as though enjoying it for the first time.

Eventually we'd fly back to Montreal, and the spell would be broken, every day becoming a series of meaningless acts, occurring in the same predictable cycle. Wake up, shower (hot water, of course), go to school, eat, break for half an hour, more school, homework, watch TV, and sleep. Repeat. Replace school with mindless, gray-matter-liquefying job once in your twenties. Repeat.

And then it dawns on me. There's something else. The army. Dotted here and there along the highway, on street corners, leaning against peeling walls are soldiers. Or maybe police officers, I don't know. Like those of the militiamen that ruled Lebanon during my entire childhood, these uniforms' patterns and colors announce to us, the civilians, and to each other, who the men were prepared to kill and who they would die for. Unlike the Lebanese gunmen, the Cubans are dressed alike and, though exuding an air of authority, seem relaxed. They swagger a little, like they're going about their daily business. I watch for them with a mixture of awe, nostalgia, and unease, but not fear. These soldiers won't be coming for me. But then, who are they coming for?

The bus stops at the edge of a bustling square—Plaza de Armas, Ana informs us. We'll be doing the rest of the tour by foot.

"Wow . . . look, you guys, isn't this awesome?" Sophie stands in the middle of the square, her brown hobo bag slung across her chest, staring in turn at each of the plaza's façades, from the old fort to the palace-turned-hotel to the dozens of stalls surrounding a park in the center of the square selling dog-eared saffron-paged books.

I'm secretly thrilled she's in just as much awe as I am. At least I'm not alone.

We weave our way through the narrow cobblestone streets of Old Havana, a veritable tourist wonderland from the looks of it, following the Hemingway path from La Bodeguita del Medio, the bar where he enjoyed daiquiris, to the Ambos Mundos hotel, where his old typewriter lays forever enshrined in a glass box, to yet another watering hole he liked to spend his nonwriting hours in.

For two whole hours we walk through narrow, dusty streets to a steady soundtrack of cars honking, kids shrieking, and a level of catcalling that would put the overweight Italian construction workers back home to shame.

Sophie and I can't stop gasping. One moment it's over the way a cascading vine of plump pink bougainvillea hangs over an ancient stone mansion, the next over inner courtyards overgrown with foliage peeping through a half-open gate. Even Jaz is won over when we turn the corner onto Calle Obispo, cobblestoned and lined with cramped art galleries trading in the colorful wares of local artists, dozens and dozens of coffee shops blaring soft Cuban music and featuring young, dark-tressed waiters in crisp white shirts and black bow ties.

We continue the tour, meandering in and out of tiny art galleries, museums, and bars until I'm so exhausted that the weight of the five-dollar bottle of Havana Club rum I picked up along the way is threatening to bring me crashing down to the ground. Every charming café we file past taunts me with its cushioned chairs and balmy interiors, so that by now I'd settle for the dingiest of cafeteria-style counters, with their wheezing ceiling fans and peeling Formica tables, boasting Cuban staples such as rice and beans, Cristal beer, and little else.

"What the hell is that?" Jaz pokes my shoulder blade as we trudge through yet another crowded, dusty, smoky, stray-dog-ridden street.

"Careful!" I swing around just in time to see what she's talking about. A bright New York City–cab yellow, egg-shaped vehicle resembling a scooter on three wheels with room for a driver and two passengers blows past us, sending the dust around my feet swirling in a tiny beige tornado and flattening me against the nearest wall.

Ana doesn't miss a beat. "¡Pendejo! ¡Coño!" she shouts after the maniacal teenage driver as he disappears into a brown cloud of dust and diesel fumes at the horizon ahead, braving sidewalk and open road alike, swerving past stray dogs, produce-laden carts, and other innocent bystanders without discrimination.

"Ana, what was that?" I need to know. The expressions pasted on the faces of the two giggling girls in the passenger seats aboard whatever contraption that was appeared to be somewhere between life-threatening fear and total ecstasy.

"A Coco Taxi. You must go on one before you leave Cuba."

I turn to Jaz.

"No fucking way. I didn't come here to die. The concept of a sidewalk obviously doesn't mean a fucking thing to these people."

"Jaz!" I whisper loudly. I know Ana heard her. It was almost imperceptible, to the point where I might just have imagined it, but her head twitched just a little bit, as though it had caught on something.

"What?" Jaz counters, loud enough for everyone within a ten-foot radius to hear.

I glare, and then turn my gaze to the road ahead. I'm not going to let her ruin this. I can't remember the last time I was so enchanted with a place in my life. Certainly not in my travel-less, fun-deficient adult life.

Not too long afterwards, the road begins to widen. One turn of a corner later, it spills into another wide open square, and the lull of multilingual conversation accompanying our eclectic group of German, French, and Canadian tourists stops dead.

Ana lets us simmer in awed silence for a minute before she speaks.

"This is the Plaza de la Catedral, and that church over there is the Catedral de San Cristóbal."

While the square is stunning in its historic serenity, gorgeous sixteenth-century hotels with picturesque first-floor patio restaurants flanking three of its sides, the main attraction is clearly the cathedral.

Notre-Dame in Paris has nothing on this thing. Well, not much, anyway.

"Wow . . ." Sophie shuffles her feet, staring down at them and back at the church, as if unable to take it all in at once.

For one thing, the gates alone are about ten feet high, and absolutely ancient. On either side of the church façade are two asymmetrical bell towers, one narrow and the other much wider. Nothing about the baroque detailing is simple—no square windows or round peepholes. Every ledge, finishing, and border is shaped to look like lace on a frilly petticoat. And all constructed out of massive slabs of ice-gray stone soaring straight into the few clouds dotting an otherwise perfect sky.

I had come here expecting to be awed by the strength of the tropical sun's heat, by the fineness of the sand on the beach; maybe I thought I'd be tasting the best piña coladas known to man. But I hadn't expected a place so steeped in sophisticated old-meets-new-world culture. It's breathtaking.

"You would like a break now, no?"

Ana doesn't wait for an answer. She steers us toward a patch of empty patio tables at the foot of one of the buildings surrounding the square. We break up into small groups and sit at the white-linen-covered wrought-iron tables, under matching white linen umbrellas. The waitstaff immediately places leafy, sweating glasses of mojitos in front of us.

"Part of the tour," says Ana.

"I could so get used to this." Especially given that on most weekdays, I tend to be seated at a gray aluminum cubicle on a gray swivel chair, surrounded by gray half-partitions sipping a murky grayish-brown substance that's meant to pass for coffee. For a splash of color, the carpet is navy blue.

Jaz smirks knowingly for a second before turning to the menu a totally edible waiter has placed in her hands. Could she be coming around?

"I can't believe we have to leave this place in just four days. It feels like we just got here. Why does my life suck so much?" Sophie is still too busy staring wide-eyed at everything around her, including the waiter, to notice the menus.

Something in my stomach sinks like one of those weights Deanna the deranged dive instructor had made me strap across my waist during the lesson. There's something incredibly unfair about this.

Everyone goes on vacation, and everyone dreads going back to the drudgery. But people often talk about being anxious to get back to people and things familiar to them, to puttering around the house, checking up on their potted tulip bulbs, their cats, their favorite news sites, to *Friends* reruns. Why can't I think of one thing I'm dying to go back to?

I try to conjure Brian's image in my head, try to cull whatever feelings of physical longing I still have for him, but all I can picture is Miguel, asking me if I am okay after hauling me out of the water, his hand on the curve of my waist as we danced under burning stage lights.

"Ali, what's wrong?"

"Huh?"

Sophie's gently rubbing my shoulder while Jaz is looking at me with an uncharacteristically mothering gaze.

"You were frowning," Sophie continues.

I need to get that under control. That and spontaneously bursting out into song when I have my headphones blaring eighties music into my ears at the gym. Just because I can't hear or see myself doesn't mean the general population can't either.

"I was just thinking . . . about work. About Diane and what I'm going to say to Brian and my mom. I need to come clean. I think . . . I mean, what real choice do I have? I'm sure they'll let me write the test again. And Brian can't feel too betrayed when he finds out the only reason I lied about Cancún was because I was so ashamed of failing the UFE. . . ."

I rattle on, hoping that the dullness in my voice would stop the questions. Even as I'm speaking, this strikes me as incredibly odd. Since when did I stop confiding in my best friends the source of my many miseries? Over fabulous alcoholic cocktails, no less?

"Bullshit."

"Sorry, what?"

"I said, *bullshit.* You were thinking about Miguel."

"I was *not!*" I say, too aware of the hot flush burning up my cheeks. Maybe it won't show through the tan.

"If you're going to lie to Brian when you get back, then I'd start practicing," Jaz says.

"Fuck you!"

"Yeah? Fuck you too. Now, answer the question. You were thinking about Miguel. It's okay, Ali, we know."

I turn to look at Sophie. She nods gravely.

I'm shocked. Am I really that transparent?

"It's true, sweetie. You're like in this constant dreamy state, everywhere you go, no matter what you're doing."

I am so not having any of this. Maybe if I stay completely

silent, they'll get so bored, they'll leave me alone. The conversational equivalent of burying one's head in the sand. Temporary, but effective.

"I don't know what your problem is. The guy could be an underwear model, and he's totally into you. Don't even try to tell me you're not hot for him too," Jaz says, completely oblivious to my increasingly reddening face. She pauses to pluck a piece of baguette from the basket in front of us. "Not to mention he's exactly your type," she adds before tearing a piece of bread and plopping it into her mouth.

Exactly my type. Huh.

Clearly, the slow mastication of baked dough is intended to communicate to me that Brian was effectively *not* my type.

Them's fighting-body-language words. The last time I checked, I'm still the most qualified person to tell who's my type and who isn't.

I clear my throat. "And what's that supposed to mean?" I raise an eyebrow.

Sophie intercedes: "Guys . . ."

"Ah! The mute wonder speaks. It means you'd make a great couple, you dork. Think of how gorgeous your kids would look." Jaz is one of those girls who measure a man's worth in terms of his genetic makeup potential. And what purpose were Miguel's genes created for if not to advance the human race, at least from an aesthetic perspective?

"Jaz," I begin slowly, "think about what you're saying here for a second."

"Yeah?"

"He's Cuban."

"So you're racist now?" She arches an eyebrow and plucks a black olive from the pizza that has just landed on our table.

"We can't exactly date if we don't live on the same continent."

"Like you'd be the first person to have a long-distance relationship?"

This is getting exasperating. It's like Jaz and I are living in two completely different worlds. The forces of reality don't figure too prominently in hers.

"He's surrounded by hot young horny tourists every single day. Hot, young, *different* tourists, might I add. There's a weekly rotation of potential cheating coconspirators."

"A guy who wants to cheat will cheat anywhere, anytime, and you wouldn't be more likely to know about it if you were living with him or five thousand miles away. You're the one who said you never want to leave this place. Well, here's your excuse to keep coming, and coming, and coming. . . ."

"That's great, Jaz. Very funny. What do you suggest I tell Brian?"

"Now, I've been waiting for that to come up. Let's see, what was he—number four down the list of excuses not to fuck Miguel? Five? I forget now—"

"Jaz!"

"So if Miguel wasn't Cuban, didn't live five thousand miles away, wasn't surrounded by fuckable women twenty-four–seven, you'd dump Brian for him, wouldn't you?"

"Jaz, stop . . . ," Sophie intercepts once more, after casting a worried look at my now ashen face.

"She needs to hear this, Sophe. Ali, you and Brian, it's not working. Wake up."

I'm going to cry. No, I'm going to kill her. I'm going to reach over the table, grab her by the throat, and squeeze all the smugness out of her beady little eyeballs.

"Brian's perfect!" Of course he is. He massages my feet whenever I ask him to. And my neck when we're watching TV at his apartment and I'm complaining about work. He holds my hand in public, and, much to Jaz's annoyance, smothers me with affection every time he sees me. And we're perfect for each other. We've mastered the whole comfortable silence thing. In fact, we can spend hours on end in comfortable silence, him playing online Texas Hold 'Em in one corner of the room while I read quietly in the other. Perfect, except my life bores the living hell out of me these days.

"Perfect doesn't mean perfect for you. Look at Carrie and Aiden."

Oh my good God. You know Jaz is in it till the bloody end when she comes out with the *Sex and the City* analogies, her life Bible. Much like disciples of Jerry Falwell take to asking, "What would Jesus do?" when confronted with life's conundrums, Jaz tends to ask herself what Carrie would do.

"Jaz, we're not going there today. We've had this discussion one too many times."

"I just want what's best for you," she pleads, leaning her body over the table.

"And, just yesterday you were anxious to point out the existence of my loving boyfriend to me when you suspected I was flirting with James."

Immediately, Jaz stiffens. "That was different," she mumbles.

"Really, how so?"

"Okay, guys, that's enough. I mean it." Sophie eyes us so sternly, we both cower. Her nostrils might be flaring. I shoot an uh-oh-we've-gone-too-far glance over to Jaz, who concurs with a reciprocal look. Like the docile parent who never gets angry, Sophie raises her voice, and we shut up.

"We're in frigging paradise, and you two can't stop bickering for one minute to realize it."

She's right. The ice cubes in my mojito have melted to nothing, and I've barely touched my pizza, which had turned out to be quite edible. If I'd had any sense left at all, I'd scarf it down in anticipation of the mass of unidentifiable goo that was sure to be our buffet supper tonight.

I reach for a slice at the same time as Jaz, our fingers smacking against each other.

"You go first." Jaz smiles weakly.

"No, you."

"I insist."

"No, I really—"

"Guys . . ."

"Ah . . . essuse me—"

Jaz and I look up, as does Sophie, who was just getting revved up to scold us.

He looks down at us, a six-foot vision of olive black eyes, sculpted arms, and sinewy goodness. All this male hotness is becoming almost clichéd. Except this particular specimen is holding what looks like a sketchbook. Is that a sliver of charcoal in the other hand?

"I'm sorry to bother you—"

"No, don't worry, it's no bother at all," I stutter.

"*Bueno,* I was walking there by the street—" He points to the open square behind him, nervous and fumbling over his words. "—and I see you and I say to myself 'I must come here and talk to you.'"

While I realize the occasional glances in Jaz's and my direction are meant to include us in the conversation, it's clear from a gaze that's having a hard time focusing on us that his words are meant for Sophie alone.

"I want to . . . ah . . . *¿cómo se dice?* My English is so bad—"

"No, not at all," Sophie says, the corners of her mouth curling up in a semi-innocent, semi-flirtatious smile. "Your English is very good."

"Thank you," he says, giving Sophie the benefit of his own, very broad, astonishingly white grin.

"I am an artist." He holds up his sketchbook as proof. "I want to . . . *pedirte* . . . how do you say . . . ask?"

Sophie nods, still beaming.

"I want to ask—" He starts his sentence again from the top, clearly proud of this new addition to his vocabulary. "—if I can draw you."

Now, under normal circumstances, a hunky, starving artist singling one out of a crowd of souvenir-hungry tourists for a portrait may induce in one a sense of skepticism. But against the romantic backdrop of Havana's old quarter, with its cobblestone streets, horse-drawn carriages, and towering sixteenth-century cathedrals, not to mention a generous dose of exotic alcohol, one risks losing oneself completely in the experience.

As Sophie does. Very visibly so.

"Of course." She blushes as he pulls a chair over from a neighboring table to join us.

"Do you need us to leave you two alone?" I mouth.

She doesn't acknowledge my presence, not even with the most imperceptible of facial twitches. Jaz and I have ceased to exist.

"Look at her," Jaz whispers. "You'd think she was getting a lap dance."

"And you would know this how?" I want it to come out like a joke, the kind of thing two longtime friends enjoying a pair of fabulous drinks against an even more fabulous backdrop can say to each other with ease and carelessness. I don't quite manage it, though. Jaz smiles at me tightly and pretends to take a deep interest in the runny remains of her mojito.

It takes the nameless hunk just a few minutes to finish the sketch. He holds it up, and Jaz and I are quick to *ooh* and *aah* over his creation. It really is pretty good, especially given that his tools aren't exactly in the best condition. The bit of charcoal he'd used looks like it may have drawn its last stroke, and the sketchbook has seen better days.

"Can I see your other drawings?" Sophie asks.

He beams and surrenders the thin volume. It seems his specialty is architecture, as page after page of beautiful building renderings reveals.

"Are you an architect?" I ask after we've turned the last page.

"I study *arquitectura*, yes, some days in the week. The other days I work as an artist in the street. For the *turistas*." He lowers his tone just the slightest hint of an octave at that last part.

I catch the flicker in Sophie's eyes. She'd noticed.

"Why? Aren't there enough jobs for architects here?"

He hesitates a minute before answering, shaping his mouth in the vowels and consonants he's trying to bring together before he speaks. "It's no the jobs . . . it's the dollars. The tourism jobs. Architects, *médicos*, teachers . . . everybody . . . they make pesos. People who work with *turistas* make dollars."

"You mean *pesos convertibles*?" Sophie says.

He shrugs and looks away. "*Es la misma cosa.* Same thing."

"I think we've lost her," I mumble to Jaz, casting my glance in Sophie's direction. She's hanging on every word the stranger clad in an overused-yet-clean T-shirt and jeans is saying.

"Why would you need dollars?" she asks.

He smirks, not without a hint of bitterness. "Some things, we cannot buy from Cuban peso stores. Only tourist dollar stores."

"Like what?" Now I'm intrigued.

"Different things. Son'times milk. Son'times meat."

"Wow." I'm not sure what else to say. Jaz is shifting in her seat, looking at her watch.

Sophie is shocked into silence, the needle on her social-conciousness barometer wiggling wildly out of control, no doubt.

Our new tablemate breaks the uncomfortable silence by reaching his hand out to me.

"Javier. Nice to meet you," he says.

"*Encantada, soy Aline.*"

His eyes widen. I love the effect my surprise Spanish has on people here.

"*¿Hablas español?*"

"Just a little." I say, blushing lightly, "I get by. Just like you and your English."

He smiles and looks down at his lap. He gives Jaz the same

vigorous handshake, but before giving Sophie hers, he holds her stare just a moment too long.

"How long are you in Cuba?" he says, drawing out the word *Cuba*—Kooba—in the same lower-intestine-melting way Miguel does.

"Just four more days." Sophie turns her pleading eyes to me, as though I were somehow in control of this situation. "It was very nice meeting you."

She looks like she might add something, but Ana chooses that precise minute to call out in her commanding, slightly satirical voice. "Okay, we are going in five minutes. Please hurry, we still have to see the Capitolio, the cemetery, and Calle Tacón market. Less' go!"

Our group, which until now had been in the throes of loosening up, being merry, and melting into the Havana background in so far as can be expected of a group of tourists hailing from three different continents, staggers sluggishly to their feet, gathering up cameras, guidebooks, souvenirs, and engaging in generally conspicuous tourist behavior.

I glance from Sophie to Javier, hoping one of them would take down the other's phone number, address, e-mail, whatever—but Sophie's chance seems to have gone by the way of our Havana morning—lost in the moment.

Javier shuffles to his feet, thanks us all profusely for letting him sit with us at our table, and leaves.

There's nothing left for us to do but follow Ana back through the maze of old colonial-era streets. It suddenly occurs to me that he'd left Sophie her portrait without actually charging her anything for it.

16

"Do you think he did that on purpose?" Sophie's slumped over the side of the lounge chair, her heart-shaped face turned toward the sand.

"Yes. For the thousandth time, yes. I don't imagine Javier goes around forgetting about his main source of revenue very often." I slit one eye open just long enough to look patronizingly at Sophie before nestling my head back into my towel, and pulling the brim of my hat lower on my chin.

Jaz rolls over to one side and tucks a thick lock of stray hair behind her ear.

"I would've said he was setting you up for a bigger financial fall somewhere down the road, but the fact that he has no way of getting in contact with you ever again kind of screws over that theory." She snorts.

Sophie's face falls.

"Jaz!" I swat her leg with the rolled-up resort-activity guide.

"What?" She shrugs. "Oh, I see. You want to take a trip down Fantasy Avenue. Okay, no probs." She shifts her bum around over her sandy towel and lies back comfortably, propped up by her elbows, one extended leg crossed over the other. "I bet . . . he's really the son of a general in the Communist party and, let's see here . . . he likes to play poor to feel closer to his people. Kind of like a present-day, in-drag version of Marie Antoinette playing milkmaid on the grounds of Versailles."

"Do you think you're funny? 'Cause you're not." Sophie's mouth curves into a reluctant grin.

I, on the other hand, am loving it.

"This is for your benefit. Please don't interrupt. Where was I?" Jaz wiggles her strawberry daiquiri back into the sand beside her.

"General's son," I say.

"Right. So he, like any self-respecting police state's general's son, has access to all kinds of files on people's personal lives and could find out anything about anybody at any time should the fancy strike him. And really, how lucky does that turn out to be when he meets and falls in love with a beautiful young tourist, all the way from the arctic lands ayonder?"

"Ayonder? Is that a word?"

"Shut up." Jaz silences me and lifts herself into an all-knowing-goddess pose, legs crossed under her, hands on her knees, palms turned toward the cloudless sky.

"As I was saying—it's really too bad you didn't leave your baseball hat or something behind, Sophe. It would've really added to the effect—so he searches in every Cuban shanty town, in every crumbling hut and four-star resort alike, until he finds his beloved."

"Why wouldn't he just get his dad to call immigration? Our hotel name is listed on those entry visas we had to fill out on the plane."

"Do you want the fantasy or not?" Jaz scolds me. "I bust my ass coming up with a nice story Sophie can snuggle up to, and this is all the thanks I get? Jeez."

"Just be consistent, man, that's all I'm saying. First we were in seventeenth-century France, then it's the Grimm Brothers. What next, *Pretty Woman*?" I burst out laughing.

"*Hola*, ladies, you are enjoying your drinks?"

I'm clutching my stomach, laughing too hard to notice that Jaz and Sophie have gone completely silent.

And white.

I turn around.

And there he is, hovering over our half-naked, coconut-scented bodies, beaming.

This *cannot* be happening. Even on a trip this weird.

I'm not sure why, but even though I have my red-and-white cherry-print bikini on, I suddenly feel naked. I yank my towel from under me and throw it over my boobs.

Oh my God. Could he have heard us? Hell, who cares whether he heard us or not—what is he doing here? Someone needs to say something. Now. Maybe this is just a mirage. Maybe it's the alcohol or the sun. Or both. Together.

"Uh . . . Javier. He-e-y . . . Long time no see."

Sophie and Jaz are still stone silent.

Javier shuffles his sneaker-clad feet in the sand, grinning like the schoolboy who hid the teacher's chalk.

Maybe he won't tell his *comandante* dad on us after all.

He sets the backpack he's been carrying at his feet.

"I know you think I'm . . . *loco*, how do you say? Crazy."

We answer with more stunned silence. He chuckles.

"I think I would think so too."

Sophie finally recovers her faculties of speech. "How did you find us?"

"You're not, like, in the government or anything, are you?"

"*¿Perdón?*" He furrows his brows at Jaz.

"Nothing." I swat her thigh surreptitiously. "We're just really surprised to see you here."

"Cuba is no so big." That coy grin again. I swoon for Sophie. "I know from the uniform of your guide yesterday that you are with Havanaturs. My cousin work in Havanaturs too. He drive a bus."

"But we weren't the only ones on the bus. There was a whole bunch of people from at least a dozen different hotels. How did you know we were here?"

186 ✳ NADINE DAJANI

"A dozen?" He smiles and shakes his head. "No. Four. I just come back from the Sol Meliá."

"How did you get to Varadero?"

"El camello."

Ah. On the road, those rusty, awkward buses that made our old charter bus look like a scrawny ballerina. And considering how many heads we saw poking out of the scum-splashed windows, it's shocking Javier looks so, well, clean.

I'm about to ask why he'd woken up at the crack of dawn, packed himself against two thousand other stinky, sweaty passengers, and spent his morning combing the twelve miles of Varadero beach for us, but the sheepish grin that's refused to leave his face since he appeared before us shuts me up.

"Jaz, I'm burning up. I think I'm ready for a swim."

The look of barely contained elation on Sophie is all the thanks I need.

"So what do you think?" Jaz and I are floating on the surface of knee-deep water, making liquid angels in the waves with our arms and legs.

"About what?" she says.

"Javier. Do you think he's really into her?"

Jaz doesn't say anything for a while. "Dunno. It's hard to say. Does it matter?"

I guess she means it doesn't really matter what anyone feels about whom since we've got only a few days left in this paradise anyway. For some reason, this makes me sad. She's right.

"Are you really asking me if I think Miguel might care about you just a little more than the two dozen different bimbos that check in here every week?"

"No!" Yes. That's exactly what I'm asking you. "Stuff like this only happens in cheesy movies and even cheesier novels. I'm not that big of an idiot." I'm beginning to seriously doubt that.

"Nobody is saying you are. He's gorgeous, coming on to you, and you're just a normal human being. He's a guy, you're a girl—isn't there a song about this? Do I need to get into graphic detail here?"

"He hasn't come on to me, you know. Not *really*."

"He did say he wouldn't let you come to Cuba on your own if you were his girl, didn't he?" she counters.

"How many times do you think he's used that line? Seriously?" I stare at her pointedly.

"I don't know . . . you were probably too nervous to notice the look on his face the night of the pageant when you picked him out of a crowd, for the whole resort to see. He was totally floored. Just because he's a stud doesn't mean he can't get flattered or giddy like everyone else. And what you did, it took guts. Confidence." She shrugs. "I think that kind of got under his skin."

Confidence. Didn't they say that was the best accessory on a woman? Hell, on *anyone*. I wonder how I managed to fake it so well that night.

"What—?"

"I swear to God, Ali, say 'What about Brian' one more time, and as God is my witness I'm drowning you right here, right now."

"I was going to say, What would you do?"

"Oh."

We stop floating and let our legs and bottoms sink into the sand. The water is so shallow that even seated like this it hardly comes up past our shoulders.

"I'm not you, so I don't know."

"I'm saying hypothetically here."

"I know what you're fucking saying!"

Wow. Where did that come from?

"Jaz . . ." I stumble, not sure where to begin. "Is everything okay?" I need to do better than that. She's my best friend. I need to point the pink elephant out and call it by name. "Does it still hurt . . . thinking about Ben?"

"I tried calling him last night."

The statement hangs between us like the pieces of algae suspended lazily just below the surface of the sea around us.

"Shit, Jaz, I can't believe you did that!"

I can't believe I just said that either. Here I am trying to be helpful. Instead I yell at her. I am *such* a moron.

"Listen, I'm sorry," I say.

"Yeah, whatever."

"No, Jaz, I'm serious."

"Forget I said anything." She jolts upright out of the water, splashing me.

"Hey, wouldn't you know, look who's been spying on us all this time."

I follow her gaze to the volleyball net, where the baked sand of the beach meets the dry crabgrass of the resort.

Miguel is refereeing a beach volleyball match.

"I don't care. Get back in the water—I want to talk to you," I say, even though my stomach had lurched nauseatedly yet again at the sight of him.

"The hell you don't. Hey, Miguel! Over here!" She waves frantically.

He waves back, whistles the end of the match, and starts jogging toward us.

I nearly melt into the cool water.

Jaz takes one look at me and snickers. "I knew it. You're just as bad—no, worse—than me. You just can't face it. Me and Ben might have a fucked-up relationship, but at least we're honest about it."

She swings around and storms across the water, taking oversized, unsteady strides until she steps onto the wet sand. I don't call out or run after her. I don't have the chance to. Miguel is now towering over me in not-quite-knee-deep water.

"*¿Qué bola?*" He bends down and pecks me on one cheek. "I

did no see you at La Bamba last night. You were no feeling good?"

"No, no," I stammer. "We spent the day in Havana, and by the time we came back and had dinner, we were totally out of commission."

"Out of what?"

"Out of commission. Tired. Exhausted."

"Ah. I did no learn that in my class."

"No, I don't imagine you would have." I look out for Jaz out of the corner of my eye. She's disappeared somewhere behind the activities hut and past the pool. I focus my attention back on Miguel and almost tumble back from the endorphins swooshing around in my brain. All over his thick torso hang droplets of moisture—whether from the sea or sweat, I don't know, and a lifeguard's whistle hangs from a worn-out rope between a set of perfectly chiseled, just-the-right-sort-of-hairy pecs. When he lifts a toned forearm to wipe the beads of perspiration across his brows, I nearly faint.

I'm such a dork.

"Did you like Havana?"

Havana. Hmm.

"It was . . ." I think back to the city. Here I am, this supposedly worldly young woman, free, at least in principle, to travel across the entire planet, yet somehow I find myself smitten with the one island he happens to be living on, one that, incidentally, he'll probably never be allowed to leave. Will he think I'm being condescending, fake even, if I tell him exactly how the crumbling city with its smoggy pollution and stunning skyline, its dirty roads and absorbing architecture had me at *hola*?

"I've never loved a place more."

He beams down at me, a glimmer of something flashing in his eyes. Pride.

"What's so weird is that even though I've never been there before, I just feel like somehow I have, you know? I don't know. I loved it too much for a place I'd only seen once, and just for a couple of hours, for that matter."

I bet all the ditzy tourists say that, I'm tempted to add for good measure.

"Like—" He pauses and throws his head back at the sky, searching his meager vocabulary for the right words. "—like they say in movies. Love at first sight."

The words smack right between the eyes, like an errant volleyball coming out of nowhere.

"Yes, something like that."

"*Bueno*, I have to go back to work. I will see you later, okay?"

Later? Later? What, like a date later, tonight at the buffet later, or La Bamba later? I can't bear another afternoon of jumping out of my skin every time a tall, thick-chested male body meanders into my peripheral vision.

"Um . . . sure . . . are you going to work the courts all day, or are you giving a dive lesson later?"

He bursts out laughing.

"Why? You want to dive again today? You need someone to catch you?"

"No," I grumble. "That's not why I'm asking."

"Why are you asking?"

"Never mind."

"Okay, okay." He lifts his arms up in surrender. "I will find you at my break."

Before I have a chance to dig for more details—what if the precise moment I decide is ideal for an afternoon shower happens to fall exactly on said break?—he leans down and kisses me.

On the cheek. Again.

And then he's gone.

⌒

"So Javier's coming back tonight? Man, the guy's got it bad."

Perched at the edge of a submerged stool at the swim-up bar, Jaz is inspecting the last-minute manicure she got expressly in preparation for this trip.

Apart from the shrill edge of overcheerfulness lacing her voice, she's acting as though nothing happened out there in the water this morning.

You can't accuse her of not being a good sport.

After Miguel went back to work—if you could really call leading a gaggle of middle-aged, spare-tired trans-continental tourists in a water gymnastics session *work*—I found Jaz here, guarding a pair of sweating plastic cups overflowing with semi-frozen blue liquid. We drank the sugary concoctions, chatting as though no nasty words had been exchanged between us. Sophie had finally joined us much later, and now we're trying, drop by painful drop, to pry the details of this morning's events out of her.

Sophie doesn't say anything. It's like the girl is drugged. She just looks meaningfully from Jaz to me, sighing heavily and rolling her eyes in luscious contentment.

"So what's the story?" I probe gently. "You didn't finish telling us."

"Nothing . . ." She shrugs.

"Nothing? Sophie, come *on*. This isn't one of those Lebanese men your mother is always trying to set you up with or some guy at a club asking you what's your sign. This is a hot Cuban who went to some serious trouble to see you."

Jaz looks like she wants to say something but checks herself.

"Mmm . . ." Sophie sucks in her breath, looking like a heated kettle on the verge of explosion.

"Sophe . . ."

"Okay! Oh my God, Ali! Jaz!" She grabs a hand of ours each and squeezes with a big chunk of her strength, which is to say, a lot. I've never seen her like this.

"He found me. Are you getting this? He *found* me."

"Yes, we know. It's wonderful."

"Fuck wonderful!" R-rated Sophie rears her oft-unseen head. "This is—no, *he* is, beyond wonderful. He's an architect!"

"We know. He mentioned that yesterday," Jaz says.

Sophie completely ignores her. "He goes to the University of Havana. Guys, how romantic is that?"

"When are you seeing him again?" I say.

"Tonight!"

"Tonight?" Jaz is either incredulous or annoyed. I can't quite tell which.

"He's going to the Varadero town square to work for a few hours and get something to eat. A cousin of his lives nearby, so he'll have a place to hang out until we're ready to go dancing tonight."

"Is he coming back here?"

"Yup. He's going to meet us at this place called Havana Café at eleven sharp, after the show. Ohmigod you guys, I can't believe this!" She's mentally skipping. "Awesome, *awesome* idea to come here for vacation, Ali . . . oh, crap . . . I'm sorry." She covers her gaping mouth behind her hands. She'd forgotten what brought us here in the first place.

"Don't thank me," I chirp. "Thank the kind folks at the Canadian Institute of Chartered Accountants."

Sophie looks absolutely mortified.

"Sophie, I was kidding. Please. How often in a day do you think I remember what brought us here, huh? But thanks for the reminder, just the same."

"I'm hopeless."

"No, just in love. For a change."

"Am not!"

"You so are. Don't even try."

"Uh . . . Ali . . . ," Jaz says.

I shove Sophie before she can throw a piece of pineapple at my hair.

"What? Oh!"

A pair of thick hands have somehow materialized over my eyes and plunged me in complete darkness. I pat them tentatively. I'd like to say Miguel, but how embarrassing would it be for all parties involved if it turned out to be James? Or (barf) Mike? Then again, if it were Mike, Sophie would be the most likely victim.

I yank hard on the fuzz-covered knuckles and twist my neck back.

Miguel.

And I'm clutching his hands.

I drop them as quickly as if they were radioactive.

Well, not quite. Even that one-second delay was just long enough to elicit the glow of having inched one step further on the path to intimacy. And it wasn't lost on the girls.

"Iss' time for my break."

"So soon?" Clearly, there are no new depths of loserdom to which I will not sink.

I can tell from Sophie and Jaz's expressions that they're giving me the visual thumbs-up.

"Erm . . . fancy a walk along the beach?" She shoots. . . .

"Yes, sure." She scoooooores.

I slide off the barstool and narrow my eyes mischievously at the girls. "See you in a bit."

Have you ever thought you were in love with someone you had no inkling how to communicate with? Forget the actual language barrier and having to contend with the vocabulary of a mentally challenged chimpanzee, where was my "in"? What are we supposed to say to break the ice? Do you come here a lot? I guess you'd have to if you worked here, huh?

Or I could try the highbrow intellectual approach. How's living under one of the last barely surviving communist regimes treating you these days? Or: Rationing—the scourge of socialism or the answer to world poverty? Discuss.

I opt for silence.

Normally, a complete lack of decent communication this early on in a relationship would be the first clue to abandon ship. The funny thing, though, is that it doesn't seem to matter. We have nothing to say to each other because the only thing either one of us really wants to do is rip the other's clothes off. No need for pretense here.

It's late afternoon and the sun is that luminescent tangerine tinged with fuchsia around the edges. Every day around this time I've been coming out to the beach for my final swim of the day, and watched the same sunset that's spurred so much bad poetry and cheesy artwork. Unlike its photographed and air-brushed replicas, this version, with all its imperfect glory, makes me, along with anyone else who happens to be walking on the beach at this hour, stop and take notice. And that's not something I'm used to doing much of. What's there to take notice of at home? The pavement with its multitude of sinewy cracks? The snow that turns to brown muck minutes after it hits the ground?

I'm so depressed, I could cry.

"What are you thinking?"

"Sorry?"

I tilt my head sideways and upward to face him. If anything, the dusk glow is making him seem even more like an apparition, a figment of my imagination rather than a man of flesh and blood.

"Nothing," I say.

"No." He stops walking. "You think of something. What?"

It's a whisper. A syrupy, spicy whisper that knocks the wind out of me. I finally know what that expression means.

Somehow in the middle of all this exchange, and without me being conscious of it, Miguel has taken hold of both my clammy hands in his. He squeezes them. Hard. And then pulls me just a bit closer.

I'm shaking. With what, I'm not sure. Joy? Fear? Anticipation? Foreboding? You'd think I'd be able to tell the difference.

Only one thought blinks loud and unmistakable, like Vegas lights, on the inner walls of my brain: This Is Wrong.

"I want to kiss you." His gaze doesn't flicker. It bores into me, steady, focused, earnest.

"Why?" I didn't mean to sound like an extra on the set of *Clueless*, honestly. I just need to know. Is this behavior the product of some bet between the social directors, some prank they play on every batch of new tourists that hit the resort, or is there something more? Like he'd tell me.

"I am not made from wood. *Soy un hombre.*"

I am a man.

As if I wasn't keenly aware of that fact.

As if I didn't find it necessary to delve into the last reserves of my willpower to keep his palpable manliness at a manageable distance from me.

Is life supposed to be this hard?

His hands creep up the length of my arms, slowly, and as much as my mind wants me to push him back, gather my sarong, and run as far away from him as I can, my body just won't oblige. It's just like that terrifying moment between sleep and consciousness when your brain is awake but the rest of you isn't. He lifts my chin and lowers himself closer to my face.

My God. When was the last time the mere suggestion of a kiss—one that hadn't happened yet—roused so many physical reactions in me? It's as though desire had been lurking under my skin, in a coma, waiting for Miguel to stroke it to consciousness.

I tilt my head up, my lips tingling in a way they hadn't since my very first kiss, my insides tumbling like teenagers in the throes of lovemaking.

Then, completely out of nowhere, my mother's angry face and Brian's sweet one ambush me. Together they launch a coordinated attack, one cursing the day we left Lebanon and other piercing me with a defeated how-could-you look.

I can't do this. No, I can, but I won't.

I jerk back, breaking free of Miguel's grasp, and sprint a few feet down the shore.

In the few seconds it takes me to get away, I feel like I'd snapped out of hypnosis. What was I just about to do there?

I slow down but keep storming toward the hotel.

Miguel trails behind. *"Amor* . . . Girl, come back!"

Girl? Did he really just say that?

Wait a minute.

I swing back and glare at him with the full force of my indignation.

Girl?

We're not dancers in a hip hop video, and Varadero isn't the set of MTV. What the hell is wrong with him? And then it dawns on me.

"You don't know my name, do you?"

He stops jogging, having caught up to me, drops his head, and pinches the space between his brows in shame. When he picks it up again, he's grinning his signature bad-boy grin.

"I'm sorry."

I have spent the last three days agonizing, tossing, turning, daydreaming, and engaging in all manner of schoolgirl silliness . . . for a man who doesn't have enough brain cells to remember my name.

"You never tell me."

"Why didn't you ask?" Even as I say this, I'm desperately fighting to repress a smile. And failing. The surreal absurdity of the situation makes it impossible for me to be angry. This isn't Montreal. There are no rules, none of the usual social signposts here. Step One: Eyes meet across a crowded dance floor. Step Two: Engage in inconsequential small talk. Step Three: Ask name and request phone number. Just like an episode of *Temptation Island*, the rules have been tossed together haphazardly and run through the rinse cycle. You make what you want out of them, whatever suits you. And I've decided the fact that Miguel, over the past couple of days, never thought to ask my name is peripheral.

"It's Ali. Aline, actually."

"Alina . . ." He savors each letter as though it were a velvety chocolate mousse. "Ali. I will not forget."

With only three days of vacation left, I certainly hope not.

17

That night, after dinner with Paul and Mike, who are finally growing on us now that they understand exactly where they figure on the love chain, the entire gang decides to leave the resort premises for a night out on the town.

For the first time since we'd set foot on the socialist isle, Sophie matched Jaz and my grooming efforts, shimmery accessory for shimmery accessory. She had even borrowed the same paisley-print Diane von Furstenberg dress she'd told me reminded her of cat puke when I wore it to the Jello Bar two weeks ago, because Javier had already seen her in the one top she owned that didn't bear an Adidas logo.

After giving his nightly entertainment performance along with the rest of the animation crew, the object of tonight's show being to pluck unsuspecting couples out of the audience and engage them in juvenile and often hilarious stunts together onstage, Miguel joins us. He arranges for a minivan to pick us up from the hotel doorsteps and take us to the club.

I'm the first to get in, and I squeeze into the back row, against the window. One by one, Sophie, Jaz, Mike, Paul, and Donatella file into the van, each of them conspicuously avoiding the vacant seat next to me. Last to hop on, Miguel tells the cabbie where we want to go, settles on the price, and then climbs in. As soon as he spots me sitting all the way in the back of the van and alone, his face breaks into a wide boyish smile.

"*Buenas tardes,* Alina." He winks, crashing on the seat next to me.

I melt. Not only did he remember my name, he Cubafied it.

"You look very nice," he says, and gently, discreetly, he rests his hand precisely on the spot where my gauzy white dress rides up to reveal my knee. Exactly the same place, the same way even, as Brian would.

This is my cue to pull my leg away. It doesn't matter that we're seated way in the back and no one can see us. Must. Pull. Leg. Away. But then again, when did this intimacy develop between us? At what point did we go from innocent(ish) flirting, the kind you'd expect to happen at a vacation village, to acting as though we were an item?

Worse still, ever since the pageant, everyone at the resort has taken to calling us a *pareja,* Spanish for "couple." And everytime someone would say it, always with that same self-satisfied smirk, as though they knew something about me that I didn't, I would either pretend I didn't have the first clue what they were talking about, or else react as though they'd just accused me of sleeping with the entire entertainment team. Rather than deter the accusing party, it just encouraged them. Which suits me just fine. I don't want it to stop.

"*Vamos, por favor,*" Sophie says hesitantly. She looks to me for approval, and I flash her two thumbs up.

After nagging the staff for help with her Spanish all day, they finally unearthed a yellowish, dog-eared language instruction manual that looked like it dated back to the perestroika days. Sophie had spent the rest of the afternoon internalizing as many vocabulary words and conjugation and sentence-structure rules as she could. And I have to admit that after only one day of self-instruction, she is well on her way to coherence.

I shift in my seat, not so much pulling my knee from under Miguel's grasp as slowly easing away from it. He doesn't insist.

The engine sputters and purrs, and seconds later the loaded

van is tottering toward Havana Café, where Sophie and Javier had agreed to meet.

Within minutes, the minivan pulls up to a gated complex that looks like it might have belonged to Al Capone back in his Mafia heyday. Just like every street on this island, the driveway leading to the nightclub is lined with proud palm trees and lush landscaping. A doorman, dressed in an elegant black tuxedo with a dark mane to match, races to the taxi, beaming as he opens the door, and lets us out.

The building is no less impressive on the inside. Gleaming chrome tables encircle the sunken glass-tiled dance floor in a stadium-style arrangement while a pair of actors in oversize wooden masks gesticulate and prance in ways I don't understand.

Very artsy.

I tilt my head and throw Miguel a quizzical look. I have no issues with broadening my intellectual horizons and everything, except on this particular vacation I was hoping to broaden my alcohol-intake-tolerance instead.

He smiles and leans to whisper in my ear, "Don't worry," and promptly lunges at the first waiter to pass us, forcing him around. From their noisy exchange, toothy grins, and painful-sounding back slaps, I deduce they are buddies, and sure enough, the waiter leads us to a table close to the stage. Before we have a chance to order, he informs us a complimentary round of mojitos is on the way. Everything is so perfect, even Jaz is smiling.

"Isn't this fun?" The dancing actors are still doing their thing on stage, so I say this in a sort of loud whisper.

Jaz nods, sipping the drink she's just been handed.

"We could've done worse," she says, an eyebrow not-so-discreetly raised in Miguel's direction. Thankfully he's too busy studying the stage to notice. Not that I think he would have minded the insinuation. He's leaning comfortably against the cushioned leather bench, an arm draping lazily across the back of my seat, the other cradling his drink. His hair is slicked back into glistening black waves, but one stubborn curl insists on swooning across his forehead. Even in his jeans and button-down shirt, sleeves loosely rolled up, his skin still looks moist. Not the kind of moist most people would experience while evaporating under the Cuban sun, but the moist of healthy, radiant, sun-kissed skin. I contemplate telling him he would make a great L'Oréal spokesmodel but figure it would take too long to translate.

"I'm going to go take a look around," Sophie says, looking fretfully over my head. I can't believe this is the same Sophie from yesterday. The one who thinks returning a guy's call after seven promising dates hints at desperation.

"We just got here. Give the man a few minutes."

"What if he doesn't see me and thinks I didn't show?"

"Who are you talking about?" Miguel asks, right eyebrow cocked. Just as I'm about to open my mouth, the room crackles into a sputtering of lethargic clapping to the bowing of the actors. I guess the show is over. The already dim lights are extinguished completely, the darkness broken only with rows of marble-size bulbs lining the staircases and walkways, and the vividly hued spotlights showcasing the dance floor. The Coliseum-style seats empty out, spilling onto the sunken marbled expanse, now shaking with pulsing Latin pop. Paul leads Donatella into the heart of the forming mob and Mike follows, no doubt hoping to salvage what's left of his thus-far booty-less sex vacation.

The spectacle is not lost on Sophie. "How am I supposed to find him now?" She moans into her mojito.

"Patience, young Jedi."

"Easy for you to say." She motions to Miguel with a swift flicker of her eyes.

"Hey, Sophe." Jaz points to a tall, lanky, tanned-to-the-core male figure emerging from the crowds of the dance floor and into the wandering spotlights.

"It's him!" Sophie squeals and jolts up from her chair.

We watch him hesitate, his eyes darting cautiously from one direction to the other, scanning the cavernous room, until they fall on the four of us. And his face breaks out into a grin that would put Miguel's to shame. He prods, pushes, and practically tackles his way to our table.

Two people have never been so happy to see each other. They hug, giggle, and babble incoherently in a multilingual cocktail. Next to them, my brief flirtation with Miguel feels more like a twenty-year-old marriage gone stale.

"Javier! We're so happy you made it." I kiss him on both cheeks and introduce Miguel. They shake hands and jump right into an easy conversation as though they'd gone to high school together.

If only James had been here.

I'd searched for him all afternoon and finally found him at the gym after I'd all but given up on the endeavor, in the middle of what looked like his seventy-fifth bicep curl. It was the first time I'd seen him since the pageant.

"Hey, stranger. Too busy to chat up nice Lebanese girls anymore?"

"Not when they're busy getting it on with the hotel staff."

My breath caught in my throat.

"What do you mean? I don't know what you—"

"Look, I don't care whether you really have a boyfriend or were just saying that to get rid of me. I just didn't peg you for a girl who plays games. I thought you were too sweet for that." Which he promptly followed with a look that said *and boy was I wrong.*

"I'm sorry." There wasn't anything else to say. It was bad enough he'd made me feel as repulsive as the patch of fungus growing in between the floor tiles, but I'd screwed it up for Jaz. That I wasn't exactly sure how or what I could've done to prevent it didn't matter.

And now I can tell just how she must be feeling, from her dejected expression, gaping from Miguel to Javier and back at Miguel, nervously adjusting her top and tugging at her skirt, looking as out of place as the fifth baritone in a barbershop quartet. She excuses herself to join the others on the dance floor. And this without once having attended the free daily salsa lessons by the pool.

"Jaz, wait!"

She files right past me without so much as a backwards glance.

I should follow her. But the sight of Miguel and Javier chatting away about whatever it is that hunky Cuban twenty-something boys chat about, and Sophie looking happier than I have seen her in eons, keeps my feet firmly Krazy Glued to the ground. A sense of normalcy is inching its way back into this whirlwind week. A normalcy I want to hold on to as tight as I can before it flutters away and Sophie and I return to our respective daily hells. Plus I'm getting tired of the babysitting game. I have enough crap on my plate to deal with. If Jaz won't stop feeling sorry for herself even in this fantasy setting, then there isn't much I can do for her.

"Come, less' dance," Miguel whispers, crouching to my ear level. I get a strong whiff of his pheromone-oozing cologne, and all blood drains out of my head. I almost want to reach up and follow his neck as he straightens himself upright again. Sophie and Javier have beaten us to the dance pit, while the music has switched back to sultry, fast-paced Latin grooves.

I line up beside Sophie and we sway side by side while the boys slide, dip, and swivel their hips opposite us. They look like they belong in a salsa video, the kind that's set up to look like a beach party in Miami or Saint-Tropez or wherever bikini-clad girls and buff guys in board shorts get together and have the time of their lives. All they need is to slip their shirts off.

"Ali . . . ," Sophie whispers.

"What?"

"Thank you."

With both hands she cups my shoulders and squeezes them, and lightly bumps her forehead against mine.

And right there, in the middle of the dance floor, grooving to Daddy Yankee and Don Omar on the Island That Time Forgot, miles into the Caribbean Sea, I plummet back twelve years to the last time I felt exactly this mixture of free, alive, and grounded in the moment. Not worried about homework or test scores or what would happen to me if I didn't get into grade seven honors math, not reenacting the scene where I tripped and made a total douche bag out of myself in gym class. Just perfectly content with where I was. Ranya was in her late teens at the time, and I was just ten. No one her age hung out with their dorky younger cousins, especially when the cousin in question was on the wrong side of chubby and sported a hairstyle that might have been fine for the members of Kool and the Gang, but looked a little out of place on a little girl. She would take me to the amusement park a few times every summer. Convinced that a pedophile was lurking behind every corner, my mother was still coming to grips with life in North America, and Ranya was the only person other than herself (and possibly my dad) she felt she could entrust me to. Once alone with Ranya and her older—and to me, oh-so-cool—friends, I wasn't a kid anymore. I was an independent entity. A person. A person having the time of her life. Every feeling was amplified as though I were on some sort of drug trip. The rides were more intense, the cotton candy sweeter—everything was imbued with the dazzling glow of sheer freedom in the company of the one human being I loved being with the most. And every time I looked up to notice the sun had dipped just a little lower in the sky, my tummy tightened a notch with the certitude that I was that much closer to the end of bliss.

The music slows, and the nimble-footed and the somewhat less so alike are pairing up. You couldn't fit a flat tortilla between Sophie and Javier right now.

Miguel wraps his arms around my waist and leads me into a slow salsa, his hips undulating Elvis-style from side to side, and slinking closer to my own.

We lock eyes, and for a second I think he's going to try to kiss me again. I hold my breath. I don't know what I'd do if he tried.

He doesn't kiss me. He just closes his eyes for a moment and rests his forehead against mine.

We continue like this for a while, rocking back and forth, not kissing or grinding, just moving. When the beat quickens, we move faster and when it slows down, so do we. One song melts into another until some time later the lights come on and I look around to discover just a handful of people around me instead of the horde that had swallowed me up earlier.

I look at my watch. Five A.M. I can't believe it. We've been dancing for four straight hours.

18

"Are you sure you're going to be okay?"

"Positive," Sophie assures me, squeezing me into a hug. "Get out of here, I'll see you later. I've got a key." She winks and turns to Javier. Together they duck into a taxi, which in turn vanishes into the foggy gray of dawn.

"This is a huge mistake. We should never have let her go," Jaz says, rubbing her hands along her bare arms for warmth. The sun hasn't really come up yet, and the nights have been more than a little breezy.

"I know." God do I know. I want to curl up into a ball and cry. "Sophie's mother is going to kill me if anything happens to her. This is all my fault. I kept telling her to lighten up and live a little. . . . What if he— What if she gets— Oh, God. I can't even say it."

But really, how could I have stopped her? A hurricane couldn't put out the light in that girl's eyes tonight.

"She's the one with the black belt." I breathe in. "I guess if any one of us is going to pull something like that, it might as well be her."

"Fine, but does she have to do it a strange country with a strange man?"

"She's not stupid, Jaz. Cut her some slack." Plus, at least one of us gets to have the time of her life, I nearly add. I won't be the one to stand in her way.

"And they don't call it a police state for nothing." I hate myself for thinking that, even more for saying it out loud. But it's true. Rather than scare me off, the men in olive uniforms and dark leafy berets wielding scary guns I've begun to notice since the day trip to Havana make me feel invincible. It's a horrible thing to take comfort in, but I now know they don't patrol the streets and shores in service to their own people. They exist to protect me, a tourist, and my sacred tourist dollars.

Feeling somewhat appeased, I climb into one of the taxis lined up outside the Havana Café with what's left of our gang. Paul and Donatella have gone back to the hotel hours ago, leaving a very sour-looking Jaz and Mike to accompany Miguel and me.

"*Querida*, I missed the last bus home," Miguel whispers as the patched-up 1959 Chevy jostles its way to the resort.

I know that cab fare to Matanzas, the closest town to the resort, where most of the hotel staff live, is more than Miguel can afford on his nonexistent salary.

"Umm, so how much do you—?"

He doesn't let me finish.

"No, no, *mi vida*, I can stay in the entertainment hut. I jus' need a blanket and a pillow."

I'm not sure why, but I find the thought of Miguel spending the night at the hotel both terrifying and comforting at the same time.

"Don't worry about it. You can stay in the room with Jaz and me." I can see Jaz shaking her head in disbelief from the front seat. I definitely should have asked her first. Stupid, stupid, stupid.

"I can't." He sighs, looking resigned. "Cubans are not allowed in the hotel if they are not working."

"What?" I'd never heard of such blatant self-directed discrimination in my whole life. Is it just the hotel policy, or is this some sort of island-wide apartheid thing between tourists and locals?

"Why not? What's the problem?"

"The *gobierno* don't want us to mix with the tourists. You know what can happen." He squeezes my elbow, and I feel myself going as red as the island's political persuasion.

"Is it like that everywhere in Cuba?"

"Here, yes. In *la Habana* or Santiago, *no se puede controlar.* It's not possible to have so much control in big cities."

"Okay, then. No problem. About the blanket, I mean."

He smiles and brushes his fingers against my cheek. *"Gracias."*

The taxi drops us off in front of the lobby, and Miguel pretends to set out for home. I follow Jaz to our room. She's still distant, speaking to me in one-word sentences, shuffling ahead without looking back. I'm not going to ask her if anything's wrong. I want to pretend there are no stormy clouds looming over my blissful evening.

The little bulb on the door lock flashes green, and Jaz and I spill into the dark room. We had left it looking more like a Soviet-era nuclear-landfill site when we took off for the club, but now it's back to its neat if somewhat sparse original self, with the addition of two pairs of white swans fashioned out of bathroom towels perched on our beds. I have to remember to tip the cleaning ladies tomorrow.

Jaz calls shotgun on the bathroom, and as soon as she closes the door behind her, I yank off my white slip dress and slide noiselessly into a cut-off denim skirt, a T-shirt, and rubber flip-flops, so much more comfortable for my covert operation. I wouldn't want anyone catching me scampering off into the night and interpret the situation all wrong. I will *not* kiss Miguel tonight. Or do anything else, for that matter. He was nice enough to take us out tonight and deserves a decent night's sleep. I'm just helping him out. That's it.

I tiptoe to the closet and pray there's extra bedding. So far, we haven't found any of the little perks you would normally expect lavished on you at most hotels around the world. In that particular respect, our functional room feels more like a Bangladeshi hut than a four-star resort junior suite. There are no little soaps wrapped in colorful paper, bearing the hotel's logo, no bath oils, no shower caps, and no extra toilet paper, a theme I'm becoming used to in Cuba.

I rummage through the closet and thank my lucky "aloha" undies that a spare beige blanket and two polyester pillows are tucked in one of the drawers. I shove everything under one arm and catch a glimpse of myself in the closet mirror.

Mata Hari, I am not.

Just as I busy myself searching for some sort of inconspicuous receptacle to hide the linens in, the bathroom door swings open.

"What the hell are you doing?"

"I'm, ahhh . . . nothing. I just—Miguel needs a place to crash, so I offered to give him some of our sheets and stuff. So he wouldn't have to sleep on a bare floor."

Jaz rolls her eyes at me. "Whatever." She climbs into her cot and rolls over to face the curtains. "You did tell him you're seeing someone, didn't you?"

"Why do you keep asking me that?" I slam the door behind me.

Her attitude is seriously starting to get on my nerves.

I tap my foot to the rhythm of my own heart pounding as I stand waiting for the elevator to struggle up to our floor, and heave a huge sigh of relief when it arrives empty.

When it stops again a few moments later, I poke my head out from between its open doors first, no farther than my nose, to check if any guards or hotel staff are around. They aren't. I scuttle across the few yards of hotel lobby that separate me from the patio doors. The only sign of life at this hour comes from the pair of orange-speckled parrots, cawing from their bamboo cages.

I'm so relieved when I'm outside, I take a moment to breathe more easily, and let my eyes adjust to the darkness. It's no use. Nothing is coming into focus fast enough. Luckily I don't have to cross the pool, just the stage area and the side steps leading up the alcove where the dancers practice their routines. I nearly wipe out on the wet tiled floor surrounding the pool.

Eventually, I make it to the awkwardly hinged wooden door of the hut. I can make out enough of the narrow stairs now to feel my way up, one very hesitant step at a time, flurries of anticipation and fear swishing around in my stomach.

At the top of the staircase is a large open space, separated by thick wooden columns. Racks of feathery and sequined costumes line the wall in compartments. The high straw-thatched roof gives the place the feel of a drafty, unkempt Honolulu auditorium, and the breeze sends a chill up my spine. Or maybe it's the fact that I really shouldn't be here.

In one corner of the loft, directly underneath a window, Miguel is stretched out on a mattress, fully dressed, with one arm propping up his head. He sits up as soon as he sees me. The moon is still shining bright through the open space, and illuminates his features.

"I brought you some stuff," I say, not wanting to look straight at him.

"Thank you." He takes the bedding from me and then graces me with that smug, enigmatic smile of his. What does he know that I don't? Can he somehow imagine how hard it is for me just to be standing next to him right now? Why am I even wondering? Of course he can.

"Sorry to keep you up so late. I know you have to work tomorrow." I stare at my feet.

"Don't worry," he says, taking care to pronounce the w and stretching out the word worry.

He's so sexy, I could cry.

"Me divertí mucho."

"I had a lot of fun too," I mumble. I don't want to admit this was the most fun I could remember having. Ever. I don't want to encourage him.

We stand there for some time, not knowing what to do with ourselves. I'm breathing faster, shallower. He's still as calm and impassive as the sea just outside the hut, which, in this silence, I can hear breaking in quiet gasps against the shore.

He inches closer to touch my face, but stops, fingers suspended in the tiny space around my cheeks. His hands travel along my shoulders and down my sides to my waist and linger there. He pulls back.

"*Yo sé que lo quieres.*"

"I do . . . I want this . . . I just can't."

"*Claro que puedes, ¿cómo no?* You can do whatever you feel," he says, taking my hand.

I am so lost in his scent, in the breeze, and in his presence, that all I can do is feel. I couldn't think, even if I tried. I don't care if love is just a complex chemical reaction, a hormonal potpourri. If it could be bottled, it would fly off the pharmacy shelves faster than Viagra. I feel envied and enviable, in a way no test score, no high-profile job, and no stable relationship could ever induce. I feel that I would be stupid to pass up this one chance, maybe one that might never come again, to . . . I don't know. Feel whole. Complete.

He backs down onto the mattress and pulls me on top of him. We're facing each other, eyes locked, ready for something. But at this moment, neither one of us quite knows what it is. I run my fingers along his still-clothed chest, my finger pads pulsing as though equipped with microscopic electric transmitters. He closes his eyes, beginning to relax, and holds me tighter against him. We rock against each other for a few moments, not daring to test our budding curiosity any further. He's no longer as calm as he was before, each breath coming as fast and as stilted as mine. He reaches for the zipper on his jeans, and I catch one furtive glance of his gray cotton briefs underneath in the white moonlight.

"I can't do this!"

In one quick maneuver, I jerk away from him and am at the staircase before I even realize what I've done. He's barely had time to adjust himself on his elbows, a bewildered expression on his face, when I've already scampered down the first few steps.

"I'm so sorry!" I hear myself say.

19

I'm jolted awake later that same morning, barely three hours after I passed out on my bed, having managed only to slip out of my
flip-flops before crashing on top of the scratchy polyester duvet.

My eyelids flap open, my head wobbles from side to side as
though the cavity that holds my brain has been emptied out and
restocked with beach pebbles, and something between my eyes
is buzzing louder than a bumblebee on acid.

It's eight thirty.

Sophie, who must have woken me while struggling to unlock
the door, pitter-patters across the tiled floor and plops into bed
next to me. Four and a half seconds later, she pokes a finger into
my ribs.

"Ali? You awake?"

"No."

She leaves me in peace for a full minute.

"Ali?" She nudges the small of my back.

"I'm sleeping."

"No you're not."

"I would be if you stopped talking."

"Aren't you even glad I made it back in one piece?"

Havana Café. Javier and Sophie, swept away in a taxi into the
first stirrings of dawn. Miguel in the hut. Alone.

The linens.

"Oh my God." I bolt upright.

"What is it?"

I put my finger to my lips. "Shhh! You'll wake up Jaz. Don't worry, I'll just be a sec."

I run to the bathroom, splash my face with cold water, smear a squirt of toothpaste onto my tongue, swish it around in my mouth with a sip of water, and dab the purple stains under my eyes with some YSL Touche Éclat.

I stare at my reflection under the glare of fluorescent bathroom lights.

Still scary, but it'll have to do.

He'd carefully folded the blanket and white sheet, and left them on the mattress in the corner, along with the pillows.

I was hoping to wake him up this morning, to be the first person he opened his soulful brown eyes to. But what I really wanted to know was how much he hated me for last night. I guess I already knew the answer to that.

At least I'd managed to evade the security guards that patrolled the resort day and night. The only people that had caught me in the act of shuffling hotel property between the sprawling pool deck and the elevators were two heavyset women in identical blue gingham uniforms, whose eyes scanned me and my conspicuous load without the faintest glimmer of interest. They must have seen the scuttle of shame across the lobby more times than they could be bothered to recount.

By the time I make it back to the room, Sophie has already changed out of my wrinkled dress and is sitting cross-legged on the folding chair on our balcony in her olive tankini, staring out at the ocean. The faucet behind the closed bathroom door is running and Jaz's cot is empty.

What is it about this place that's made morning people out of the three of us? The enticing breakfast buffet? Highly doubtful.

"Hey, you." I slide the glass door of the balcony open and shut it behind me.

"Hey." She's still staring straight ahead, over the tops of palm trees and red-tiled bungalow roofs, to the shoreline at the end of the cobbled path from our complex to the beach.

"Did you do it?" I sit down beside her.

She doesn't need to answer. She shakes her head in embarrassed disbelief and then grins like someone who'd pulled a winning lottery ticket out of a garbage can.

"How did this happen to me?"

"Tell me you used protection."

"Of course we did."

I breathe out. "Okay. Good. Now I'm ready to hear this. Go."

"I don't know where to start—"

"Tell me about him first. What's so great about this guy that he's managed to snag the one Arab woman in the cosmos that would flabbergast the entire expatriate Lebanese community by turning down rich, young, and not-too-shabby-in-the-looks-department men like Yasser?"

Sophie doesn't say anything. She keeps looking out at the sea.

"What's he like?"

She clutches her face in both her hands like she's going to cry. "Like no one I've ever met."

I rub her folded knee and wait for her to go on.

"He says he doesn't want to leave Cuba."

"Well, it's pretty easy to say that when you've never been anywhere and you don't have a choice."

"He's been all over Europe."

"How?"

"He spent a semester studying in France last year."

"Can they do that here?"

"Apparently so."

"Wow."

How many times had I wished I'd done something like that in university? All that dreaming and plotting of where I'd go and what I'd do never amounted to anything. I never did squat about it. It would've meant an extra semester and the possibility of not finding a job straight after graduation. Audit firms don't wait till you graduate to hire you. They do it as soon as you've got Auditing Principles 101 under your belt and can be employed to photocopy files, count widgets, or do whatever it is they don't want to pay a qualified accountant to do. And the John Labatt School of Business isn't exactly the kind of faculty that encourages you to find yourself before you commit to a specific career. They leave that up to the Arts department. Because they're in business too—the business of providing a steady supply of corporate-drones-in-training to large consultancies and multinationals. And if you didn't like it, well, you could always major in Philosophy.

"So he speaks French?"

"And German, and a bit of English . . . Ali, he's so different from the guys back home, you'd love him. So . . . I don't know . . . grounded. What bugs him the most about living in Cuba is feeling so cut off from the rest of the world. He says he'd love to be able to buy a ton of different newspapers one day and figure out for himself what he wants to think rather than have it spoon-fed to him. Kinda makes you wonder about the things we take for granted."

"So how come he decided to stay in Cuba when he had the chance to leave?"

"I asked him the same thing, although honestly, Ali, couldn't you think of one thing that would make you want to stay here now that you've seen what it's really like?"

We stop to scan the open space around us, taking in the swaying palm trees, the tender warm air, the sun that hasn't once stopped smiling on us since we got here. To think, just a short three-hour plane ride to the north of this very spot, people we know are scurrying around, wrapped in quilted parkas and clutching thick scarves against their faces as they race from their cars to the nearest door.

"It's different for us, Sophe. We're in Varadero, in a nice clean hotel, on a nice stretch of beach that regular Cubans don't get to see unless they're on the cleaning staff. This is not reality."

"I know, but what about Havana? That was real. A whole lot more real than a place where malls get decorated for Christmas a full three months ahead of time. Seriously, can't you see yourself here? Just for a little while?"

"Sophie, I *cannot* believe how delusional you are sometimes. What would I say to my mother? What would you say to yours?"

"Don't you wish, just once in your life, you could actually carry on an honest conversation with her? What do you two ever talk about?"

"Mostly she just gossips about who's getting fat or whose daughter got a nose job while I nod and pretend I care. She's on to me though. That's why she'd rather hang out with my aunt Maryam and Ranya.

"At least we both like to shop," I add as an afterthought. It's true, we do. It's the only level we've connected on since I was old enough to brush my own teeth.

"Ali, what else are you going to pass up because you're too scared to be yourself in front of her? You're going to live your whole life lying to everyone?"

"Not everyone . . . just my mother. And anyone who knows her."

Sophie drops her head back, exasperated.

It's not the first time we'd reached this sort of deadlock over the issue of what I should or shouldn't tell my mother. I like to err on the side of less is more, but Sophie has these lofty, New Agey delusions about the truth setting you free and all that crap. She can afford it. Her family's had a few generations to shake off some of the Old Country bullshit people insist on clinging to. I don't have that luxury.

"Listen, we don't all live in this fantasy world where people are happy with us because we're honest. She really would disown me for picking up and running off with Miguel." Assuming he ever wanted to speak to me again, of course. "And where would that leave me when the infatuation wears off and one of us dumps the other?"

"Is that what you're afraid of? That you don't have a safety net?"

"Isn't that what you're afraid of too?"

Silence.

"You know it wouldn't be impossible to spend a few months here. There's a middle class. Javier's mom is a history professor at the university." Sophie steers the conversation back on course. "He says his family's had their Havana apartment since before the revolution. He gets to study what he loves in a city that's known for its great architecture, plus there's a lot of opportunity for him what with the restoration of old buildings and everything."

"So why was he so bitter that day in the plaza?"

"I think the effect of tourism on the country is rubbing him the wrong way. On one hand it's pulled them out of a major recession, but now they're starting to see differences in classes again, people with access to *pesos convertibles* and those without, lineups for tourists and different ones for Cubans."

"And he told you all of that in broken English in between gasps of ecstasy?" I arch an eyebrow at her.

She stares me down. "We spoke French, I'll have you know, and—"

"And what? Tell me before I explode!"

"Yeah, and what?"

Sophie and I jump at the sound of Jaz's voice emerging from behind the glass.

"What did I miss?"

I can tell from Jaz's tone she is trying hard to cover up the hurt of being left out. I feel like a complete shit.

"Nothing. You came at the perfect time. Sophie's just about to talk dick."

"Ali!" Sophie yelps.

Jaz lets outs a snort. "Yeah, right."

"No, really, she was." I stand up and lay my hand on Jaz's arm, a plea for truce. I sense some of the tension inside her seep out.

"I think this topic would be best discussed over runny eggs and stale bread," she says. "C'mon, I want to get an early start on my tan."

With that, the three of us hop back through the room and down to the cafeteria.

It turns out Sophie had the most memorable night of her life to date, right there on the beach in front of the resort. How she got this past the guards on dune buggies and other tourists with the same bright idea, I don't know.

"So where is he now?" asks Jaz, between mouthfuls of fresh pink papaya.

"He had to catch the early *camello* back to Havana. Class. And then work. Yesterday wasn't too productive for him."

"But we're leaving in two days. Is he coming back to party with us on our last couple of nights here?" Jaz looks genuinely concerned for Sophie.

I can't manage to get my lips to move.

Four nights up already. Two to go. Didn't we just step off the plane yesterday? But then how could so much have happened since then? I'm suddenly overtaken by a vision of throttling the hemp-clad, pink-fluo-dreaded Jocelyne for not having tried harder to get us on that Sunday-morning flight, buying us just one more day in paradise. In just four days, my life had been

picked up and thrashed around like the seashell pieces littering
the Varadero shore, and yet, in just over forty-eight hours, I'm
going to be back to the same spot, exactly where I'd left off, a
hamster on a running wheel, stuck in the same cycle. Nothing
has changed—the envelope containing my dismal UFE scores
packed in a side compartment of my hand luggage hasn't disappeared in a cloud of smoke, my mother still doesn't know I
flunked, and neither does Brian.

Brian! Poor, unsuspecting Brian. Brian who still thinks I'm on
a well-deserved party week in Cancún, figuring how badly can I
behave when I'm getting hammered with the same people I'll
have to see at the office—day in, day out—for the foreseeable
future. And this while he's slaving away at his office, probably
pulling in as many overtime hours as he can manage so he can
afford a bigger, better ring when the time comes. . . .

A shiver runs up my spine.

I have to stop. I'm getting way ahead of myself. Plus I've still
got one day of glorious freedom left, and I refuse to spend it
thinking about my miserable life. Things will blow over. They always do. Like the time my mom found my diary when I was seventeen, forced the lock, and greeted me with a tearstained face
when I came home from school that afternoon. Going through
those nightmarish couple of weeks, cringing every time I thought
about those pages about Tino Tortorricci and what went on in his
'95 Nissan Z3, with her just crying in my presence, or worse,
leaving any room I walked into, it was hard to imagine that the
torture would ever end. But it did. Eventually.

"There's actually something I'd like to ask you guys." Sophie
looks at both of us apprehensively. "Javier's mom is leaving for
Rome today. She's visiting his sister who married an Italian and
moved there. . . ."

I put my fork down and turn to look at her.

So she wants to ditch us for Javier on our last couple of nights
here. Even though God knows when we're ever going to have the

chance to do this again. My heart sinks at the thought, but I really can't blame her. If I could spend one last night next to Miguel, grooving to the sultriest, most sensual music I'd ever heard in my life, or even just sit in the same room as him and watch him coerce unsuspecting tourists into playing drinking games, would I have the willpower to say no?

"It's okay, Soph." I pat the back of her outstretched hand. "We understand." I'm hoping Jaz will jump in and back me up. She doesn't.

"What are you talking about?" Sophie stares at me. Then something seems to dawn on her and she cocks her head to one side. "Did you really think I was going to take off to Havana and leave you guys here?"

"Don't look at me like that. This is the first time I've seen you so smitten. How am I supposed to know what to expect?"

"I was going to tell you that Javier's invited all of us over. Tomorrow evening, after he's done with class. And Miguel too!" Sophie squeals that last part.

"Shh!" I scan the drafty cafeteria furiously with my eyes, just in case he might have walked in without my noticing.

"What's wrong?" Jaz asks.

Satisfied he's not anywhere in sight, I turn back to the girls.

"We might have had a bit of a spat yesterday . . . I don't know. Maybe. I'm not sure."

"Spat?" Jaz eyes me incredulously. "*Spat*? Only you, Ali, could make a hot holiday fling sound like a marriage. What did you 'spat' about?"

I tell them, as briefly as possible, and with the least amount of self-incrimination, about the not-so-happy dénouement of the previous night.

"So you didn't do it." I can't tell if Jaz is relieved or disappointed at the outcome of the fling that never was.

Sophie stares at me, eyes drooping at the corners, lips downturned, completely crushed.

"Stop giving me those puppy-dog eyes, Soph. You can still go. In fact I'll be mad at you if you don't."

"It won't be the same. I want you there with me. Both of you. Remember how much fun we had in Havana? And that was with a busload of old people. Imagine just the five of us—"

"Assuming Miguel's forgiven me for last night's blue balls episode."

"I think you're jumping to conclusions. You haven't seen him this morning yet," Sophie presses.

As if on cue, Miguel walks through the glass doors of the dining room. As for all the entertainment crew, mingling with guests at mealtimes is part of his job.

All activity at the table is suspended, including my heartbeat.

We watch him quickly scan the room and stride past the buffet line. He stops to say hi to Mike, Paul, and Donatella, seated close to the entrance. He strolls right past James, and pauses in front of the next table. He pulls up a seat. Right next to Xena, Warrior Princess from the first night, who even at this time of the day is painted three inches thick with makeup.

Even Sophie can't put a positive spin on this one.

I didn't come all the way to paradise to pine over a guy whose motives in attaching himself to me were suspect from the outset. Even less to watch the same guy ignore me. On her way out of the cafeteria, trailing right behind Miguel, Xena threw me one of those looks that said, Your loss, moron.

As far as I'm concerned, she's done me a favor. I don't have a choice in the matter anymore. The problem is I'm stuck on this resort with plenty of time to feel sorry for myself. And fantasize over what the two of them are going to be doing when the first sign of the moon shines in the saffron sky.

But if that's what he wanted, what he was after from the beginning, why did he waste so much time on me? And this when he's got an entire resort full of skinny, young, horny bimbos from every conceivable nationality west of Turkey at his disposal.

Is it possible that he actually feels something for me?

Jaz looks up from her *Vogue* holiday issue.

Whoops. Did I just say that out loud?

"I think he does. How many unaccompanied young women say no to this guy, you think? You're one up on that older brunette chick who's always hanging around him just on that score." She lays her magazine on the sand beside her. "I guess the question is what you're going to do about it."

"What do you want me to do? You keep giving me the evil eye whether it's Brian or Miguel I'm talking about without once offering me some real advice. What's up with you, anyway?"

It's true. She's been so hot and cold on this trip, I never have a clue what's going to come out of her mouth next.

"What's the point?" she huffs. "You're just going to do what you want anyway and then lie to us about it."

"Excuse me?"

"Why not? You lie to your mother all the time, you lied to Brian, everyone at work, why not us? Tell me the truth, Ali. Did you sleep with Miguel last night?

"I don't believe this!"

"Is that a yes?"

"It's a none-of-your-fucking-business if that's how you're going to be. Jeez, Yasmin." I gather my towel, book, and suntan lotion and stand up, wiping sand off my legs and butt. "I'm going for a walk. Catch you later."

I pick up the pace of my jog before she can see the corners of my bottom lip begin to quiver.

Sophie wanted to spend our last day on the resort taking part in all the activities she'd missed over the course of the week. I haven't seen her since archery.

224 * NADINE DAJANI

The three of us had spent Thursday in a daze, Sophie hardly seeing straight in anticipation of seeing Javier the following night, Jaz annoyed and giving me the quasi-silent treatment after our spat, and me too terrified of leaving my room for fear of a chance encounter with either Miguel or the Amazon Lady. It was the first night since we'd arrived that none of us wanted to go out. We just collapsed in bed at a very sober hour, each left to her own haunted dreams, and didn't bother to have breakfast together. In a continued effort to avoid Miguel and now Jaz, I spent the morning aimlessly combing the beach, and now my feet are killing me.

It's shocking how little time doing this activity wastes, especially when you're so angry, your leisurely stroll is more like a vigorous power-walking session.

I'd lost count of the funny looks I'd gotten from fellow vacationers every time my face twitched at one gut-wrenching memory or another, whether it was of Miguel's briefs under the glimmer of the moonlight, or Jaz's preposterous accusation.

How could she? With everything I've been going through? When did this holiday get hijacked by a pack of hormones tripping on a PMS high? And where did I get off wondering if Miguel actually has feelings for me or not? It seems the more time I'm spending in close quarters with Jaz, the more I'm starting to sound like her.

The thought both depresses and disgusts me.

She's my best friend. I should be helping her get over Ben, build her self-esteem, reminding her of his high-ranking status in the land of Loserdom if that's what it took. Not feeling resentful over having to babysit her tonight when Sophie drives off into the sunset in a '57 beat-up Chevy, hand in golden sun-baked hand with Javier.

Sophie. At least one member of our pathetic trio seems to be enjoying herself.

I sigh and drop my meager load on the soft sand. I'd try to

read, but not even the latest Marian Keyes is potent enough to hold my attention right now.

I know. I'll go for a swim.

I strip off my sarong and wade into the water up to my waist, and then let myself sink, until somehow I'm floating on my back, looking up at the sky, dotted here and there with clouds that look like squirts of whipped cream suspended against a backdrop of gentle blue.

"Alina."

I jerk around with about as much grace as a cat fallen in a bucket of soap water.

"What are you doing here? And where's Xena?"

Miguel just frowns at me, obviously confused.

"Never mind," I say. "I asked you why you're here."

More puzzlement. He takes a hesitant step back. "You are angry with me?"

"Where were you all day?" Oh, God. This is so not how I envisioned our first exchange following that night in the hut would go. Not after what was almost—

"I was looking for you."

"The hell you were. I saw you with her!" I'm fuming. Why, I don't know. Okay, I know, but I never imagined I could have such little control over my feelings. What happened to cool, collected Aline from Montreal? The one who's in a sensible relationship with a sensible man following a sensible career path, and with an absolutely glowing future ahead of her? Oh right, the UFE. At least I had managed to momentarily forget about that.

"Listen, if you want to fuck her, you have my blessing. You really do. Just stop . . . stop whatever it is you're trying to do to me. Leave me alone."

I'm going to lose it. I want to take a swing at him, push him in the water, or maybe bang my own head against something. Something hard. Just anything that will stop the torrent of emotions running through me, emotions that run contrary to everything that's ever been hardwired into my brain. *This is his job.* It's what he does all day, every day, with different girls every week. Making them fall just hard enough for him to get into their bikini bottoms. Not that I have any issues with casual sex—hypothetically, that is, since I'd never had the occasion to experience it myself. It's just you're not supposed to actually be *falling in love* with the other party.

Did I just say falling in love? Fuck.

I bury my head into my hands like I'm about to start wailing at an old-style Muslim funeral march.

"What's wrong?" He takes a step toward me.

"Nothing. I don't want to talk about it." That's it. Enough melodrama. I'm going home tomorrow, and in a week's time this'll just be a really embarrassing memory. I hope.

"Why you say you saw me with her? Who?"

"That woman. The French woman that's been making funny eyes at you all week long."

"Georgette? This is why you are so angry?"

That better not be a hint of a smirk on his face.

"*¿Estás celosa?*"

"No, I am *not* jealous. You, on the other hand, are completely full of yourself."

He laughs even though I'm sure the only part of my retort he caught was the bit about me denying my feelings toward the overpainted Amazonian.

He inches even closer, this time grabbing me by the waist and letting his fingers linger inside the curves.

"How could I be with her when I have spent every night since the show . . . the *competición* with you? Well, almost . . . last night I could not find you." I think back.

Admittedly, his schedule this week has been pretty predictable. By the time Jaz, Sophie, and I are up in the morning, he's already preparing for one activity or another, waiting for the guests to stream past the pool and take their places on the lounge chairs. Then it's a series of organized games until five, which is when the staff trek back to their homes in Matanzas to change for the evening. And at eight every night, he's working the seating area of the buffet, mingling with guests, making sure they're having a good time. Then it's off to the show. And ever since that pageant night, he's been spending his few hours of freedom between 10 P.M. and dawn showing me the time of my life. Well, in so far as I've let him.

Maybe I am being a bit unreasonable.

"I jus' saw Sophie playing volleyball. She is very good," he says in response to my prolonged silence.

"Before Engineering, I think she aspired to be the next Jackie Chan."

"Jackie Chan, yes!" He chuckles, either because he's finally managed to make out one of my jokes, or else at the thought of Sophie pulling a kung fu move.

"She tell me you are going to Havana tonight."

She what?

"Uh, we're still in the planning stages."

"She ask me if I want to come."

Okay, now she's really dead.

I stare up at Miguel dumbfounded.

"You don't want me to come with you?"

I still can't get my lips to move. Do I want him to come along? Of course. Is it really the smartest idea to pop into my head? Well . . .

"Okay, I don't come."

He turns around, pretending to be crushed but failing miserably, with lips upturned the tiniest bit at the corners.

"No! Wait . . . I mean—" Sigh. All my life up until this very moment seems riddled with regret. Regret over going into the wrong major, over being too preoccupied with graduating ahead of the game to bother with a semester abroad, the kind that would've shown me what I was made of. Regrets about my career.

I was damned if I was going to spend the rest of my life regretting what might or might not happen tonight. Jaz is going to be right there with me. That should be insurance enough.

"I do want you to come." I fix my stare down at the water.

"What?"

"I know you heard me."

"No, no te oí bien."

I glare at him, exasperated. "Will you please come out with Sophie, Jaz, Javier, and me tonight?"

"You will let me kiss you?"

"No."

He laughs and pulls me against him, completely closing the gap between us. "Okay, I will come anyway."

"Let me go!" I struggle against his chest, but it's about as useful as fighting off a brick wall.

He responds to my yapping by dipping my entire body beneath the waves, hair too, and lifts me back up, wrapping his arms as tight around my waist as physics will allow him.

"Smile!"

I flick my neck up to find Jaz standing in front of us, a waterproof camera practically shoved under my nose.

She snaps a picture.

"Jaz, you're fucking dead!"

Too late. She's way ahead of me, sprinting toward an awaiting Sophie on the shore, both of them in hysterics.

20

It seemed that Jaz had forgiven me for whatever had set her off in the first place. Which is making the next few words to come out of my mouth that much harder to articulate. I hadn't exactly told her I was going to Havana tonight. Not yet. I was hoping she'd change her mind all by herself, but that was looking less likely by the second.

"What do you think, Ali, tube or halter?" She holds up both dresses to my face.

"Definitely the halter."

I glance pleadingly at Sophie. She is already dressed for Havana in another one of my outfits, there having never been any debate as to whether or not she would leave for the city tonight. She responds with a tight smile, and a tap on her wrist signaling that I should just bite the bullet and get on with it.

Pheeeeeew. I exhale. This is great practice for when the Air Canada 747 lands in Mirabel Airport tomorrow evening and I begin my slew of confessions to absolutely every person I know.

"Jaz . . ."

"Mmm?" She's holding up two pairs of sandals, one black and strappy, the other a cork-soled wedge. "I've worn these three times already." She holds up the thick-soled shoe. "Too bad I'm not your size, Al. Have you even worn *half* the shoes you brought along?"

If I don't do this now, we're going to be seriously late. There's still a chance she'd want to come, and if I didn't give her enough time to get ready, I'd pay for it.

"Jaz, are you sure you don't want to go to Havana tonight? We've already been to every club worth seeing on the Varadero strip. . . ."

She narrows her eyes at me.

"Didn't we already go through this? I thought we were staying here tonight." She glowers at me. "Together."

I force myself to meet her icy stare. "I promised Miguel I'd go." Ambushed into promising, more like it. But really, who am I kidding? I'm positively thrilled Sophie triple-karate-chopped me into it. "Jaz . . . I really want you to come too. Please."

"You're joking, right?" Her mouth hangs open. "You want me to tag along on a double date with you two and the Cuban Wonderboys?"

"You were invited. . . ." I glare at Sophie, cowering in a far corner of the suite. I need backup.

"Of course. Javier made a big point of saying so," Sophie squeaks from the far corner of the room.

"Oh, so I'm officially the pity-case desperate loser friend?"

Crap. I've never seen Jaz get so angry with Sophie before. Sophie looks like she might burst into tears.

"Jaz, don't be stupid. We really don't want to leave you here alone, but you have to understand—" Understand what? I'm at a complete loss. "—it's, this . . . it's a big deal . . . for Sophie."

"Then why do you have to go too? You were happy enough to let her drive off to God knows where that night after the club."

Right. There's no way out now.

"I like him, Jaz. A lot."

"Story of your life." She flings both sandals on the floor and storms out of the room, slowing only to scoop up the room card and a pair of yellow sunflowered flip-flops. "I'm sick and tired of listening to your stupid sob stories!"

The clang of the slammed door reverberates throughout the room.

"*Stupid sob stories?* What?" I whip around and glare at Sophie. "What's with all the cryptic bullshit?"

"She's pissed off and lashing out at you. Don't take it personally."

"How else am I supposed to take it? She won't be reasoned with, won't meet me halfway, she won't even relax and try to enjoy it here. She just wants to make me feel guilty all the time. What for? I don't get it."

Sophie slinks on the floor next to me. We both stare out into the empty space ahead of us.

"Sophe?"

"Hmm?"

"Don't sit like that in my dress. It's Catherine Malandrino."

She chuckles, then sighs, and leans against my shoulder. "That's why I love you, Ali. You know how to keep things in perspective."

Miguel was waiting for us in the lobby at 5:30 sharp, exactly when we'd asked him to. He'd swapped his day off with Chino just so he could have the rest of the evening free for us.

"You smell nice." I pull away from his chaste one-sided cheek kiss.

It's a bit of an understatement.

"And you look very nice." He eyes me from my wild curls down to my sandaled feet in a way that makes a tiny nook deep within my gut tingle with anticipation. Anticipation for what, I don't know.

I'm feeling the effects of five days on the inedible-resort-cuisine diet and loving it, having shed those stubborn five-pounds-away-from-body-bliss everyone seems to complain about.

So tonight, I've decided to flaunt my newly flat abs in a stretchy ocean blue dress.

Javier's tour bus driver cousin had agreed to take us to the city in the Havanatur minivan the company lets him keep when he's not busy shuttling tourists around, so we had actually landed a pretty sweet deal. A roomy, air-conditioned ride, for half of what we would have paid a tour operator.

And, as it turns out, at twice the speed.

"This can't be legal." Sophie screws her head back to face me, the fear of God on her face. "This isn't a cab. It's a freaking jet."

"He does this for a living, Sophe. We're going to be fine."

21

One hour and fifteen minutes after we'd left Varadero, the mini-van drops us off in front of a neat-looking building in a residential quarter of Havana. On top of the forty *pesos convertibles* that the fare cost, I press a crisp twenty in Guillermo's hand. I figure he deserves at least that much for cutting the traveling time by half and delivering us to the capital alive to boot.

Sophie lets out a mini yelp at the sight of Javier waiting for us at the foot of the building. He folds her into his sinewy arms and lifts her off the deeply cracked pavement.

"No he podido dejar de pensar en ti."

Oh, boy. If after a mere day and a half of separation he already can't stop thinking about her then his future after this evening is looking decidedly gloomy to me.

And even though I'd bet my last Pepto-Bismol chewable tablet that Sophie didn't catch one word of what he'd just said, I could swear I saw all the stars of the Havana sky glint in her eyes.

Javier manages to tear himself away and takes her hand instead, turning to face Miguel and me. *"Vamos,"* he says, and leads the way ahead of us down the same street that brought us here.

With long, hurried strides we turn the corner of Calle 21 onto La Rampa, a clean, wide street that looks nothing like the cobble-stone alleys of Old Havana we'd visited on the tour. It's more modern looking, lined intermittently with inviting coffeehouses and small shops selling everything from clothing to appliances. I stop to peer into windows of spacious, airy boutiques and tiny tiled enclaves where people are lined up by the dozen to buy cigarettes, sodas, or spicy-smelling pastries. Miguel lags behind with me, while Sophie and Javier hurry ahead, lost in animated conversation and lingering gazes.

"We should keep up the pace, we wouldn't want to get lost," I say.

"Why you worry so much? Always, always, you are worried about something. Even when you don't say it, I can see it, *en tu cara, en tus ojos color miel.*"

Color miel. Honey colored. My heart tickles in my chest. I didn't think anyone west of the Wailing Wall considered "honey" a valid eye color. Something you could put on your driver's license or birth certificate. Age: 22; height: 160 centimeters; eye color: honey.

"You mean *assali*," I tease.

"*¿Cómo?*"

"I thought it was just an Arabic thing. Honey color. *Assali.* They say 'hazel' in Canada. Honey is so much more . . . I don't know. Romantic. Am I being silly?"

He chuckles. *"Claro que no."*

He reaches for my hand but suddenly, before his fingers can caress mine, he tenses. The sun has just set behind a veil of foggy gray blue. Sophie and Javier are way ahead of us and except for a pair of police officers, conspicuous in their olive-green garb, and the odd gaggle of raucous revelers, we're pretty much alone.

"What's the matter?"

He shushes me with a glare, tucks his hands in his pockets, and quickens his pace.

We're nearing the policemen, now on our side of the street. Miguel's stride picks up. My mind races: What is he afraid of?

What has he done? What have I gotten myself into? My mother was right. Well, she'd be right if I were to fly home, confess to the whole pathetically sordid Cuban-love-god-versus-Brian-the-dependable-sweetheart love triangle mess and afford her the chance to comment.

One of the men in uniform eyes Miguel the way guys do when they walk into a bar and scan the scene for potential competitors, sizing each other up. Miguel bows his head a tiny bit and squeezes his thick arms against his sides as if he would dissolve into nothing by doing so.

One more step. Another. The policeman shoulders Miguel with a padded thump. I realize I'm holding my breath. We take another step and so do the officers, our paths diverging once again. Exhaling slowly, I hear their footsteps stop a few feet behind us. They're speaking, but not to Miguel and me, asking someone for ID.

I turn my head just enough to see.

A mixed group of fifteen- or sixteen-year-old boys in faded jeans and girls in bright spandex are leaning against a wall, smoking, drinking clear liquid straight out of transparent glass bottles. One of the guys is strumming a guitar. I'm too far away to hear what they're saying, but they're digging through their jeans and their purses, looking for something to show the police. ID.

"*Lo siento.*" Miguel takes my hand and squeezes it a few steps further. "I'm sorry."

"What happened? Why were you afraid?"

"This is the problem in Cuba." He kicks an offending pebble out of his way. "You are not free to do what you want, to say what you want, to speak to who you want. They think when a Cuban talks to a tourist, he must be a *jinetero*." Here he pauses, turns to look at me, smiling sweetly. I want to ask him what he means, how can such a thing as not being able to choose who you associate with be, but he doesn't give me the chance.

"Come, let's hurry before we get lost." He pulls his hands out of his pockets and grabs hold of one of mine. Together we race across La Rampa, passing a travel agency, a movie theater, and a handful of traffic lights before catching up with Sophie and Javier, who barely register our presence.

"Miss me?" I yank on a lock of Sophie's hair.

"Er, actually . . ." She winks. "Just kidding! What were you doing back there, anyway?"

I consider telling her what happened, and think better of it. I'll just make sure to steer her to the other side of the street should we happen on another pair of patrolling police officers.

A few blocks later, Javier makes a sharp turn at an inconspicuous corner onto a narrow, dusty alley that smells faintly of garbage.

I glare at Sophie.

"Uh, Javi . . ." She'd read my mind.

"¿Sí, mi vida?"

"I thought you were taking us to a restaurant," she says meekly.

"Not a restaurant. A *paladar*."

"A what?"

"Trust me." he winks at her. "In Cuba, it is the *gobierno* that owns all the restaurants, the hotels, anything for tourists. You know Cubans cannot have their own *negocio* . . . business?"

She nods.

"*Bueno, paladares* and *casas particulares* are the exception."

Gobierno or no *gobierno*, I somehow find the idea of a state-owned eatery much more reassuring than some sort of mom-and-pop start-up run by people out of touch with the standards of competition and a free market.

"Sophe . . ." I nudge her.

"Don't pull a Jaz on me. Relax." She grins mischievously, like that's supposed to make me feel better.

We near the end of the alley. No restaurant in sight. None that I can see, anyway.

"I thought La Rampa was really nice . . . ," I squeak, hoping someone cares enough to listen.

"Don't worry." Miguel grins. *I'm here,* his tickled expression says. He doesn't seem to have any more of an idea where he's headed than I do, but I don't think it's weighing so heavily on him. I guess that's one of the perks of being six foot two and buff. And male.

"Aquí." Javier halts abruptly, in front of a fifty-ish man slumped in a white plastic patio chair, his huge belly cradled on top of his lap like an oversize bowling ball tucked under his thin shirt.

"El Hurón Azul. ¿Está por aquí?" Javier says.

"Momentito, muchacho."

The man with droopy bulldog cheeks grips both edges of the chair and pulls himself to his feet, hovering midway to hike up his trousers. He sighs as though the fate of the entire *paladar* were resting on his tired shoulders, and trudges two steps to the nearest door, painted electric blue.

He raps twice, and waits.

My breath is caught somewhere between my upper ribs and collarbone. The suspense is more absorbing than *InStyle*'s annual Top 150 Beauty Products exposé.

The door opens, releasing a slice of dim yellow glow into the pink twilight.

"Entren, entren, por favor." A waiter in a neat black vest and trousers over a white shirt rolled up to the elbows appears behind the now wide-open door and ushers us in. Javier and Miguel step aside, allowing Sophie and me to walk in together.

Sophie sees it first. She gasps.

"Ali, look . . ."

The "restaurant" is in fact a room that might have been someone's den in its previous life, just big enough to hold three tables of four. It leads directly to another similar room on one side, and a kitchen with a swinging door on the other.

Aside from its diminutive proportions, the place is a different world from the dingy street on the other side of the threshold.

Every exposed space is virtually wallpapered in paintings of all sizes, having only their energy and bold color in common, with exposed brick poking out in between the gilt frames and wood canvases. Though no two tables or chairs are exactly alike, they are matched in their antiquelike appeal and intricate detail. Even the knickknacks belong to another era altogether, a small crowned Jesus statue perched atop a polished mahogany console with wrought-iron handles, next to a porcelain baseball player and a Grecian vase holding a single gardenia strand.

"This is stunning. . . ." I scan the far wall of the adjacent enclave, a bartender's wet dream, lined with row upon row of bottles of amber liquid with labels like Hennessy, Courvoisier, Johnnie Walker, and racks of dark red wines, all on display behind sheets of glass sprouting from the floor and reaching up to the ceiling.

The waiter seats us at the only empty table, beside two distinguished-looking couples, probably my parents' ages, firing emphatic Spanish repartee at each other in a different accent from Miguel and Javier's.

Other tourists, I'm guessing, South American maybe, or even Mexican.

The table is a beautiful solid oak, adorned with two crisscrossing table runners, and the most colorful fruit bowl I've ever seen.

"Are these edible?" There are pieces of pineapple cut into star shapes, fresh papaya wedges, mangoes, and stuff I don't even recognize. Each one is so perfect, I can hardly believe it isn't a piece of molded wax, placed there for decoration.

"*Claro, ¿cómo no?*" Javier snatches up a mysterious orange ball and pops it in his mouth.

Giddy with excitement, Sophie follows suit, except she picks a papaya star.

Even Miguel studies the room appreciatively.

"Have you been to Havana before?" I ask him.

"A long time ago, I came here with my mother to visit my uncle, her brother. We are from Holguín. Iss' very far."

"Varadero must be pretty far from Holguín too, then. Do you mind living so far from home?"

He shrugs. "I go to see my mother every month. And my job, it's not so bad." He winks at me.

I roll my eyes and swivel toward the waiter who has just appeared at our table with menus.

I take one and sigh. Sophie smiles tightly at me. We're on the same wavelength, I know it—if only the quality of the food could match half the charm of the place. Certainly not if the tasteless resort buffet we were subjected to was anything to go by.

I flip open the leather cover and am pleased to see an English translation underneath each item.

"Please . . ." Javier lowers my menu and stares straight at my face from across the table. "You must try the Cuban specialty."

I'd love to. Really. It's just that I left the Pepto-Bismol at the hotel, and if my stomach could hardly withstand the bland resort fare, I shudder to think what it would do with a full-blown authentic local meal.

"Javier, I . . ." really don't know how to put this.

"Oh, just try it, Ali," Sophie says. "We're already here, let's do this all the way." With that, she snatches the menu from my hands and gives both hers and mine back to the waiter.

"What if the national dish happens to be a big fat pig stewing in its own juices?" I say slowly in Arabic, hoping that Sophie understood despite her meager vocabulary in that particular language.

"So what?" The words are slow and deliberate, and sound like they've been spoken by an articulate canary. Somehow the pitch of Sophie's voice always shoots up several octaves when she's forced to make use of her mother tongue.

"Sophie, I don't eat swine!"

"But you've been knocking back mojitos like they're mineral water."

"That's *so* not the same thing."

"I promise you will love it." Javier lays his hand over mine like we're old high school friends. The intimacy feels nice. Like he's letting me into this incredible pocket of the world, showing me its secrets.

"Okay." I gulp audibly. "Can you tell me what it is first?"

"*Ropa vieja.*"

"Sorry, what?"

"Old clothes."

That really doesn't help.

I look over to Sophie. She nods reassuringly. "It's okay, Al. It's an adventure, remember?"

Right.

Miguel acquiesces wholeheartedly to the old clothes suggestion, and the waiter shuffles to the kitchen, returning a few minutes later with our drink order. Mojitos all around. It's our last night here, after all.

They come in fancy highball glasses, the mint leaves hovering in the top tier of the silvery liquid. The price list says they're two dollars each. Unbelievable. The same drinks would cost three times as much in Montreal. At least.

"So . . . How did you find out about this place?" I feel stupid asking. It's his city, after all. It's just that when the only time you hear anything about Cubans is when a couple of them are trying to make it across shark-infested waters in a recycled inner tube, it makes reconciling all this with the images on CNN a lot harder.

"Cuba is famous for *paladares.* This one is owned by two artists." He gestures to the walls in a sweeping movement. "I think to myself that you will like it."

"You thought right. It's lovely. But—" I lean in and lower my voice. "—who eats here? Is it for tourists or Cubans?"

Javier grins. "This is why iss' important to see other things than Varadero or the Cayos. Anyone can eat here. Iss' very expensive for us in Havana, but iss' possible. In Varadero, iss' not possible. You should see other places in Cuba as well, Pinar del Río, Santiago, Trinidad—"

"Holguín . . ." Miguel grins.

"I'd love to see Holguín."

There's a lull in the conversation, each of us retreating to our thoughts. I'm picturing myself in a great Michael Kors Resort sarong, wide-brimmed hat, and nothing else, à la Rene Russo in *The Thomas Crown Affair*, lying on the sand in front of a rustic Holguín cabana, Miguel dozing by my side. I wonder what he's thinking about.

"Sophie." Javier is the first to snap out of it. "*¿En qué estás pensando?*"

"Nothing . . . ," she stutters. "I was just . . ." Deep exhale. "We're leaving tomorrow."

Javier's shoulders heave. "Iss' not a problem. When will you come back?"

"I don't know. . . ."

Neither do I. Most likely never. And even if we do, it won't be anytime soon. Things would have changed. Who knows where Miguel and Javier would be? Maybe Javier would have graduated, started dating one of his classmates, matured, gotten engaged . . . A bright guy like him isn't going to do tourist portraits in Cathedral Square forever. And Miguel? In a month's time, I'd be an unpleasant shadow of a memory in the back of his mind, the one girl who didn't cave. I wonder how many horny tourists it would take to get the rotten aftertaste of me out of his brain. Then again, I'm probably just flattering myself.

"Why you don't know? You can come here when you want, no? Iss' very expensive?"

"It's not that simple, Javi. . . . Well, yes, actually, money is going to be a bit of a problem since I'm basically unemployed, but I can scrape enough to get here. It's actually my . . ." Sophie squirms in her seat. "It's my parents," she finally says. "I've never been on this kind of vacation alone, so if I go twice in a row to Cuba, they'll think something's up. And then there's the scholarship—"

"Scholarship?" Javier's eyes flicker with attention. "You did not tell me."

Sophie stares down at her lap.

The waiter rescues her with four plates of heaping, steaming food.

Old clothes.

I guess the name comes from the fact that the marinated beef is shredded into spaghetti-thin strips. Tomato, onion, pepper, and garlic aromas travel up from the dishes and tickle my nose. It smells great. And the portion is gigantic. Another waiter swings through the kitchen door bearing deep terra-cotta bowls of black beans, white rice, and fried plantains.

"I don't like bananas," I say, mostly for my own benefit.

"Try it first," Miguel says, his tone both gentle and commanding.

Whoops. I didn't think anyone had heard me.

Sophie glances up from behind her plate at me, and beams broadly, wincing as though she were on a roller coaster and the metal safety belts had just been lowered, announcing the beginning of the ride.

Here goes nothing. I pick up my fork and dig into the "old clothes." The first bite makes me swoon.

"Oh my God. What's this again? Old clothes? Why the hell don't they serve this at the resort?"

This is unbelievable. It almost reminds me of Lebanese food, so pleasantly spicy it is. The meat tastes like it's been aged and marinated for ten years.

"Official hotels like the one in Varadero, they think tourists want food like they have at home. *Hamburguesas, pizzas, y todo eso,*" Javier says. "Here, it is the owners who prepare everything. They pick the best food from the *mercado* every day. In Cuba, the problem is that we cannot always get what we need, even if we have money. So, one day you come here and there is no chicken, or no beef. But Cubans are the best at making a lot with very little." He holds up an imaginary string between his fingers, and stretches it.

Miguel nods gravely, like he knows all about making do.

I feel like telling him that my family, who endured fifteen years of civil war, would empathize. I want to tell him how much more we have in common than he thinks. But this is not the kind of dinner-table conversation that can be had in broken bits of English and Spanish, over mojitos and *añejo* rum.

Sensing my fixed stare, Miguel looks up from his *ropa vieja* and smiles sweetly. "You did not try the *plátanos maduros.*"

"I will." I smile back, sighing, not because I want to jump his bones right here right now like any other time he's anywhere within a five-mile radius of me, but because I'm aching to tell him about me, my life, my stupid job, my mother, Lebanon, even Brian. I want to point at the latticed windows and say how I remembered seeing the same ones at my aunt's 150-year-old flat in Beirut. I want to discuss the paintings on the wall and confess how much I liked to sketch when I was younger, how much I still wanted to do it if only I weren't so afraid to discover that I sucked, and that all I was and would ever be was a miserable accountant. I want to tell him about the nagging little voice in my head that keeps telling me that Brian isn't The One, that I'm nowhere near knowing enough about myself to commit to a life of bland sameness. Above all, I want to ask Miguel how I could explain all this to my mother without her looking at me like she'd spawned the child of Satan.

I sigh. I have no idea how much of this he cares to hear, or if he'll indulge me and listen attentively despite being bored to tears. I don't remember not being able to trust my own feelings like this in a long time. Not being able to read someone else the way I can't read Miguel. Or is it that I'm so afraid of what it is that I'm reading in his animated eyes, his easy smile?

"Alina, you are not eating. . . . You don't like it?"

I snap back to the table, the conversation, Sophie and Javier gazing at each other through a drunken haze of hormones, and Miguel's eager face.

"I love it." I shovel a huge forkful in my mouth to illustrate my point. I even tear off a piece of sticky fried banana and bite into it.

"It's fantastic." It is. It's not so much a side dish as a dessert. "Sophie, try this." I slide the plate across the table. "I don't understand how Cubans aren't enormous. Think of the carbs. . . ."

Javier chuckles. "Actually, we have a problem with obesity in Cuba." He wipes the corners of his mouth with a burgundy linen napkin, as though suddenly self-conscious about how much he'd eaten.

"Could've fooled me. I'm used to the *Jerry Springer* style of obesity. Not quite the same thing."

Miguel's certainly not worried about the epidemic. I watch him raise his loaded fork to his mouth, and I'm in complete awe. I've barely made a dent in my heap of rice, and he's already polished off two-thirds of his plate.

My insides stir at the sight of him. I really don't get it, but there's something about the way he's going about it that's—God help me—*sexy*. He eats like a proper man's man should. Shoveling everything in his mouth at once, taking in the fuel that makes his body so broad and strong, that feeds the bulging muscles under his skin. Not at all like Brian, taking bites that wouldn't satisfy a sparrow, scrutinizing every spoonful for evidence of the onions, garlic, or peppers he's specifically requested be removed from his plate. Brian has no appreciation for spice. And watching Miguel attack his food with so much ardor, I wonder if he takes everything else in life with the same passion.

22

"I can't believe how beautiful the *Malecón* is at night." I sigh.
Miguel and I are strolling along the wide stone boardwalk, shoul-
dered against a ghostly street on one side, and frothy white
waves atop ink-black ocean on the other.

I say ghostly because none of the majestic buildings I've seen
along the *Malecón*—from its beginning at the Morro Castle to
this spot, halfway to Javier's apartment—appear even remotely
inhabitable. Some are even propped up outright by enormous
wooden beams, like something out of a history book depicting old
military forts. The paint on the ones left standing has long since
peeled away, leaving slabs of gray in its wake. It's hard to know
what got these structures in this sorry state in the first place. De-
cades of salt water, erupting from beyond the thick stone barrier,
leaping over the sidewalk, across the street, and unleashing its
fury on the sad buildings. Or maybe just plain neglect.

But they are very much inhabited, because through tiny
spaces between blinds and under balcony doors, scraps of artifi-
cial light escape into the night. And yet, despite the beaten-
down look of things, it's hard to call this squalor. Not when I can
imagine how much the charity-ball-hosting and nouveau riche
society back home would pay to have balconies this intricately
welded, stone moldings so artfully sculpted, and soaring columns so stately that you'd swear you were looking at a Renais-
sance château instead of a middle-class Cuban home.

The wind blowing off the ocean brushes my face and tousles my hair, pasting a few strands against the remnants of my sticky lip gloss. I sweep them away, and shudder. The combined effect of the breeze against skin that's spent the past two hours oozing sweat from every pore in an overcrowded Centro Habana nightclub is firing shivers throughout my body. I knew I should've brought a sweater.

"You are cold?" Without so much as a moment's hesitation, Miguel pulls his long-sleeved knit over his head and gently rests it across my shoulders.

I should give it back. He's going to freeze in that thin white T-shirt. Plus, I don't know how long I can stand having his heat, his scent, a crisp aftershave mixed in with sea and salt, enfolding me.

As much as I don't want to, I let the sweater slide down my back and hand it to him.

"Here. I don't want you to catch cold."

"Alina, *por favor.*"

I'm obstinate. "No, take it."

He inhales sharply and takes it from me, turning to look far into the distance ahead, his gaze floating above the bend carved into the rocks over the course of millennia.

"You never told me what you do in Canada. Do you work or study?" he says after a moment of strained silence.

It's true. We'd never broached the subject. How ironic, considering the reason I came here in the first place, a reason that keeps fading further and further from my consciousness.

"I'm an accountant. An auditor, actually."

His eyebrows jolt upward. He seems impressed, even though I'm pretty sure he doesn't know what an auditor is.

"It's not a big deal," I add quickly. "It really sucks, if you want to know the truth."

He furrows his eyebrows while an amused smirk plays across his lips.

"I used to think it was a big deal." I have no idea why I'm still rambling. He doesn't care. Not to mention the tackiness of discussing unfulfillment with a man whose most promising career prospect is to entertain hammered tourists at a resort he's too lowly to walk into unless he's on duty, when I myself am decked out in Marc Jacobs from head to toe.

"When you're on the outside looking in," I continue, "it seems like a big deal. You imagine yourself living in a great downtown penthouse that an interior designer made to look just like the spread you saw a few *InStyle*s ago, driving a Passat or Mercedes Coupe or something. You think about how proud your parents would be, and how they'd snatch up any opportunity to gloat to their friends about how successful you are. But then you do it and you realize it really sucks. You see that everyone in the office walks around with the same slouch. Nobody cares, least of all you, and you finally realize that you're really not that special after all. The special ones are those that have the guts to go after what they really love, what they're really good at. Then you wonder why no one ever told you that in the first place."

I have no idea how much of that he understood, or how much of it even made sense. He stops, takes my hand, and guides me to the side of the seawall. He backs into it and pulls me so that I'm leaning against him. I start to feel light-headed.

"*¿Por qué no te valoras más?*" He says this so softly I feel none of the defensiveness I normally would if a virtual stranger had just questioned my sense of self-worth. Maybe it's because he's a virtual stranger that I can't argue. . . . Could I be so transparent? Does he see something in me I don't want to see?

"Why do you pretend to like me?" I want to follow this up with *Do you really think I'm going to marry you and earn you a one-way ticket out of this place?* but I manage to hold that thought in.

He hangs his head back and sighs. Then he focuses back on my face, taking it in his hands. "You are a very smart girl. And sexy too." At this he smiles mischievously. "There are many sexy girls in Varadero. But not many girls who are smart too, and kind, *y que nos entienden.*"

His eyes had hardened into seriousness at his last words, girls who understand them, who understand what it might be like to be one of them. To be Cuban. To have the rhythm of African-inspired beats coursing through your veins like blood, filling you with passion and exuberance. To hear the music in the language, instead of the accent of maids and drug dealers in American movies. Or perhaps I understand what it's like to be brown and different, in a sea of privileged whiteness.

The wind blows my hair into my lip gloss again. Slowly, he pushes the errant strands away from my face and tucks them behind my ear.

Please, God, don't let him try to kiss me again. I don't think I'll be able to stop him this time.

Why I don't just let it happen is starting to elude me. I had a good reason. . . . I know I did. . . . Is it Brian? Or is it the fact that we're leaving in a matter of hours and I don't want to be one of those tacky tourists that come out here just to get laid by a hot Latin stud, no strings attached? But what if I wanted strings? . . . There. That's why I won't let him kiss me. I knew there had to be a reason. Because I'm completely, unabashedly, unapologetically in love with him.

"You are not happy."

I'm not sure if this is a question or a statement.

"No. I'm not."

"I don't understand why. *¿Qué hay?*"

I snort out a half laugh. Didn't I just tell him what the problem was? Insanely demanding parents? Luxury penthouses? Not wanting to condemn myself to a life of poverty?

"I make a lot of money as an accountant. It's hard to say no to that."

"But still you are not happy."

"Is anyone ever really happy? Isn't it just our tragedy as humans to keep wanting more?"

"I am."

"What, happy?"

He laughs at my expression, a mix of surprise and sarcasm.

"Why? What is it that makes you so content? Your job? Your . . ." I couldn't think of anything else to finish the sentence with.

"I am happy with you. Now. We are on the *Malecón*, there are stars in the sky. Iss' a little cold," he chuckles, "but you are very warm. . . ." He pulls me closer. "I wish I could kiss you."

My body breaks into a full-out throb, heat pounding through every nerve ending, making me feel radioactive. His hands on the curve of my waist are burning through me.

I hear footsteps gently tapping the pavement, and jerk backwards, the thrashing of my heartbeat making my whole body tremble.

Sophie and Javier are standing a few feet away from us.

"Sorry . . ." A faint blush animates Sophie's cheeks. Javier just looks amused, as though he'd anticipated an awkward moment like this all evening long, and was smug in the knowledge that he was right.

"We flagged down two Coco Taxis and figured we'd take them back to the apartment." Sophie continues. "Wanna race?"

I glance back at Miguel, one eyebrow arched.

He nods.

"You are so on!" I screech, and run to the nearest of the twin egg-shaped yellow cabs.

"I wonder what's taking them so long." Sophie sighs, looking out across to the majestic Hotel Nacional, with its palm tree–lined driveway and palacial balconies.

We're at Javier's apartment on the top floor of an old but well-maintained building with a temperamental elevator. Besides her job as a professor, his mom runs a *casa particular*—a private bed and breakfast. I guess that's why they seem so well off. Both rooms she has to let out are vacant tonight, and that's besides the wing of the apartment Javier, his mother, and her helper occupy, so there's plenty of room for all of us.

We watch the Caribbean Sea behind the hotel swell into a solid sheet of water, rise up, and splash against the wall of the *Malecón,* water spilling over the stones and halfway to the buildings on the other side of the street.

"I'm glad you had the foresight to flag down those cabs. And I can't say that racing down a famous Havana boulevard in glorified scooters at four A.M. was the worst way to end a perfect night . . . ," I say.

"It's not over yet. At least I hope not."

"*Sophie!*" I mock-gasp. "I'm shocked! What's happened to you?"

She doesn't laugh with me. She just stares out to sea, a new habit I'm beginning to expect every time I ask her anything remotely important.

"What? What is it?"

"Do you like him?" She turns to face me, anxiety clouding her features.

"Who, Javi? He's great, Sophe." And I mean it. Going around Havana tonight first by foot then in a horse and buggy, he took the time to point out obscure monuments to us, buildings, things we hadn't seen on the tour. He took us to the very spot an Oscar-winning Cuban movie, *Fresa y chocolate*, was shot, brought us inside to show us pictures of all the famous people who'd dined at the movie-site-turned-*paladar*. Jack Nicholson, Danny Glover, Oliver Stone, and a slew of others. He even showed us the university where he studies. I could swear Sophie swooned when the buggy pulled up to the ancient complex, with its chipped statues and winding stone steps. You could tell how proud he was to show off his city, to make sure we understood why he couldn't imagine leaving with only dim hopes of ever coming back.

"They're going to think we're crazy." I know she means our parents, our friends, even Jaz.

Jaz! I wonder how she's getting along. I won't let guilt get to me. Not tonight. I'll make it up to her tomorrow. I will. Definitely.

"Ali, can I ask you something?"

"What?"

"How bad would it be if I turned down the scholarship?"

Shit. Sophie's happiness, as well as that of her entire family, was hinging on the next few words to come out of my mouth. Me, who couldn't even be trusted to make simple packing choices for this trip. I can't imagine who in their right mind would consult me with a decision of this magnitude.

"This wouldn't have anything to do with Javier, would it?" I tread cautiously.

"Nooo . . . Not really . . ."

"Sophie!"

"Ali, I'm serious. I know accepting the scholarship is the safe, sensible thing to do, but I've done three years of engineering and I hate it. Isn't that a sign?"

"You might change your mind entirely once you start working."

"Oh, like you did?"

"Fine. If you're going to be that way."

"You always do this."

"Do what?"

"Clam up whenever we start getting somewhere. What about you? What was that I saw on the *Malecón*?"

"Oh, come on. I know you didn't see anything because nothing *happened*."

"Only because you noticed I was there."

I open my mouth to protest, but it remains suspended in a speechless *O*. Is she right? Is that why nothing happened?

"Alina, *toma*." Miguel strides through the wide-open veranda doors holding two glasses of a syrupy brown liquid. It looks like Tu Cola, Cuba's version of Coke. Javier is right behind, another two glasses in his hands and a guitar under his arm.

"Oh, no. You're not going to serenade us, are you?"

"Yes, of course," Javier says.

Miguel, Sophie, and I can barely contain ourselves.

"Javi, this is too cheesy for words," I wail.

"You want to sing for us, then?" Javier hands me the guitar.

I can hardly stop laughing long enough to push the instrument back at him.

"I don't think so."

Javier sets his drink down on the floor beside him, and I take mine form Miguel. I was right. They'd mixed us Cuba Libres, the local version of rum and Coke. Strong ones.

"Are you trying to get me drunk?" I poke Miguel's shoulder blade.

"Why? Iss' too strong?"

"No, it's fine. I was just kidding." Not to mention touched by the shadow of concern that fluttered across Miguel's face.

The balcony's not wide enough for us to form a circle with the chairs. I gather my dress around my knees and ease myself onto the hard floor. Sophie needs to give Javier some space to man the guitar, which means I'm pretty much squished against Miguel. It's not too bad. Especially when his fingers wander up to my hair, down the length of my shoulders, then rest at my waist.

Javier starts strumming what I think are the opening chords to "Hotel California."

"Oh God, no! Not that, please." It was the song Sophie taught herself to play guitar with. That and "The Sound of Silence."

When he parts his lips and starts singing, it gets worse.

Sophie's clutching her sides in pain, she's laughing so hard. I hear what might have been an insult from another apartment hurled at us across the darkness.

"I think maybe you should retire the guitar before you get evicted," I say.

"Wait." Sophie takes it from him, nestles herself in his lap, tunes the guitar, and starts playing. Though she's not quite a pro, her fingers dance artfully across the strings and the scraped wood surface. She looks so happy sitting there, so angelic. She even sounds like an angel, especially next to Javier's off-tune croaking of a few minutes ago.

I'm not sure when the sky around us begins to lighten, but it suddenly dawns on us that we should maybe get some sleep before the minivan of death comes to take us back to the resort.

Javier stands up first, and pulls Sophie to her feet.

"There are two bedrooms on this side of the apartment. You can use any one—or two—if you like." Embarrassed, he looks away. *"Buenas noches."* He disappears behind the opaque glass of the balcony door.

"You'll be okay?" Sophie asks, glancing anxiously toward the threshold.

"Get out of here. Someone's waiting for you."

"I'll see you in a bit—"

"Go."

"Okay. Night, Miguel. Ali." And then she disappears too.

Tap, tap, tap . . . my fingernails play a mysterious beat on the clay floor tiles of the veranda, not knowing what else to do.

It's so quiet.

Every once in a while we hear the growl of a motorbike thundering down Javier's street, or else the buzzing of the cicadas in the trees, but that's it.

I wait for Miguel to pronounce himself done for the night, and claim ownership of one of the two rooms. He doesn't.

Nor does he take advantage of our complete isolation and try to slide his hand under my dress.

He just picks up the guitar, fiddles with the tuning, and begins strumming. It sounds like a ballad.

Slowly, softly, seamlessly, he sings the lyrics that match the music, just one notch above a whisper. I can't make it all out, but I catch a few words here and there.

"Why didn't you say you could play?"

He doesn't let me interrupt the flow of the song. Something about the sun and reaching for it, about it being easier to reach it than this woman's heart. The woman who I presume inspired the music.

"Miguel . . ."

He stops strumming, and looks at me. His stare welds me into place.

I don't know why this happened to me out of all people, or whether the same thing happens a million times over to a million people, every single day around the world. I just know it did. I was given a perfect night. A perfect ending to a perfect vacation.

Perfect, except for one thing.

I still hadn't let him kiss me.

For everything he'd made me feel since we met, for every pang of longing I hadn't known in years, I owed him at least that. I don't even care who knows about it. I've earned my kiss.

With the music stopped, the two of us are plunged in conspicuous silence again. The bristle of my dress as I steady myself on my knees and inch toward him hisses in the night. Miguel lets the guitar slide off his lap with a soft thud that sounds too loud in the semi-darkness.

With just inches separating us, he lifts one hand against my cheek and pulls me just close enough so that our faces feel suspended in anticipation, our nerve endings enflamed and throbbing. I can feel the heat of his closeness.

This is it. I close my eyes and breach the last tiny space, laying my lips against his. The simmering buildup of a week of repressed desire ignites us both. His mouth crushes mine, his tongue parting my lips, his hands circling up and down my sides, setting the whole of me on fire.

When a stray finger sweeps across the side of my breast, he stops, looking straight at my face, as if waiting for me to push him back.

A few seconds tick away, and I don't say anything. The same finger then snakes up my arm, along my shoulder blade, and with his thumb, he pushes the strap of my dress aside. Instead of hiking it back up, I flick the other strap and reach around to unhook my gauzy, barely there bra.

He gapes for a second, as if he really didn't expect this to happen, before catching himself. *"Te llevaré al cielo,"* he whispers.

He holds me as delicately as though I were a porcelain doll, and lifts me up and over his lap so that I'm straddling him.

That's when I feel him. And the realization submerges me under a wave of pure panic.

I've only really ever seen one real live penis in my whole life. Pictures don't count. Sure, there were isolated events in the backseats of cars, which may have involved some over-the-jeans action, some vigorous rubbing maybe, but really, Brian was it. I feel like some sort of born-again virgin.

I'm suddenly so nervous, I'm sure he's going to think I've never done this before. I feel like a bad joke.

But when he kisses me again, his tongue taking me like it could fill the whole of me, sending the cars, motorbikes, the dim glow of dozens of balconies surrounding us into soft focus, my anxiety fades along with the rest of world. All that's left is now, this night, this balcony, and this man who wants me just as painfully as I want him.

He moves in sync with the sucking and pounding of the sea against the stones of the *Malecón*. His touch betrays both the deftness of a man who's never met a woman he couldn't seduce, and the tenderness that made each one feel as though there had never been another.

And when my body convulses with the kind of pleasure I thought I was just not equipped to feel, I hear the last words he said to me play over and over in my head.

Te llevaré al cielo.

I'll take you to heaven.

23

Something slimy and vaguely disturbing induces me to flutter open an eyelid, braving the hazy early-morning rays. And I'm not just talking about the drop of bird shit that just splattered on my forehead, although I have to say that's pretty disgusting too.

It took me that nanosecond between sleep and dead-to-the-world unconsciousness to put a name to it, but that uncomfortable sliminess sloshing around in the pit of my stomach is dread. I ought to know all about that feeling by now, and its cousins, fear and foreboding, but then again, it's not every day you wake up to the pink light of dawn and the distant chattering of housewives from the balconies and rooftops around you. Next to a man who even in the middle of deep, blissful slumber, with what looks like a small pool of drool forming at the corner of his mouth, is still the most beautiful creature you've ever laid eyes on.

You would have been dazed and confused too.

I gently reach over to the closest potted plant, snap off a leaf, and use it to wipe my forehead before the greasy glob slides down my temple.

A cool breeze blows over us, making me shiver, and I feel him stir beside me.

Oh God, what have I done?

I squeeze my eyes shut and pull my knees toward my chest, bare under my flimsy dress. It doesn't work. Snippets of last night, the *paladar*, the dancing, the *Malecón*, and then . . .

Dread isn't just washing over me now, it's flogging me, choking me, searing through my head like a violent migraine.

How could I have done this? In three years of admittedly less-than-perfect togetherness, I've never sunk so low. I've never even come close. I thought about it—how could I not with a guy like Tom working not three feet away from me—but to go from there to waking up half-naked on someone's balcony, someone I've known for all of a couple of days, next to a semi-stranger . . .

This is beyond awful.

Miguel stirs again, this time yawning audibly. Beside me, his body stiffens into a long stretch, and when it finally relaxes, he drapes an arm across my jutted hip.

But despite feeling lower than pond scum over what I've done to Brian, to our relationship, I don't feel one ounce of regret over the indulgence itself.

Not for all the world would I take back last night. Intermingled with the pangs of foreboding in my gut are stirrings of delicious lust every time my mind flashes up a snippet of a heated memory.

And no matter what happens when Miguel wakes up and realizes that the conquering is done, that he can drop the act, I don't care. I still wouldn't take it back. And as for what kind of girl that makes me, I care even less. I've spent my life making sure everyone thinks of me as a nice, sensible, accomplished young woman, and for what? Because for all of my parents' good intentions, or anyone else who's ever felt compelled to share with me their opinion on what I should or shouldn't do, they don't actually have to live with the consequences. I do. And if this fear, this uncertainty, this hovering-over-the-edge-of-an-abyss feeling is what comes after the most incredible night of my life—well, that's tough, I guess.

I reach down toward Miguel's hand and squeeze, curling my back into his chest. This must have woken him up, because he squeezes my hand back. We lie together, listening to the increasingly animated sounds of the street below us, trucks laboring up the hill to the Hotel Nacional, drivers calling out to each other in quick, lively tones, sporadic honking, in complete peace and quiet.

"No podemos quedar más, mi vida," he whispers in my ear after a few minutes of blissful morning laziness.

But just the thought of getting up, leaving this place, and going back to face reality is enough to send painful cramps searing through my gut.

I turn around and wrap my arms around his neck. "What are we going to do?"

He strokes my hair. "You can call me at the hotel, send me *cartas.*"

"I don't suppose you have an e-mail address I can use?"

He laughs, not dignifying my stupid rich North American–ass question with an answer.

Honestly, you're a good Lebanese girl your entire life, and the one—*one*—time you throw caution to the cedar-scented winds, it has to be with someone who can't afford to pick up the phone and call you, much less scrape together enough money for a five-minute stop at an Internet café. Fate, with a sharp kick in the shins and a crackling, evil laugh, is mocking me once again. Dangling total and utter bliss in front of me like a swaying pendulum and snapping it back just when I reach for it.

There's a timid knock at the veranda door. It must be Sophie.

"Just a minute!" I straighten up next to Miguel and prepare to make myself somewhat presentable to the world, given that I don't have so much as a toothbrush with me, let alone a tube of lipstick or a mascara wand. And my panties are nowhere to be seen.

I don't exactly feel comfortable asking Miguel where he tossed them last night.

Speaking of whom, he's still lying on the ground, his hands now webbed behind his head, looking up at me through half-closed eyelids.

"Stop looking so smug." I swat his thigh.

"*¿Cómo?*" He raises an eyebrow at me, though I expect my body language gave away my full meaning. If his Cheshire cat grin is anything to go by, then I'm right.

And in one swift movement, he raises himself beside me, smacks my bottom loud and hard, and them plants a long, crushing kiss on my lips before jumping to his feet.

I love this man so much.

"She's going to kill us, isn't she?" Sophie eyes me with sprightly resolve. She's feeling guilty over leaving Jaz behind on our last night here, but not so much that she would take back her own blissful—if fleeting—experience. And Guillermo, true to his promises and wacky driving style, had gotten us back to Varadero in a record-setting one hour and ten minutes, making up for the time we lost stopping for a breakfast of croissants and strong Cuban coffee from the bakery around the corner from Javier's building.

"She might be a little scary for a day or two, but she'll come around. It's just one night, after all," I say as much for my own benefit as for Sophie's.

I reach into my bra (recovered—thank God—but sadly, no news on the panty front), extract the plastic room key, and slide it into the slot. I ease the heavy door open, and as quietly as humanly possible, Sophie and I tiptoe onto the coral tiles—and find the familiar shape of Jaz's back hidden under the sheets in one of the double beds.

"Great, she's still asleep. Hurry up and get in the other bed. . . . Maybe we'll get lucky and she'll think we just came in really late last night." Miles beyond modesty and already half-naked, I unhook my bra and search under the covers for a T-shirt, not bothering to dissimulate my chest from Sophie, but keeping the bottom half of my body camouflaged.

"Ali . . . you hear something?"

"Shh! Just get in bed."

But then I hear it too. A sort of clinking sound coming from the bathroom. Like someone tinkering around with eye-makeup remover or a toothbrush or something. Before the connectors in our supposedly higher-educated brains snap together, the bathroom doorknob twists open, unveiling a very stunned, very naked (and clearly very chilly) Mike.

"*Aaaahhhhhhhhh!*"

I can't really say who started screaming first, but at any rate, Sophie's shrieks and mine, intercepted with repeated bursts of "what the fuck" courtesy of our friend Mike, were soon joined by Jaz's, whose morning was clearly getting off on the wrong side of a pick-me-up shag.

"What the hell are you two doing here?"

My only consolation is that Jaz is too underdressed at the present moment to go hunting for sharp objects to hurl at us.

"It's our r—"

"Get out! Out! Out!"

As if we couldn't do that fast enough, Sophie and I both scurry backwards toward the door and narrowly miss tripping over a still dumbstruck and still denuded Mike, who upon catching us staring at him in disbelief for a split second, shuffles both hands over his shriveled button mushroom before we spill out of the room and slam the door behind us.

"I can't believe she'd do this." Sophie squints at the early-morning sunbathers stretched out on the shore from under the shade of a straw-thatched umbrella. In our extreme haste to get the hell out of the room, we forgot to snatch our sunglasses from the top of the bamboo dresser.

I sigh. I really don't know what to say. Why wouldn't she do this? I had known all along this wasn't exactly the kind of vacation she'd expected, given that she's mostly into scouting the bars, clubs, and restaurants with the hottest media buzz, and lying on a stretch of beach that Paris Hilton or Lindsay Lohan may have treaded on before the spot was discovered by the paparazzi. This is a girl who religiously reads *InStyle*'s top getaway locations to me out loud over the phone. I should have known Cuba's rich history and off-the-beaten-track flavor wouldn't figure as a major attraction compared to, say, the *Sex and the City* New York Tour.

And then, of course, there's the small matter of Ben. I should have listened better. Paid attention more every time she went on an angry Ben tirade. Isn't that what friends are for? Who was I to pass judgment on her love life? Like mine's the picture of honesty and respect. *Not.* No wonder she felt compelled to run off with the first male, no matter how sorry a specimen, to show her any attention.

I totally suck.

I lie back on the lounge chair, looking conspicuously out of place in my outfit from last night. As stupid-coked-out-tourist-passed-out-on-the-beach-after-too-much-partying as I must seem to the lifeguards and water sports staff meandering along the shore, I'm glad for the last few precious minutes I've stolen to stare at the sparkling blue expanse in front of me, to rub my feet in the soft powdery sand, to feel the scorching sun beat down on my face one last time. . . . Wait a minute, where did the sun go?

"Jaz! You found us." I sit upright, stuttering and gaping like the clueless idiot I feel like.

She hovers above me for a few seconds, eyeing me angrily, not saying a word. This isn't helping me feel any less shitty. Or nervous.

"It was easy," she says. "There aren't too many white girls in whorey outfits prowling the beach looking like they spent last night getting busy against a dirty alley wall."

Ouch.

My jaw drops. So does Sophie's. For one thing, after five and a half days of baking in the sun, I can hardly be described as white anymore. Second, there's nothing whorelike about my appearance, except maybe the day-old-caked-mascara spread around my general eye area. That's it. And honestly, if you were to take one look around the beach, you'd see that save for the inappropriate attire, Sophie and I have fared much better than, say, the topless German chick over there who's so hungover, she couldn't be bothered to haul her sorry behind to the toilet to puke up last night's booze binge.

I take a deep breath, reminding myself that it's the fury talking, and that I've already established that Jaz has every right to be furious.

Still.

"Jaz, I think we need to talk," I say slowly.

"Why?" She runs her hand through her curls distractedly. "So you can give me a quick and dirty lecture about my sorry love life and then get back to giggling and gossiping about your fabulous Cuban studs? No thanks. I need to pack. I just came down here to tell you this vacation's been a complete disaster, and that this friendship is clearly over. You've both been selfish, especially you, Ali—after all, the whole reason I agreed to come here was to make you feel better over flunking the UFE, and then you go off like we're on some sort of booty ride. Let me ask you, did you give one thought to Brian this whole time?"

As I'm listening to her, the pulsing glow of my face transfers to the rest of my body. I'm flashing hot, then cold, feeling sweat form along my brow and chills running up my back by turn. I start to shake from the sheer unfairness of everything she's said.

"How dare you!" I dart up from the lounger, losing all control of myself.

I feel people around us turn to look.

"Ali, relax." Sophie rubs my back, whispering softly as though crooning to a baby. "Not now. Don't make it worse."

"Make it worse? How much worse does it get?"

Sophie reaches for me again, but I silence her with my hand. I said we needed to talk. No time like the present.

Jaz is staring me down, her arms folded over her chest.

"Tell me, Jaz, exactly how do you know what I have or haven't thought about Brian? Just how do you think I've felt about everything that's happened to me here?"

"Seemed to me like you loved every second of it." Her glare would freeze the polar ice caps to pre–global warming levels.

"It was torture."

"I'll bet."

"I love Brian—"

"Really? It shows."

I hold back the venom for one second. One second only. Then it comes spewing out.

"And how the fuck would you know when you haven't had one meaningful relationship in your entire life? You want to know if I ever spared a thought for Brian? I never stopped thinking about Brian, and my parents, and what I was doing, but I don't expect someone whose most long-term commitment is a booty call arrangement to understand."

There.

In the space of about a second and a half, Jaz's face has gone from haughty to ashen. My heart turns into a gooey blob and drops somewhere in the vicinity of my knees. Some girl-bonding vacation.

Sophie sinks back into the lounge chair and clutches her temples between her hands.

"Well." Jaz's voices shakes with barely contained rage. "I'm sorry we can't all have a bevy of guys falling at our feet at any given point in time. Some of us have to do the best with what we've got." With that, she swings around toward the hotel.

"Jaz, wait!"

She doesn't stop. I lunge after her and manage to get a hold of her shirt.

"Finish what you started. What *we* started. You've had a problem with me from the beginning. From the first day you set foot on this island, you had issues. Do you expect me to believe that one guy and one evening spent by yourself is all there is to it?"

She doesn't look at me, but neither does she try to break free of my tight grasp on her T-shirt. I take it as a positive sign.

"Jaz . . . you and Sophie are my oldest friends. You're my family. You can be as angry with me as you like, but I love you. That's why I can't stand what Ben does to you. You're smart and pretty and young and so outgoing and just . . . fabulous. We wouldn't have been friends for so long if you weren't. You're not going to find the right guy if your mind can't let go of that piece of scum that doesn't deserve you."

"What about you?" She turns around, and I can see she's crying. "You keep saying you love Brian, but if that were true, how did you fall so hard for Miguel?"

I open my mouth to offer a ready-made, manufactured, and packaged response, just like I always do, but it won't come out. They're both staring expectantly at me. I'm cornered.

"Brian's perfect . . . on paper."

"I know he is. That's why I hate it when you flaunt your perfect relationship under my nose all the time."

"But you just admitted you think my love life is in shambles—"

"You have someone who loves you. And he's not exactly riffraff. On top of that, you get to live the hot Latin lover fantasy. You get to choose to go back to your safe, predictable little life with someone who's probably going to propose any day now, or give it all up and run away with Cuban boy toy to Spain or Bolivia or some ridiculous place like that. It's like, 'Gee, Jaz, what should I do? And oh, by the way, Ben's an asshole. Dump him.'"

I look into her tear-streaked face, unable to believe what I'm hearing. Somewhere hidden among all those words, I think she admitted to being jealous. Of me. I'm too stunned to react. Not that I don't know better than to actually accuse her of jealousy out loud. I don't have a death wish. Yet.

Do I admit that Brian already proposed? Somehow I'm not convinced that she'd take the revelation for the life-complicating, gut-wrenchingly unwelcome development that it was. She'd probably yell at me for having it too easy again.

"I know I'm not one to talk when it comes to guys," she begins, "but you're my friend. I want what's best for you, and it kills me to see you short-changing yourself."

"Me too, Jaz." I sigh.

We gape at each other, defeated, exhausted from the emotion and the tears.

"It's not as easy-breezy at it looks from the outside . . . ," I say.

"Yeah, and I really do care about Ben. Look, I know there isn't a therapist out there that would condone my attitude, but the truth is that it's too hard to end it when I have absolutely no prospects. . . . You've never known what it's like to be lonely, Ali. How old where you when you and Brian started dating? Eighteen? Nineteen? You were a baby. You still are. Just run away with Miguel into the sunset and don't look back."

"It's not that easy either. He proposed." Bombshell dropped.

Two sets of eyes widen at me like I'd just sprouted a pink fluo Mohawk.

"When?" Sophie's first contribution to the face-off.

"At Ranya's wedding."

"That was weeks ago," Sophie says.

"When were you going to tell us?" Jaz looks appalled.

"It's not that I didn't want to tell you, for God's sake, of course I wanted to tell you! I was afraid . . . I was afraid you'd get all excited and gushy and girly and get me wrapped up in the excitement when all I wanted was to forget it ever happened." I sink into the sand and muffle my sobs into my palms.

Almost instantly I feel two pairs of arms wrap around me, rocking me back and forth. It was an unfair statement. How could I have such little faith in my best friends that I didn't think they would understand? I deserve to be flogged. They should get in line.

"And then M-Miguel happened—" I can barely get the words out through the sharp intakes of air and the violent sobs. "—and now I'm so confused—"

"Shhh . . ." Sophie's voice is firm and reassuring. "We need a round of drinks before we can even think of having this conversation."

"I'm thinking champagne on the plane. What are the odds we can get an upgrade to business class?" Jaz offers.

"We can always say she was dumped at the altar. Who would be so heartless as to resist?" Sophie counters.

"S-so does that mean that you still want to be my friend?" I manage between sniffles.

"Pull yourself together, you sound like a kindergarten kid with serious self-esteem issues." In Jaz-speak, this is a profound apology. I smile through my disheveled, frizzy hair, my dirty face and day-old makeup.

"Just do me a favor," she continues. "Please don't give Brian a big slurpy kiss at the terminal when you see him like these past six days were some kind of dream. You've just single-handedly confirmed my theory that couples that are into major PDA are really just compensating for deficiencies in their relationship. It makes me sick."

"No worries there. I made sure to get Sara to pick us up from the airport."

As if I'd have any clue what I'd say to Brian if I saw him now. I stand up and wipe the thousands of clotted sand specks from my legs and butt. My life as I know it may be over by the end of this day. It's probably already over, except that I haven't really felt the ramifications yet. And now my last solid pillar, the "thing" so preciously amorphous for words that I've taken it for granted for so long, is on shaky ground. My friendships.

⤸◯

I have no idea if I'll ever see Miguel again. But that thought is too depressing to bear right now, so I have to tell myself that I will. Even if I have a hard time believing my own words.

Hi, Mom, Dad, Sara, Sami, Auntie Maryam, Ranya . . . Dodi! Nice of you to join us. Have you met my husband, Miguel? No? I brought him back with me from Cuba. No, I couldn't have just brought a souvenir. He's a person with thoughts and feelings, and I love him. No, actually, I don't really know what they are, seeing as communication can be a bit spotty sometimes. But he's great in the sack, so it's all cool. What? What about Cancún? Oh, that's a long story.

Right.

Saudi Arabia, here I come.

"Anything to declare, miss?"

Why do they automatically assume I'm a miss? Couldn't I just be a really spiffy Mrs.? That's what I could be a year from now. (No way you could book a venue in Montreal in under a year—not unless it's the Bar-B-Barn Chicken n' Ribs.) Mrs. Brian Hayes. Or, Mrs. Miguel . . . Miguel what? It must be on the scrap piece of paper he tore off the side of a sailing brochure in the hotel lobby and scribbled his address on.

"Miss?"

"I'm sorry, what was the question?" I flash high-alert red as the immigration officer inhales sharply and graces me with a look that says, *I'm this close to slapping you with the Customs Special right about now.*

"Did you bring back anything from Cuba?"

I wonder what he'd do if I said, "Yes, as a matter of fact. A husband."

"No."

"No cigars?"

"Nope."

"Rum?"

"Oh, right. One bottle. Sorry."

He glares and scribbles something on the card. "Souvenirs?" More than my mind can handle.

"A painting. Twenty-five dollars."

He doesn't look convinced, but stamps my passport anyway and motions me to pass with a curt nod. I'm free. Sort of. There's still the luggage to look for. I meander over to the sliding conveyor belt, in no particular hurry. Oh, look, the baggage handlers are picking up the luggage off the rotating rubber surface and tossing each jam-packed piece to the side, presumably to clear the way. How thoughtful.

I spot my Guess monogrammed carrying case from a mile away (see—it pays to get distinctive luggage), cut through the scavenging hordes, and roll my way to the gate. I'll find Sara while Jaz and Sophe look for their own bags.

I push myself onto the tips of my toes in search of a tall, lanky seventeen-year-old with wild Lebanese hair that's never seen a bottle of anti-frizz cream or an ionic flatiron.

Instead, I see a man, young, average height, with sandy blond hair, his steel gray eyes boring right into me.

Brian.

Part THREE

24

Brian. Shit.

We stand a few feet apart, motionless, while the travel-weary masses brush against our stiff bodies in slow motion. What can I possibly say to make this awkward, frozen silence just a little less . . . well, awkward and frozen?

"Where's Sara?"

Not quite the sparkling fix-all quip I wished I could have come up with, but it's better than the alternative: more awkward, frozen silence.

"That's it, Ali? That's all you have to say?"

I let the plastic handle on my carrying case go and rush toward him. My arms, like twin magnets, lock tightly, if stiffly, around his neck. I hold my breath. The half minute it takes him to return the hug feels like forever. But he does. I exhale. My world won't come crashing down on me just yet. Not yet.

My relief is short-lived, though. Brian pulls back with much greater ease than it took him to reach out to me.

"When were you going to tell me about Cuba, Ali? Would you have told me at all if I weren't standing here right now?"

I don't understand how he can look at me so intently, without wavering, when all I want to do is run as far from here as I possibly can.

I could pull the shifting-blame stunt I seem to be so adept at, the same one I resorted to the night he proposed, but I can't do it.

274 * NADINE DAJANI

All my strength has drained right out of my pores, right through my mismatched khaki gauchos and Juicy tube top, ridiculous-looking under the winter coat and scarf I'd pulled out of my luggage just minutes ago.

Do I ask him how he knew when and where to pick me up? What must have gone through his mind when Sara told him to watch for a flight from Varadero instead of Cancún? Poor Sara. I'd put her between the proverbial rock and a hard place. Physically stop Brian from greeting me at the airport or come up with some fantastic lie as to why he shouldn't surprise me. Not everyone's as great a liar as I am.

Or maybe my phone call tipped him off. Maybe he'd spent the last week scouring the newspapers for a mention of my name on the UFE pass lists and then put two and two together.

No. I won't ask. It would just make matters worse, I think. If I've learned anything from years of lying to my mother, it's this: When cornered, don't say a thing. Let the other person do all the talking.

He doesn't know about Miguel. This is just about Cuba and the UFE results. I can still fix this.

But do I want to? Maybe this is my chance, the one I've been subconsciously waiting for . . . well . . . for a while. I can walk away. Right here, right now. Actually, I can confess, and then watch *him* walk away.

"Brian . . . I . . . there's something I need to . . . Oh my God." I try to grab my right temple with my hand, but it's shaking so violently, I can't control it. "Do you think my parents know?" I manage to say before dissolving completely in tears right there at the arrivals gate, sobbing and gulping in huge quantities of air.

He doesn't budge at first. I wonder if he's going to slap me. Of course he'd never do anything like that, no matter how far I pushed him. Then again, who doesn't have their boiling point?

I want to stop crying, to pull myself together, but I can't. This is it. I'm going to get dumped. In an airport terminal. No matter how dysfunctional our relationship had been at times, I never imagined Brian and I would end up like this.

What seems to me like an eternity later, I'm conscious of being steadied by a pair of slender but strong arms, Brian's, and being led, my face buried in the sleeves of my soft cashmere coat, across the mezzanine, then a blast of air so cold that it practically freezes my tears on impact. The sound of different footsteps reverberates off the concrete surfaces of the sheltered parking lot. If Sophie and Yasmin are near, they're as stone-cold silent as the walls around me. Someone hands me a tissue.

"It's okay, Ali. Just take it easy for now. We'll talk about this later."

Brian. So I'm not getting dumped right this minute. I'm not sure whether this is a relief or not. Wouldn't it be nice if I didn't have to decide? If some outside force acted for me.

Brian eases me into the front seat of his very sensible, very plain beige Corolla, and fumbles with the seat belt. The passenger doors behind me open and close, and the car purrs quietly to life, as though it too didn't want to upset me in my condition.

I wipe my nose and steady my breathing and tell myself I'll tell him tomorrow.

25

I haven't told Brian yet. To his credit, he's been giving me some much-needed space. Then again, it's only been a day.

What I have done, though, is think about Jaz. A lot. We'd bickered before but never anything like that last day in Cuba. Am I really that self-centered? Narcissistic? I always thought I was out to please everyone around me. Why else would I have gone into accounting? Because of that zany buzz I get every morning when I wake up, ready and eager to take on the financial world?

That must be it.

And what about Sophie? Why didn't Jaz lash out at her like she did at me? If it were anyone besides those two girls, I might call foul play. A devious *Survivor*-style alliance. But I've known them practically all my life—the part that counts, anyway. I owe it to Jaz to sort out this . . . this *thing* that happened between us, one way or the other. Thing is, I've never been terribly good at confrontation. I've never been convinced that people really mean it when they claim all they want from you is the truth. I'm with Jack Nicholson on this one. Most people can't handle the truth. Exhibit A, my mother. Twenty-two years old and three years into a relationship, I'm still not allowed to sleep over at Brian's place. Honestly, what does she think we do when we're together? Hold hands?

Speaking of my mother, if she knows anything about this

mess—any of it, the UFE scores, the Cuba trip, my troubles with Brian—she hasn't shown it. She just asked me how my trip was when I walked in last night, and went back to watching her usual soaps on the Arabic-language satellite channel. Denial ain't just a river Egyptian literary heroines and B-list actresses hurl them-selves into to end their tragic lives. It's also a place most Arab mothers call home.

"Good morning, Aline." Soula brushes past me on the way to Sid Cohen's office, the one she seems to have usurped in light of his golf addiction, a jumble of keys in her palm, a dishwater-gray trench coat draped over one arm, and half a dozen files in the other.

Oh my God.

I hold my breath. This is it. I'm going to get canned. Can't say I didn't come mentally prepared, in as much as you can be when you know you're showing up to the office just to hear the words, *You're fired.*

There's no way *The Apprentice* is worse than this. I'll take Donald Trump's comb-over and his stiff acting over Soula's mer-ciless scowl any day of the week.

With all the bustle and hurry of an eighty-five-year-old Ital-ian matriarch brewing her signature tomato sauce, Soula unlocks the room, releases the stack of files onto the rich mahogany sur-face of the desk, hooks her coat behind the door, and snaps her laptop open.

She fumbles some more around the desk, opening and closing files, hooking up a mouse to her laptop, staring at the screen, and scrolling.

I'm torn between gaping and pretending it's just another ho-hum day in the life of a lowly junior accountant. What the hell is wrong with her? Why won't she just call me into the office and put me out of my misery?

Finally, a few minutes later, she lowers the screen, stands up, and saunters over to my cubicle.

I hold my breath.

"I have a meeting in a few minutes"—she glances at her watch—"and then another one this afternoon. The files on my desk need photocopying before the second meeting. I also need you to compile a list of outstanding creditors and other pertinent stakeholders for each one of those files. You know how to do that, right?"

Actually, I don't. Too busy logging hours at the Xerox station to do much, you know, *accounting*.

"Yes, of course." Tom's bound to walk in here any second now. He'll show me. I can trust him.

"Tom's in Phoenix this week doing some on-site testing. I'm counting on your help in the meantime. That means some over-time is going to be expected of you."

This exchange could not be any less coherent were it taking place on the set of *Pee-wee's Playhouse,* with Hulk Hogan as a guest star.

"Um, sure. I mean, I don't see a problem with that."

"Good."

Could it be that she still doesn't know I failed the UFE? It hardly seems possible. For a fraction of a second, my heart leaps at the possibility, however remote, that I might still have a few days in my fool's paradise. But at the same time another part of me is fuming. I can't put up with this charade a minute longer.

Soula nods curtly and disappears around the corner.

What was that? I need information, and I need it now. I had come in extra early this morning in the hopes of running into as few people as I could manage. It had worked—for the first hour I spent in this building today, tiptoeing along hallways and sprinting from behind one large plastic plant to another, I was convinced it was just me and the janitor. Until Soula showed up. But the faraway beeping of phones and the humming of desktops coming to life tells me that this state of seclusion is about to come to an end.

Must make contact with home base. Aphro. She'll know how to break even the bleakest news to me without either lying or crushing any remaining microcosms of hope left in my soul.

I lurch for my phone and dial. She doesn't even wait for a full ring before picking up.

"What. The *fuck*. Happened to you?"

"I know you've got call display and everything, but is that really any way to speak in a professional environment?"

"Ali, don't mess with my nerves. I can't take it. I've just spent the last week imagining either your parents found out about the UFE and shipped you straight back to Lebanon, or else you had emptied your bank account and made off to some island in the middle of the night. I had no idea what to do."

"You didn't tip off my parents, did you?"

"Are you kidding me? You forget I'm Greek, almost thirty, and still living with mine. I'm shocked they haven't arranged my marriage yet. And stop changing the damn subject. Where were you, and why the hell couldn't you at least send me an e-mail?"

"So I guess everyone knows about the UFE?" My heart sinks deeper with every syllable.

There's a brief lull in the conversation. I can imagine Aphro shrugging at the other end of the line.

"Yes. So what? This isn't exactly a literacy test where you have to come up with two hundred and fifty words about your first pet. It's the UFE. People fail. Smart people. It happens."

"But I've never failed anything in my entire life. My parents are going to want to kill themselves. I'll be forever known as the kid who showed all that promise and then fell flat on her face."

"Now you're talking crazy. You think anybody here cares you failed? That's old news. They are, however, in awe of the sheer size of your balls, my friend. Who just doesn't show up for a flight with, like, thirty of their friends and colleagues? And then disappears off the face of the earth? It's like straight out of a movie."

"I just switched my Cancún ticket to one for Cuba. I spent the last week in Varadero. See? Nothing mysterious or ballsy about it. If anything, I couldn't handle their pity for a whole week. Not exactly what I'd call a mature, rolling-with-the-punches response to adversity."

"At least you've given everyone something new to talk about. So how was Cuba?"

"I can't talk about it right now." Mostly because every time I think about Miguel, I feel like the guy who's having his still-beating heart ripped out of his chest and then shown to him in *Indiana Jones and the Temple of Doom*. But I don't say that. "We'll save that discussion for happy hour. By this I mean an afternoon when I manage to get out my pajamas and meet you at Thursday's after you're done at work."

"I'm hearing random words coming out of your mouth that mean nothing to me."

"I'm talking about my impending unemployment, dork." I make a "duh" face even though she can't see it.

"Why? Did Soula say something?"

"That's just the thing . . . no."

"Then what's your problem?"

"Diane said they can officially send me the way of Betamax technology if I flunked."

"Diane's still on her mysterious personal leave thing. My money's on plastic surgery. Evelyn thinks it might be an abortion. She swears the guy she's been dating is a New Agey aromatherapist dude. Not exactly husband-and-potential-father material . . ."

"Aphro, focus!"

"Sorry. Yeah, anyway, so she's still away, and really, she gets the last word on who stays and who goes, unless, of course, a partner has it in for you. Who's the partner in charge over at your area?"

"Sid Cohen, I think. That's what the plaque on the office door says. I've never seen him. I guess when you've been around as long as he has, showing up for work is optional. Soula's running the show."

"So don't piss her off. Sit tight, work your ass off, and who knows. Maybe you'll get a break."

I mull that over for a second. Maybe the reason Soula didn't make a fuss about the UFE results is because she really doesn't know. Or she knows and doesn't care. After all, Tom's out for the week, right? What good would it do her if I got the boot at this particular point in time? And who knows, if I show her I can do just as good a job as Tom, what's to stop her from fighting to keep me? The way to a workaholic's heart has got to be, well . . . through work.

"Thanks, Fro, you're the best."

"What? What did I say?"

"Listen, I gotta go, but we'll talk later."

"What about Cuba? You didn't tell me—"

"Later, Fro."

And I hang up. I've got work to do.

It's funny how it sounded so easy at the time, but really, if I have to read one more insolvency memorandum I might just have to impale myself. And I've been at this twenty-seven minutes. I think I need some more coffee.

"Hey! Ali, you're back. Nice tan! Makes you look really . . . ethnic."

Penny whips around the corner, her cheeks still red from the cold November air, and flops into her swivel chair in the cubicle beside mine.

"Thanks," I mumble into my cold, half-empty Ernsworth mug.

"How was the trip?" she asks, sprightly as a Katie Couric clone on speed.

Where's my manufactured, premediated, question-quelling response? I don't have one.

"Um. Fine." How much does she know? Everyone who would've been with me on the trip is from the Audit department. Penny's never been in Audit.

"Take any pictures?" she soldiers on.

"I did, tons, but I lost my camera in the airport somewhere on the way back. I think it was the airport, anyway." *Moi:* one; dignity: zero.

"Oh God, that's terrible!"

"I know." I still haven't said pictures of what, so I can't technically be accused of lying.

Thankfully, Penny's cell phone breaks into a tinny version of Gwen's "Hollaback Girl" before she can continue.

"Jem! Where have you been, you naughty girl? . . ."

I tune out and turn to my screen, clicking on the tiny postcard-shaped icon on the bottom left corner of my laptop, silently pleading with the Goddess of Corporate Mercy to save my bored and weary soul. Nothing. Not even spam. I would have at least expected something from Sophie, the only person capable of understanding the depths of my depression. Well, almost. She doesn't have to explain to her boyfriend of three years that she . . . er, experienced a minor slip of judgment mere days after he proposed.

Must not think about inevitable demise and possible excommunication from Lebanese community, not to mention the sharp kick back into the world of Singletondom. This is surprisingly not so difficult to do. Somehow my mind zeroes in on the pitifully disorganized state of my workspace and decides it can't go on unless the lapse in cleanliness is remedied.

I busy myself gathering all manner of writing tools scattered haphazardly around my cubicle and group them into piles: red pens, green pens, yellow highlighters, paper clips, while trying very hard to tune out another one of Penny's social life bulletins, being broadcast as we speak.

"Bollocks, Jemima, I know very well that you can make it. . . . Well, I can't be expected to cancel with Alistair, can I?" Long pause.

"But, Jem! I've bought a new dress and everything! Fine, then. I'll just have to take poor Simon out myself and tell him that his date is out snogging some other bloke!"

Click.

Well. That's the end of that. It's also my cue to get some work done myself. But . . . wait a minute . . . could this possibly be the answer to at least one of my problems?

"Umm . . . Penny, you all right there, sweetie?"

I'm not being selfish. A tad opportunistic, maybe, but really, I just don't see Jaz objecting to this brand of selfishness. Not when she stands to benefit. At least I really, really hope she will.

"Oh, it's nothing, really," she says, shrugging her shoulders and sucking enthusiastically at the tattered pencil between her teeth. She turns her chair slowly toward her computer like she's toying with the notion of perhaps doing some work, but then she swivels back, crosses her legs, and leans forward conspiratorially.

"It's my cousin Simon," she begins, pulling the pencil out of her mouth. "He's visiting from England, and I was supposed to spend Saturday night showing him around, you know, not that anything here could ever impress him, of course, being a Londoner and all, but he's thinking of doing some graduate studies at McGill, so I thought he would appreciate a little stroll about the city. It would've been brilliant if Jem could take him, seeing as she's from Hertfordshire and Aunt Joyce wouldn't want him getting too attached to the local girls—"

"Of course." I smile and nod politely, gently prodding her along to the crux of the master plan.

"Anyway, she's decided she'd rather spend the evening sucking face with an imbecile she met on the Plateau. Honestly, he's one step up from those squeegee hooligans."

"The bitch!"

"I know. So that leaves me to babysit poor cousin Simon when I've got a delectable dinner date of my own." Penny pouts then smiles deviously at me and opens her mouth to rant some more, but I cut her off.

"You know, my friend and I were planning to go out for a casual dinner tonight. We certainly wouldn't mind if . . . I mean, I'm sure I could persuade Brian to come alo—"

"That's a marvelous idea! Oh, Ali, you're the best!"

"Me? Please, don't mention it."

So, besides securing a peace offering for Jaz in the form of a blind date—who I seriously hope is not an ax murderer or a dead ringer for Steve Buscemi—I've bought myself one more day to think about what I'm going to tell Brian. Unless, of course, he rips the guts right out of my plan and turns me down.

26

It took some serious convincing, along with multiple promises that we would finally have The Talk tonight after dinner, but I'd managed to drag Brian to the Koji's Treehouse, one of Montreal's hippest sushi bars. As to whether or not this was the best idea, the jury's still out.

"Cuba, Ali? And you couldn't bring yourself to tell me?" Brian's eyes flicker with controlled anger. "Didn't you think I'd understand?"

He's sitting next to me on one of the straw tatami mats laid neatly around the sunken wood table. Behind us, elegant rice-paper screens are drawn firmly together, distancing us from the tapping of chopsticks against china and the gentle murmur of the restaurant's general dining area. Under normal circumstances I would have found the seclusion, framed by the soft light of paper lanterns and mural depictions of Japanese warriors, to be roman-tic. But today I sit here, with my legs tucked under me, a stiff gin and tonic in my hand, wishing I were anywhere else.

This was *such* a bad idea. Something was bound to go wrong. I hadn't expected that Simon might turn out to be a gentleman and insist on picking up Jaz himself. His gallantry has had the unfortunate consequence of leaving Brian and me alone together when I'd hoped for just a little more time to summon up what little nerve I have left.

"It's not like I planned it, you know. I just . . . panicked. I couldn't think of anything better to do than run away." I'm having a very hard time meeting his stare.

"Like you did that night at your cousin's wedding?"

Crap. The proposal. I was trying so hard to forget.

I flash red hot and then break into a cold sweat that soaks the right armhole of my silk Joie tunic while damp spots sprout across the back of my neck. "I have no idea why you're bringing this up now."

"Ali . . ." He takes a slow, deliberate breath, as though meditating on how best to deal with my childishness. Then, sliding closer to me on the mat, he takes my clammy hand in his. "What's happening to us?" His eyes search my face pleadingly. For what, I don't know. "I thought we were going somewhere. That we wanted the same things."

He raises his free hand to my face and with all the tenderness he can muster, pushes a loose strand of my hair behind my ear. Far from having the desired effect, the simple gesture catapults me back to the sound of waves crashing against stone, to a salt-and-sea-scented night, to Miguel's fingertips on my face. With Brian holding my hand and Miguel in my head, guilt shoots into my chest like venom and tightens into a ball of poisonous rage, directed squarely at the man in front of me. I hate him because he isn't Miguel, and I hate myself more for thinking that.

But what's mind-bogglingly infuriating is how nice Brian is being about all of this. Why doesn't he get up and stomp around and shout out at the top of his lungs the first cruel thought to cross his mind? Somewhere inside I'm waiting for him to say something insensitive, or petty, or clueless—anything that'll give me an excuse to fight back. But I might as well be waiting for the Manolo Blahnik fairy to leave a little something high and pointy under my bed. It just isn't going to happen.

"Maybe what I want has changed. Am I not allowed to change?" I snap my hands back from his grasp with more vigor than I intended.

Immediately I check his face for signs of renewed anger, afraid I might have gone too far. But he doesn't react. The poor boy must have resigned himself to my bipolar disorder.

Quietly, I place my hand over his knee. There's no need to make this breakup any more difficult than absolutely necessary. Maybe if I summon all my feminine mind-bending powers together, I can gently prod him into thinking of this as a mutual decision. Maybe even get him to see that we were never really right for each other, that our relationship is about as fresh and exciting as a three-day-old tuna sandwich.

Actually, now that I think about it, I don't know what good it does anyone to bring up Miguel at all. If Brian and I were meant to be together, I would have jumped at his proposal. And that was even before Miguel was a twinkle in my consciousness. No, clearly Miguel has no part in any of this. In fact, I'd be doing Brian a colossal favor by keeping this bit of superfluous information to myself. It's the only decent thing to do.

"Of course you're allowed to change," Brian says after a few seconds of silence. "It's just, how am I supposed to keep up if you won't tell me what you want?"

Because I have no idea what it is that I *do* want. I just know this isn't it.

Nope. Can't say that. Too mean. It would be like saying the last three years meant nothing to me, which isn't true. Brian's such a nice person, I sometimes think my mother would have married him herself had she been twenty years younger and, let's face it, living in a parallel universe where a Muslim woman didn't go straight to Hell for hooking up with an "infidel." And if a perfectly decent, sweet, high-potential-earner man isn't what I want, then what is? A life of poverty in a squalid Cuban shantytown with my fifteen kids and a husband who hosts karaoke Thursdays at Club Med? If my family didn't kill me first, rabid jealousy of every horny female tourist, real or imagined, that Miguel might meet on the job would.

"Ali . . . ," Brian gently prods. "Ali, what is it? What do you want?"

How bad would it be if I let it all out? Would the truth truly set me free? Or would the mere thought of it make me gag every time it crossed my mind?

I open my mouth to say something, but my lips twitch downward. Oh no, no, no, no, no. Not now. I can't cry now.

"I don't want the detached bungalow in the suburbs with the plastic toys out front and a white picket fence," I burst out. Fuck. Where did that come from?

"Fine." Brian raises his hands in mock surrender. "Cramped studio apartment in the most run-down corner of the city, with stinking garbage out front it is. Better? Ali? Hey . . . I was just kidding. Honey . . . what's the matter?"

Just like him. Making light of a serious situation with his lame-ass jokes. Exactly the kind of thing that I loved about him when we first met. The kind of thing that's squeezing my heart like a dirty kitchen rag being wrung out and hung to dry. Am I ever going to meet anyone who can make me laugh like Brian does ever again? Or will I die bitter and alone, shunned by my family and my fifteen half-Cuban, half-Lebanese kids?

"Don't you get it?" I don't know why I'm shouting. Or how I can get so angry when Brian's done nothing but sit there and try to make sense out of me. "I just . . . I want . . . I don't know. I was just so . . . *free* in Cuba." I melt into the straw mat, my elbows sliding in opposite directions across the shiny cherry wood surface of the table. I wish I were invisible.

"What are you talking about? Free to do what?"

Funny, that sounds exactly like something my mother would say. She and Brian share this uncanny knack for seeing right through bullshit. Unfortunately for them, this power comes hand in hand with a serious penchant for denial, which explains how they can both be so close to me yet know me so little. Still, everyone, even someone as patient as Brian, must have a saturation point.

"Ali, answer me! Free to do what? Did something happen in Cuba?"

Damn that man's perceptiveness. Blood rushes to my head; my heart starts pounding to the rhythm of footsteps marching to a scaffold. I can hear it beating right through my eardrums.

I'm not ready to be outed. I need more time.

I press my lips together to keep the corners from turning down, and sniffle loudly.

Jaz and Simon are going to be here any minute, and I can't have anyone see me like this.

"Ali, look at me!" Brian takes me by both shoulders and swings me around to face him. Even as everything seems to slow down around me just like it did at the airport, as I taste something not unlike puke rising up in my throat, the thought that I could make someone, normally so good-natured and kind, want to throttle me sits in my stomach like a bad piece of sushi.

I open my mouth to protest, but I'm interrupted by some awkward fumbling with the screen doors.

And in walks Jaz, followed by a medium-height, lanky guy with cropped blond hair.

"Thank you, miss, sorry about that . . . After you, Yasmin."

A diminutive waitress in a navy blue kimono speckled with orange blossoms bows to us, keeping her gaze firmly tilted to the floor, and slides the screen door shut behind her.

Simon.

Brian drops his arms to his sides instantly.

"Apologies for our tardiness." Simon extends his hand to swiftly recovered Brian. "We made a short stop along the way."

Jaz, dressed plainly but elegantly in a black turtleneck and a knee-length moiré skirt, steps around from behind Simon and lowers herself onto the mat, across the table from me.

Though I'm really not the sort of person usually prone to out-
bursts of spontaneous prayer, I still mutter a thankful *nushkur'allah* under my breath while my pulse returns to normal.

I have at least a whole hour, probably two, to pull myself together and figure out exactly what I'm going to say.

✎

"Don't be daft, man. Man U are simply indestructible. And I'll
tell you why. . . ." Simon launches into an enthralled explanation
of why Manchester United are set to beat Arsenal to the top of
their soccer division this year. The boys have already covered
hockey, golf, and even touched slightly on American football,
though Simon declared himself early on not to be a huge fan of
the sport. Somehow he's managed to maintain the delicate bal-
ance between bonding with his date's girlfriend's boyfriend,
while being charming with me and completely attentive to Jaz. I
smile at her from across the table and throw her a look that says,
in no uncertain terms, toy with this guy and it'll have to snow on
Havana before I set you up again.

I adore Simon. All throughout the preliminary round of
drinks, the appetizers of edamame and vegetables tempura, I
keep battling the urge to lurch over the table and give him a noo-
gie. And what he lacks in killer looks he amply makes up for in
an offbeat style and a quirky sense of humor. Friendly, congen-
ial, and absolutely hilarious, he's the kind of person you make
an effort to add to your inner circle of friends rather than assign
to that sea of more or less interchangeable people caught somewhere between mere acquaintanceship and true friendship.

For starters, he's all over the Arabic thing. Unlike many people
who through the course of normal conversation find out I'm
Lebanese, Simon seems to know a thing or two about that part of
the world and actually wants to get my take on things. Most of my
encounters with non-Arabs go something like this: "I don't know
much about all that stuff but . . ." followed by a monologue

where the speaker, rather than attempt to remedy his or her self-professed ignorance by asking me a question or two about the subject, proceeds to lecture me about the sad state of Middle Eastern politics, peppered with a few strategically placed "bunch of crazies" and "Why can't these people just get along?" here and there. While I used to think it was my duty as the token Arab in any gathering to provide a short geopolitical history of the many conflicts plaguing the region, lately I just smile and nod. No one likes complicated answers to complicated issues. They just like to have their notions of good guys and bad guys confirmed. That much I've managed to figure out in my young life.

"Were you living in Lebanon during the civil war?" Simon asks me between bites of tuna sashimi.

"Mmm-hmm." I nod my head, my mouth being completely stuffed with an oversize California roll. I wash it down with Sapporo in anticipation of the next question.

"Jesus. How did you get through it?"

"It wasn't so bad, really. I was very young, and my parents went to a lot of trouble to make sure we weren't exposed to what was going on. We left before it got really bad."

"Surely you must have seen something unsettling at some point?"

I put my chopsticks down for a second and think. There is one image of the war that I still carry around etched in my brain. I muse over whether or not I want to dampen the conversation by bringing it up.

Simon seems taken aback by my momentary silence. "You don't have to answer." He flusters. "I'm really sorry, I didn't mean to pry."

"No, no, you didn't. It's a fair question. It seems like with all my waxing poetic, I've managed to convince myself there was never a war." I smile in an attempt to dispel the awkwardness that had settled over the four of us.

"I was looking out once and I saw this young man walking down the street. I was probably only five or six at the time, but I was enough of a little flirt, even back then, to think he was cute. He was wearing a long-sleeved shirt in a bright color. Orange maybe. Or red. Anyway, in the place where his arms should have been, the shirtsleeves flapped in the wind as he walked down the street and past my balcony. Empty. He wasn't the only maimed war victim I'd seen. There were tons of them, usually begging outside of mosques or open markets. But for some reason he stuck. He was walking with purpose, like he was trying to get somewhere quickly. I remember wondering how he'd managed to get into his neat clothes, where he was going in such a hurry . . . I remember being really curious, and not in a pitying way. I just really wanted to know more about him. I guess you might call it my first conscious memory of empathy."

We sit in awkward silence for a full minute before Jaz breaks it. "Thanks, Al, that was really uplifting."

I pick up loose rice grains off my plate and pitch them at her with my chopsticks. She ducks behind her napkin for cover.

"No, no. I asked." Simon lifts his hand to defend me.

"People, relax. It's not like that." By turns I peer intently into each pair of eyes looking back quizzically at me. "Every Lebanese person—sadly most other Middle Easterners too—has their own war story, or at least one their parents of cousins or uncles told them. But our lives aren't wasted for it. When I picture that cute armless guy, I don't imagine him sulking and wondering what he did to deserve his fate. I picture him sitting around with his buddies, laughing and catcalling the girls who walk by. I think what I'm trying to say is that you learn to get on with life and that it's really about enjoying the simple things while you can."

Did I really just say that? Wow. And minutes ago I was ready to kill myself over being in love with one guy and near-engaged to another. Maybe I need to take the words coming out of my mouth somewhat more to heart.

"It was just like when we were in Cu—"

Shit. I *cannot* believe I let that slip. In between bites of yellowfin snapper sashimi and memories of Beirut, I'd managed to lose myself, to forget that my whole life was on the verge of crashing down around me.

Jaz's eyes widen in complete shock. She lunges for her cosmo and gulps it down. She has no idea what I have or haven't said to Brian. I feel so horrible for her right now, I could stab myself with this chopstick.

"What was that?" Simon asks, his eyes brimming with innocent inquisitiveness. Brian turns red. With shame or anger, I can't say.

I follow Jaz's lead and down my Sapporo in three gulps. And choke.

"Are you all right?"

"Fine . . ." I cough loudly and gasp for air. "Fine, Simon. I just . . . need . . . cough it out . . ." I know I'm turning as pink at the cherry at the bottom of Jaz's martini glass.

Brian taps me a few times on the back, and I pray to God they've all forgotten about my unfinished sentence.

I recover and reach for the white linen handkerchief on my lap, still feeling a little flushed, and dab at the corners of my mouth while smiling at Brian. *See? Everything is just fine,* I try to tell him without resorting to words.

Unfortunately, if his facial expression is any indication, he's regressed right back to that frightful place we were at when Jaz and Simon joined us nearly two hours ago.

"You were going to say just like when you were in Cuba, right?" he says without the slightest hesitation or flicker in his voice. "How did you like it?" He turns to face an ashen-looking Jaz.

Oh, no. It's one thing for me to lie through my teeth, but to ask my best friend to do it for me? Unconscionable. I can't do it. But then what am I supposed to do? Confess to everything right here in front of Simon and Jaz?

"Brian, honey . . ." I tug at his sweater sleeve, the same sweater I'd picked out for him two years ago. The one that brings out the warm specks of gray in his eyes. Except when he turns to pat my hand, the gray is more like hard steel.

"In a minute, sweetheart. Don't you want to hear what Jaz has to say about her trip?"

My cheeks go from oven-burner hot to glacier cold. I know it's because every drop of color in them has drained away in the space of an instant. The instant it took me to realize that Brian wasn't going to let it go this time. I did it. Like the drunkard who curses that last drink, the one that toppled him over the edge, I curse out this double date, the mention of Lebanon, even poor Jaz and Simon. Maybe if I'd just stayed home, spent more time at the office, avoided his phone calls. Maybe I would have had more time to think. Now I feel control slipping eerily out of my hands. There's nothing I can do anymore.

"It was . . . really fun. Relaxing." I can sense Jaz weighing each word carefully.

"You girls went to Cuba together?" Simon chirps, utterly oblivious to the temperature in the room having dropped to chilling depths in the last minute and a half.

"They did." Brian says in a tone you'd never guess was completely sarcastic if you weren't the object of his sarcasm. Jaz and I hang our heads slightly. I'm feeling a little bit like I imagine Dr. Frankenstein must have felt upon seeing his creation. Sarcasm doesn't become Brian at all. Neither does meanness. He's never been deliberately nasty to me—or anyone—before. From the doorman of his building to the squeegee kid who insists on wiping his Corolla's windshield with mucky brownish water. Even that guy gets a smile and a buck.

"They went with another friend too. A girls' vacation," Brian adds.

"Right," says Simon. "Girls-gone-wild vacation, you mean!" He's the only one to laugh out loud at his own joke. "Wait a minute—is that what you stopped for on the way here?" He twists around to look at Jaz.

Jaz adopts the semblance of one of Robin Williams's catatonic patients in *Awakenings*. She gapes at me, her mouth opening and closing a few times before she manages any sound.

"I think I need to go to the bathroom. Ali, you coming?"

"Sure." I prop my frame on my toes, ready to jerk up, but Brian lays a firm hand on my shoulder.

"One second. What was that, Simon? You guys stopped somewhere along the way? And here I was thinking you guys hit it off *really* well and just made up a lousy excuse."

"No, man. Jaz made me stop at the pharmacy and came back with a stack of prints. It was massive, man, you should've seen it." Simon chuckles, holding both hands up in the air.

"Ali, I . . ." Jaz swallows hard as though her throat were dipped in plaster and let out to dry. "They were ready for pickup today, and I was just so excited to see . . ."

I can't hold her responsible for this. I honestly can't. No matter how much I'm craving an outlet right now, I just can't. There's no way she could have anticipated this. I was the one who slipped up, not her.

In any case, she looks like she's in as much pain as I am.

"Why don't we take a peek while you ladies powder your noses or whatever it is women feel compelled to do together in a public restroom."

I glower at Brian. He's taking this too far. It's between him and me, and there's absolutely no need to drag anyone else into it.

"Brian, I think we should go," I say quietly. "It was lovely meeting you, Simon—"

"What the fuck is wrong with you, Ali? What are you lying

about now?" He whips around and grabs me so hard by the arm that I wince. "And don't try to tell me you aren't!

"Jaz, give me the pictures." Brian stretches out his arm, the expression of a schoolyard bully etched all over his usually serene features.

Jaz hesitates, but regains her composure. "Don't tell me what to do! How do you even know they're from Cuba?"

Simon, who has sat in stunned silence for the past two minutes, finally utters a few fumbling words. "Listen, Brian . . . I don't know what's going on, but I think we should all cool off for now. I can take the girls home if you like." He tries his best to calm Brian with his own gentle tone. "Ready to go, Ali?"

He offers me his hand.

"Not yet." Brian turns me around to face him, this time a bit more gently, but I can tell he's doing everything in his power to stop himself from bursting with rage. "I'm asking you to please let me see those pictures. Please."

The *please* comes out hoarse. Not nearly so hoarse as my response, though.

"Okay."

Jaz and Simon fade away into the soft yellow of the walls, swallowed up by ink warriors gouging each other with curved swords while shy geisha watch from behind spread fans.

I could have kept on fighting, I could have tried to manipulate him the way that comes so easily to me. I bet I would've won too. But for how much longer would we keep up the act?

As if seeing myself through a dream, I reach over the table and pick up Jaz's hobo bag. Slowly I unzip it. No one stops me, so I slip my hand inside and fumble for an envelope thick with prints. Even if there weren't one picture of Miguel and me together, it's over. I know it, and so does Brian.

For so long now, I'd tried to insulate myself from the truth. It seemed to me that if I pushed it into a far-enough corner in my brain, then I could convince myself it didn't exist. If Brian never found out about Miguel, then would my infidelity ever have happened? I never fully grasped the meaning of the tree falling in the forest until this moment. Do I want to be one of those people who don't know—or care—what is happening around them, or do I finally open my eyes, even if I don't like what I see?

I find a stack that feels like it may be the proofs, pull it out, and hand it to Brian. Still, no one says a word. I'm not even sure Jaz and Simon are in the room anymore. My lap is looking blurry and a little damp in spots.

Out of the corner of my eye I see the pictures cascading to the floor at a furious pace, one by one, by Brian's side. There's the tarmac when we first stepped off the plane. The baggage handlers—man that girl is snap-happy—Lenin, our first bus driver. There's the beach, Sophie smiling in front of the pool, holding a coconut with a straw sticking out of it in her hand, then one of the three of us together. My heart drops to my knees when I see one of Miguel float to the ground. Except in this one he's surrounded by most of the entertainment crew. It was taken the night of the pageant.

And then he reappears. Tall, muscular, and handsome as a movie star, waist deep in azure water, and with his arms wrapped around me, his lips on the curve of my neck.

This time I force myself to look up. Brian is completely expressionless. I half expect him to yell out *whore* loud enough for the entire restaurant to hear. Slowly, his features soften and change. Oh, God. Is he going to cry? I really don't think I could take that. I'd rather he slap me and be done with it.

He doesn't cry, or shout obscenities at me. He looks like the Brian I left behind when I went to Cuba. A contented, self-assured Brian. The kind of person who goes through life with a completely clear conscience. In other words, the total opposite of me. All traces of meanness are gone, which makes my heart plummet with a sense of loss. If I didn't know better, I'd think he's almost happy to have his suspicions confirmed, to know that he wasn't crazy or delirious over nothing. I'm not saying that he doesn't seem utterly torn and dejected in equal measures, but at least he knows now.

"Brian, I'm so sorry. . . ."

"Please don't touch me, Ali." He shrugs his arm away and pulls himself upright.

"Listen, I just want to explain—"

"I don't want an explanation. You said you wanted to be free. Well, you are now."

"This is what you wanted too," I whisper. "I know it."

He had gotten up, ready to storm out of the room, but he whips around. "What?"

"Are you happy?"

"Ali, I've had it with your games. I've had enough of you stringing me along like I was . . . like I was a fucking dog or something."

"I'm *not* playing games . . . not now. I'm asking you if you're happy. If you ever were."

He runs a hand through his hair, sending locks of it jutting out from behind his ears. He looks so sad, it's killing me.

"I was happy. When I thought we wanted the same things out of life. You weren't always like this. You wanted to be married with kids, remember?"

"I was nineteen. I was an idiot."

"Are you saying I'm an idiot for wanting that?"

"No! That's not what I meant. I meant . . . I mean . . . I don't think I really knew who I was back then. I'd grown up thinking my options were pretty much the same as all my cousins'. You know: do well in school, marry a nice Arab boy from a good Arab family, have babies. My parents might as well have never left Lebanon."

"What does that have to do with us?"

"Everything . . . I had to struggle for every bit of freedom I got. Everything was always a showdown between my parents and me. Staying out late, getting a part-time job so I could pay for my own clothes, going on this trip, dating you . . . The truth is . . . I don't know how much of our relationship was me rebelling against my parents' expectations and how much of it was that I'd picked you, *you*, Brian, out of all the people in the world to be with for the rest of my life."

His face twitches and his eyes take on the hardness they had when he met me at the airport.

This is raw pain. For both me and him. But it's also the real, honest truth.

27

If you are reading this, chances are you are over thirty-five and have yet to find that special someone.

Hmpf. I don't think the over-thirty-five-and-unattached crowd should have the monopoly on complete cluelessness when it comes to relationships. I may only be twenty-two, but I feel I'm clueless enough to fit your narrow target market, Dr. Goldenblatt, thankyouverymuch.

Maybe you've already spent your most vibrant, attractive years focused on your career.

Yeah, no. Not quite.

Maybe you're divorced, widowed, or you've wasted too much time with the wrong man.

Now we're getting closer. Except judging by chapter headers like "The Bridget Jones Complex: Setting Impossible Standards" or "Man-agement: How to Keep Him Interested in Your Portfolio," I have a feeling I've already failed Dr. Goldenblatt's no-nonsense twelve-step program to snagging (and presumably keeping) a man.

Hardly a week after Brian stormed out of the tatami room, I'm still so depressed, I can barely get out of bed in the morning. I thought that once I figured out what I didn't want—which is to know exactly what every day of the rest of my life would be like—I'd be less neurotic. I'm not. Not nearly. I'm just as lost as

I ever was, except now I'm riddled with the added anxiety of having purposely ended what might have been my best shot at happiness. My only shot, maybe. Hence, Dr. Goldenblatt. I'd picked up the thick self-help tome from Chapters on my way to meet Sophie and Jaz at Aïsha's store.

"What are you reading?" Sophie interrupts her inspection of the dress rack with one eyebrow raised at my book.

I quickly stuff the manual back into my Matt & Nat faux-leather tote. No need to take my inner despair public.

But I'm too late for Jaz's eagle eye. With the shameless skill of a sixteenth-century gypsy, she swipes my bag from under my arm and relieves me of my less-than-literary tome faster than I can say crazy banshee.

"*Mergers and Man-quisitions: The Business Woman's Guide to Marriage after Thirty-five,*" she reads out loud. "You are aware this makes you a loser of the highest order?"

"Give me that." I snatch the paperback out of Jaz's hands and plop it into my newly recovered purse.

Sophie drops her shoulders and cocks her head to one side, looking at me as you would at a toddler who'd just walked into a doorknob in his haste to catch the opening bars of the *Sponge-Bob SquarePants* theme song.

"Why would you read something so . . . so . . ."

"Loserish?" Jaz offers.

"Jaz! We're supposed to be helping."

"That's exactly what I'm trying to do. Who's going to go out with someone who reads this self-help bullshit?"

"She's only been single for a week!"

Ugh. A week of utter misery. Since they're such relationship experts themselves, I leave the girls to debate how best to get me out of my rut and wander across to a rack crowded with bejeweled tunics, the sound of my Fornarina boots clanking against the blond wood floor of Aïsha's shop. It's Thursday, meaning the stores are open till nine, but with the hours I've been clocking in at Ernsworth lately, it's a wonder that I was able to make it here at all.

I thumb a gauzy black halter top, cinched under the breasts by a black-and-silver beaded band. I turn over the price tag. Hmpf. I could afford it. I won't be able to once Diane gets back and I'm on unemployment insurance, but I can now. I certainly don't need it. But if retail therapy ever needed a poster girl, I've got to be it.

Whoever said that garbage about the truth setting you free must have been on drugs. If anything, the truth has cemented in me the certainty that I'm going to die a lonely spinster. Not unless I decide to toss out my last shred of dignity and sign up to Islamicpersonals.com.

And yet. Something about the finality of the whole restaurant episode feels strangely comforting. Not the kind of comforting that makes me want to rush home and interrupt my mother's daily viewing of *The Family of Hajj Mutwalli* with an outpouring of the truth like something out of a bad sitcom, but still . . . I think maybe once I stop feeling nauseated every time I hear Brian's voice echoing in my head, ordering me not to touch him, once I stop remembering how he jerked away from me when I tried to hold him back, I think maybe I might be ready to open up to my mother a little more. Who knows, once she gets over the shock of having raised a Jezebel, she might be grateful for the potential of a friendship between us. A real friendship, based on mutual honesty and trust.

Right. And Condoleezza Rice will have a nice sitdown with Hamas and declare a complete truce over figs and Turkish coffee.

I cringe at the thought of telling my mother the real reason that Brian dumped me. Because I slept with Miguel. And if she managed to compose herself from the blow that not only was I no longer a virgin, but that my "number" had now shot to two, she'd surely ask me about Miguel, what he does for a living and if he comes from a "good family," whatever that's supposed to mean.

And that's when she'd really want to kill herself. I guess I have to be grateful we don't have nuns where I come from, because if there were a Muslim equivalent to a convent, that's where I can expect to be sent.

There is, of course, an obvious silver lining to the truth. I'm now free to carry on with Miguel in so far as I can get away with it, without guilt looming over my shoulder like a vulture waiting for that fateful swoop. The funny thing is that now that I find myself one obstacle short of what I would've considered bliss two weeks ago, I see the total impossibility of any sort of relationship with my Cuban love god more clearly than I ever did before. What would Dr. Phil have to say about that?

I've written Miguel more than a dozen letters since I've been back, all filled with nothing. Lines and lines of nothing. A paragraph about the latest snowfall, a few semi-optimistic ones about work designed more to humor myself than him. Not once did I mention my family, naturally. Does he even know what a Muslim is, let alone what our family values are like? How would a man for whom sex is more like a recreational sport than something you do to consummate a bond between two families react to not being able to hold my hand in public lest it get back to my family? Would he laugh me back to the Stone Age it would seem I come from? How do you explain to someone how all your life you've let the burden of achievement placed on you, the child of struggling immigrants, dictate your every decision, when he's suffered the crime of being actually, physically trapped on an island with little hope of ever leaving? I couldn't.

It dawns on me now how little I know about Miguel. I'm no less lovesick for this nugget of enlightenment, of course. Plus I now know where the word, love*sick*, comes from, said feeling still running wild in my veins like a viral disease. I can't say I've ever felt this way before, not even when Brian and I first met. In the past year of our relationship, I would have carved out my heart with a spoon just to feel something—anything—rippling through my body in a fury of heart-fluttering, insides-churning emotion.

My mind continues to wander as I stop to pull a velvet cropped jacket off the hanger. Is that why I'd been so irritable with him those last few months?

But with Miguel, it's as though I've been hurled to the complete opposite side of the emotional-intensity spectrum. I'm consumed with insecurity and racked by a depression brought on by not being able to be with him. Almost to the point where I wish I'd never met him.

And yet . . . If I concentrate hard enough, I can still conjure up electric jolts—sometimes just an imperceptible nudge, other times a powerful punch—deep within my insides.

So I guess I can't say that I wish the night of the pageant, the dive accident, Havana, even that night on the balcony, had never happened.

What, then, is the answer?

I place the velvet jacket back on the rack and drag myself to a corner of the airy space where a cream leather sofa sits on top of a Moroccan rug. The boyfriend couch. I plop down on it with a sigh of pure resignation. I'm all thought out.

"Oof!" A few feet away from me, Aïsha steps out from behind the cash register, wiping her hand across her forehead in exhaustion. She'd just rung up the last member of what had sounded to me like a squadron of Valley girls. In twos, the young demoiselles file out of the store, each holding at least one—some of them two or three—of Aïsha's signature pink carrier bags.

"Congratulations." I turn to her, happy for the distraction from my thoughts. "You look like you're doing really well."

"Yes, well. It's a tougher business than I thought. I'm hanging in there." She swings a lock of her annoyingly gorgeous hair behind her and gives me a harried smile.

"It must be very rewarding. Not having to answer to anyone, I mean." By anyone I strictly meant a shrew with an overachievement complex called Soula, and a walking terror-machine by the name of Diane.

"*Oh, non, surtout pas.* There is always someone you must answer to. In my case, the bank." She shrugs. "And my customers," she adds as an afterthought. "I wish I could spend less time worrying about the bank and more about them. *C'est la vie,* I suppose."

Aïsha must be right. It's her store, her vision. She knows better than me. Still . . . I run my hand along a row of cashmere tees, decadently delicate to the touch, and let myself indulge in a brand-new fantasy, one that has just formed in my mind and nuzzled up against the one of me and Miguel, married, living together in a flat just like Javier's, overlooking the deep blue Caribbean Sea.

What if—and I know this is crazier than the idea of my aunt Selma flashing her boobs at a Rio street carnival—*I* were to run a clothing shop one day? And not just run it, but maybe own it too.

I lift my gaze to the mannequin in the window, dressed in a bouffant burgundy tulip skirt and crisp white shirt with a silk sash tied around the waist.

I could totally put that outfit together. And didn't I invest in winter white a full season before *Vogue* declared it the new red? Which was, of course, the new black before winter white made its debut.

What else do you need to run a successful clothing store, besides a good eye for what would and wouldn't sell? A mind for business? At least I've got the accounting side of that subject, and really, isn't the rest just plain common sense?

I feel a smile curling the corners of my lips. I quickly repress it before Jaz or Sophie catch me and declare me completely certifiable.

My own store. What would I call it? How would I decorate the

306 ✳ NADINE DAJANI

place? I'd be responsible for the buying, naturally. Oh, God. My knees go weak at the thought of having tens of thousands of dollars to spend on shopping. And wholesale prices too, for stuff that other people won't see for weeks—even *months*—down the line. All I need is some money.

And that's where my short-lived dream takes a neat nosedive, much like Wilbur and Orville Wright's 1903 *Kitty Hawk Flyer*, smack into the fields of reality.

Money. However much I had of it was already invested in a wardrobe whose value had declined 95 percent at point of purchase. If only I could count a vintage Chanel box suit or perhaps a Balenciaga sack dress, say circa 1960, among my assets. Then eBay might have been an option. Bebe and Banana Republic, sadly, won't cut it. Even my Marc Jacobs, Diane von Furstenberg, and Catherine Malandrino pieces aren't likely to fetch a tidy sum, seeing as these designers are still alive and very much kicking.

My parents, of course, would be of no help, since they need every penny they earn for running the house and putting back into their own business. And while I could probably impress my dad with a snazzy business plan, I doubt I could induce him to gamble the family's livelihood on my hazy vision.

My parents. Auntie Maryam, my uncle Munir, Ranya, even that moron Dodi. The rest of the Hallaby clan. What would they say to quitting a stable day job and getting up to my eyeballs in debt? They'd raise their hands to the heavens and curse the day they moved to North America, that's what. And even if they didn't come out and say it, I know what they'd be thinking. That they didn't leave their country, their friends, their home, all that behind, so their daughter could become a shopkeeper. I could have done that in Beirut.

"Hey, Aïsha . . . ," I call out.

She lifts her gaze from the stack of sweaters she's been folding. "Mhhm?"

"How did you get this started?"

She doesn't need to ask me what I mean.

"My mother worked at the house of Dior in Paris. She was one of the *petites mains* before she retired."

I don't ask her to explain. I'd recognized those words from some of the biographies of famous designers I have on my bookshelf. They're the women who toil in the ateliers of famous French couturiers, the ones behind the intricate hand-stitched detailing, beading, and appliqué on the suits and gowns of the world's elite. The hundreds of hours of their manual labor is responsible for the outlandish price tag of haute couture.

"She taught me to sew young, and taught me well too. I was making my own clothes when I was just fourteen. My father was a tailor. He owned the atelier where he worked. It did very well, but then he fell ill and I wasn't interested in hemming men's trousers for the rest of my life. So he sold it, not long before he passed away."

"Sorry."

She waves me away distractedly, moving on from stacking sweaters to rearranging the clothing on the racks in size order. "It was a few years ago. Anyway, he left us the money from the sale of the business, plus his own savings. Our home had already been in the family for two generations, and I'm an only child. I'd graduated from Parsons Paris by then, so opening this shop seemed like the logical thing to do."

"So why'd you leave Paris and your family?" I peer through the window looking out onto the street. The lights from the store are casting shadows against the thin layer of powdery snow on the sidewalk. Why anyone would leave Paris for this is beyond me.

"It's very difficult in France. Designers are a dime a dozen, not just French ones but from all over the world. There's still the idea, even now, that America is the land of opportunity, where anything is possible. I suppose Montreal isn't what is traditionally thought of as America, but that's why I chose it. Different, a fresh start, while still reminding me enough of Paris that I wouldn't feel so homesick."

"And does it?"

At this she laughs. "They tell me come February it won't, but I think I can handle it. Of course, I find the North American custom of only two weeks of holiday a year perfectly barbaric."

She would, coming from a place where six weeks is the standard.

"In France hardly anyone works in August. Just the people who are necessary to attend to the tourists."

I sigh. "Must be nice."

"There are nice things about Montreal too, *tu sais*. Everything is so . . . *je ne sais pas* . . . so young and vibrant. You can almost feel that you are in a city that's in its infancy, especially when you come from a place like Paris. I thought I would have a better chance of making it here, but . . . I don't know." The space between her thin brows furrows, and her face takes on a distant look.

"What is it? Is something wrong?"

The expression fades away as quickly as it had appeared.

"It's nothing. Just the everyday ups and downs of business. Nothing that would interest you."

It does interest me. Very much so, actually. But I wouldn't want to make her ill at ease, so I keep my mouth firmly shut.

"Ali, you all done here?"

I stare at the heap of clothes in Sophie's arms in complete shock. "Who are you, and what have you done with Sophie?"

She smirks at me, mild embarrassment narrowing the outer edges of her eyes. "Hey, life's too short."

"You're right about that at least. Is that a bikini?"

"Yes." A squeak more than a word, really.

The girl can't even look me in the eye. "He texted me again yesterday. It's cheaper than calling, I guess."

"And?"

"He says I have an open invitation to come back whenever I want."

"But we knew that already. Next?"

"I'm thinking Christmas."

Christmas. Holy shit. That's like one month away.

"Your parents are going to flip, you realize."

What I'm dying to know, of course, is exactly how she plans on accomplishing this feat. So I can take notes.

She simply shrugs. Not very promising. "Look, Ali, I'm twenty-two. I'm almost done with my bachelor's. They're going to have to realize one day that I won't be a kid forever."

Such simple words, yet so ludicrous to my ears. When you're an Arab, your parents own you. For life.

"What about the scholarship? Made a decision yet?" With my own life in virtual shambles lately, I'd nearly forgotten to ask.

"Nope."

"Don't you have to have your mind made up by next month?"

"Yup."

"And this doesn't worry you how?"

"Ali—" She lets the clothes drop next to me on the sofa in a tangled, messy mound. "—you think too much."

28

The one happy side effect to being single and miserable, as far as I can tell, is that overtime hours clocked in at the office tend to be mistaken for a passionate zeal for your job instead of the natural outcome of having no love life—or any life, really—to speak of. At least that's the only explanation I can find for Soula's sudden thawing to me. I'd say warming up, but that would suppose that she was merely cool in our earlier dealings, as opposed to a perfect Popsicle.

True, when I started in this department, I didn't know my job requirements from the Patriots' three-four defense, but thankfully, I haven't been completely without resources.

For one thing, a thorough search of Tom's cubicle has yielded, among other things, a thick procedures manual replete with meticulous notes and helpful contacts. Among my less amusing findings was a photograph of his exquisite self, standing behind a disgustingly attractive strawberry blonde, with both his hands proprietarily draped over her hips. Humph. I can only assume the reason it was stuffed all the way in the back of his drawer rather than displayed prominently on his desk was because the mere sight of the woman was so disconcerting to him that he had to find a less distracting home for the picture or else risk losing his job.

And once Penny had gotten over the shock of seeing her private-schooled, polo-playing cousin Simon take an uncommon interest in Jaz, she seemed quite willing to help fill in the gaps in Tom's training manual.

I guess witnessing the train wreck that was my public breakup turned into a cataclysm for bringing Jaz and Simon together. Good for them. Maybe this'll be the guy to break Jaz's vicious circle of low self-esteem and bad relationships. And then she'd be well placed to return the favor and set me up. Oh, the irony.

I glance up at the large circular clock on the wall over the filing cabinet where we keep the legal correspondence, a clock that wouldn't look out of place in a school cafeteria.

Five thirty. I could totally leave now. In fact, Penny's halfway out the door already.

"Bye, Pen, see you tomorrow."

"Tootles!"

And off she goes. Except Penny isn't battling possible unemployment. Though Soula's confidence in me may have inched upward somewhat, HR director Diane still has the final word. And I'm not likely to last past the length of time it takes her to tick "fire Aline Hallaby" off her to-do list, once she gets back from leave. Which hasn't happened yet, so I should really cool it. Sophie's right. I think too much.

But that's not the only thing keeping me here. I'm actually finding all this new stuff, learning about the differences between Chapter 7 and Chapter 11 and 13 bankruptcies and talking to bankers and lawyers—God help me—fun. Not Friday-night-at-Club-Rouge fun, but not mind-numbingly boring at least.

Unlike my ticking and bopping days at Audit, there's something vaguely rewarding about what I'm doing now. Going over the bank covenants, making sure the numbers add up, that all the legal docs are drawn up and enclosed, assembling the file, and then handing it to Soula for verification before she contacts the client and tells them their papers are ready to be filed with the government. Granted, I'm sure the people Soula talks to can think of happier times in their lives than the day their bankruptcy papers were finalized, but not unlike a doctor seeing a patient through a difficult illness, we actually help make a tough process just a little bit easier. I can think of worse things to be doing. Like, say, ticking and bopping.

In my overzealous haste to be a good little worker, I'd missed the fact that my desk was actually bereft of files that still needed tending to. My "to do" stack had surreptitiously dwindled down to nothing and risen in a towering pile over on the "done" side.

Well. I suppose I could call it a night, then. Go home, maybe catch the tail end of *The Family of Hajj Mutwalli* or else the opening theme music of Umm Kulthum while my mother shapes a mixture of beef, spices, and bulghur into kibbe balls, the Lebanese version of meatballs, in front of the TV set. And if I found that to be less than enthralling, I would be welcome to shut myself up in my room and replay the scene at the sushi restaurant over in my head, again, or else cry over what Miguel and I could've been in another life.

I lift my eyes discreetly over the top of my laptop screen and find Soula still hunched over Sid Cohen's mahogany desk. Well, his ex-desk, since for all intents and purposes, the man isn't coming back. She hasn't moved from that position since at least three this afternoon.

Grabbing as many files as I can manage and securing the stack firmly under my chin, I quietly push back my chair and tiptoe toward her office.

"Erm." I clear my throat. "Hi, Soula, need any help?"

For a fraction of a second, I don't think she heard me. Maybe she's gotten so used to my self-effacing presence in the office that my diminutive figure in the doorframe doesn't even register in her consciousness. Then I spot a flicker of movement in her eyes, before they open up, wide and hopeful.

"Well, okay. If you don't need me, I'll be off, then." I lay the files on the corner of a nearby wood filing cabinet and spin on my heels as fast as I can when her voice booms after me.

"No! No, wait. Thank you, Aline. There's certainly a lot more where that came from." She fumbles around her workstation, not quite sure what to unload on me, and after some considerable rummaging, she settles on a thick stack of client files. "Are you all done with the Madison Group files?"

"Yes. That's all of them here." I point to the stack I've just deposited in the room.

"I have to say, Aline, I don't know what Diane was talking about when she warned me to keep an eye on you. So far you've proved yourself quite the self-starter. Motivated and reliable. I'll have to have a word with her when she gets back next week."

Despite the tepid dry air of central heating buzzing quietly throughout the room, I feel a glacial shudder jolt my insides awake. I tuck my trembling hands behind my back.

So she's back next week.

What if a good word from Soula isn't enough to move Diane's Darth Vader–black heart? It's anyone's guess at this point.

"Here you are. All yours." Soula steps out from behind the desk and plops about a dozen fresh folders in my arms.

"If you could have these prepped by tomorrow afternoon, I'd be pretty impressed," she says.

"Not a problem. I'll get to work on them straight away." I nod curtly by way of a self-dismissal and saunter back to my desk. At least she'd given me a tangible goal, something I know I can work toward. Maybe there's hope for me yet.

It's eight thirty, and I'm still at the office. Soula's stare, boring through my back, has kept me chained to my desk even though my mental capacities shut down two hours ago. Didn't anyone ever tell her it's counterproductive to micromanage your staff?

Wait. I think I hear something. . . .

Could she be packing up to go home?

I risk a tiny peek in the direction of her glass-paned office and discover that she does indeed seem to be gathering her things and throwing them into her boxy briefcase.

She locks the office door behind her and pauses at my cubicle on her way out. "Ali, you're still here? Go home, you shouldn't stay here all by yourself."

"Don't worry, I'm done for the day. I'll just take a minute to pack up."

"Alarm goes off at eleven," she says, somewhat skeptically, I think. "Good night." She then graces me with one of her smiles, as rare as the vision of two humpback whales mating in the icy waters of the Atlantic, and heads for the exit.

A funny thought crosses my mind as I watch her turn the corner past Penny's abandoned desk and disappear down the corridor.

She called me Ali. For the first time since I've known her. Maybe she really is starting to like me.

I scan the stack of remaining folders—substantially dented— still in front of me, and mentally prepare to push them to the to-be-dealt-with-tomorrow corner of my cubicle.

Then again . . . Soula said the alarm wouldn't go off until eleven. That still gives me a chance to do some prep work for another file or two. And honestly, the less chances I have of running into my mother when I come home, the better.

She still has no idea. None. Not about the UFE or even about Brian. I'll tell her soon—of course I will, as if I could keep this secret much longer—it's just that I've decided to adopt the need-to-know technique reserved for those occasions where I've bought something ridiculously expensive that I'm sure I'm going to get hell for. Like a pair of three-hundred-dollar boots. My mother may not know Tod's from Talbots, but she can sniff a pricey purchase from a mile away. So I just hide my latest indulgence for a few weeks, typically three, after which time I can safely declare the purchase old news. What was that, ma*ma?* My boots? Oh, I bought these ages ago. . . . How much, you ask? Er . . .

Sometimes when declaring something was bought eons ago isn't enough, I resort to skimming a few dollars off the price tag. Half is a good rule of thumb. Unfortunately, there are limitations to this method's applicability to UFE scores, but at least it's a start.

I surrender to my inner voice and grab the first bound file from the top of the stack, noting the client's name, scribbled in blue ink on a white label poking out from the side of the pile.

It's not like the dozens of others I've gone through today— typically identified by a slew of numbers followed by the suffix *Inc.* Nor is it an obscure name I've never heard of and am unlikely to ever see again. It's one I recognize.

Aïsha Saint-Jacques.

I slump against the back of my chair, my mouth gaping open. I don't believe this. She'd said business was difficult, but this? How could it happen? I'd never seen the woman's store empty, and shit, just from my business alone she should be breaking even. Honestly.

All traces of my earlier exhaustion evaporate like water off a scalding sidewalk. I just can't wrap my head around this. I need to see her. It's only eight forty-five. If I run, I can make it by closing time. Maybe I can still catch her cleaning up.

"Aïsha? Aïsha, are you there?" I glue my face against the icicle-cold glass and peer inside. The store's empty, and only the lights in the window are still on. I rap four times against the heavy glass door and wait. Seconds later, an elegantly coiffed head pokes out from behind the back curtains bearing a look that says *I've got a baseball bat, buddy.*

"It's me, Aline. Open up." I mouth, not sure if she can hear me. I wave frantically, then wrap my arms around my shoulders and shudder violently to signal that I'm freezing.

This has the intended effect. Aïsha scurries across the hardwood floor to let me in, her forehead still creased in a puzzled sort of way.

She must think I'm crazy.

"I'm sorry, Ali. You'll have to come back tomorrow," she says, cracking open the door and releasing a tiny sliver of heat. "The store's closed. Besides, I haven't put any new merchandise on display since you were here yesterday, and you've already tried all that on."

"No, no, no. It's not about that. Really, though, you haven't got anything new?" Focus Ali, focus. "Never mind that. There's something important I have to talk to you about."

"What is it?"

"Can I come in first? I've lost feeling in my left pinkie toe."

"Oh, yes, of course. I'm sorry." She swings the door just wide enough for me to walk through and then promptly locks it behind me.

"Can I get you anything to drink? *Un café, peut-être?*"

"Yes, please." I rub my gloved hands together. Damn this cold. What was wrong with Cuba again?

"Turkish?"

"Sure. How come you're always drinking that, anyway?"

"It's the way my mother always makes it. She grew up in Algeria before she moved to France and met my father."

Aïsha lifts the thick white curtains at the far end of the shop floor and leads me into her atelier. Bright fluorescent lighting shines down on sturdy wooden worktables and chairs, the kind you're likely to find in an elementary school art room, all draped with swaths of materials of wildly different colors and textures. The contrast between the understated chic of the boutique on the other side of the linen curtains and the no-frills utilitarianism of the back room is startling. Every available wall space is carpeted in fashion sketches and fabric swatches. It occurs to me that Aïsha may even be living in a tucked away room here somewhere to save on rent.

She motions me to grab a seat at one of the tables and puts a kettle on in the small kitchenette wedged into a corner of the workshop.

"Tell me you're not ready to pack up and go back to France yet." I slump onto a wooden workbench still shaking from the cold, and glare at the frost etchings forming on the windows.

"Yes, well, it may just come to that," a resigned voice answers me.

Crap. That's so not what I meant. I'd let the depressing weather distract me and forgotten for just a fraction of a second why I'd come here in the first place.

"I may as well tell you, Aline. I'm going broke."

I almost choke on the coffee she's just handed me. "That's what I came here to talk to you about." I set the espresso cup on the table and look up into her tense features. "What's going on? I thought you were doing great."

"So did I." She sighs, easing into the chair opposite me, and takes a cautious sip of the thick black liquid. Her eyes glaze over, and she looks like she might burst into tears.

I don't know why, but something inside me wants to cry right along with her. Maybe all this business with Brian and Miguel is making me sentimental, but maybe it's something else altogether. Maybe somewhere in the back of my mind I had been rooting for Aïsha ever since she opened shop. I think I must have seen her as my own flesh-and-blood incarnation of hope. Hope that it was possible to know what life you were meant to be living, and then actually make it happen. What's she going to do now? Go back to France, just to work as a mere employee in someone else's atelier when she had run her own? Would she have to face her family and friends with the humiliating knowledge that she'd failed, as I was going to have to do very soon?

"Listen, I want to help you. I'm going to help you. I'll need your cooperation, though."

"What can you do?"

"I work in the insolvency department at Ernsworth and Youngston's, the firm you filed bankruptcy with."

"What? I knew you worked in finance, but I had no idea—"

"Yeah, it's not exactly my favorite topic of conversation."

"You never really seemed like the accounting type to me."

"I never really thought so either, but that's beside the point. I'm actually supposed to be filing your Chapter Eleven papers right now but—look, I'm not an accounting genius or anything, I really shouldn't be doing this without asking Soula's permission—"

"*Soula?* You know her? She's the financial consultant that was supposed to get me out of this mess. Oh, I could just kill her!"

I stare at Aïsha, slightly bewildered. She's usually so calm and composed. It's really strange to see her like this. I half expect her to light aromatherapy candles and chant for the eventual enlightenment of her enemies rather than just curse them out like the rest of us.

"Er . . . Soula's my boss, actually. Are you upset with her about something? She's really very competent. And dedicated—"

"I'm sure she is," Aïsha says, regaining some composure. "But, well, you know how some doctors can be geniuses but are completely bereft of a bedside manner? That's exactly what she reminded me of. She's been to see me only once, and just to inform me that there's little hope for my tiny boutique when huge, mass-market retailers are taking over fashion, and how competition in this field is so fierce, and blah, blah, blah. She actually cited Wal-Mart's foray into fashion as an example. Ha! *Mais ça alors!* I couldn't believe I was paying her to sit right where you are sitting now and tell me how lucky I am to have gotten this far without a financial backer. She said I was too unknown to even contemplate selling out to a conglomerate like LVMH or the Gucci group. As if I've worked so hard and invested so much of my money just so I could hand over my creation to a faceless corporation and lose all creative control." She lets out a dainty, outraged snort. Even that sounds Parisian.

"I could read it in her eyes, Ali, even if she wouldn't tell me in plain language: She had absolutely no faith in me, or this label, so what was the point in me even trying to get anywhere with her?"

As much as I want to help Aïsha, I'm still an Ernsworth employee. I wouldn't want to give Diane one more reason to give me the ax when she has so many to choose from already. I have to weigh my words very carefully.

"Did she offer you any alternatives to bankruptcy?"

"Nothing."

I'm really confused now. I thought this was our job. At least that's what I'd managed to pick up from all that eavesdropping on Soula and Tom's conversations with clients. I thought— mistakenly, I suppose—that financially viable customers were more worthwhile than the flat broke variety. I must be underestimating how much we're charging for filing the paperwork.

I stand up and pace around the workshop, fingering a beaded silk skirt here, pieces of an embroidered shirt there. A row of sewing machines reach all the way to the back of the room, and I envision *les petites mains*, the seamstresses, hunched over designer scraps, their livelihood utterly dependent on Aïsha's creativity with fabric and fashion trends. I'm almost on the brink of tears myself.

"The worst part," continues Aïsha, "is that business is just booming. I can't restock fast enough. I need to expand if I want to stay afloat. But for some reason, my sales figures aren't translating into solid profits, and the bank won't extend my loan. I've already gone through my inheritance—I used up most of that just in start-up costs—and now I just need some cash to keep the company running until it can turn a profit. I'm close. I'm sure of it. I just can't prove it."

During her impassioned monologue, Aïsha had been stomping and pacing all over the workshop floor. Spent, she slumps on the chair beside me, her head buried in her long slender hands.

A couple of key words from her speech strike a chord of recognition in my harried brain. Sales? Profitability? Long-term earnings potential? A dim recollection of a university lecture about the implications of these notions eases languidly into my head. But why is this important? I know I know this.

"Aïsha, this doesn't make any sense to me. Can't you have another financial analyst take a look at your books? There's got to be a way to make the bank see your potential."

"I wish I could, but I'm already down to the wire, financially speaking. I have no money left. I thought that if there were anything that could be done, the people at Ernsworth would have found it. I called that awful Soula Adrian but she wouldn't give me the time of day and when I tried to get in touch with her boss instead, all I ever got was his voice mail with instructions to contact Soula for 'any urgent matters.'"

Sid Cohen. Soula's boss. I imagine him on the green, somewhere in Southern Florida, banging his Bergdorf Blonde wife in between golfing sessions with the old boys from the country club. No wonder Aïsha can't reach him. There's only one thing left to do.

"Aïsha, d'you think maybe I can take a look at your books? I'm not promising anything—" Hell, I'm not even certified yet.

"Please." She silences me with a shrug and a wave. "What do I have left to lose at this point?" She pulls herself to her feet and shuffles to the other side of the room, where she steps behind a pine desk buried under mounds of sketches, swatches, and charts of every conceivable size and color. In sawed-off tin cans, coloring markers share crowded living space with scalloped fabric scissors, yellow highlighters, and measuring tape. I don't know why, but I somehow expected something more orderly, more pulled together from Aïsha.

"I try to keep it neat around here." She blushes. "But I have a hard enough time supervising the seamstresses and managing the shop that some things just seem to fall by the wayside."

The poor woman sounds like she's in need of an intervention. I feel an unexpected surge of gratitude for having Sophie and Jaz in my life. Even if neither one of them could sketch or sew their way out of a DKNY hobo bag, they'd still throw themselves headfirst into helping me, whatever manner of first aid I happened to be in need of.

Aïsha reaches into a drawer and removes a thick leatherbound notebook, the kind I often see Mr. Khalil, the purveyor of meat products to the entire Lebanese community of our neighborhood, scribble in while one of his five sons tends to the customers.

"Thank you so much for doing this, Aline. It means a lot to me."

"Please don't thank me." Especially since I haven't exactly informed you that I've already failed my professional exams, and will most likely be out of a job soon. I should probably slip that in somewhere. Maybe I'll wait till I've had a chance to check out her books.

"I have confidence in you," Aïsha says, studying me earnestly, her expression having returned to its usual Zenlike serenity.

I wish I could say the same.

I manage to get through all the work Soula has delegated to me by noon the next day. Positively thrilled, Soula drops a fresh double load on my desk, utterly oblivious to Aïsha's file tucked surreptitiously under my in-tray, behind the bamboo plant.

I've got only a day—a week maybe, if I'm really, really lucky—before she realizes I haven't turned it in for review. And with all this extra responsibility she's throwing my way, I'm beginning to feel the heat.

So, when eight o'clock rolls around and everyone, including Soula and the janitorial staff, has called it a day, I decide it's safe enough to remove Aïsha's file out of its hiding place.

I turn the cover and scan the bright orange table of contents. Let's see here . . . legal documents . . . bank statements . . . creditor info . . . financials . . . I think I'm getting a headache. This is entirely unacceptable. I have to get out of here before I pass out of boredom. I owe it to Aïsha to do a good job. I stow the file away in my work tote, along with my sunglasses and keys, and head for the exit.

This mission calls for a double chocolate mousse cake hit with a frothy caramel cappuccino on the side at my favorite java haunt. It's going to be a long night, and I'll be needing all the caffeine I can get.

29

"Doesn't this remind you of high school?" Sophie peers at me over the edge of her Advanced Electromagnetics textbook. "Remember when we would study together in your parents' basement, and I'd help you with Cal while you helped me with . . . What did you help me with Al?"

"Nothing. You're brilliant, remember?" I sink my face into the 475-page book spread open on the table in front of me. Financial Accounting III.

It's Saturday morning, and Java-U is bustling with the usual crowd of students either cramming for midterms or tending to their social lives. Social lives that are doubtless light-years ahead of mine in coolness. What do you expect from someone who'd only just figured out what an MP3 player was around the time Apple came out with the iPod nano?

"This feels nice," Sophie continues. "I kind of wish we could do this more often. I miss you, man. You turn hot shot businesswoman and forget about your peeps?" She thumps her chest in fairly believable gangsta style.

"Plus when you were seeing Brian, we'd go out clubbing, sure, but you never had any downtime left over for us. Like now."

I'd hardly call scrambling to find the answer to Aïsha's conundrum before the weekend's up and Soula discovers the missing file "downtime," but I have to admit there's a ring of truth to Sophie's words.

Isn't it funny how it takes being single again to realize how much your friends mean to you? I mean really realize it, down to the core of your soul. Both Sophie and Jaz had been alone the entire time I'd been with Brian, but it wasn't until that last day in Varadero, the day Jaz let all the silent resentment seep out of her like venom out of an open wound that I saw the effect of my romantic dramas on my friends. And now I'm the one who needs them.

I lift my face and force a guilty smile at Sophie. "I'm sorry, Sophie."

"For what?"

"For not really being there."

She shrugs. "It's normal."

"I know. It's so weird . . . after spending so many years on the same path, our lives are starting to drift off in separate directions. I don't think they'll ever be on the same track again."

"We kind of have to get used to that."

I let the thought simmer in my head for a minute. What if Brian and I hadn't split up? What if we'd gotten married instead, and then had babies right away while Sophie and Jaz kept to the party circuit? Would the fact that I'd be tied up with playgroups and PTA meetings ruin our friendship? Or what if it had been Sophie that left me to study Swahili in the plains of Kenya while Jaz accepted a transfer to New York? I'd be the one nuking mac 'n' cheese by myself on a Friday night and reminiscing about the good old days when I had friends.

I shudder at the thought.

"Maybe we just have to change our idea of what friendship means," I say cautiously. "Maybe it's not about clubbing together every weekend or knowing every little detail about each other's lives like we used to. Maybe it just means that wherever we are in the world, whatever we're doing, we stay in touch and make sure we each know that the other is there for us."

Sophie's eyes cloud over with a film of moisture, but she blinks it away. "You're so right."

"Why? Why am I right?" My heart skips a beat. God, please let me be wrong. "Are you thinking of running off somewhere without telling anyone? Don't think I won't hunt you down and pulverize you." I'm only marginally kidding.

Sophie just throws her head back and laughs. "Oh, God." She dabs at the wet corner of her eye with her pinkie. "Ali, you kill me. What if I did? What would you say?"

"Seriously?"

"Seriously."

"It depends. You could start by telling me what you're thinking."

She takes a breath like she's about to launch into a Shakespearean soliloquy. "I was thinking . . ."

"Yes?"

"This whole scholarship thing . . . I think I might be able to delay it another year, if I could prove to my professors I wasn't just taking time off to bum around Europe or something."

"So you think taking a year off to bum around Cuba with Javier is going to go over better?" I am *waaaaay* ahead of her.

"Well, not exactly bum around. I was thinking of joining Habitat for Humanity. Maybe I could help with wiring houses or something, I don't know, but if after three years of engineering, I can't be useful to an organization that builds homes for the poor, then what am I good for?"

Now this I hadn't seen coming. Although I should've. Ever since we were kids, Sophie's been looking for the chance to make a difference. She never really knew how, but I have to give her credit for recognizing an opportunity when she saw one. The sensible side of me, the one that usually ends up sounding exactly like my mother, wants to tell her she's nuts, that you can fantasize about this kind of stuff, but no one actually goes out and does it. But really, is that true?

No one we know would do this, but isn't that just because our parents were too busy trying to make it in a new country, struggling with a language and customs that weren't their own, deflecting racism away from us whenever they could while simultaneously forcing us to grow thicker skin so we could deal with it on our own?

Who has time to even think about joining Habitat for Humanity, or saving the humpback whales, or lowering emissions standards when you've got that to worry about?

But Sophie and I are different. We're just as Canadian as the guy who does the Molson Ex "I am Canadian" commercials on CBC. This is our country, and we'd found our place in it long ago. Whatever obstacles our amber-dusted skin sometimes thrusts in our faces, we are perfectly capable of dealing with them.

"Do it."

While I'd been momentarily lost in thought, Sophie's gaze had sunk back down to her textbook.

Her eyes narrow at me as though she hadn't heard me right.

"I said—" I lean over and place my hand over hers. "—just do it."

Her faces swells in something like glee right there in the café, and I'm afraid she's going to start hyperventilating.

"But if you and Javier get married on a secluded beach somewhere in Cuba and you don't invite me, I swear to God, my friend, I will get you."

I can't do this.

It's one thing to follow a set of standard procedures spelled out in a manual, the result of years of other people's expertise, compiled and distilled for my convenience. It's also one thing to work out the solution to a complicated accounting problem when you know exactly which chapters from the textbook you're being tested on. It's another thing altogether to find a solution to a questionless problem with no resources to speak of except for old class notes and a useless file.

The look of utter defeat must have been etched all over my face because Sophie interrupts me with a gentle tap of her foot under the table.

"Tell me again what the issue is. Maybe I can help."

"You can't."

Now if Sophie would somehow magically morph into Brian, we'd be talking. He'd know exactly how to approach this.

"Try me."

I sigh, preparing to say out loud the words I'd been churning in my head over and over again for the past God knows how many hours.

"The bank is calling in the loan. It seems Aïsha is in breach of some of the covenants."

"What's a covenant?"

"It's like a stipulation. Say, you need to borrow some money from a bank, and they're, like, 'Yeah, sure, just make sure you follow these rules.' If you break any of the rules, they can technically recall the loan. Unless they're reasonably sure that you'll eventually turn a profit."

I can already see Sophie's eyes glazing over, but she tactfully blinks the boredom away and ponders the new information.

"Why would they lend you money if they're setting you up for a fall?"

"They aren't. They want you to succeed just as much as you want to so they can keep collecting their interest charges. But they don't want their money to disappear into a big black hole either, so they keep close tabs on you the whole time you're still indebted to them."

She bites her bottom lip. "Sounds rough."

I shrug. "Not really. I just have to show that Aïsha's making money. Well . . . not money. A profit." I see the look of confusion creep across Sophie's face again. "You can technically be making tons of money, but if you spent a lot of it just setting up your store or your factory or whatever, then it's gonna take a while before you actually start seeing some of it in your pockets, right? It's called an investment."

"Right."

I'm not convinced she got it. Genius or no genius, accounting is in a realm of logic all its own, so you can hardly blame the girl. But still . . . she's managed to get me thinking. . . .

"Sophe, you saw all the people in Aïsha's store the other day, didn't you?"

Sophie nods.

"And practically all of them walked out with a carrier bag." I bang my hand down on my textbook in frustration. "I just don't get it."

All those years of business school followed by nine months in Audit, and I hadn't learned anything useful. More likely, I'd spent the last four years dreaming up outfits in my head instead of focusing on the print under my nose, so to speak. And when at the end of my half-assed studies I managed to get a stuffy, important firm to pick me, *me* out of countless hopefuls, did I drop to my knees and thank my good luck and sound genes? No. I didn't. I slacked off, never thinking it would come back to bite me in the butt quite this way. I couldn't care less about my job. I'm slowly beginning to think that losing it might be a blessing. But that I can't help someone I really like, someone who's put her faith in me . . . now *that* is the definition of hitting rock bottom.

"Let's look at this like a physics problem." Sophie's got that crazed look in her eyes now, the one that takes over her when someone buys her one of those 150,000-piece 3-D puzzles. "What do we know? The shop is clearly making *some* money, so why is the bank calling in the loan now?"

"Because of the covenants. They've been breached."

"What kind of covenants are we talking about, here?"

"Are you really interested in this?"

"Yes. Stop asking me that."

"Fine. Suit yourself. There's a whole bunch of covenants about minimum inventory requirements and interest payment terms and crap like that. The big enchilada of bank covenants, however, the one that's got Aïsha in a bind, is the one concerning the current ratio. It has to stay at a certain level."

"You lost me."

"Look, there's nothing too funky about it. It's a kind of fraction that compares how much money you have with how much you owe. Well . . . sort of."

I suppose I could get into the discussion of how a current ratio is actually current assets divided by current liabilities and then list what's an asset and what makes it current, but Sophie's textbooks were making her drowsy enough without my help.

"Bottom line is that Aïsha looks like she's spending more than she's earning, which still doesn't seem to make too much sense to me."

"Uh-huh." Sophie had fought valiantly, but the morbid stench of a battle lost hangs in our corner of the café. The battle against Death by Accounting. I'd really lost her this time.

"All this java juice is making me hyper." I get up from the hard steel chair and arch my back, rubbing it at the base, right where it's aching from seven hours of inertia. "I can't think anymore. Let's call Jaz and see what she's up to."

I catch the flicker of relief in Sophie's face. "Sure?"

"Yup."

"Okay." She starts gathering the books, pens, and loose papers on her side of the table. "You know about Jaz and Simon . . . they went out twice this week." Sophie raises an eyebrow at me. "Think this might be going somewhere?"

"If Ben doesn't come out of the woodwork and Jaz manages to remember what a dick he is if he does, then maybe."

"Maybe we should get her really drunk one night and have

'Ben is a dick' tattooed on her chest so it's there in case they decide to get it on. Just, you know, as a preventive measure."

"The idea has merit. Maybe we can get it henna-tattooed. That'll teach her without the effects of permanent scarring. Now let's see if she can get us into Club Rouge."

30

It's Monday morning, and I'm not any closer to finding a way to save Aïsha from the end of her brief tenure as an entrepreneur.

At least Tom's back from vacation, more tanned and beautiful than ever, so I'm free to take comfort in gazing at him whenever I don't think he's looking.

Tom's not the only one who's back in the office today, as I was reminded by the blinking red light of my answering machine this morning. Diane's secretary had left a message to call her back and schedule a meeting at my "earliest convenience."

"Athanasios! You're back." Somehow Soula's voice had bounded ahead of her, resounding between the inner walls of my brain. "How was your trip?"

Athanasios. I don't think I'd heard anyone call him that before. I like it so much better than dime-a-dozen Tom.

"Too short." He grins with just the appropriate mix of I'm-so-suave confidence and warm approachability.

"Aren't they always?" Soula sighs in a rare show of humanity. Then she notices me like one notices an insect that's crawling over their new shoes. "Good morning, Ali." The edge of her clunky brown audit bag whacks my shin as she passes my desk. "Nice weekend?"

Oww.

"Ahh . . . yeah, fantastic." There's really no need to tell her I spent so much time glued to a coffee shop table this weekend that a homeless man tried to pick me up sometime around 4 A.M. And this so I could secretly pore over a file I had smuggled out of the office and dissected to pieces at a campus coffee shop. If only squandering my last chance at corporate redemption had been worth it.

"Good, I'm glad. But take it from me, Ali—" She leans conspiratorially over the partition. "—don't let too much partying affect your career. You're a professional now."

The bags under my eyes. More like a complete set of Louis Vuitton luggage, signature collection. I must look like something out of an eighties zombie movie.

Tom looks up from his screen with one eyebrow and a tiny corner of his mouth raised.

Thank you, Soula.

I force a meek smile and hope she interprets it as gratitude for the nugget of professional wisdom she's just imparted. At least she's going to her office.

"Oh, one more thing, Ali," she says, turning back to face me. "I can't seem to find this one file." She closes her eyes and pinches the bridge of her nose in thought. "I can't recall the name just now. You wouldn't happen to have anything sitting on your desk, would you?"

Oh, God. She knows. She's just toying with me, the cheap harpy.

"No, nothing. I haven't got anything here besides what you assigned to me last Friday."

"Hmm."

I wonder if you can hear teeth chattering from three feet away.

"Just keep an eye out for me, will you? Hold on, let me get the name for you." She calls out, her shapeless jersey shift disappearing behind her office door.

How many weeks of unemployment insurance is an Audit junior entitled to these days? Wait, I forgot—they're calling it "employment insurance" now. Like semantics are supposed to make me feel better. Was it a 60 or 70 percent top-up? I didn't pay much attention to that section of the contract when I signed on. I was more interested in how long it would take to save up for a Dior saddlebag on my new salary.

"Shit! What do you mean, the client wants me there?"

I'm jarred out my quasi-delirious state by Soula's manly voice thundering out of her office. "Can't you handle this on your own? For fuck's sake, John. . . ."

The rest is a jumble of insults and orders.

One minute later I hear the phone slam in its cradle with that shrieking sort of ring phones make when they're being physically abused.

"I'll be in a meeting the rest of the morning." Soula blows past Tom and me like a howling hurricane. "Just carry on with whatever you're doing and I'll catch up with you this afternoon." And she promptly disappears down the hall leading to the main client boardroom.

Saved.

But for how long?

An hour later, I still haven't found anything that's even remotely useful. It's half past ten, the thirteenth round of a twelve-round boxing match. I could lick my wounds and try to get up one last time for good measure, but I'd rather just stay down and play dead.

And I really can't face Soula right now. She said she wouldn't be back until the afternoon anyway, and Aïsha deserves to hear it straight. Straight from the person who failed her.

"Ali . . ." Tom propels his swivel chair in my direction.

"Hmm?" Should I bother to bring the backup along? Does it even matter anymore?

"Thanks for covering for me this week. I've thumbed through a couple of client files this morning. Everything looks great."

"My pleasure." It really was.

I gather the legal drafts, the bank recs, and financial statements into a neat pile and stuff it into my Marc Jacobs alligator tote, leaving the company-assigned mud-brown audit bag to gather more dust under the desk.

I may be an auditor, but I don't have to look like one.

Well, *was* an auditor.

"Bonjour! Quelle belle surprise." Aïsha rushes to greet me as soon as I set foot in the shop.

It's still too early for most shoppers, the only activity along the busy downtown avenue coming from passing office-dwellers—you can always tell them apart from the rest of the world by the sallow greenish undertones of their skin. Every once in a while one of them interrupts her frantic pace to peer into Aïsha's storefront window, a mishmash of rich burgundy, brocade, and velvet cascading over the wire-ribbed torsos of mannequins.

I've decided I'm going to be blunt. There's no time to drag my feet anymore.

"I've got some bad news." I brace myself for the colorful mix of multilingual curses to come my way. I won't fight it.

"Oh, no . . . what's happened?"

"I didn't find anything."

"What?" It comes out more confused than angry. "Oh, don't worry about that," Aïsha says. She shrugs and turns to grab a broom from behind the counter.

I'm dumbfounded. Where are the tears? The insults? The infamous Gallic temper?

"I don't understand. . . . You're not angry?" My mouth gaping, I watch her sweep the polished floor with long, careful strokes, her curtain of black hair swinging languidly with each stroke.

"I wasn't expecting miracles from you, Aline. I'm just glad someone cared enough about me and my little store to help."

Before I walked over here, I had decided that no matter what, I wouldn't let my emotions take over. Whatever it came to. But now, in spite of myself, I feel the stirrings of frustrated fury stinging me from under my skin. Where's the mother tigress determination to keep her dream from dying? Where's her anger? I never imagined she'd give up so easily.

"You could complain, you know. You could take them to court!"

"Whatever for?"

"Because! Because . . . because they were negligent! And don't try and tell me they weren't. Hell, I'm Ernsworth too, you know, and I didn't come through for you either." I bite my lip to keep it from trembling.

"Oh, Aline!" She drops her brooms and hurries to my side. "I hired them to handle my bankruptcy claim. They're—you are, actually—doing your job, precisely what I'm paying you for." She smoothes my hair as if I were a small child and leads me to a stool by the cash register.

"Here, sit down. I'll get some coffee going." She disappears behind the curtain of the workshop.

I breathe in, deep, and hold it before I exhale again. I'm suddenly aware of my leg, bopping up and down like I was on speed. Maybe the strong-enough-to-stun-a-horse Middle Eastern brew isn't what I need right now. A martini, maybe. More coffee, probably not. I decide to take a stroll around the store instead while trying to mimic deep-breathing techniques I'd seen on TV. I want to take it all in before big burly uniformed men drag whatever's salable out the door to the sound of Aïsha's wailing.

I walk the length of one wall, stopping to run a finger down a pretty tweed trumpet skirt, paired with a Victorian-inspired cotton blouse. Aïsha should really carry more of this businessy type of merchandise with all these office buildings around here. Not that it matters at this point.

I swing my arms to distract myself. Aïsha was right when she said I'd already tried on the entire shop. Except . . . The storefront window is stocked full of merchandise I haven't seen before. Cocktail dresses, bejeweled tunics, and decadent costume jewelry. The Holiday collection.

"Hey, Aïsha, is that new stock in the window?"

"Yes," she calls out from the back. "The production was already under way when I realized I wasn't going to meet the minimum profit figures set by the bank."

Wait a minute . . . but if . . . No! Surely no one could have missed something so obvious. And so simple.

With a sudden burst of energy, I lean over, reach for my bag, and pull the entire stack of enclosed papers out and spread them all over the cash register area.

My mind is racing faster than my fingers can turn the pages. An eternity later, I find a section marked with a yellow Post-it. The bank covenants.

I flip to another section, this one outlining all her expenses since she opened shop.

And my hands freeze.

There it is, in the notes to the financial statements, in tiny writing.

"Aïsha, why did you expense all these . . . these costs over here? . . ." I pull back the folder holding her invoices, the one I was poring over just last night. "See here, 'Fabric—cotton/viscose blend, velvet knit, paprika, seventy-five meters.' Is that the fabric you used for the new collection?"

"Ah . . . yes, it is, actually. Why? Does it matter?"

I completely ignore her and move on to the next item in the file. "And those over there, you bought two extra machines."

"They're special for producing some of the finishings on the pieces. It takes the seamstresses so much time to do the same work that these machines can do in a matter of minutes. I figured I'd be saving myself money down the line by having fewer seamstresses eventually."

"And you *expensed* all this stuff?"

"Ali, are you okay?"

"Just answer the question!"

"*Mais, bien sûr.* I thought I'd lower my taxes that way. This is how it works, no?"

"If they were real expenses, maybe. But they're not. You're running a business. These are assets. There's a difference. Didn't your accountant say anything?"

"I do my own accounting on this special software I bought just the other . . . Ali, seriously, are you okay?"

"Aïsha, do you realize that all these expenses are what's making it look like you're not making any money? The bank thinks you're tossing good cash out the window. That's why they're cutting you off."

Her pretty face draws a complete blank. Honestly, don't these artsy types know *anything*?

"Okay, let's start again. Have you ever heard of the saying, 'You have to spend money to make money'?"

"Y-y-es . . ." She eyes me cautiously.

"You've clearly spent lots of money getting your collection started, but it's going to take some time before you get it all back. You know, for customers to pass by, see the stuff, try it on, and hopefully buy it. These aren't expenses, Aïsha, they're assets. The bank can't know that if you don't tell them."

"They didn't ask," she replies with genuine bafflement.

"*You* don't tell them, Aïsha, your financial statements do. You've prepared them all wrong. Look, if we deduct all your assets from the expenses section . . ." I quickly punch some numbers into the calculator and double-check the nasty letter Aïsha received from the bank.

"Look! You see!"

I watch Aisha peer at the numbers in confusion, feeling myself slip into a dreamlike state. Not unlike the kind I get into when I've had one too many martinis.

"What? Do I see what?"

"Your current ratio. Look—it beats the bank's minimum requirements. You passed! You made it!"

I almost want to pick her up and twirl her by her tiny waist around the room. Even if she still doesn't really know what I'm talking about.

She's saved. And so am I.

31

I stumble to a clumsy stop in front of Soula's office, struggling to catch my breath. My face feels flushed with the strain of having half jogged, half sprinted all the way from Aïsha's shop to the foot the Ernsworth building.

My reflection on Soula's glass wall pants back at me, flyaways and frizzles forming a fuzzy halo around my head. Meanwhile my crisp white cotton shirt, fresh from my mother's flawless ironing, sticks to my skin like cheap leather in August.

I look like a lunatic. Not the best condition to be in when attempting to present a serious case. But then again, who gives a shit what I look like? I'm about to prove to Soula, to Diane, to every single audit junior who snubbed their snooty little noses at me when I flunked the UFE that I wasn't just an average screwup in a fabulous pair of shoes.

Alerted by my heavy stifled breathing, Soula drops the red pen with which she was so furiously pockmarking an open file and lifts her face to me, her schoolmarmy reading glasses slipping down her nose.

"Where were you?"

"I'm really sorry—" Why am I apologizing? I was doing my job, for fuck's sake. "I had to step out of the office for a bit, but that's actually what I wanted to talk to—"

"Step out of the office for a bit?" she snaps, trapping me in a glare that would freeze Hell over. "This isn't university. You can't just 'pop out' for a cappuccino and a biscotti in between insolvency files. This is work—"

"But if you'd just let me finish!" Whoops. That had come out a few notches louder than it should have. "Sorry. What I meant was, I'm sorry I didn't tell you before I left, but it was really unexpected and you were in a meeting anyway." I pause for a short breath. She doesn't yell. Good sign. I keep going. "You know that Aïsha Saint-Jacques file, the one you were looking for earlier? I went down to see the client—"

"You mean to tell me you had that file all along? Even when I asked you about it?"

It's hard not to cower in front of your superiors, especially when you were conditioned by years of schooling and overcautious parenting to think that they held the key to your entire future. But Soula's complete volte-face is *Exorcist*-grade scary, even to me. Last Friday I was motivated, self-starter Ali. Today I'm lower than shoe vermin.

"Yes, but I really don't understand how that's a big deal."

"You don't see how this is a big deal?" she mimics. "This is going straight to Diane. And to think I was ready to vouch for you."

I can't believe what I'm hearing. It's not possible this is the same person from last week. Not if she's sane, anyway.

"I figured out a way to save her from bankruptcy!" I blurt out, unable to hold it in any longer. Despite Soula's hurtful words, the knowledge that Diane was now back in her office readying my pink slip as we speak, my heart is bursting with pride. I could recite the entire soundtrack of *The Sound of Music* backwards right about now.

Soula stares at me, her mouth frozen in a bizarre oblong oval, her facial expression betraying a mixture of confusion and disbelief.

"There's a mistake in the preparation of the financials. Could you believe she's been doing all her own accounting? Of course you would, you've met her, but the point is the business is perfectly sound. We just have to present the restated financials to the bank."

I'm shaking and completely out of breath, my voice faltering at the end of each sentence. All the stress of the past few weeks is nothing compared to the tension of this moment. This is it. It's either a promotion or a big brown cardboard box to pack my pink slip and picture frames in. I doubt they'd let me keep the stapler. But really, how could anyone fire me right now? Even Diane, the gatekeeper to the Underworld, wouldn't dare.

Soula doesn't budge. My feet are beginning to go numb, and my knees can't be far behind.

"You mean you haven't filed her bankruptcy papers yet?" she says carefully, her voice calm and sedate, as though we were discussing what brand of highlighter we liked best instead of deciding on my future. It almost sounds like she'd completely blanked out everything I said after *hello*.

We continue to stare at each other in silence, all movement beyond the square-foot-and-a-half of space separating us completely suspended.

"I'm sure you'll make filing those papers your top priority now. I expect them on my desk by eight thirty tomorrow morning." I half expect her to add, *And why don't you get me a nice cup of chai tea while you're at it* next.

I don't move.

I'm waiting for Tom, Penny, and everyone else in the office to jump out of the shadows and yell "April Fools" or "Happy Birthday" or something. Then I'd calmly explain that it was neither April Fools' Day nor my birthday, and we'd all have a good laugh about it and go back to our desks. And the bank would come through with Aïsha's loan, and Diane would get hit by a bus and all would be well with the world.

But no one scurries out from behind the blinds, or underneath the desk.

"Well, what are you waiting for?" Her voice is dripping with annoyance, but her furtive glances betray a strange sort of expression I'm not used to seeing in her. If I didn't know any better, I'd think that Soula, the next senior-manager-vice-president-of-the-whole-fucking-company-in-training looks embarrassed. But what could she possibly be embarrassed about?

It occurs to me that I have to move, say something at least, but I still can't budge. Somehow, the tattered pieces of my spine manage to collect themselves enough so I can mumble something resembling coherence. "I just said I've found a way we could prevent Aïsha from going out of business. If you like, I'll go get the f—"

"I heard you the first time, Aline." Her eyes bore into me, cold and menacing. And a little bit scared. "I suggest you go back to your cubicle and do exactly what I said, or you can expect to be looking for another job tomorrow. And please don't think that another major consulting firm will look at you twice after they've heard what Diane and I have to say."

That's it.

Something starts to tingle right under my skin, a spreading numbness I haven't let myself feel in a long time. Not fear, not foreboding or dread. Not the pitiable sentiment of wanting to be anywhere but here.

It's rage.

"I don't give a flying fuck anymore."

Soula blinks twice at me. Did she honestly think I was going to cower into my little corner when I'd done nothing wrong? Ha. As if.

"I worked my ass off for you and this company even though I hated every second of it." My voice is steady yet seething. "One whole weekend, forty-eight hours, I slaved over that file, and this is what you have to say to me? Not even an explanation, a reason. Nothing."

"Aline, I'd be careful what I say right now."

"What, are you threatening to fire me? Again? Is there some sort of running bet between you and Diane to see who could threaten me with the boot the most times before I went postal? Fine. You win. I've had it. I'm sorry if I'm not more devastated, but I've actually been expecting this for quite some time now and the suspense's been killing me. The only reason I'm still standing in front of you is because I'm trying to help someone I care about and you're ready to rip her dream to shreds, you—" Do I say it? I've been dying to say this to her since the day I met her. "—you bitch."

Soula's mouth twitches, and she goes from the excited pink of a few moments ago to a scary purple. Almost eggplant. She springs from the leather chair like a liberated Jack-in-the-box.

"I'm going to pretend you didn't just say that. Now march back to your desk and get back to work."

"No. I won't do it." Soula looks like someone might have nailed her feet to the floor. Dazed and confused. And utterly clueless of what she's supposed to do next.

"I told you what I came here to say, and if you're going to squash a poor woman's life under the soles of your hideous shoes, then you can perfectly well do it yourself."

I don't wait for an answer. Stumbling out of her office, I snatch my purse from under my desk and break for the exit.

"You just wait one minute, Aline Hallaby!" I hear Soula calling out the corridor behind me. "Wait till Diane hears about this. And every audit manager in town. Accounting's a small world, you know, and this is the last you'll be seeing of it."

"Ali, are you okay?"

Tom pokes his head from around the corner, his face clouded with concern. Or is it pity? I don't have time to wonder.

"Sorry, Tom, can't talk right now." I swing away from his grasp. I'm too angry to speak, too angry to see straight, so angry, I want to fucking scream. Where's the damn elevator?

I punch the triangle pointing downward for the twenty-seventh time in the last five seconds. It's no use. I'm better off taking the stairs. Tom is right behind me.

"Hey, Ali, listen to me. . . . Ali, wait, dammit!"

He grabs hold of one of my shoulders like he's ready to pin me to the wall.

"What the hell do you want from me?" I scream straight into his face. I don't care what he has to say or how he's looking at me, his eyes softening as they peer into mine. All I care about is that he's loosened his grip on my shoulder.

Just like I learned in the odd kickboxing class I'd taken at the gym, I summon all my strength and plummet toward the ground, using the surprise effect to break loose of him, and then rocket back up on the other side of the arm that had pinned me to the wall.

"What the—?"

By the time he's recovered, I'm already racing down the fire escape, the startled look on Tom's face as I nearly assaulted him coming back to me in flashes.

At least I didn't knee the guy.

Within minutes, breathless and swimming in my own sweat, I spill out of the building and onto the sidewalk. The setting sun is shining painfully bright, and the entire cobbled square in the middle of the city's financial center is brimming with activity. Courier boys zip past me on their bikes so fast, I'm sure they're going to kill themselves; motorists are busy outdoing each other with their obnoxious honking; and pedestrians, talking, as it would seem, to themselves through affixed headsets push past me casting one glance at my tearstained face before shrinking away in embarrassment.

I don't blame them. I'd do the same. I'd stare at the pitiable oddity on the street, pretending not to have noticed. I feel like a modern-day Quasimodo with no medieval bell tower to hide myself away in.

Familiar faces from the office begin to trickle out of the revolving glass doors, people from other departments, from other firms, the guy who works the day shift at the Energy smoothie stand on the second floor. Any second now, someone's going to notice me, notice the look on my face, and ask me what's up. Either that or ignore me completely. I don't know which is worse.

For the first time in a very long time, I don't want to see Sophie. Or Jaz. Or anyone, really, except for one person. My mother.

32

The train screeches to a halt, snapping me right out of my marginally suicidal thoughts. I dodge my way around the other passengers and step onto the platform into a mix of schoolkids and sallow-cheeked business people.

My typically suburban street, with its looming maples and identical brownstones, is oppressively quiet. So quiet, in fact, that I'm left with nothing to do but fantasize about assaulting Soula with the back of my sharpest stilettos. But before I can come to a conclusive decision as to which one of my forty-six pairs would cause the most damage, I'm already standing at the threshold of the split-level duplex I share with my parents.

I slide my key into the lock and let myself inside, out of the cold and drizzle of the late afternoon.

Instead of the silence I was expecting, I'm greeted by the sound of shouting Arab women coming from the kitchen. The yelling alone doesn't set off any alarm bells in my head—I'm used to hearing the three wives of *Hajj Mutawalli* curse each other out on the portable TV most days of the week.

But the voices don't belong to the trio of Egyptian soap queens. They belong to my mother and Auntie Maryam.

I tread nervously across the vestibule, then the den, and carefully poke the top of my head around the kitchen wall.

Auntie Maryam is gesturing wildly, arms flailing, head bopping from side to side. Perhaps the most glaring indication of her current mental state is that she appears to have left her house clad in an orange jogging suit with white socks and fuzzy slippers on her feet.

And she has lime green curlers in her henna-tinted hair. This from a woman whose favorite form of entertainment is hanging out at the mall café and making fun of housewives in last season's hemlines. I wish I had my camera.

"Calm down, Maryam." I can see my mother struggling to relax her own nerves. Her face is blotched red and puffy as if she'd just stopped crying herself. "We don't know anything yet."

"What's there to know, *ya Muna?* If only the kidnappers had left a note! What are we going to do? *Allahu'akbar . . .* " And with that, my aunt Maryam resumes her outrage, by turn imploring God to smite those who took away her poor innocent daughter and asking Him why in His infinite wisdom He had deemed it necessary to pick on our family.

My mother leaves Auntie Maryam to her ranting, lending moral support by standing close by and holding her head down in shared grief.

Neither one of them has seen me yet. Should I say something?

I open my mouth to ask what's happened, but before I can say anything, a mechanical tango number rings conspicuously throughout the kitchen.

My cell phone.

I reach instinctively for my purse, but oddly enough that's not where the noise is coming from. I look up and lock eyes with my mother.

Her face, pinched and harried as it was a second ago, now seems to be swelling with rage. Her chest is heaving with it, as if she can hardly hold the anger in.

"Go ahead, pick it up." She grabs the phone from where it's sitting on the counter and hurls it at my head. Luckily, I can catch. "Maybe it's your boyfriend again."

Oooo-kay. Now she's really flown off the sanity cliff.

348 * NADINE DAJANI

What could she possibly be talking about? She's never re-acted this way to Brian before, not that there's any chance he'd call me again anyway.

The phone's stopped ringing. Mildly annoyed that I might have missed an important call, I flip it open to check the number. Two missed calls. The last one from Aphro. Great. Word must be all over the office.

The other one is from an unknown number. Whatever. I clamp the chrome top down on the number pad and stuff my sleek Motorola back into its designated slot in my purse.

I look up to find my mother still glaring at me like she was a fifteenth-century English peasant and I were a condemned witch about to be lit on fire.

And that's when it clicks.

Sweet Mohammed, I am going to die.

Right before I boarded the bus to the airport, I gave him my cell number. The one phone I thought no one else would ever pick up.

Miguel.

My kneecaps wobble like jelly and I feel my legs go numb. I grab the wall before they can buckle under me.

Maybe she suspects something but doesn't really know. She's probably just trying to scare me into spilling my guts. Lebanese mothers can be a lot like the KGB in situations that involve strange men and their unmarried daughters. I need to concen-trate on breathing. And on keeping my big mouth shut.

Her eyes are still firmly locked on me, the corners of her mouth and her shoulders trembling in sync. Finally she parts her chapped lips to speak. *"Meen hayda Miguel?"*

Who's this Miguel person?

God have mercy on my soul.

33

As much as she would have liked to throttle me right then and there, my mother had no choice but to drop the whole Miguel line of questioning when my father and Uncle Munir, Ranya's dad, let themselves in by the back door just moments later. There was a real tragedy at hand. My execution would have to wait for a more opportune moment.

Ranya, it seemed, had disappeared today while her husband was busy inspecting a piece of land out in Industrial Park.

How convenient.

Less than an hour after I walked in on my aunt and mother wailing like a pair of wildebeests in heat, we were all seated in Ranya's football-stadium-size den, sipping tar-black coffee out of tiny espresso cups and making strained small talk with Dodi's mother. The men of the family were still arguing with Constable Giroux out in the hallway.

The gist of the discussion went something like this:

OFFICER GIROUX: I think we should hold off filing an official missing persons report until tomorrow. Maybe she was upset about something and needed some time to think. [Insert accusatory glance at Dodi.]

UNCLE MUNIR: My daughter is a respectable married woman. She would never do something like this to her family. Perhaps this is how people from your country behave, but certainly not a woman from a good Lebanese family. [Insert reassuring nod toward Dodi's father.]

And that's about as far as the young policeman got with the assembled clans.

I had my own opinion on the matter. If foul play had anything to do with my cousin's disappearance, I was ready to eat my left shoe. And since I have my Sergio Rossi slouchy boots on, that's saying something.

For one thing, Ranya's Nadya Toto mink, the one she couldn't stand on the grounds that it made her look 120 but that Dodi insisted she wear, was gone. So was every item of expensive jewelry she owned.

"Of course it's theft!" Auntie Maryam cries, wringing her hands in her lap. "Why couldn't they just take everything and leave my poor Ranya alone? May God burn down their houses, curse their wives with infertility and their children with cerebral palsy."

No one beats Arabs when it comes to creative cursing.

"They must be holding her for ransom, the heathen donkey offspring," Auntie Maryam mutters before breaking down for the sixteenth time tonight.

I might have been more concerned had I not noticed that Ranya's favorite coat, a gorgeous yet perfectly worthless Narciso Rodriguez satin trench, the one that always hung in the hall closet when it wasn't on her back, was also missing. As was her brand-new Roland Mouret dress, the one she developed an unhealthy obsession for after she saw it on Demi in *OK!* Also MIA was an assortment of Manolos and Louboutins, and perhaps the most telling of all, her Kate Spade makeup case.

Whoever these supposed kidnappers were, they not only knew their modern designers but clearly had a fetish for women's cosmetics too.

And then, of course, there was the minor fact that no signs of forced entry were to be found anywhere. If Ranya and Dodi's

Westmount penthouse were the set of *Law & Order*, this is where
Detective Green would have Dodi against the wall, one hand
pressed firmly against the weasel's throat while the other one
fished for handcuffs.

Unfortunately, the way this investigation was going, it
sounded more like a scene from *Pride and Prejudice* than one
from *CSI: Miami*.

Girls like Ranya, virtuous Arab girls from good Lebanese
families, did *not* run away and leave their husbands behind.
Maybe Canadian women did these sorts of things, went the pre-
vailing logic of the room, but good Arab girls certainly did *not*.
Ergo, Ranya had to have been kidnapped.

There was simply no other explanation.

Being somewhat less delusional about what "good Lebanese
girls" did or didn't do than the rest of the family, I opt for the
wait-and-see approach. I was going to wait and see if there really
was something worth being concerned about.

Sitting in Ranya and Dodi's plush apartment, decorated with
bejeweled mirrors and tasseled cusions like something an Arab
Martha Stewart might have put together, I decide to focus on my
own plight instead.

So Mom knows about Miguel. Damn. She had to find out
about the toughest one first. If she'd somehow discovered that I'd
failed the UFE instead, then maybe I wouldn't have had to say
anything about Miguel or even Cuba. Sure, I'd have to confess to
the Brian debacle at some point, but I could have come up with
a better reason for being dumped than because of a one-night
stand.

By this time, the coffee has been drunk, the cups turned upside down so the thick residue left at the bottom could snake
down the sides, drying in intricate reddish-brown patterns like
latticework on a mosque window.

In every gathering of Lebanese women, there's always one
among them that doubles as the designated All-Seeing Coffee-

352 ✳ NADINE DAJANI

Cup Reader. This task often came down to my aunt Maryam, but
since no one would let her anywhere near the enchanted cups
lest she read something too disturbing in the mystical dried-up
grains, the job fell to Raja, a friend of Dodi's mother who'd
tagged along for moral support.

"I see a beautiful young woman in the prime of her youth, a
married woman with dark flowing hair." The old crone is clearly
talking about Ranya. "She is distressed but not afraid. She has
faith, and her faith will see her through. I see her laughing."

Gag me.

If this is Raja's way of making my aunt feel better, it is pathetic.

I try to excuse myself, something about needing some air, but
the withered fake blonde in head-to-toe-pleather insists on doing
my cup first.

"I see a fork in the road ahead of you," she says.

I see someone who's been watching too much Psychic Network TV.

"It is very difficult. People will advise you to follow the first
road, the one covered in blossoms and fragrant roses. It will be
difficult to turn away, but at the end of this road lies a bottomless
hole."

Wow. That's a lot going on in a teeny tiny espresso cup.

"There's more."

Ooh, more! If she says I'm going to make my parents proud
with a fortuitous marriage and bear my husband many sons, I
will seriously have to go barf.

"I see a man."

I knew it.

"An *ajnabi* of fair hair. He is standing behind you in the
shadows, following you, but you can't see him. But take heart,
habibti, he has one foot stepping forward. He will soon step out
of the shadows."

Ha! This is so sad. I just smile and nod even as I'm thinking how I'll probably never see my fair-haired Brian again. And Miguel has dark hair, so that's two strikes.

"Thanks, Auntie Raja. That was really . . . mystifying."

She smiles at me through her cataracts and her cakey makeup. *"Sha'toura."* She taps my knee, beaming. *Good girl.*

My mother snaps her head around at the sound of that word as though she'd forgotten I was there. Her eyes bore right through my face and into my skull.

Sha'toura, my ass, I can almost hear her cursing in her head.

"Aline, I need to talk to you." I guess she figured she might as well, since it was looking like we were going to be here for a while. She ushers me inside a bedroom on the other side of the apartment and shuts the door behind us.

With the door closed and without the slightest inkling of a hint, my mother turns around and slaps me.

34

It takes me a moment to feel the sting of it, another for my brain to register what has just happened. I haven't been slapped since . . . since . . . since I have no idea how long ago. My face burns where she'd hit me, and the tears erupt completely by themselves, without the slightest inducement from me, as though the moisture-producing glands themselves had somehow burst.

"I asked you who's Miguel," she says in Arabic.

The notion of time as it usually applies to human beings ceases to exist in the vacuum of space around us.

Utterly unmoving, it mocks me, makes me aware of the ticking of my wristwatch, of every line in my mother's face as she stares me down.

"Well? Aren't you going to speak?"

I can still feel the tingle where her hand made contact with my skin. I want to run away, but there's nowhere to go. Not anymore. And since I can't run away, there's only one thing to do. Something I've never dared do before. Reason with her.

"Mom, sit down. Please."

"I asked you a question, answer it!"

"That's exactly what I'm about to do. But not if you're going to get all psycho on me." I glare back at her with every ounce of determination left in my body.

She stands motionless, shooting darts at me with her eyes. "Is this how living in this country's taught you to speak with your mother?"

Oh, for fuck's sake. If I have to hear her curse out "this country" one more time, I might just explode.

I take a calming breath. I *can* reason my way through this.

"Mom, please—"

"Don't 'Mom, please' me! Who do you think you're talking to?"

Okay, so that approach didn't work.

"I'm talking to my mother. You know, the person who supposedly loves me and wants what's best for me?"

"Oh, so I don't want what's best for you? Is this what your friends say to their mothers?"

I can't help but let out a muffled giggle. "Why are you bringing up my friends? What am I, five?"

"Look! Now she's laughing at her own mother. Listen to her, listen to the ill-mannered ingrate. . . ." And she rants a while longer in Arabic, using words I don't really understand but that I vaguely recognize from old Egyptian movies.

There's something about the rhythm of her speech that strikes me as odd, even though I've heard it a million times before. . . . She sounds like she's speaking to herself instead of to me. It never struck me before, because that's just how Arabs speak sometimes, a little cultural quirk. I've heard Auntie Maryam speak this way to Ranya.

But it does get me thinking.

"Mom . . . It's okay. No one's going to fault you for not raising me right."

My muscles tighten in anticipation of being smacked again, but it doesn't happen.

Instead, my mother stands before me, her eyes wide with shock, motionless, save for the slow rise and fall of her chest.

I search her face for signs that she understood what I meant.

Even if women of my mother's generation were studying in

the same universities as men, even if they were free to dress pretty much as they pleased, there remained at that time the residue of a cultural belief that these girls were the safekeepers of the family honor and, as such, would always need someone to watch over them.

I knew this from the jokes my mother and her friends would sometimes exchange. Like the time Auntie Selma had been reporting a comment one of her elderly Lebanese relatives had made about a young girl sitting in an outdoor Beirut coffee shop, laughing and carrying on in a mixed group of *shabab*, young men and women.

" 'Look at that *sharmouta*,' she said," I heard Aunt Selma tell my mother. "I thought, if this girl was a whore for sitting in a coffee shop with boys, what does that make my daughter?" And they both burst into hysterics. Which explained why my mother didn't dare tell her parents that their granddaughter may very well marry an *ajnabi* one day. A foreigner.

That kind of thinking wasn't my mother's. It was leftover residue from my grandmother's generation. The woman who raised my mother. And who bequeathed her all of her insecurities and her fears, just as my mother had bequeathed me mine.

But I'd seen my mother's confident, fun-loving grin in old pictures. I'd seen her with Farrah Fawcett hair and Jackie O. sunglasses, sitting on a beach in a terry cloth sundress that wouldn't look out of place in a Juicy Couture collection, my dad's arm around her waist.

If I can break through to the woman in the pictures, I can maybe get somewhere.

"No one's going to report you to *Téta* Amira because I did something bad."

Her arms drop limp and lifeless to her side. She seems to shrink at the tone of my voice.

But the nanosecond of weakness is short-lived.

"What's all this nonsense? Honestly. Next you're going to tell me you want to go on Dr. . . . Dr. Whatshisname. You know who I'm talking about. The bald one with the mustache who's always yelling."

"Dr. Phil?"

"Yes, him."

I smother a laugh that comes out sounding like a snort.

The tight line of her lips softens a tiny, near-imperceptible bit.

It's time. If there is ever going to be any hope for an honest relationship between us, then I have to go for it. Right now.

"Mom, I failed the UFE." I say it fast, before I can stop myself.

It hangs in the air around us, sucking up the oxygen bit by bit until I think I'm going to faint.

"Mom . . . did you hear me?"

"I heard you."

I'm afraid she's going to cry again, but it's my own tears that start spilling down my cheeks in an unchecked torrent. What's even more shocking is that my mother, the woman who had it in her to hit me just minutes ago, decides that this bit of news warrants a hug. I cry all over the sleeve of her cherry-print housedress while she strokes my back. I cry for what I had done to Brian, for what could've been with Miguel, and for what I'd let Ernsworth do to me.

With the worst of it now out there, there's no point in delaying the rest any longer. I let it all out, not allowing myself to stop, everything after I found out I'd failed, Diane's threats, the class excursion to Mexico turned trip to Cuba. I pause here for a second, knowing she'd want a proper go at me for having breached her trust the one time I'd been allowed on an unsupervised vacation.

But she doesn't say anything, even to this.

I slow down again when I get to the bit about Miguel, wondering how much I should disclose. I choose to keep this bit of information waddling around in a gray area, leaving it up to my mother to decide how much she wants to know.

Then I tell her what I think must be the hardest news of all for her to hear, that Brian and I have broken up. At this her eyes widen with shock and—dare I say—concern.

"Are you okay?"

"I'm fine. Honestly. We should have broken up a long time ago. We were both boring the life out of each other. He just didn't want to admit it to himself, and I didn't either until Cuba. I think maybe . . . maybe I'm not ready to settle down."

I half expect her to take this opportunity to smack me again and tell me how *Téta* Amira had married *Jiddu* Abd'allah when she was thirteen.

"I told you that, but you wouldn't listen," she says instead.

For a second I'm not sure I heard her right. "What? When did you say that?"

"I've always said it. You have selective hearing just like your father. You Hallabys hear only what you want to."

My mind is reeling. I know I didn't just imagine the adoring looks my mother would throw her favorite pick for future son-in-law.

"Mom, I know you loved him. Don't give me that."

"What's not to love about the poor boy? He's lovely, and kind, and a good man. Everyone could see that. Why would I object?"

"Because he's not Arab? Or even Muslim at that?"

She sighs again, this one seeming like it's coming from the deepest part of her. "What do you want me to say? That it never bothered me? I can't tell you how many times I would cry about it to your aunt Maryam, but what am I going to do? I know that . . . that life changes and we have no choice but to change with it. We can't move to North America and pretend we're still living in Lebanon."

Stop. Hell has officially frozen over. My mother, after over a decade of denial, had somehow come to terms with what it means to immigrate.

"But then why aren't you angry that Brian and I broke up?"

She squares her shoulders back and gapes at me, her left eyebrow arched. I pissed her off again. And we were doing so well. "*Ya Allah ya,* Aline! Really, you're going to drive me mad." She flings both arms high in the air, bringing them down on her thighs with a loud smack. She would've made a great Egyptian soap queen in another life.

"Everything is always your mother's fault! This whole lecture you gave me, weren't you trying to tell me that you're old enough to make your own decisions now? Isn't that what this is all about?"

I nod.

"And so in this one area, the one place I didn't let myself interfere, you make it sound as though I forced you to act against your will. Honesty, Aline, this is too much." She rolls her eyes at God imploringly.

She gives her blood pressure a moment to return to normal and then picks up where she left off.

"It took me a long time to warm up to Brian, not because he isn't a wonderful man, but because I know that others in our community might not look at the situation as kindly as your father and I have. I knew it would be difficult for me to constantly have to defend your lifestyle to the rest of the family. But I did it. And I would do it again. If I believed in living your life for others, I would never have left my parents and crossed an ocean to come here."

I try to think back. Did she ever pressure me into staying with Brian after I started to have my doubts, or was that something my own mind had come up with because I preferred to stay in a bad relationship rather than venture out on my own?

Liberated woman of the West, my ass. All my talk of wanting to break out from under my parents' iron grasp turned out to be a load of crap. I just wanted someone else to take care of me instead.

If my mother could come to terms with being an immigrant, then surely I can come to terms with being an adult.

"I married your father because I loved him," she continues. "Not because I thought I should. Why would I want any less for my daughter?" She squeezes my leg affectionately, but only for a second. Then her face takes on that grave stony look I'm used to whenever I've disappointed her.

"Now, about this Miguel person. What exactly did you do with him?"

I just love how the warm glow of our honest mother–daughter exchange lasted about half the lifespan of a fruit fly.

"Can we talk about this later? I think Auntie Maryam needs us right now."

I'm treated to the warning glare, the one that used to be a signal to me when I was five that a major spanking was on the way, but at least the subject was dropped.

I didn't get a chance to ask my mother how she'd feel if I weren't an auditor anymore. Which is actually a lucky thing because the follow-up question to this of course is, "Well, what are you going to do with your life, then?"

I still don't have an answer to that unless you consider *I have no fucking clue* to be acceptable.

Move out. Though this is my first pick for Step One toward true independence, it isn't exactly clear of obstacles: (a) I will be disowned. Make no mistake about it. No matter how sappy and sentimental my mother had gotten just an hour ago, she remains a woman set in her ways. And those ways include children who stay glued to the nest until they're either married or dead. (b) I've never been in a worse financial position to be contemplating this move, seeing as I am soon to be unemployed.

I wonder when that's going to happen. Officially, I mean. The last words I'd said to Soula on my way out were *you bitch*. It would be a bit of an understatement to say that I harbor no delusions about my impending sacking.

The thing is—for the first time, I truly, honestly, couldn't care less.

I'm just in no particular hurry to hear it from the horse's mouth either.

"Mom? It's three o'clock in the morning. I think we should go home."

She's sunk into the winter white love seat beside me and has her hands wrapped around her temples. She looks exactly like she did when I first walked into the kitchen earlier today.

"There's nothing we can do now." I prod gently.

"We can't leave your aunt and uncle alone."

"You need to rest. We'll be back first thing tomorrow."

"Don't you have to work tomorrow?"

"I'll take tomorrow off."

It's not like I could possibly get into any more trouble.

35

It was really hard getting up for work this morning, especially since I'd unilaterally given myself Tuesday off. The smell of re-heated Egg McMuffins escaping from the lunchroom and wafting through the Corporate Recovery department greets me on this sunny yet freezing Wednesday morning. I'm getting fired today, and I couldn't be any happier if I'd been voted sexiest auditor alive by *CA Magazine*.

The happiest news of all is, of course, that I was right and my mother, as well as the entire Hallaby and El Hoffi clans, were wrong.

Ranya called yesterday. From London. As in England.

What I really want to know is how that repository of human waste also known as Dodi thought we weren't going to find out. It turns out that not only were "good Lebanese girls" perfectly apt to run away when their husbands were found to be as gay as a Wham! reunion, but they were also capable of concocting some pretty impressive revenge schemes to boot.

Being the naïve virgin that she was on her wedding night, it took Ranya a little longer to realize there was more to Dodi's lack of enthusiasm in the bedroom department than it would have taken your average thirty-one-year-old. Also, being a good, not to mention resourceful, Muslim, she prayed for patience while simultaneously scouring La Perla for the most fetching visual aids money could buy. Not that either action proved helpful.

But it wasn't until the day Dodi got careless and neglected to sign out of his Hotmail account that things took a sharp turn up Ugly Alley. One particularly sordid .jpeg attachment was all she needed to forward every piece of incriminating evidence she could lay her manicured hands on to a confidential e-mail account as well as onto a handy jump drive now safely guarded by her lawyer. She then proceeded to empty every bank account she had access to, as well as perform a strip job on the apartment worthy of the *Ocean's Twelve* gang. The jewels, the mink, anything portable. And then she bought a one-way ticket to London.

I'm so proud of her, I could burst.

She even asked to talk to me.

"I'm scared," she'd said.

"Of what?"

"I've never done anything like this before. . . . What will people say?"

Sigh. You can take the girl out of the Middle East, all the way to the land of Big Ben and the Sex Pistols, but you'll never take the prude out of the girl. Well, maybe not never. Ranya had been on her own for all of twenty-four hours, most of them spent sipping orange juice (no, not champagne, even at a time like this) in a first-class cabin aboard British Airways. One must not expect miracles.

"You think Maya and all those other girls at your wedding won't find ways to criticize you even if this whole mess had never happened? Come on, gossip is our national sport. Besides, by the time they're finished with Dodi, everyone will have forgotten all about you."

It's true. Dodi was guilty on more than one count. The most grievous was that of being gay. It's pretty much the only sexual sin an Arab man can commit that's worse than a girl "losing it" before she gets married. I almost felt sorry for him on that one. Almost. Going against the grain of a constricting society is something I'm only too familiar with. Playing my cousin Ranya for a fool and dragging her through the mud with him, however, I'm not about to forgive in this lifetime.

Funny the lengths people will go to hide their true selves from the world.

As though that weren't enough, Dodi had also committed the second biggest sexual sin known to traditional Arab society. He'd left his bride as innocent as the first night she'd crawled under their nuptial duvet. Now that's bad. But being the smart cookie that she was, the .jpeg file she still had in her possession as well as the slew of hot and heavy e-mail exchanges with a gentleman who may or may not have been paid for his services meant that she would also get a tidy settlement in exchange for her—and our—discretion.

"What am I supposed to do now, Ali?"

The girl has it all—looks, brains, and now, more money than even she could spend. And she is asking me for advice?

"What have you always wanted to do?"

"That's just it. . . . I don't know anymore."

"Well, there's your answer. Go figure it out."

"You know I can't. *Mama* and *Baba* will never be able to show their faces in public again."

"And how do you think Dodi's parents are feeling right now?"

Silence.

"Ranya, stop worrying. Just go with the flow, for once in your life." Oh, the irony. "Your parents will understand, and so will everyone else. And you know I'm here for you, whether you need me or not."

It gave me a warm glow, deep within my gut, to know that after all the years of Ranya doting on me, I'd been given a way to pay her back.

"So you'll come visit me, then?"

"Only if you promise to have the time of your life and fuck the first hot Englishman that lays eyes on you."

She promised. Not about the Englishman part, though. She yelled at me for that one.

So today, the biggest gray cloud in my otherwise clear sky is that I can't take to the Internet and air out every last bit of Dodi's rank laundry to the world.

That, and the likelihood of running into Soula any second now.

Instead of Soula, it's Aphro who smacks right into me the second I turn the corner to my cubicle.

"Did I get off on the wrong floor?"

"What the hell happened to you?" She grabs hold of my vintage gabardine blazer by the collar and yanks it toward her face.

"I took a day off. I figured they owed me one. At least. Now let go of me, please."

"Couldn't you have called? You won't believe the shit that went down—"

"Ali! There you are."

"Morning, Penny."

I plop into my chair, switch on the computer, and wait for it to boot up.

"Your little stunt caused quite the stir yesterday. What exactly happened?"

"Pen, sorry. Ali can't talk right now." Aphro tugs at my top again, this time with more urgency. "We have to get out of here."

"You wait your bloody turn, I'm not leaving till I get the scoop," Penny huffs.

I look from one deranged lunatic to the other. I swear I was never this popular before. The girls must be dying for some of my fuck-the-system mojo to rub off on them.

"So, why is Diane combing the entire building trying to find you?" Penny parks both elbows on the width of my partition like she intends to spend quite some time in that spot.

"Probably to fire me. Anyone have a spare cardboard box lying around? Anything will do. I don't have much. A few frames, some postcards. Who wants dibs on my two-hole puncher? How about my 'Revised' stamp? Pink highlighter, anyone?"

"Ali, I mean it. I need to talk to you. It's important."

"Hang on, Fro. I just walked in."

Before I can do anything else, the flickering red light of my answering machine catches my attention. I pick up the receiver and punch in my numerical password. Fourteen unplayed messages. Wow.

I'll call you, I mouth to Aphro and grab a pen and a scrap piece of paper.

She gestures wildly at me to stop while I try my best to tune her out. She'll remember this day when I'm sitting at home in my pajamas at three in the afternoon, watching *Oprah* and calling her office every twenty seconds out of the sheer mind-blowing boredom of unemployment. It *is* my last day, and though I don't plan on doing much work, I intend to go down in dignity, tying up whatever loose ends I can.

The first couple of phone messages are routine office stuff— one partner has sent out a general message asking if anyone's seen the wallet file for one of his clients. A couple of messages later, there's another one from the same partner. This time he tells us to forget he asked and hangs up the phone curtly. Guess he must have forgotten it in the can.

The last message on Monday afternoon, probably delivered just moments after my ignominious escape from Soula's lair, is from Diane.

"Aline, Diane here. I just received your test scores. Call my secretary and schedule a meeting immediately." *Beep.*

I thought I had mentally prepared myself for the inevitable, but my body is unwilling to cooperate. My left knee breaks into convulsions while the other one goes numb. I look up, hoping to find Aphro, but I guess she must have given up trying to wrench me away from my desk and gone back to hers.

Messages ten, eleven, and twelve are attempts from Diane's

secretary to reach me and schedule an appointment. By message thirteen, Diane is back on the line.

"Aline, Diane here. You must know why I'm calling you by now. Give me a call on my mobile as soon as you get this message."

The last message consists of Diane apologizing for not having given me her mobile phone number, and then leaving it for me with more instructions to call her.

And that's it.

I guess I'm going to have to call. Sooner or later. I'm more partial to later.

I'm ready for that coffee right now. My computer's booted up, and the minuscule digital clock at the bottom right corner of the screen reads 8:45. I lean over to get a better view of Soula's—or should I say Sid's—office. It's empty. Not like her at all to be late. With any luck, her alarm clock didn't go off today and she'll scamper in just as I'm bidding my last good-byes. Or she's busy avoiding me. It's not every day one of your underlings calls you a bitch to your face. Maybe she just couldn't hack it.

Oh, who am I kidding?

"Miss Hallaby."

I know that voice. Shit.

I slowly turn my neck just enough to catch a glimpse of the short bespectacled woman standing on the other side of the half-partition.

"Miss Hallaby, Ms. Cloutier has been trying to get in touch with you for some time now."

"Ahhh . . . er." I stall for some time to weigh my options. I remind myself there's nothing to freeze my blood in my veins over, but old habits die hard. "I was . . . ahhh . . . sick yesterday. I couldn't make it. Sorry."

"I checked with the receptionist for your group, and she didn't report any illness-related absences for that day," she says, using the least amount of facial muscles possible to actually produce speech.

"I had the Chinese flu," I quickly blurt out, remembering something in the news about some sort of flu that was going around these days. It came from somewhere in the Far East. Or was it the bird flu? No, that was so last year.

"You were too sick to call?"

"It's funny you should say that," I say after a spurt of forced giggling. "This flu attacks the muscles in your body and makes them ache unbearably. My ears were the most affected, actually."

An arched eyebrow followed by a curt "Please come this way" is all I get for an answer.

I guess they'll just have to cut my minor indiscretion from my severance check. That's if I even get a severance check in the first place.

36

Nothing in Diane's office seems to have changed since the last time I was here. Except for some new picture frames on her desk, everything appears to be in its usual impeccable state.

"How was the wedding?" I say as breezily as I can manage under the circumstances.

"What are you talking about?" Her brows furrow in annoyance. So much for the friendly approach.

"The pictures on your desk, they're new. You're standing next to a girl in full pouffy white glory with matching headgear and a three-hundred-tiered cake behind you. I just figured—"

"I was just redecorating. Never mind about that," she snaps.

I certainly won't be asking about her mysterious leave now.

"Aline, I'm sure you know why—" She's interrupted by the mechanical bleating of her phone. "Oh, for Chrissake! Ali, excuse me."

Ali? I can't remember her calling me anything other than the über-formal Aline, and even that was an improvement on "you . . . whatsyourname?"

I scan Diane's desk while she berates her secretary over the speakerphone for not having taken a message. The sleek dark wood surface is minimally covered, the thick stacks of employee records securely stored in matching cabinets behind her. My eyes wander over her fancy pen in its chic platinum-plated cradle, a business card holder at the head of the desk, and then I freeze.

There it is, glaring at me, holding its tongue out and yelling, "Gotcha!" The Canadian Institute of Chartered Accountants crest on the upper left-hand corner of the brown envelope is unmistakable. My exam results—my failing results—are staring up at me from Diane's desk.

On cue, the pit of my stomach sinks to new, unexplored depths. I'm not sure why. It's not like I didn't know this moment wasn't coming. It was just a matter of time, really.

After a full two minutes of berating the woman who'd led me here, Diane switches off the speakerphone and turns to me. "Don't worry, we won't be interrupted anymore."

That's too bad, I feel like adding, because I was really hoping that we would be interrupted. As many times as possible.

Diane clears her throat. Apart from the cursory niceties, I've barely said a word since I filed behind the secretary and followed her through these doors. Diane too, I notice, isn't saying much. If I didn't know better, I'd think she was having trouble launching the Pink Slip Speech. Instead of fireworks and colorful expletives, I get fidgeting and more silence. I'm almost disappointed. How many times must she have done this by now? Seriously.

"There's no easy way to put this, Aline, so I'm just going to have to come out with it."

Don't let me hold you up. Please.

"On behalf of all the partners here at Ernsworth and Youngston, as well as the entire management staff—" And here she inhales slowly and deeply, her piglet eyes reluctantly meeting mine. "—I apologize."

All the while that Diane had been talking, my brain had shifted into duck-and-search-for-cover mode. It was the mental equivalent of curling up into a fetal position with your two ears burrowed firmly between your knees.

In other words, I hadn't really listened to a single word she'd said. But it didn't seem to me that she'd uttered those words I'd been dreading for the past month or so.

"I perfectly understand your silence, Aline. I'd do the same if I were you. Still, I hope you'll hear me out before you make the decision to leave or not."

By now my ears could not have been more perked up to full-attention mode had they been privates reporting to their sergeant before battle. What could she possibly be talking about? Many years of ingesting pop culture via movies and TV have taught me that the best course of action at this particular moment is not to fight the current and just let it drag me where it may.

"We can't offer you a promotion just yet," she begins, "especially given your test scores, but you'll be given a second chance to write and put at the top of the list for potential candidates next year. We think this is a fair offer."

I realize that at this point I should be asking for some sort of explanation, but I'm a sucker for comedy, and the lunacy of this situation is beyond anything I'm likely to experience ever again. I *have* to play along and see just how far Diane is planning to take this joke.

"What about salary?"

Diane ruffles some of the papers in front of her nervously, but then her face tightens and she squares her shoulders, adopting that let's-talk-business stance I've seen on her so often. "We feel that a bonus equivalent to ten percent of your salary as well as a five percent raise over the next year is more than fair."

"But we're willing to negotiate," she adds after a pregnant pause.

I would have rolled to the floor, clutching my stomach in a convulsing fit of laughter if not for Diane's deadpan delivery and the national-emergency-level seriousness of her expression.

She begins tapping her short nails on the hard surface of the desk, in apparent anticipation of an answer. I'm guessing that any sign of life from my side of the room would be welcome at this point.

I lean forward and open my mouth, not quite sure how I'm going to assemble my thoughts into a coherent sentence. "First of all, I'd like to say apology accepted. I've had some tough times with Ernsworth, but overall, it's been an . . . invaluable learning experience." I was about to say *great* but decided that *invaluable* sounded a lot more like Detached Ice Queen, Mistress of Her Emotions, than just plain *great*.

"And while I do appreciate this opportunity that Ernsworth has been so kind as to offer," I continue, "I think my interests lie elsewhere."

In other words, O Supreme Czarina *Biatch*, you couldn't pay me enough to keep working here.

I wait for the hailstorm of Diane's wishes for eternal damnation to rain down on me, but I'm met with her usual cold stare, certainly nothing out of the ordinary.

"Well, while that's certainly your decision," she stumbles, "I think—*I know*—this is the best offer you're going to get from any of the Big Four. I advise you to take it under consideration before you make any hasty decisions."

"That won't be necessary. But thanks for the advice." I feel like leaving the conversation at that, as payback for all of Diane's superior airs not just toward me, but toward every underling that's ever had the misfortune to deal with this walking, fire-breathing drone. But a strange feeling of magnanimousness grips me. Maybe the idea that this is really the last time I'll be sitting here, in this seat, taking this brand of haughty crap from Diane is finally sinking in, imbuing everything inside and around me in a happy, rosy glow I'm dying to share with the rest of the world. I don't stop. I give her a semblance of an explanation instead.

"I know that it's hard for you to comprehend that there might be a world beyond the Big Four, beyond Best Practices and the

UFE, beyond this company even, but there is. I don't know why I didn't imagine I could do better than this before, but I just have. Don't ask me how, or why now—I don't know—but that's why I can't accept your offer. In case you were wondering."

"I wasn't."

"Okay. Just checking."

"Is there anything else, then?"

I've made it this far without having any idea what the big joke is. What's one more push? "Actually . . . there is."

"Well?"

"I was wondering, since you were going to offer me a raise and all for my trouble, what kind of severance package are we looking at, here? I mean, it's the least Ernsworth can do after all . . . after this ordeal." And this was the only sentence, as far as I was concerned, that was said in full sincerity during this surreal exchange.

Diane takes a deep breath.

She doesn't answer. Just glares, the kind of glare someone throws you when they know they've lost.

37

After what was arguably the weirdest conversation of my entire existence, I step off the elevator, onto the Corporate Recovery floor, and wander to my cubicle in a complete daze.

What am I possibly going to *do* with all that money?

Pay off all my credit card debt? Finally purchase the entire set of Louis Vuitton luggage I've been dreaming about since I was three and travel the world in a headscarf and sunglasses, pretending to be a famous movie star?

I kid.

It's not that much, really.

But it's enough to cover Visa, rent, and utilities for about two months with some left over for a few pieces of furniture. For my new apartment, that is. Because I *am* going to move out, no matter how many Arabic expletives and threats of eternal damnation my mother hurls my way. Now that I know Ranya's going to be richer and happier than even she imagined, I can safely indulge in getting something out of that scandal myself. Not only did my cousin's train wreck of a marriage prove that even the most carefully plotted plans can blow up in your—or more aptly, your parents'—face, but it conveniently allows me to argue that unlike Ranya, I'd be moving just six metro stops away as opposed to six hours by Airbus. That's got to count for something.

I'm still waiting for Ashton Kutcher to leap out from behind a plastic potted plant and yell, "Punk'd!" right into my face, even though I'm just an insignificant plebeian.

But no one leaps out from behind anything as I casually float down the hallway back to my desk, except for Aphro, who nearly tackles me to the ground when I turn the corner.

"I've been waiting for you for a fucking hour! Jeez, don't you know I have work to do?"

"Then what are you doing assaulting me? Anyway, guess what just happened . . . no forget it, you'll never guess. I'll tell you what happened—"

"Diane just offered you a raise and another chance to write the UFE?"

"Er . . ." I'm definitely expecting some sort of camera crew now.

"How did you know that? Is Soula in on this too? Where is she, by the way? It's almost eleven."

"She won't be in today," she says matter-of-factly.

"Why? Is she sick or something?"

"Or something. Come, let's go down to Starbucks."

The sheer absurdity of this day is making the idea of Pam Anderson and Nicole Richie as novelists seem perfectly logical. I follow Aphro down the hallway and past the receptionist's desk at the front of our floor.

She beams at me. "Have a great day, Ali! See you soon!"

"Uh, yeah. See you soon, Chantal."

A few moments later, Aphro and I are comfortably seated in plush green-and-burgundy couches in a dark corner of the coffee shop on the first floor, nursing two frothy cappuccinos.

"Spill."

"You know that file you've been working on?" Aphro fingers the rim of her mug, purposely stretching out her ten seconds of Knowledge Keeper to the fullest effect.

"Can you try to be more precise, please? I have—*had,* actually—about five billion active files on my desk."

"The clothing store one, Ashley something or other."

"Aïsha Saint-Jacques?"

"Sounds about right," Aphro mumbles between two gulps of foam.

"What about it?"

"Soula fucked it up. Royally. She hadn't looked at the file twice when she asked you to draw up the insolvency papers. Ernsworth was technically liable for professional negligence. The client could've sued. Not that she would've had the money to, but still, it doesn't look good."

This isn't making any sense. I grab both my temples, letting the new information sink in. The first stirrings of nausea rumble in my stomach. Could someone do something like that *deliberately*? Would Aïsha have been destroyed out of mere negligence if it weren't for me?

"Why would Soula risk her good name like that? For what?"

"Two words, babe: Zieber Securities." Aphro smacks her plum-tinted lips together after a bite of blueberry muffin.

I stare back blankly.

"Zieber Securities? The Swiss brokerage firm? Ali, man, where have you been?"

Okay, so maybe I'm not so in tune with financial industry news as I should be, but hey, I've got a life. Not to mention, I don't care.

"They're one of our biggest clients. Soula was working her ass off for these guys in the hopes that they'd make her CFO."

"What?" I jolt back against the sofa and stare at Aphro incredulously. "You sound like some sort of delusional corporate conspiracy theorist."

"I'm not spouting this stuff out of my ass, here. This comes from way up." She points a thumb upward as she says this. "This is straight from the horse's mouth."

"Which horse?"

"The one whose office you were in this morning."

"No!"

"Yup."

"How? . . ." I'm speechless. The creatures of the Black Lagoon had turned on each other. Who knew.

"The shit hit the fan when Sid Cohen called your buddy Amelie."

"Aïsha."

"Whatever, to tell her the good news."

"Wait a minute, back up. I thought Sid was retired."

"Not exactly. Let's just say his schedule is flexible. The office is still his until he makes his retirement official. Why would he when he can waltz in once every three months and call it work? Anyway, he happened to stop by last Friday to check his messages and who knows what else, gloat over his golf handicap or whatever partners talk about when they're not barking orders at us. Whatever. Anyway. So he notices that this Aïsha chick had called him a bunch of times and left pretty desperate messages. So he calls Soula into his office and asks her to brief him on the file. She does, and takes all the credit for finding the whole mistake thing while she's at it. Now Sid can't wait to call up this lady and tell her the good news himself. I'm telling you, Ali, I've never seen Soula sweat it out like that. You should've seen her, practically groveling to make that call herself. 'Oh, Sid, don't trouble yourself this, don't trouble yourself that.' Anyway so he calls, barely gets started with the Standard Ernsworth Bullshit speech when his face begins to change color. Oh, man, Ali, I saw the whole thing through the glass. It was awesome. I mean, you could totally tell when the shit hit the fan."

"Wait a minute. What were you doing up in Corporate Recovery anyway? Audit's two floors down." I cock my head and raise an eyebrow when she doesn't respond. "Were you hitting on Tom again?"

"I was trying to, but all he could do was talk about you,

biatch." She throws a piece of blueberry muffin at my hair. "He saw you storm out the other day, and he seemed really worried."

"Thanks." I pick a speck of muffin out of my hair. "You were saying?"

"Right. So after a good twenty minutes of straight listening— the man hardly said a word—he hangs up, walks over to the office door, shuts it behind him, and then the fireworks begin."

"What do you mean? What happened?"

"I don't know, I couldn't hear a thing, but it didn't look pretty, I'll tell you that."

"What about Diane?"

"She came down to Sid's office a few minutes later. It seems Soula might have gotten away with a warning if the puck had stopped at Aïsha's store. But *nooooo* . . . Sid had all her files pulled and, get this, got a bunch of partners to personally review them themselves. Lo and behold, what do they find, but that dozens of them, especially all the ones filed on behalf of small businesses, had evidence of negligence. Can you just picture the lawsuits? So now Sid's up to his ankles in shit too, since he's still technically in charge." Aphro pauses for another sip of cappuccino. "Knowing the partners, though, all he'll get is a polite invitation to retire, with a little bit of extra padding to his pension, of course. These people don't turn on their own crew. Soula, on the other hand, is toast."

"What happened to her?"

"JP swears he saw her leaving the office yesterday with a security guard holding her by the elbow."

I'm utterly speechless. Stun-gunned into place. Of all days to play hooky, I had to pick yesterday.

Honestly.

Aphro studies me, a self-satisfied smirk painted on her face while she waits for everything to sink in.

Soula was shirking her responsibility. She must have thought spending her energy on Aïsha's little shop was beneath her. Why waste time on small potatoes when you can go after the big fish? And when she was found out, she tried to pretend she was the team player all along.

Bits and pieces of this morning's interview come back to me in short, pointed waves. The raise. The chance to write the UFE again. The prospective promotion dangling at the end of another year of corporate servitude. For one tiny second, something inside me sinks. It's that familiar feeling of faltering over the edge of uncertainty. Was I stupid to turn down Diane's offer? I mean, it *is* pretty fabulous when you think about it. I could afford a bigger apartment, for one thing. I'd even have enough parental goodwill stockpiled that they might be able to let my momentous move pass just under the radar without a fuss.

I turn my head toward the floor-to-ceiling windows at the far end of the coffee shop and watch the people go by. Whoever coined the expression *suits* to mean businesspeople was on to something. I see so much gray, dark blue, and black, from shoes to pants to jackets and briefcases, that the entire street seems to blend into one giant blob of Dark. The Suit Blob. Rendering everything and everyone faceless in its wake. I wonder who am I to think that I could escape the force that is Corporate America. Did all these people really just want to be nobodies in a crowd of sameness? What kind of dreams do they harbor under all that sameness? Which one wanted to be a rock star when he grew up? Who goes crazy for interior design?

Then I think of Aïsha, of someone who plunged headfirst into a dream, regardless of the potential for dire consequences. She made it. Why not me?

"So what did Diane offer you?" Aphro says.

I just stare back at her for a full minute. "Fro, there's still one thing you haven't told me."

"What's that?"

"How do you know all this?"

"What? Have you *seen* the way that woman treats her secretary?"

After I wipe the tears of laughter out of my eyes, Aphro does something I've never seen her do before. She stands up from her seat, walks over to my side, and pulls me into a hug.

"You'll make it. Don't worry. Whatever you decide, I know you have it in you to make it."

"Thanks," I squeeze her back, and when I pull away, I spot a perfectly still, perfectly beet-faced Tom standing behind her.

"I'm sorry. . . ." He flusters. "I didn't mean to interrupt you. . . . I'll come back later."

"No need to, Tom. Manny must be going mental looking for me by now." Aphro grabs him roughly by the shoulders and shoves him down into her now-vacant seat. "I've been gone a full fifty-five minutes." She rolls her eyes and mutters "loser" theatrically.

And then very discreetly, she winks at me when Tom isn't looking, turning me the same shade of red as the Valentine's Day underwear I have on. (Hey, it was clean.) I'm going to kill her.

"You okay?"

I can't look at him. My cheeks are still burning. Plus he's got one of those blue shirts on that turn his pupils the same color as the water in Cuba. Times like these you'd think he's Irish instead of Greek if it weren't for his perpetually tanned skin.

"I'm great," I say, meaning it for once.

"I heard you turned Diane down."

"Yeah."

"That's too bad."

My right eyebrow twitches involuntarily. I look up at him, conscious of a warm glow emanating from my tummy. "Why's that?"

He shrugs and flicks a lint ball off his navy blazer sleeve. "I'll have to train someone else now."

Jerk.

"Why are you smirking at me like that?"

Damn those involuntary facial twitches. I'll have to see someone about that. A hypnotist maybe.

"Nothing. I was just wondering . . . how that girlfriend of yours is doing," I say playfully, waiting for his standard "she's doing fine" answer.

He looks confused for a second. Just one second, and then he gives me that grin that continually makes Aphro as well as half the population of this building swoon every time it flashes across his face. "We broke up, didn't I tell you? It's been a while, actually."

I can't speak. I want to, really I do, I've got my mouth open and everything, but nothing will come out.

"How's Brian?" he says in response to my apparent unwillingness to partake in the conversation.

"It's, um, a long story. . . . Care for a cappuccino?"

38

It turns out I have less stuff to take home with me from my (now old) cubicle than I thought. The small things I'd used to carve out a sense of individuality at Ernsworth over the past ten months take up about half a Gap carrier bag's worth of space.

Tom and I had spent almost an hour talking before he realized that though I may have the rest of my life to sit around sipping expensive coffee and munching on biscotti, he still had a job to get back to.

We talked about his girlfriend Athena, another good girl from a good Greek family. I reluctantly talked about Brian. I hated discussing him with another guy—one that I have a crush on, no less—but it did feel nice to speak to someone who seemed to know what I was feeling.

Athena, as it turns out, had been planning a big Greek-style wedding from day one. At least that's how it felt to Tom. I didn't say anything, but even though I'd never met the girl, I could tell him he was absolutely, 100 percent right. A Greek boy who looks like him and has his kind of job—if the girl herself hadn't wet her panties at the mere mention of him, then her mother had. I was sure of it.

So the wedding pressure, looming over the couple like a satu-rated cloud, had dampened the relationship. Sucked all the spontaneity out of it. I told him that it didn't necessarily take be-ing with someone from your own ethnic background to feel that way. Two years into my own relationship with an *ajnabi*—a *xeno*, where Tom's from—and I was feeling the same way. Except I couldn't put my finger on it. Or maybe deep inside I could, but being the neurotic girl that I am, it wasn't so easy for me to throw in the towel as it would have been if I were I guy. I had been needy and afraid.

Of course, I had kept that last bit to myself. Nor did I tell him that it took a certain Cuban someone to show me I wasn't ready to settle down and wait for the suburban house, the two-point-five kids, the minivan, and maybe the cruise every winter. In the words of the hooker with the heart of gold, I want more. I want the fairy tale. Even if I have to ride into the sunset on my own. Well. For the time being, at least.

When Tom left to go back to the office with a promise to stay in touch, I realized I had the whole afternoon ahead of me with nowhere pressing to go. And so I decided I might as well see how Aïsha was handling the great news.

"Got some new stuff, I see." I step into the sunny shop, glancing at the freshly dressed window.

"*Eeeek!*" Aïsha materializes out of a puff of white dust before me, and squeezes me so tight, I'm afraid I might suffocate.

"Wow, I don't think I've ever seen you this happy."

"And why wouldn't I be? I feel like I've been resurrected. All because of you."

"Well, I wouldn't go that far—"

"Stop it. You're wonderful. End of discussion." She silences me with a firmly raised hand. "Want some champagne?"

"Why not?" I can't think of anything better to be doing on a Wednesday morning at eleven.

Behind Aïsha, all the way to the back of the store, four big cardboard boxes are scattered around the floor, overflowing with pink tissue paper and clear plastic.

"What's all that?"

"New stock from France. Want to see?" Aïsha scurries over to the boxes with the anxious enthusiasm of a three-year-old showing his parents his first artistic creation. "I've been thinking, you know, after my near-business-death experience, this doesn't have to be just about me. It could be much bigger, you know. I've been so obsessed with making a name for myself, I think I've had tunnel vision."

"What do you mean?"

"Well, for starters, I've got so many contacts back in Paris."

"And?"

"My friends are all so talented, but not really as entrepreneurs."

The wheels in my head slowly begin to turn, and I can see from Aïsha's face that she's noticed.

"*Mais, c'est super!*" she yelps in her sexy accent. She grabs hold of both my arms and clings to them. "*Je le savais!* I knew it." She doesn't let go. "You and I, we think exactly alike."

"You're going to start importing clothes from France and selling them here?" I say, my enthusiasm pushing my voice up a few octaves.

"Why not? I don't know why I never thought of the idea. This way my contacts don't have to leave France in order to sell their creations in Montreal, and they get to do business with someone they trust. If it works out, we can even become distributors for the rest of Canada and the States. Of course, I'll have to make sure to keep the costs down. That might be difficult—"

"You know something, Aïsha? I have this crazy theory. . . . I think that deep down, *waaaay* down, people actually like to pay more for stuff. It makes them feel special. You just have to convince them it's worth it. It's called 'trading up' in business."

Aïsha backs away and examines me up and down, like those construction dudes three blocks up the street.

"For months now I've been noticing that the more expensive

merchandise was flying off the racks while the cheaper stock was a harder sell. I thought that was maybe because my store is still a bit of a novelty. I can't believe it."

"What, you can't believe that people can be such sheep? Have you taken a look at my latest Visa statement?"

"No, not that. I can't believe I never thought to offer you a job here. Not that I expect you to leave your glamorous position at the firm. I'd never be able to match the pay anyway."

I'm completely silent for a moment.

Of course. Somewhere in the back of my mind, that very thought had occurred to me and was dismissed almost as soon as it appeared. What would the salary be like in a place like this compared to what I'd been making? A joke. Advancement opportunities? Ha. I'd have to forge my own path, taking tentative steps to figure out which way was up. At least I'd always have health insurance.

And yet . . . it makes complete, perfect, and utterly delicious sense. Everything fashion is already my hobby—why can't I make it my life?

"What exactly are you saying?"

"That if circumstances had been different, I might have made you a job offer."

"What kind of job are we talking about, here?"

"Keeping the books, for starters." She blushes pink under her already rosy complexion. "I think I could use some help in that department."

Bookkeeping. Huh. Not exactly what I'd had in mind for my first foray into the fashion world, but it's a plan at least. Which is more than I had two minutes ago.

If I show her how responsible I am, how eager I am to learn (perhaps I should hold off asking her about store discounts), maybe within a few months she'll let me tag along to Paris on buying sprees every once in a while.

"Of course, that wouldn't be the only thing you'd be responsible for. As I'm sure you can imagine, the accounting for a place like this isn't too complicated, just basic day-to-day stuff."

"So, what kind of other stuff should I—I mean, the potential candidate—expect to do?" Mop floors, dust countertops, help old ladies get into the latest rhinestone thong underwear . . . you name it, I'm your girl.

"I have to go to Paris four times a year to see the shows—"

This is it, the moment it all comes together, the fairy tale . . .

"—so I need someone I can trust to put in charge of the store while I'm away."

Oh, so close.

"But there are also the New York and Toronto fashion weeks, which I have to make an effort to attend to keep an eye on the local competition, so I'll need someone who's fluent in English and has a great eye for fashion to send in my place. There are only so many shows I can be bothered to sit through in one year."

Me, me! Pick me! I want to throw myself at her feet and beg, but the basics of business negotiations won't let me. I've got to play it cool. I tuck a loose strand of hair behind my ear and shift my weight from one foot to the other.

"Is there anything else the hypothetical candidate would be expected to do?" I toss my head back, attempting my most nonchalant countenance.

Aïsha's eyes narrow and the corners of her mouth curl up in a half smile. "I suppose this candidate, the hypothetical one—" She peers at me meaningfully. "I suppose he or she would be expected to help with the selling aspect when they aren't attending to the books, or helping with the window displays or sewing samples. You know, that sort of thing."

I clear my throat. "And, um—" I feign a few coughs to buy time. "—what kind of compensation would we be talking about for this still-nonexistent applicant? You know, should he or she materialize."

"Ali, are you trying to ask me something?" Aïsha says, her

voice laced with a twang of whimsical mischief. "Is there some-one you know who might be interested in the position?"

My heart leaps. This is it. This is the moment. I feel like every success, every failure, every path taken in my life so far has led me to this point. But there it is, the abyss of uncertainty looming on the horizon, beckoning me into its dark belly.

Am I doing the right thing? What's my life going to be like five, ten, fifteen years from now?

Oh, just gag me.

"I do, actually." I cough, the butterflies in my stomach flutter-ing furiously. "Me."

"But you have a job already. A great one, in fact."

"Not anymore. I quit this morning." I shrug my shoulders as if the whole ordeal were a plan hatched and carried out by cosmic forces beyond my control, and not something I had done when in complete control of all my faculties.

"How did this happen?"

"It's a long story. I'll tell it to you sometime when business is slow. More importantly, you still haven't mentioned anything about the pay—"

She lunges at me with the full force of her tiny frame, and nearly tackles me to the ground.

Epilogue

The breeze blowing off the Caribbean Sea ruffles my hair and tickles my neck just like I remember. I close my eyes and breathe in the salt air, letting memories of late-night partying with the girls in Varadero clubs, of meeting Javier in Plaza de la Catedral, of strolling on this very boardwalk, hand in hand with Miguel, swirl around in my head.

Has it really been almost a year?

I had been scared to come. I still remember the first time I walked into my family home in Beirut after so many years of being away. I remember feeling betrayed by even the smallest changes—naked tiles where once there had been carpet, the boarding up of the attic where we kept provisions during the years of the civil war. Of course it was summertime, and so my aunts didn't need wall-to-wall carpeting, and the war had long since been over. But I still felt betrayed as if I'd expected that time would have stopped and waited for me to come back.

Havana, though, hasn't changed. Not one bit. The rocks below the *Malecón* look just as forbidding as they did last year, and little boys in tattered shorts are still leaping over them and plunging ten feet over the wall and into the ocean. The grand buildings along this street are still in serious need of a paint job, and the Hotel Nacional still proudly overlooks the city in all of its Old World glory.

I think this is what bewitches the tourists who come here. No matter what happens around the globe, it will always be 1959 in Cuba.

But something *has* changed. Or rather someone. Believe it or not, despite the knowledge that I'm going home to a fresh twenty-five centimeters of snow—or so Aïsha claims—a part of me is eager to go back. Don't get me wrong—the palm trees are still as hypnotic now as they were last year, with their lazy swaying and their leaves, bunched together like pom-poms that explode into a million vibrations every time the wind blows. The sidewalk cafés are all there, all the ones we'd seen the first time. And the mojitos and Cuba Libres are every bit as bittersweet as this complex country.

Still, I'm anxious to take back my place in my comfortable routine. Get up, shower in a bathroom that's probably one-tenth the size of the one in my parents' basement, slide into the latest hot item that's freshly arrived from Paris, pick up two cappuccinos from the Starbucks at the foot of my building, and then walk the three blocks to the shop. To my little corner of bliss.

It's not bliss every day. Especially when a customer strolls in, attempting to return something she claims is two sizes too small when it's clearly seen the inside of a washing machine. Or, in some cases, the bottom of a dusty closet. The more subtle ones will get the merchandise dry-cleaned but forget to tear off the tiny piece of paper stapled to the tag.

Classic.

My favorite days—besides the ones I spend taking orders on showroom floors in Vegas and New York—are the ones where we're expecting a new shipment. Inspecting the stock, counting, and then tagging it while trying to imagine how best to present it and which customers I'd recommend it to. That's my favorite part. And it only gets better when I catch the brief glimmer in the eyes of our most loyal clients when they come in and see that we've got new stuff.

What I feel for Aïsha's store is not unlike how I imagine new mothers feel toward their babies. I stay up nights worried about it, I can't sleep when it's not doing so hot, and I'm elated when it gets a favorable mention in the local press, as proud as if I were the one being photographed and praised.

Of course I don't plan to work at someone else's shop for the rest of my life. Aïsha and I each have our different visions. She's more into the really creative, not-so-practical stuff, which is fine for people like me, but I'm not most people. They prefer the safety—and price range—of Banana Republic over Behnaz Sarafpour. I'm starting to think bigger than that. I realize now how invaluable my experience at Ernsworth was. All those months I assumed were wasted when really I was guilty of having tunnel vision—I thought I had to be either fully immersed in fashion, like Aïsha is, or business, like Soula or Diane. It seems pretty silly to say I never saw the potential in combining the two into one perfect job, like a buyer or a product developer, but then again, I'd gone through my life thinking there was only one way of doing things. One right way. I couldn't have been more wrong.

It's taken my parents a predictably long time to get used to the fact that I won't be making nearly as much money this way as someone with my education typically does. But I think they also see I'm much happier now. My dad was only mildly concerned, being a business owner himself. He doesn't believe in retail and would rather I work for him if I'm going to go down that path. But beyond that, he could perfectly relate to my feelings of having my spirit wither and die as a random office drone. He used to be one himself.

As someone who'd suffered the practical consequences of my father's switch to entrepreneurship—the money shortages, the late nights, the absentee coparenting—my mother was less amused by my choice. But as I explained, I don't have anyone to take care of but me right now, so that's not really an issue. I'm more astonished that she's still talking to me now that I've moved out, so who knows, maybe one day she'll come around on the fashion thing too.

The only thing I miss about Ernsworth is Aphro, but she does manage to visit the store as often as her crazy schedule lets her. There was a bit of reshuffling after Soula's unexpected corporate demise. Manny took over her role, and Aphro was promoted to his job. I couldn't be more thrilled for her. She can finally afford all those designers she idolizes.

Even Diane went through—well, *a change,* shall we say. Like those die-hard anti-gay politicians, it turns out Ms. Cloutier was harboring a terrifying secret of her own. She was—gasp!—a human being under the corporate Medusa exterior with aspirations of being a wedding planner. I nearly choked on my chicken dumpling à la George W. Bush when Aphro told me. Apparently she'd been dabbling in the profession for a while when she took that mysterious personal leave. It was so she could plan one of Montreal's most high-profile weddings. She got the job only because of a friend of a friend of a friend who wanted to piss off her mother-in-law and hire an unknown. It turned out to be the wedding of the decade. Who knew the Ice Queen had such a flair for flower arrangements and Fabergé china? It wasn't long after I left the firm that Diane chose to come out of the closet, so to speak, and reveal herself to be a human being with actual emotions, feelings, and aspirations. She was promptly fired.

It couldn't be a more perfect day for a wedding, although honestly, I could've done with a little less sun.

I had a fight with my mother this morning in the hotel—the Hotel Nacional, no less. That's where everybody's staying. It was about my outfit. A Marc Jacobs blush sundress glammed up with a pair of silver Stuart Weitzman sandals. It's a beautiful dress, really, if a little on the flimsy side, but what do you expect for an outdoor wedding in Cuban weather? I think it's the white bikini top I opted to wear underneath instead of a bra that drove her over the edge. Well. We'll see who melts out here in this heat first. Me in my bikini top, or her in her sequined tunic. Arabs. Honestly.

My mind drifts over the blue of the water at the horizon and back to thoughts of home. After a long day spent on my feet, knees, hands, and whatever else was needed for the labor at hand, I always come home to a message on my machine. A message of love.

"Hey, you."

I jolt around, startled, and on reflex, Tom reaches out to steady me.

"Careful. Those rocks down there look sharp."

"Aren't you supposed to be with the rest of the boys?"

He hangs his head and sighs. "They don't understand half of what I'm saying. And I can't understand a damn word they're saying either."

"Still, the wedding's going to start any second now, and you wouldn't want anything to hold it up, would you? Certainly not an annoying guest disappearing."

"Oh, so I'm annoying now?"

"A little . . ."

"Would you think better of me if I kissed you?"

"Maybe."

Instead of stooping down to my eye level as he normally would, he wraps his arms tightly around my hips and lifts me off my feet and onto the low stone wall.

He leans in close to me so that all I'm conscious of is his smell.

I can't help it. For just a brief fraction of a second, a whiff of Miguel blows through my head and swooshes around in my insides.

I grab Tom by his two cheeks and pull him to me, crushing

our mouths together. I part his lips with my tongue and inhale sharply, kissing him as deep as I've ever kissed anyone.

"Wow." His eyes still closed, he pulls back. "I didn't even have to tell you how great you look. If I weren't convinced your mother's watching us from her hotel room, I'd rip your clothes off right now."

"There's five hundred rooms in there. And five dozen people out here. She doesn't have X-ray vision."

"Ali, I know your mother. Don't try and tell me she doesn't watch me like a hawk."

"I won't. I don't have time to, anyway. I should probably go see the bride."

At this he sighs again. "Does that mean I have to go back to those guys? I never thought I'd say this, but if I never have to smoke a Cuban cigar again, I'll die a happy man."

"Javier doesn't smoke."

"No, but between his uncles, cousins, and buddies, I'm surprised there's anything left to sell to tourists."

"Okay, Mr. Stand-Up Comedian. Go away. I'll see you at the ceremony."

"I love you."

"Me too. Bye."

I stand there and watch the man that still makes my insides churn after a year of couplehood walk away, and I thank my lucky stars for Miguel, though the gratitude is mixed with twinges of guilt. I never did call back the man who'd shown me a glimpse of the Possible, the one who taught me to delight in my dreams as if I were a kid again. I refused to spoil the perfect memory.

No matter how much we want to believe something sometimes, I think the truth is always lurking somewhere inside us. If Miguel had pursued me only because I was, for him, the embodiment of another chance, a different life . . . did that really make him evil or conniving? Realistic, maybe. Pragmatic. Opportunistic at worst. But not evil, at least I don't think so. Then again, maybe he singled me out because he cared, just a little bit, and figured if the only way he could escape his paradise prison was to marry a gullible tourist, that tourist might as well be me. We may even have had a chance. Maybe. But I didn't want to know. I still don't, even though finding out would be as simple as stealing away to Varadero for a day.

I'd rather hold on to my perfect memory, drawing strength from it to face my future.

I didn't know what would happen after Brian and I broke up and after I left Ernsworth. I never had any designs on Athanasios. But then again, neither did I have any on Miguel. I never dreamed I would be helping Aïsha run her boutique, and that Sophie would find happiness living in Havana with a Cuban architect. She was such a great fit at Habitat for Humanity that they took her on as a paid employee. There were a few immigration snags, of course, but that's all taken care of now that she's going to be married to a Cuban.

Even Jaz has managed to let go of Ben with the help of Simon. He had to go back to England after a few months in Montreal, but not before the two had a whirlwind romance. They're doing the long-distance thing now, since she's too happy with her job to leave. I don't know what's going to happen with them. I just know that Jaz is beginning to see what an amazing person she is. It almost glows out of her. I know—whether or not it works out with Simon—that she's finally ready to be happy.

I never imagined we would all be assembled here, in Cuba of all places, about to embark on such diverging paths. I'm not sure where I—or Sophie or Jaz—are going to be in a few weeks, let alone a few years. What's incredible is that for the first time, I realize how much it doesn't matter.

Discussion Questions for
FASHIONABLY LATE

1. Ali is one of those lucky people who knows exactly what she wants to do with her life—and yet she ended up as an accountant, the polar opposite of her hopes and dreams for the future (she admits she doesn't even like math!). What made her do it, in the face of mounting evidence she should be doing something else? Do you think she would have eventually switched careers had she not been pushed by circumstance?

2. The pursuit of freedom is an important theme in this novel. What does freedom mean to Ali? Do you think Ali feels more free than her more tradition-conscious cousins, especially Ranya? How are Ali's notions of freedom challenged when she meets Miguel?

3. Throughout most of the novel, Ali's parents seem to be living in the past, almost as though they'd never left Lebanon. What do you think compels immigrants to cling to old customs and reminders of their old homeland once settled into their adopted country? Do you think Ali's parents are especially hard on her, or is she the one being hard on them?

4. Ali bristles when James tells her he's from New York City. She feels a need to explain her position regarding the terrorist attacks of 9/11. Do you think she's being paranoid or is her reaction to be expected? Ali also mentions the creation of Japanese internment camps for the detention of Japanese-Americans and Japanese-Canadians during WWII. Do you think something like that could happen today?

5. While Ali and Jaz clearly love each other, their friendship is often strained, especially when talk turns to relationships. Do you think Ali has a right to be critical of Jaz's love life?

What about Jaz—what do you think is the motivation behind her dislike of Brian? Why does she push Ali toward Miguel?

6. Sophie plays the role of eternal peacemaker between her hot-tempered friends. What is it in Sophie's personality that makes her adopt this role? Do you think every group of friends has a "Sophie"?

7. Yasmin's self-esteem issues are a major impediment in her pursuit of relationship happiness. This is the struggle of many young women in their twenties. Why do you think this is? What effect did the trip have on Jaz? Where do you see her going from here?

8. Cuba represents the "forbidden" in more ways than one. What are some of those ways? What was it about Cuba that made Ali open her eyes to possibilities? Did the portrayal of Cuba in the novel conform to your expectations? Have you ever been on a trip that changed your outlook on life or opened you up to new experiences?

9. When Ali recounts the story of her relationship with Brian, it sounds like an idyllic romance—at least at first. What do you think went awry? Do you think Ali herself was wrong in cheating on Brian? Do you think she should have felt guiltier than she did? What would have happened had she managed to resist Miguel's advances?

10. The pursuit of "true love" is another important theme in the novel. What do you think attracted Ali to Brian when they met? What was the glue that held them together for three years? What attracts her to Miguel and Tom? Ali admits that one of the things she and Brian have in common is that neither believes in the idea of soul mates. Do you think Ali has found a soul mate in Tom? Does it matter to her? Why or why not?

11. Ali's preoccupation with what her family might think of her choices weighs heavily on her mind. Do you think this is a cultural quirk, or is it a symptom of Ali having not yet blossomed fully into an adult? What was the turning point for Ali? Do you think bending your life to conform to parental expectations is unique to certain cultures, or is it universal?

12. What did you think of Ali's spur-of-the-moment decision to quit her job? Would you have done that in a similar situation? What does this novel say about the way we choose our professions?

13. This novel deals with young women and their struggles to find a place in the world for themselves, be it professionally, romantically, or within their families. Even though the three women featured in *Fashionably Late* are Arab, do you think their struggles are universal?

14. For most of the novel, Ali chooses to follow the path of satisfying other people's expectations rather than pursuing what would make her truly happy. By the end of the book there is a reconciliation of sorts between Aline and her mother, but it's not your typical happily-ever-after ending. What do you think the future holds for these two? What do you think the future holds for Ranya, whose blind pursuit of others' expectations landed her in an unhappy marriage to a gay man?